The Big Lie

ALSO BY JAMES GRIPPANDO

The Girl in the Glass Box★   Got the Look★

A Death in Live Oak★   Hear No Evil★

Most Dangerous Place★   Last to Die★

Gone Again★   Beyond Suspicion★

Cash Landing   A King's Ransom

Cane and Abe   Under Cover of Darkness

Black Horizon★   Found Money

Blood Money★   The Abduction

Need You Now   The Informant

Afraid of the Dark★   The Pardon★

Money to Burn

Intent to Kill   **Other Fiction**

Born to Run★   The Penny Jumper

Last Call★   Leapholes

Lying with Strangers

When Darkness Falls★   ★ A Jack Swyteck novel

The Big Lie

A Jack Swyteck Novel

James Grippando

HARPER LARGE PRINT

An Imprint of HarperCollinsPublishers

THE BIG LIE. Copyright © 2020 by James Grippando. All rights reserved. Printed in the United States of America. No part of this book may be used or reproduced in any manner whatsoever without written permission except in the case of brief quotations embodied in critical articles and reviews. For information, address HarperCollins Publishers, 195 Broadway, New York, NY 10007.

HarperCollins books may be purchased for educational, business, or sales promotional use. For information, please e-mail the Special Markets Department at SPsales@harpercollins.com.

FIRST HARPER LARGE PRINT EDITION

ISBN: 978-0-06-297927-8

Library of Congress Cataloging-in-Publication Data is available upon request.

20 21 22 23 24 LSC 10 9 8 7 6 5 4 3 2 1

For Tiffany

The great enemy of the truth is very often not the lie—deliberate, contrived, and dishonest—but the myth—persistent, persuasive, and unrealistic.

—JOHN F. KENNEDY

The Big Lie

Chapter 1

Balloons. Countless balloons.

Jack lifted his gaze to the domed ceiling above the jumbotron, his attention drifting from the monotony onstage. Suspended high in the rafters, nestled in giant nets that stretched from one end of the arena to the other, thousands of shiny latex balloons hovered like red, white, and blue storm clouds ready to burst and bury the 4,763 delegates on the convention floor.

It had taken nearly a half century for the Democratic National Convention to return to Miami, and probably with good reason. The convention that had sent Senator George McGovern off to slaughter was remembered only for air-conditioning so faulty that delegates passed out from the South Florida heat, and organization so lacking that the acceptance speech was delivered after most of America had gone to bed. So uneventful was it that, just four years after clashing with Chicago Police and shouting, "The whole world is watching," leaders of the antiwar movement spent most of the 1972 convention at the Poodle Lounge or the Boom-Boom Room at the Fountainebleau Hotel in Miami Beach talking about the good ol' days.

"From my first day in office to my last," the nominee droned on, "my primary mission as president will be to create more opportunity and more good jobs with rising wages."

It was yet another stock line from Florida's junior senator, which drew dutiful applause from the nation's most enthusiastic Democrats, who were determined to make their nominee's uninspired speech worthy of prime-time television. Some delegates on the convention floor looked on with adoration in their eyes and tears streaming down their faces. Jack could only guess what moment in party history they were reliving in their minds to tap such emotion. As for Senator Evan Stahl Jr., history would record that his ninety-minute speech had hit its high point roughly eighty-nine minutes before its ending, with "I accept your nomination with humility, determination, and boundless confidence in America's promise."

Jack was still counting balloons. There appeared

to be an equal number of red ones, white ones, and blue ones. He wondered why. The American flag was mostly red and white.

"God, this is awful," his father muttered.

Harry Swyteck had been Jack's ticket to the convention. The former governor and his wife were guests of honor, but Jack's stepmother was feeling under the weather, so Jack got the former First Lady's ticket. Father and son joined distinguished Democrats in a mezzanine-level box that came with theater-style leather seats, flat-screen TVs, a wet bar, and waitress service. Had the arena been rocking for basketball instead of politics, not even a second mortgage on the house could have put these seats within Jack's financial reach.

"So it's not just me?" Jack whispered. He and his father were standing in the back by the bar, a semi-private area that was perfect for business talks that couldn't wait until after the game, the concert, or whatever the event.

"I've heard filibusters more interesting."

That was quite an indictment. Decades earlier, Harry had served in the state legislature with Senator Stahl's father, where they'd once combined to read the entire Tallahassee phone book into the record to filibuster a bill.

"What's wrong with him tonight?" Jack asked.

Harry didn't answer, but Jack's question was sincere. Evan Stahl was a skilled politician, and by all accounts he was living a charmed life. Stahl had been a three-time NCAA scholar-athlete at the University of Florida and a Rhodes Scholar, then earned a law degree cum laude from Harvard. He'd returned to Florida with big political aspirations. Marrying the daughter of a Cuban immigrant turned multimillionaire, the ultimate American success story, certainly didn't hurt his meteoric rise from state legislator to congressman to junior U.S. senator. As if to complete the presidential package, his wife had her own career as a hospital-based psychiatrist for the Florida Department of Law Enforcement, treating institutionalized inmates, but still finding time to raise a nine-year-old daughter who was as smart and passionate as her mother.

"I'm serious," Jack whispered. "Something's not right here."

Some said that the senator was most effective in a town-hall setting, where he could engage directly with people. But never had he fallen on his face at the teleprompter the way he had tonight. It was the biggest speech of his life, and he was as flat as the Florida Everglades, his words lacking heart, as if his mind were elsewhere.

"America is once again at a moment of reckoning," the candidate continued. "Powerful forces are threatening to pull us apart. Bonds of trust and respect are fraying."

Jack felt his father's hand on his shoulder. "Moments like these make me truly sorry you had no interest in politics. You could do better than this with no script."

Harry was right on one count: the political bug had never bitten Jack. Like three and a half million other Floridians, Jack was an independent with no party affiliation—a fact that Harry had kept quiet to get his son inside the building under the honored-guest invitation to the former governor "and guest." Jack wasn't exactly passionate about the Democratic candidate, but he was no fan of the incumbent, Malcolm MacLeod, whom Democrats had been threatening to impeach since retaking the House of Representatives in the midterm election. The House never did vote on impeachment, instead making a calculated strategic decision to oust him through the ballot box. MacLeod's base rallied behind him, but rumors of corruption were so pervasive that most experts proclaimed him a one-term president. Heading into the summer conventions, pollsters projected a Democratic cakewalk to the White House. Pundits quite seriously proclaimed that it didn't matter who the Democrats nominated, as long as the nominee managed to avoid indictment for a capital felony between the convention and the general election in November.

The worry lines on his father's face had Jack wondering if, as usual, the pundits were dead wrong.

"You know something, don't you?" Jack said in a serious tone. "What is it, Dad?"

They retreated deep into the corner, farther out of earshot from the other guests. Harry kept his voice low as an added measure of privacy.

"I had a chat with Senior before dinner tonight," said Harry, meaning Senator Stahl's father. "He's trying to talk his daughter-in-law out of suing for divorce."

The news surprised Jack. He'd met the Democrats' First Couple earlier in the campaign. They'd seemed happy, no sign of tension. "What happened?"

"The story will break tomorrow. Turns out, the senator has been having an affair."

"I'm sorry to hear that."

Jack glanced at the jumbotron, where two hours earlier a DNC video had extolled the nominee as a family man who stood for family values.

"We have to decide whether we're going to work together, so we can all rise together!" said Stahl, speaking in a voice that didn't boom the way it should have.

Harry just shook his head, lacking the enthusiasm of

the floor delegates, who at least pretended to be moved. "This affair is the answer to MacLeod's prayers," said Harry. "I honestly don't think Evan's campaign is going to survive."

"I don't mean to sound cynical," said Jack, "but don't you think you're being a little old-fashioned? Plenty of politicians have survived extramarital affairs."

"Not like this one."

Jack's imagination ran for a moment, but it was hard to conjure up anything in the nature of an "affair" that would shock the modern political world. "Who is she?"

Harry glanced at the stage again, then looked Jack in the eye. "That's the problem. Rumor has it that the 'other woman' isn't a woman."

The senator reached for a big, fiery finish—and it sounded like a reach.

"My fellow Americans, there's a clear choice ahead of us. One that looks at the future with fear and hatred, or a new vision of courage and confidence that builds a better tomorrow for our beloved children. That honors our beloved country. And that makes America greater than ever!"

The crowd erupted. Stahl thrust his arms in the air, but his gestures, like his words, lacked heart.

"Thank you! And may God bless the United States of America!"

On cue, the music blared, and the bulging nets fell away from the catwalks to release the colorful finale. Balloons poured down from the ceiling, covering the candidate, the stage, and the screaming throngs of delegates on the convention floor. Jack noted that the would-be First Lady did not join her husband onstage, which left the candidate awkwardly alone, knee-deep in inflated latex, engaged in a silly game of balloon volleyball with his supporters in the first row.

"You get the picture?" asked Harry.

Coming from his father, the question had Jack thinking of two other governors, Sanford of South Carolina and McGreevey of New Jersey—one who served out his gubernatorial term and was elected to Congress after he went missing in Argentina with his mistress; the other who resigned his office and disappeared from politics after announcing that he was gay.

"I get the picture, all right," said Jack.

November

Chapter 2

It was the first Tuesday after the first Monday. The morning sun was a distant orange sliver rising from the Atlantic as Jack emerged from the bedroom dressed and ready for work. His wife and daughter were in the kitchen. Jack grabbed his car keys from the pewter dish on the counter, kissed his family good morning and goodbye, and headed for the door.

"Why you leaving so early, Daddy?"

Ever since her kindergarten teacher had introduced the concept of time, Righley found any occurrence outside the normal rhythm of things to be worthy of comment.

"I want to go vote before work," said Jack. "Daddy has to cancel out Nana's ballot."

Andie popped a couple of frozen waffles into the

toaster. "Just because my mother is a Republican doesn't mean she's voting for MacLeod. I'm a Republican, and I'm not voting for him."

Jack liked his mother-in-law, and the fact that her heart was big enough to have adopted Andie out of foster care only elevated her in his eyes. But he had her pegged as someone who talked progressive and voted her pocketbook.

"No matter how many different ways I ask, your mother refuses to tell me who she's voting for."

"She's a firm believer in the Australian ballot system."

"What's an Oztrain ballot?" asked Righley.

"It's when kangaroos elect our president," said Jack.

"Daddy's so funny," Andie said with a roll of her eyes. "It means that you don't have to tell anyone who you voted for. It started in Australia a long time ago, so it's called the Australian ballot system."

"Mommy's right. And the good thing about a secret ballot is that it stops bullies from telling you how to vote."

"So stop telling my mother how to vote," said Andie.

It made him stop and think. People said MacLeod was a bully, but both sides were guilty. "Fair enough," he said, and he started toward the door, then stopped.

"Oh, I almost forgot. Dad asked me to watch the election returns with him tonight."

"Where?"

"Somebody's house in the Gables. Not sure. It's a watching party."

"Jack, I really don't feel like going anywhere tonight."

"Actually, it's invitation only. Dad got invited, and Agnes isn't feeling up to it. He asked me to join him."

"Seems like Agnes is playing the 'not feeling well' card a lot lately. Is she okay?"

"I wouldn't read anything into it. I think she's just tired of the campaign."

"Or maybe Agnes is voting for MacLeod," she said, teasing.

It wasn't outside the realm of possibility, and it wouldn't have been the first point of disagreement between Jack and his stepmother. Not by a long shot. "Guess I'll have to vote twice."

"Daddy, you can't do that!"

"That was another Daddy joke," said Andie. "They're easy to spot because you have to remind yourself to laugh."

Jack opened the door. "So you don't mind if I go tonight?"

"Honey, if this race is as close as it's supposed to be, I'll be in bed hours before we know the winner. Go. Have fun."

"Thanks. I hope we will."

Jack and his father were at Miami International Airport when the Stahl campaign jet touched down at 6:35 p.m., Eastern Time.

The senator had started the day by casting his vote three blocks from his house in Coral Gables. Then it was off to morning rallies in Michigan and Ohio, followed by quick hits in Tampa and Orlando, all in a last-ditch effort to turn purple voters blue before polls closed at 7:00 p.m. A cheering partisan crowd was on hand to welcome him home.

"I'm still not a fan of those caps," Harry said.

Stahl and his staff never wore them, and there was no official campaign cap, but almost every supporter who'd turned out to greet him at the airport was wearing a pink baseball cap with the post-convention campaign slogan: MAKE AMERICA FABULOUS AGAIN. It had started after President MacLeod got caught up in the moment at a campaign rally and turned on an effeminate accent to say that Senator Stahl wanted to "make America fabulous again." It immediately caught on with Democrats. The caps were a nation-wide sensation.

"What don't you like about them?" asked Jack.

"I have no problem with gay pride. But this man cheated on his wife. Those hats disrespect Mrs. Stahl, and you don't disrespect a wife and mother who's hurting."

Jack took the point. The caps would have been fine if an openly gay man were running for president. Nobody knew if Senator Stahl was gay, straight, or bi-sexual. The only thing for certain was that he was an adulterer.

The candidate and his team piled onto the campaign bus. Jack and his father went to the car, and Jack got behind the wheel. "Where to?"

"Just follow the bus," said Harry.

Jack hesitated. "You said we were going to a watching party."

"We are. At Senator Stahl's house."

"Dad, I'm not even a registered Democrat."

"Nobody's perfect," said Harry.

"I'm serious. I felt awkward enough as the stand-in for Agnes at the convention."

"You're my son. Relax."

Jack couldn't help but be impressed that his father

was on the invitation list. The run-up to the election had made it clear that the senator from Florida couldn't win the White House without carrying his home state, so it only made sense to pull a popular former governor into the inner circle.

"How many people will be at the house?" asked Jack.

"A dozen or so."

"Seems like a small group. Maybe I should just drop you off."

"Are you nuts? I've already gotten you Secret Service clearance. Stahl is going to win, and this is your chance to be in the room with him as it happens. Be a part of history."

It was indeed an excellent fly-on-the-wall opportunity, so Jack stopped protesting.

The drive to the Stahl residence took about twenty minutes. A Secret Service agent directed them through the gate to overflow parking on the other side of the fountain, and another agent checked their identification at the front door. Harry was instantly recognized by guests who'd arrived ahead of them, and even though Jack and his father were greeted with smiles, Jack could feel the tension in the air.

The final months of the campaign had been a bloodbath. Before the conventions, most analysts had given President MacLeod a better chance of being indicted than reelected—and that included analysts who were of the view that the Constitution probably prohibited the indictment of a sitting president. When news of an extramarital affair transitioned to rumors of a gay lover, support for Stahl in certain demographics dropped like a stone. It wasn't just older voters. The biggest hit was among fiscal conservatives who embraced progressive social policies—the twenty-first-century version of "Rockefeller Republicans"; their progressivism had a limit, and for many that limit fell short of "His and His" bathrobes in the Florida Governor's Mansion. By Election Day, the race was a dead heat. It would all come down to Stahl's home state.

"Florida, Florida, Florida," television analysts proclaimed as the polls closed.

It was the refrain made famous by NBC's Tim Russert and his low-tech whiteboard in the 2000 election, when "hanging chads" and Florida's twenty-nine Electoral College votes put Bush 43 in the White House. The squeaker of 2000 was only the first of three presidential elections of the new century in which the margin of victory in Florida was 1.2 percent or less. With a fourth in the making—the second to involve MacLeod—Florida again was the nation's focus, with analysts on every network borrowing the late Washington bureau chief's three-word mantra.

"It's going to be a long night," said Harry.

The doorbell rang, and Jack made himself useful by answering it. A team of caterers wheeled in enough hors d'oeuvres and refreshments for a weeklong watching party. Last in the line of excess was a cake in the shape of Senator Stahl from the shoulders up, so lifelike that it was downright creepy. Fondant struck Jack as the perfect political confection: it looked amazing, but in the end, not nearly as good as promised.

The senator's father walked over to check out the cake. "My granddaughter would absolutely love this," he said, a hint of sadness in his voice. "Such a shame she can't be here tonight with her father."

The senator's divorce was filed but not final. Last Jack had heard, Mrs. Stahl and her daughter were waiting out the campaign from an apartment in Singapore, where homosexuality was a criminal offense punishable by caning, and where freedom of the press lagged behind countries like Egypt and Afghanistan—which made it the perfect place to insulate a nine-year-old girl from constant media speculation about her father and his alleged boyfriend, her father and a male prostitute, her father and a gay porn star, her father and a bacchanalian orgy of young boys and centaurs.

Harry walked over to greet his old friend. Behind them, in the living room, were four flat-screen televisions brought in for simultaneous viewing of different network coverage. Senator Stahl and his closest advisors had choice seats on the overstuffed couch. Senior was about to reintroduce Jack, but the group was suddenly gripped in awkward silence, as *the* attack ad of the campaign aired one more time before the polls closed on the East Coast. It began with Senator Stahl standing before a bouquet of microphones at the historic press conference he'd called just three days after the convention, his wife nowhere to be seen as he delivered his prepared words.

"The truth is that I did break my wedding vow to a woman I love very much. I had an extramarital relationship that was not appropriate. In fact, it was wrong."

The image froze, locking onto a strategically selected frame in which the senator seemed to be winking at the camera. Voice-over followed:

"Why won't Senator Stahl tell us who it is?"

The senator slowly faded into the background, as if hiding from the voters. A man and a very concerned-looking woman replaced the senator on the screen.

They were seated on a bench at a playground, a group of preschoolers behind them climbing on monkey bars.

"If you ask me, there's more to it than cheatin' on his wife," the man said into the camera. "That's why Stahl won't tell."

"Honestly, I don't even want to know who it is," the woman added. "I've heard enough."

The voice-over returned: "Haven't we all heard enough?"

The ad ended with the American flag flying over the White House and the voice of the president: "I'm Malcolm MacLeod, and I one hundred percent approve this message."

To say that Stahl survived the ad was to say that Michael Dukakis neutralized convicted killer Willie Horton and the revolving prison door, the 1988 mother of all fear-mongering attack ads. The campaign's initial response—"We see no reason why gender matters"—only confirmed that Democrats had no clue what mattered outside a Democratic primary. Finally, after an eleven-point swing in the polls, the Democratic narrative shifted to "the senator's affair was with a woman, but we still believe gender shouldn't matter." By then it was not only too late, it was laughable. Late-night comedians turned it into a twenty-first-century version of the old Seinfeld joke, "Not that there's anything

wrong with the senator having an affair with a man."
The ad didn't explicitly accuse the senator of having a
same-sex extramarital affair, but the gay dog whistle
called home millions of lukewarm MacLeod supporters who had voted for him once and vowed never to do
it again.

"I need a drink," said the candidate, and he started
to the kitchen.

Stahl and everyone else had seen the ad countless
times, but it never seemed to lose its effect.

"Evan should have paraded out a former *Playboy*
model and shut down this gay talk from the get-go,"
said Senior.

Jack understood the cynicism. "For what it's worth,
my wife liked his explanation in the final debate—that
he got involved with a woman who regrets it and wants
to save her marriage."

"What's to like about it?" asked Senior.

"Naming her would make it impossible for her to
reconcile with her husband. It's not an honorable situation, but in a way the senator did an honorable thing by
respecting another family's privacy."

Senior seemed to appreciate Jack's attempt at a silver
lining. Then he looked at Harry. "You think we'll ever
find out who Evan slept with?"

Harry shrugged—not that he didn't know, but because it was inevitable. "Certain people would pay a lot of money for that information. Everyone has his price."

It was grammatically correct, but in this context Harry's use of the male pronoun left an awkward silence hanging over them.

"*Her* price," said Senior. "Everyone has *her* price."

Chapter 3

President MacLeod and his wife were home, in their Fifth Avenue penthouse apartment, in time to hear the first media projection of the night. Paulette Barrow, Florida's attorney general, phoned the president with the news. Barrow was a rising star in the party and one of the president's favorite people—"and not just because she's a gorgeous blonde," the president had said more than once on the campaign trail. Barrow had delivered the "why women love MacLeod" speech at the Republican National Convention.

"Great news, Mr. President. MSNBC projects that Michael Moore will move to Canada if you're re-elected."

"Good riddance. Communist."

"Best of luck, sir."

"We don't need luck. We need Florida."

Of his final twenty-four hours of campaigning, Mac-Leod had spent eighteen in the Sunshine State. Florida's I-4 corridor—the nineteen-county, 132.3-mile swath from Gulf-side St. Petersburg to ocean-side Daytona—was arguably the most valuable political cache of swing voters in America. Political consultants called it "America's corridor of power," paved with presidents made and contenders broken. It was the six million registered voters in the middle third of the peninsula that put Florida up for grabs: Republicans racked up votes in the conservative north and southwest, Democrats cleaned up in the southeast population centers, and the two sides battled it out in the high-growth "purple" areas along Interstate 4. Prior to the conventions, MacLeod's campaign strategists had all but conceded Florida to Stahl. Then everything changed.

"How we looking in Florida?" the president shouted across the room.

His campaign manager checked the latest numbers on his tablet. "It's literally fifty-fifty, Mr. President. But that's with less than one percent of precincts reporting."

"One percent? What the hell good is that? They could have just polled Senator Stahl's parents. No way

Evan Senior voted for anyone but the straight candidate. There's your fifty-fifty."

The eighty-inch flat-screen television suddenly turned bright red. A real projection was about to be made, and it was the right color.

"Where's the remote?" MacLeod shouted.

There was only one remote, and only one television, because MacLeod watched only one network. He found it wedged between the couch cushions and raised the volume to hear the important announcement.

". . . is projecting that President MacLeod will win the key state of Ohio, adding another eighteen Electoral College votes in his march to the magic total of two hundred seventy he needs to win reelection."

The living room erupted with joy, MacLeod shot two fists into the air, and high-fives were slapped all around. Ohio was just one of three "toss-up states"—Pennsylvania and Florida the other two—that strategists said the president needed to win. But MacLeod was feeling momentum.

"Where's the First Lady?" he asked, popping a handful of Tic Tacs into his mouth. "I deserve a kiss!"

"She's getting her hair blown out, sir."

"Good. We all need to look our best. Oscar, bring me my victory speech!"

Oscar Teague was the president's chief strategist

and senior counselor who, in life before the White House, founded an online news platform that brought the alt-right out of the shadows. Even Teague conceded that no one ever knew what the president might say at any given moment, but Republicans and Democrats alike agreed that if anyone could hold him to a script, if only for a little while, it was Teague. He took a seat on the couch and handed the president the latest draft, which was freshly bleeding with red ink.

MacLeod skimmed the first page and then laid it aside, scowling. "Where's that line I liked so much? You left it out."

"What line, sir?"

"The one you texted me right after midnight. 'It's morning again in America.'"

"Sir, I wasn't suggesting we use it. That was President Reagan's 1984 campaign slogan. 'Prouder, stronger, better. It's morning again in America.'"

"Oh. I knew that."

Political slogans were not MacLeod's strong suit. MacLeod was a businessman, not a politician. He'd made his first millions in multilevel-marketing companies, but his real fortune had come later in life, when at the age of forty-nine he was literally the old man in the digital world, pioneering the multibillion-dollar industry of peer-to-peer (P2P) file trading on the so-called dark side of the Internet. It was "the dark net" that had come back to haunt him, unleashing a chain of events that led to the appointment of a special counsel and threats of impeachment by the House of Representatives.

"Can I have a minute in private with you, Mr. President?"

Andrew Blake was right behind him, the president's personal attorney—personal criminal defense attorney. The president excused himself from his guests, and the two men retreated to the library. MacLeod closed the double doors of dark mahogany, shutting out the buzz of excitement from the watching party.

"I've always been straight with you, Mr. President. And I'm being very straight with you now."

"Straight" was Blake's favorite word. Straight talk. Keep to the straight and narrow. At times, MacLeod felt like telling him to go straight to hell. But Blake was irreplaceable. Against strong Democratic opposition, he'd convinced the Justice Department to stick to its long-standing position that the U.S. Constitution prohibited the indictment of a sitting president.

"Tell me," said MacLeod.

"There are millions of Democrats who still think you dodged a bullet when the House decided not to bring impeachment proceedings. They had the votes."

"But they didn't have the votes to convict in the Senate. That's politics."

"Correct. But that's not the end of the story. I spoke with the U.S. attorney in New York. There's no doubt in my mind that if you lose this election, you will be indicted on the day after Stahl is inaugurated as president."

"All this P2P file-sharing nonsense was over twenty years ago. At some point, the statute of limitations has to run on those crimes."

"Those crimes" were identity theft. MacLeod had been an early investor in file-sharing software and platforms that allowed complete strangers to connect online to search for shared files on the computers of their "peers" on the same network. Most people shared music or video, prompting the lawsuits over illegal trading of copyright-protected material that shut down Napster and others in the early 2000s. Of greater interest to law enforcement was the fact that, on most of the P2P networks, roughly two-thirds of downloadable movies and other files contained malware—viruses, worms, Trojan horses—that turned personal information on a home computer into the cyberspace equivalent of an unlocked and unattended vehicle with the keys in the ignition and the motor running. P2P became a virtual smorgasbord for identity thieves. MacLeod cashed out of the P2P industry at the right time, before Silicon Valley discovered that stealing personal information was completely unnecessary, that people would happily shovel everything about themselves into the social-media maw, as long as their friends would "LIKE" it.

"The indictment won't be based on the violation of any cyber-security laws," said Blake. "The offense is lying to an FBI agent in violation of Title Eighteen of the United States Code."

"What's the lie?"

"There are actually thirty-one of them, sir."

MacLeod grumbled. "I should never have agreed to sit down and talk to those bastards."

His lawyer's expression said it all: *I told you so.*

"What's done is done," said MacLeod. "What's our strategy?"

"Win the election."

"I mean if I lose. What's Plan B?"

Blake paused, which was what he always did before delivering news the president didn't want to hear. "You should resign, sir."

"What?"

"Vice President Kincaid will become president for the final two and a half months of your current term. There's no guarantee, but it would be within his prerogative to issue a full pardon before President-Elect Stahl takes office. In the best interest of the country, of course."

MacLeod rose from his chair and began to pace, considering his lawyer's advice. Then he stopped and looked at Blake. "I much prefer Plan A."

MacLeod hurried from the library, walking with purpose down the hallway to the living room. Election coverage continued on the television screen, but MacLeod went straight to the whiteboard in the corner, where his advisors had been doing the election math all night long in two columns, blue for Democrat and red for Republican. So many numbers had been crossed out and recalculated that it looked more like a physics equation than an election tally.

"Am I going to win?" he asked his chief strategist.

Teague struggled, there being no doubt what the president wanted to hear. "Right now, the only thing we know for certain is that we're getting clobbered in the popular vote. We'll lose by at least four million. Probably closer to five."

"We didn't run our campaign to win the popular

vote. Not in the last election, and not in this one, either. Where are we in the Electoral College?"

"None of the networks have called Pennsylvania yet, but we're hearing good things on the ground. We're going to win there."

"And if we do?" asked MacLeod.

Teague grabbed two erasable markers and put two numbers on the board. "Two sixty-five," he said, writing in blue for Stahl. "Two forty-four," he said, switching to red.

MacLeod walked to the window, buried his hands in his pockets, and gazed out over the city lights. It was simple math: 509 of the 538 Electoral College votes were sewn up. The winner needed a majority of 270.

"So, it comes down to Florida," he said—not a question, but a mere restatement of what he'd heard at least a thousand times in the final stages of the campaign.

"Yes, sir. Twenty-nine from Florida puts you over the top with two seventy-three. Or it puts Stahl over the top—way over the top—with two ninety-four."

"How close is it?"

"As of this minute, you're up by about eight thousand votes. With total voter turnout pushing ten million, that's a dead heat. Shit, Roseanne Barr got over eight thousand votes when Romney lost Florida to Obama by less than a point."

"I voted for Roseanne," said MacLeod. "What's wrong with Roseanne?"

"That wasn't my point," said Teague. He grabbed a black marker and circled a different number on the board. "Five million. That's still the number that concerns me. If you win Florida by just a few thousand votes, and you lose the nationwide popular vote by five million, it'll be Gore versus Bush all over again. We need a strategy."

"Get me Paulette Barrow on the line. I need her to shut down the cries for a recount before they get started."

"In Florida I don't believe the attorney general has any say over recounts," said Teague. "It's up to the secretary of state."

MacLeod was losing patience. "Oscar, the Florida secretary of state is a Democrat, am I right?"

"Yes, sir."

"Can you name a more loyal Republican in the state of Florida than Paulette Barrow?"

"No, sir."

"And not to put too fine a point on it, but how many blow jobs do you think I've gotten from the Florida's Democrat secretary of state?"

He'd never gotten one from the Republican attorney general, either, but the president rather enjoyed the way his backhanded innuendo made his staff squirm.

Teague nervously reached for his phone and dialed. "I'll get General Barrow on the line, sir."

Chapter 4

"I know this is not what you want to hear," said Harry. "But I believe you should concede."

Senator Stahl was polling the group in his living room. Reality had reared its ugly head at exactly 11:34 p.m. Eastern Time, when the Associated Press called the state of Florida for MacLeod. The loss of those twenty-nine Electoral College votes made it mathematically impossible for Senator Stahl to reach 270. It wasn't hard to imagine the euphoria at MacLeod's penthouse on Fifth Avenue. What Jack couldn't grasp was the reason for his father's advice.

"Why concede?" asked Jack. "MacLeod's margin of victory is two-tenths of a percent, if my math is right. Anything less than half a percent triggers a mandatory recount under Florida law."

Until that moment, Jack had offered little more in the way of election advice than had the untouched election cake. Perhaps it wasn't Jack's place to speak out in this group, but healthy disagreements with his father were somewhat second nature, a positive offshoot from the bad old days of mutual verbal assault.

Senator Stahl reached for his phone and dialed his campaign manager, who was running what was supposed to have been a victory party at the Miami Beach Convention Center. "Turn off the election coverage, Irwin. Cue the campaign video."

Stahl put his phone aside and looked the former governor in the eye. "Harry, what's your answer to the younger half of the Swyteck contingent?"

"Jack and I had this same disagreement with Gore versus Bush. The certified results on election night had Bush ahead by less than eighteen hundred votes. Even closer than this race. What did the Democrats get by challenging the result? Nothing."

"You can't frame the issue in terms of whether it's good for one party or the other. People are fed up with the Electoral College. The idea that the candidate who wins fifty-point-one percent of the vote in Florida gets a hundred percent of Florida's twenty-nine electors is just wrong."

"Those are the rules, Jack. That argument is not even on the table."

"I understand. All I'm saying is that if you have a winner-take-all system, it's even more important that every single vote is counted. Asking for a recount makes sense."

"Son, you're being wrongheaded."

"What's your point, Harry?" asked Stahl. "Don't try, because we might fail?"

"First of all, you will fail," said Harry. "A recount might turn up a few hundred votes, but not eight thousand. Number two, we have a midterm election in two years. Sure, we can cry 'do-over' tonight and be labeled the party of sore losers. Or we can accept reality and be the party that puts our country above our party—and hopefully take back the Senate the way we took back the House two years ago."

There was silence in the room. If it had been just Jack and his father talking over beers, Jack would have argued the point further. But this was Harry in his element, and the advice was coming from a two-term governor of Florida who had never in his political life been forced to deliver a concession speech—not once in forty years. Harry Swyteck might have been old and retired, but he understood Florida politics.

Everyone in the room seemed to understand that much.

"Bring me a landline," Stahl told his assistant. "I need to congratulate our president."

Jack and his father were the first to leave the Stahl watching party. Everyone else in the candidate's living room had invested too much, hoped too much, and worked too hard over the past sixteen months to push themselves up from the couch and be the first ones out the door.

"Was I right?" asked Harry. He was in the passenger seat, glancing over at Jack in the glow of dashboard lights.

"I don't know. But I respect you enough to say you made sense."

"Thank you. I think."

It would have been enough for Jack to call it a night and head straight home. His father wanted to witness the concession speech, however, so Jack went with him.

To Jack's knowledge, there had never been a funeral at the Miami Beach Convention Center. A funeral would have been jolly compared to the mood at the Stahl election party, as election night turned into the early morning after.

The Stahl campaign video—not live election coverage—was playing on the jumbotron, exactly as the candidate had directed. But there was no hiding the fact that Florida had gone Republican, and that there was no road to victory. Thousands of sad faces, many washed with tears, told the story. Some folks had already left, as evidenced by the pink and blue MAKE AMERICA FABULOUS caps left behind.

The campaign video cut off. Governor Greer of Wisconsin entered, stage right, in the company of his wife, three sons, two daughters-in-law, and two grandchildren. The midwestern governor had done his job and turned the Dairy State blue, but it wasn't enough.

It would have made sense for Greer to introduce his running mate, but the governor and his family simply lined up behind the lectern, waiting, smiling, and waving in response to applause. A moment later, Senator Stahl stepped out without introduction, probably to save himself the embarrassment of walking onstage without his wife and daughter.

"How the heck are ya?" Stahl shouted in his trademark greeting.

The crowd cheered and hollered with whatever voices they had left. Jack had watched plenty of concession speeches on television, but the heartbreak of loyal supporters was palpable when you were actually in the room. Stahl waited for the applause to fade—it took a while—and then began.

"I have so, so many people to thank," he said, "not the least of which are the sixty-seven million Americans who gave us an impressive five-million vote majority in the popular vote."

That was the proverbial red meat to the partisan crowd, and Stahl allowed them a moment of revelry. Then, with a pained smile, he pushed forward.

"But first, let me take care of business."

"Don't do it!" a woman shouted, joined by others with similar pleas.

The senator's smile drained away, and his expression turned serious. "In every campaign, often at the very moment political tension threatens to tear us apart, there comes a time to stop serving one side or another and serve democracy itself."

"No!"

"Please, please," Stahl said, quieting the crowd. He swallowed the lump in his throat, and then he continued.

"History is a great teacher," he said, "and our country is rich with great history. In 1824, Andrew Jackson won a plurality of the popular vote and the electoral vote, yet the House of Representatives chose John Quincy Adams president. Despite having much to say about the process, Jackson conceded.

"In 1876, Samuel Tilden won a majority of the popular vote, but the electoral vote was disputed in four states. Not surprisingly, one of those states in dispute was Florida," he said with a smile, drawing a few sad chuckles from supporters. "Congress appointed a commission that made Rutherford B. Hayes president. Tilden conceded.

"Twelve years later, it happened again. Grover Cleveland won the popular vote. Benjamin Harrison won the Electoral College. Cleveland conceded.

"In this century, Al Gore won the popular vote, but lost the state of Florida by a few hanging chads, costing him a majority of Electoral College votes. His fight went all the way to the Supreme Court. But in the end, he, too, conceded. 'Just as we fight hard when the stakes are high,' Vice President Gore told us, 'we close ranks and come together when the contest is done.'

"Many of us still feel the sting from just four years ago, when Senator Hillman won the popular vote by a bona fide landslide. But it was Malcolm MacLeod who took the Electoral College, and so Bernadette did the right thing. She picked up the phone and made the call no presidential candidate wants to make.

"In that same spirit, I called President MacLeod about thirty minutes ago. Unfortunately he was unable to come to the phone."

The candidate paused to allow a chorus of boos to pass. He gathered himself, on the verge of concession, when his campaign manager approached and handed him a note. Stahl reviewed it and gazed out toward his sea of loyal supporters.

"Well, what a surprise," he said with a wry smile. "I see that the president just tweeted."

A few laughed through their sadness, but the candidate fell silent. The crowd waited. Jack watched from a distance, sensing change in the air. Jack was too far from the stage to read the senator's expression, so he checked the close-up on the jumbotron overhead. What he saw only fueled his sense that something was afoot. A transformation seemed to be bubbling up from deep inside the candidate, breathing life into a political soul that had been dying day by day, starting with the press conference that had turned a Democratic cakewalk into a political death march.

Stahl cleared his throat and read aloud. "The president's tweet says as follows: 'I will take Senator Stahl's phone call and accept his concession only after he apologizes to the American people.'"

The boo-birds returned, but the candidate quieted them, signaling that there was more.

"Hashtag—" Stahl stopped, biting back his anger,

and then he finished reading the president's tweet. "Hashtag 'Sodom and Goliath.'"

A split second of silence followed, as collective confusion—*Goliath? WTF?*—fell over the audience.

"I'm guessing he meant 'Gomorrah,'" said the senator.

Silence gave way to shrieks of outrage, and then a man in the front row shouted, "Five million matter!" He said it again and again. It quickly caught on. Two women joined him, and it spread across the entire row. In a matter of seconds, the whole crowd was chanting, "Five million matter! Five million matter!"

On it went, the crowd refusing to let their candidate finish his concession speech. As thirty seconds became a minute, and as a minute grew into two minutes, the senator seemed to come back to life and embrace the message.

"Yes! Five million do matter!" Stahl shouted, and the crowd erupted with a roar of approval.

"We live in a tech-savvy world in which dirty politics has gone high-tech," he said, speaking with newfound energy. "As a businessman, Mr. MacLeod made billions of dollars mining your personal data. If you're on social media, his campaign knows what you like, what you share, what you buy—maybe even what you think."

A wave of suspicious boos cascaded across the convention center.

"Now, no candidate, no matter how strong his social-media campaign, can trick five million voters in fifty different states into voting for him."

"Five million matter!"

"But what if he can win the White House simply by convincing eight thousand voters in Central Florida to hate me enough to vote for him?"

"Five million matter!"

"When the votes of five million Americans are ignored—and when a presidential election is won with hate-filled e-mails strategically targeted to eight thousand voters in Polk County, Florida—something is wrong!"

"Five million matter!"

"When five million votes are ignored—and when the White House is won with bald-faced lies strategically targeted to scare the living crap out of eight thousand voters in rural Brevard County—something is wrong!"

"Five million matter!"

"No, Mr. MacLeod. I will not apologize. Nor will I concede. This fight is not over! Not over by a long shot! Hashtag 'Five Million Matter!'"

The roar became a crescendo, and the confetti that had been intended for the victory celebration fell by the bucketful from the rafters.

Jack watched in amazement. Not since the Pope's first visit to Miami had he seen such mob hysteria, when the Hispanic faithful unleashed their wrath against an unwitting street vendor for hawking T-shirts that should have said EL PAPA—the Pope—but instead said, LA PAPA—the potato.

The noise inside the convention center was deafening, but Jack could see his father's lips moving. Maybe Jack heard what he was saying, or maybe he just intuited what his father was thinking.

"It's political Armageddon" was what Jack thought he had heard.

Chapter 5

I t was 2:00 a.m. when Jack texted his wife. He didn't intend to wake her, but she answered his text with a call.

"Looks like I'll be with Senator Stahl at his house the rest of the night," said Jack.

Andie yawned into the phone. "Isn't it victory parties that go into the wee hours of the morning?"

"So hilarious," said Jack.

Immediately after the non-concession speech in Miami Beach, Candidate Stahl—he was still a candidate—convened his inner circle at his house. This time, Jack was not merely his father's guest. He and the senator were in the kitchen with Matthew Kipner, a gray-haired Washington lawyer and nationally recognized expert on election law. Jack's father and the rest of the Stahl team were brainstorming in the living room.

"I want you involved in this," said Stahl.

The framed needlepoint on the wall, HOME IS WHERE THE HEART IS, made Jack wonder how Mrs. Stahl was handling all "this."

"Involved how, exactly?" Jack asked, though he had a general idea.

The 130 million Americans who voted on Election Day didn't actually vote for Stahl or MacLeod. They voted for a slate of electors chosen by the respective political parties. By law, the nation's 538 members of the Electoral College were scheduled to convene in their respective state capitals on December 14 and vote. Until that happened, there was no president-elect.

"Right now we have 265 Democrats in the Electoral College," said Stahl. "That leaves us thirty-nine days to convince five Republican electors to break ranks and vote for the winner of the popular vote—yours truly."

Jack paused. It seemed like high time to clear the air. "Maybe my father hasn't told you, but I'm—"

"An independent," said the senator. "I know."

"I'm sorry you lost. But if you're asking me to lean on my father to help you change the minds of Republican electors, I'm not your man."

The senator took a seat at the barstool, looking at Jack from the other side of the granite-top island. "This isn't about politics."

Jack couldn't count the number of times he'd heard those words from a politician. But he let the senator finish.

"If we find Republican electors willing to break ranks and vote for me, it's going to be an epic legal battle. MacLeod and his team of lawyers will come down on them like a sledgehammer. Matt can tell you. He's the expert."

Kipner elaborated. "Most states require their electors to vote by party line. That means if voters in the November election went Republican, the entire slate of Republican electors is expected to vote for the Republican candidate in December. The same is true in states that went Democratic. Any elector on the slate who crosses over to the other party is considered a 'faithless elector.'"

"I'm familiar with the concept. My dad and I have had umpteen arguments about the Electoral College since *Gore v. Bush*."

"Then you're aware that when it comes to binding its electors to vote along party lines, Florida has a strange law."

"Why would Florida be anything but strange?" said Jack, and the remark required no explanation. From "hanging chads" and Cocaine Cowboys, to the Versace killer and the "CNN-Sucks" Bomber, Florida was a sanity-deprived society, the continued existence of which defied evolutionary theory.

"Amen to that," said Stahl.

Kipner went to the coffeemaker on the counter and poured himself a fresh cup. "Our legal position is that Florida's statute allows electors to vote their conscience. They don't have to vote on party lines. But the statute is goofy enough for MacLeod to make a persuasive counterargument."

"Are you asking me to be part of your legal team?" asked Jack.

"Not exactly," said Stahl. "Matthew is my lawyer."

"Then where do I fit in?"

Kipner answered. "We don't know where we'll find our so-called faithless electors. It could be Florida. It could be Alaska. Michigan. Nebraska. Wherever we find them, those electors will need their own local lawyer."

Stahl leaned forward, making "the ask" more personal. "Can I count on you, Jack? If there's a fight in Florida?"

"Can I ask why you want me?"

"Obviously you're a very talented lawyer," said Stahl.

"I also like that you're an independent. No affiliation with either party blunts the claims of partisanship."

"And?" Jack prodded.

"Kipner finished the thought. "Let's be straight: your name carries weight in any lawsuit in Florida with political implications. There's nothing wrong with that."

"I appreciate your honesty," said Jack. "But I've never accepted a case because of my last name."

"Senator Stahl needs a go-to lawyer whom he can trust, and we need that person in place, ready to step in on a moment's notice."

"So, what do you say, Jack?" asked Stahl.

Jack considered it. "If there's a faithless elector in Florida who wants to hire me, and if I think I can help, there would be no reason for me not to take the case. But I would be the lawyer for the elector and only for the elector. I won't take directions from the campaign." Jack looked straight at Kipner. "Or from the candidate's legal counsel."

Stahl glanced at his lawyer. "That good enough for you, Matt?"

If Jack was reading Kipner's expression correctly, his response was well short of "good enough."

"Jack, you don't seem to understand," said Kipner. "This battle is going to be high profile. Lawyers will be begging to play on this national stage."

"And I'd love to be involved—on my terms. I won't be offended if you steer the case to someone else."

"Hold on," said Stahl. "Take a minute to talk to your father, Jack. Then give us a decision."

"I call my own shots when it comes to my law practice. What do you want me to ask him?"

The question was directed to the senator, but Kipner took an assertive step forward. He seemed ready to move down the list to one of those lawyers who would "beg" for the job.

"Ask your old man if he knows any lawyers we can trust," said Kipner.

"Got it," said Jack. "Gentlemen, it sounds like this interview is over. But thank you."

Jack started out.

"Jack," said the senator, stopping him. "You're making a big mistake."

It was late, Jack was tired, and, for his father's sake, Jack didn't want to say the wrong thing to a man who still had a legitimate shot at the White House. He kept it short.

"You're probably right," Jack said, and he left the kitchen.

Chapter 6

Ground Force One, the president's armored motor coach, rolled into Florida like a jet-black fortress on wheels. It was day three of President MacLeod's victory tour.

MacLeod's chief strategist loved history, and his inspiration for this road trip was George Washington's 1,887-mile stagecoach tour following his inauguration in 1789. Heading south from Washington, MacLeod's tour sailed right through Virginia, which had gone for Stahl, and officially began in Raleigh, North Carolina. Then it was on to South Carolina and Georgia. The original plan had been to hit every state the president had carried in the general election and to do it before the meeting of the Electoral College on December 14. MacLeod's mission was an in-person meeting with each Republican elector—all 273 of them—to reinforce what the president's lawyers characterized as a "binding legal commitment" to vote for him. "Thirty-one states in thirty-one days" was the slogan. But like so many plans the MacLeod White House had rolled out in the previous four years, this one had barely begun before it was scrapped and completely rewritten. The press reminded MacLeod that he wasn't a president-elect with nothing to do but hit the road and thank everyone who voted for him; he was the sitting president with a country to run. Thirty-one states were whittled down to the nine battleground states that had pushed MacLeod over the top in the Electoral College. Chief among them was Florida.

After breakfast with his chief strategist on the bus, MacLeod stopped for a stump speech at Tallahassee Community College, also known as TCC, disparaged as "Tee Hee Hee" by luckier students who got directly into nearby Florida State University without having to spend a semester or two at TCC. About a thousand passionate MacLeod supporters crammed into Eagle Field baseball stadium near the TCC campus. Most were seated in the bleachers and grandstands. Others grabbed a patch of the Bermuda grass infield, getting as close to the president as the Secret Service would allow. MacLeod had no prepared words. The president's penchant for free-flowing thought gave his staff indigestion on a regular basis, but his base loved the way he waxed on without a script. MacLeod was on his favorite topic: winning.

"Look at the electoral map," he said, though he had no map to show them. "I won thirty-one states. If you go county by county and color in every one that went for me, over eighty percent of the map is red! What did Stahl win? Basically, the liberal population centers around New York City and Washington and certain cities in California. That's the Democrats' idea of democracy. Let a handful of big liberal cities pick your president and forget everyone else. That's what they mean when they say 'the popular vote.'"

MacLeod paused for the usual showing of love and support through friendly booing.

"By the way, have you been to San Francisco lately? You can't walk two blocks down the sidewalk without stepping in a pile of human waste or being assaulted by a mentally deranged homeless person. Is that the best America can be? No, thanks, Mr. Stahl. Voters rejected you and your elitist views. You say, 'Five million matter'? I say elections matter. You lost. Get over it. There are no mulligans in politics. Thank you all very, very much!"

Like a rock star, he waved to his adoring fans and started offstage. A pair of stone-faced Secret Service agents escorted him back to Ground Force One. The president climbed the steps quickly, still energized by his speech. The pneumatic door closed behind him, and he took a seat in the captain's chair by the dark-tinted window. His chief strategist sat across from him in the other chair.

"That was awesome," said MacLeod.

"I'm glad you enjoyed it," said Teague. "But there's no time for any more speeches. We have to stick to the schedule. I don't see how we're going to get through twenty-nine meetings today before hitting Alabama tomorrow."

"Stop and think about what you just said, Oscar. Do you honestly think we're going to find an unfaithful elector in Alabama?"

Teague thought about it, but not very long. "Well, no, actually."

"My point exactly. If we have to stay over another day in Florida, so be it. We can do a group meeting with all nine Alabama electors and get right back on schedule."

"That's fine. We'll need two full days in Florida. I have some specific concerns."

"Tell me."

Teague set up his notebook on the table and positioned it so the president could view it. Thumbnail photographs of Florida's twenty-nine electors populated the screen in yearbook fashion.

"Good-looking group," said the president, and then he zeroed in on the brunette in the second row. "She's actually pretty hot."

"I'll get to her in a minute. By and large, the slate is filled with hardcore Republicans who wouldn't vote for a Democrat if you put a gun to their head. Obviously, I'm not worried about the chairman of the Florida Republican Party. But there are a handful of wildcards we need to focus on."

"Like who?"

"This guy, for one," he said, pointing. "Alan Schwartz."

"Who's he?"

"He won the Florida Lotto six years ago. Eighty million dollars, lump sum. Every year he gives a ton of money to Republican candidates, which I presume is how he ended up on the Republican slate of Electoral College voters. But it turns out he uses his spare change to buy politicians of every stripe, Republican and Democrat alike. So I don't know how loyal he is."

MacLeod grabbed a pen and made a note on his list of names. "I'll put a question mark by him. Who else?"

"Irving Bell."

"The former football player? That Irving Bell?"

"Yeah. A solid Republican, but he gets a lot of grief from the black community for supporting you."

"Do you seriously think a Republican NFL star who grew up in Miami's toughest black neighborhood is going to vote for a homosexual?"

"Senator Stahl is alleged to have slept with a man. Even if it's true, that doesn't make him a homosexual."

"Give me a break, Oscar. Now you sound like those liberal lunatics who came down on Rami Malek at the Academy Awards for saying that Freddie Mercury was gay. I get it. The man bit the bullet and slept with a woman at some point in his life. He's still a killer queen in my book."

"I'm just saying that Mr. Bell could feel some external pressure to abandon you."

"Irving 'the Bell-Man' can handle pressure. Who else? Do any of these electors have a brother who's gay, a lesbian daughter—that sort of thing?"

"I don't have that information, but the answer is probably yes. We're talking about twenty-nine people from one of the most diverse states in the nation."

"I guess we'll find out when I talk to them," he said, and his gaze drifted back to where the conversation had started. "Tell me about this brunette."

"Charlotte Holmes. Thirty-three years old. Lives right here in Tallahassee."

"How did she get to be an elector?"

"She works with Madeline Chisel."

"The gun lobbyist?"

"The one and only."

MacLeod's gaze returned to the on-screen headshot. "Damn, now I'm in love."

"You may want to cool your jets, sir. So far I've been able to line up twenty-eight of Florida's twenty-nine electors to meet with you. There's only one who hasn't gotten back to me. Care to guess who it is?"

"Maybe Ms. Holmes likes to play hard to get."

"Maybe Charlotte Holmes is somebody we need to worry about."

"That's the difference between you and me, Oscar."

"What's that, sir?"

"Beautiful women don't scare me." MacLeod smiled and popped a Tic Tac into his mouth. "Ever."

"Another one of your many virtues, sir."

MacLeod laughed. "You're such a tight-ass, Oscar."

"I've been called worse," he said, letting it roll off his back. "More important, I want to start moving on Charlotte Holmes. I suggest a call from you to Madeline Chisel."

"That's a great place to start," said the president.

"That woman has kept Tallahassee in line on guns for forty years. She can certainly get her own employee in line."

MacLeod's praise for Chisel was no exaggeration. It was Chisel who'd crafted the Florida statute that allowed anyone who legally owns a firearm to carry a concealed handgun in public, after payment of a small permitting fee and completion of a rudimentary training course. Florida's law went on to be duplicated, in some form, in almost every state. Chisel's fingerprints were also on the country's first stand-your-ground law, which did away with any duty to retreat and authorized the use of lethal force as a first option in response to a perceived threat.

Teague retrieved the contact information, dialed up Chisel on an encrypted line, and handed the phone to the president.

"Madeline, good to hear your voice. How long has it been?"

"Since your speech at the NRA convention, Mr. President. I'm honored to take your call."

"We're having some trouble setting up a meeting with your associate, Charlotte Holmes."

"Yes, and I apologize for this mess. You know, I turned eighty this year."

"Congratulations. You sound as young as ever."

"I don't feel so young. This is the first year since Bush forty-one that I declined to serve on the Republican slate of electors. I've spent the last two years passing the baton here at my lobbying firm to Charlotte. So I gave her the honor of being an elector, just to build up her street cred, so to speak. She was my golden girl."

"Was?" MacLeod asked with concern.

"Yeah," she said, her voice halting. "Charlotte resigned about twenty minutes ago."

"What? Why?"

"She didn't give a reason. I got a one-line e-mail this morning, and she didn't answer when I called her. Pretty inconsiderate of her, after all I've done for that girl. I was getting my thoughts together to call Oscar when my phone rang."

"Obviously it's more important than ever that I speak to her."

"She has to clean out her office at some point, but I'm not sure it will be today. I can drive over to her house right now, if you want."

"Yes, please do that. Let us know."

"Will do."

The president thanked her and then ended the call. He laid the phone on the table and looked at his campaign manager. "I guess there's a first time for everything, Oscar."

"Sir?"

He sat back in his captain's chair, gazing pensively out the dark-tinted windows of Ground Force One. "Charlotte Holmes is starting to scare me."

Chapter 7

Jack was in his office when his father called. Harry's wife was in the hospital.

"Just for some tests," said Harry. "We need to know why she's feeling tired all the time. I'm sure it's nothing."

Agnes had been "feeling tired" since July, when Jack had taken her seat of honor beside the former governor at the convention in Miami Beach. Jack suspected it was more likely something than "nothing," but that was probably the last thing his father needed to hear.

"I'm sure you're right," said Jack.

"It would do her good to see her granddaughter. Could you bring Righley by for a visit?"

Jackson Memorial Hospital was a world-renowned teaching and tertiary-care center just across the Miami River from Jack's office, less than a mile from the Criminal Justice Center. Jack wasn't the only criminal defense lawyer in Miami who'd stood in a courtroom defending a client whose victim lay in a hospital bed at Jackson, quite possibly with a view of the courthouse. There were definitely parts of his job that Jack didn't like.

Visitation hours at Jackson were until 9:00 p.m. Andie swung by the office to pick up Jack. Righley was strapped into her car seat behind him.

"Daddy, why would anybody want arms like a bear?"

"What, sweetie?"

"Wouldn't they be all hairy and gross?"

"Wouldn't what be hairy and gross?"

"Bear arms."

Andie stopped at the intersection. "I think our little girl's been listening to those TV ads—the ones that say Senator Stahl's attempt to hijack the Electoral College is a left-wing attack on the Second Amendment and the right to bear arms."

"The right to keep and bear arms," said Jack. "Not the right to bear arms."

"As distinguished from the Third Amendment and the right to frog feet," said Andie.

"I want frog feet!" shouted Righley.

Jack laughed, then stopped. "What the heck is the Third Amendment, anyway?"

"I don't know. You're the lawyer."

"I must've missed that day in law school."

Self-parking was virtually impossible anywhere on the medical campus, so they valeted at the main hospital entrance. A patient was waiting in a wheelchair at the curb, attended by a nurse. She was barely conscious, too weak to hold her head up straight. Jack took Righley's hand to hurry her along and keep her from staring with the innocent but nonetheless intrusive curiosity of a child.

"How old is that lady?" Righley whispered.

No older than Andie, Jack guessed. Jack hadn't come looking for a teaching moment, but later, probably when they returned home, would be an appropriate time to talk more about diseases that robbed people of their best years. "She's very sick, honey."

They checked in at the visitation desk. Jack wanted a candid update from his father, which he wasn't likely to get in front of a child, so Andie sat with Righley on the couch and Jack waited by the elevators. The chrome doors parted and Harry stepped out, but before Jack could even say hello, a reporter jumped out of nowhere and cornered Harry by a potted palm tree.

"Governor, how is the former First Lady?"

Harry was surprised but gracious. He told the reporter

exactly what he'd told Jack: tests. It took only a moment for the journalist to pivot to the real purpose of the ambush. "Sir, is it true that you advised Senator Stahl to concede the election and not take this fight to the Electoral College?"

Jack tried not to react in the presence of a reporter, but his father's advice had been rendered in the limited presence of the candidate's inner circle on election night—which meant that this reporter had one very high-ranking source.

"Whatever I told the senator is between him and me," said Harry. "I'm a private citizen these days."

"What do you think of the latest news out of Michigan?"

"What news?"

"The Republican elector who said he was threatened with death if he doesn't switch his vote to Senator Stahl."

"I've not heard that report. If it's true, it's terrible, and whoever made such a threat should be prosecuted to the full extent of the law. Now, if you'll excuse me, I'd like to take my son and his family upstairs to see my wife."

"Just one more question, Governor. Does Senator Stahl have your full support in his efforts to convince Republicans to be faithless electors and vote Democratic?"

Harry hesitated, and Jack wondered how his father was going to handle this one.

"I would never criticize any American for voting his or her conscience," said Harry.

"Including members of the Electoral College?"

Righley ran across the lobby and wrapped her arms around Harry's legs. "Hi, Grandpa!"

Harry scooped her up. Jack glanced across the lobby and silently thanked Andie for having the good sense to send Righley over to rescue Grandpa.

Harry excused himself and carried Righley into the open elevator. Jack and Andie joined them, Righley made a big deal out of pushing the button, and they rode up to the fourth floor, sans reporter. Jack's cell rang as they walked down the hallway. It was his assistant calling from the office. Jack never ignored a call from Bonnie. He let Righley and Andie go inside the room without him and took the call in the waiting area by the nurses' station.

"Sorry to bother you, Jack, but it's a potential new client, and this is definitely an emergency."

"Who is it?"

"Her name is Charlotte Holmes. She's one of the Florida electors."

"Bonnie, are you sure this is not a practical joke?"

Jack could think of at least one friend who would think a stunt like this was hilarious.

"It sounds legit. She said she already spoke to Senator Stahl's lawyer and mentioned Mr. Kipner by name. Maybe she wants to change her vote."

"If she spoke to Kipner, she wouldn't be calling me. The last conversation I had with him made it clear that if any of the electors needed a lawyer, I wouldn't be at the top of the referral list. They want someone they can control."

"Should I tell Ms. Holmes to call someone else?"

Jack had his doubts, but what if this was real? "Put her through, I guess."

Bonnie made the connection, did the introduction, and then dropped herself from the call. Jack went straight to the issue that was at the root of his suspicions. "Ms. Holmes, I'm told that you were referred to me by Senator Stahl's legal counsel, Matthew Kipner."

"That's not exactly right. I said I spoke to Mr. Kipner. I told him I was considering voting my conscience and that I expected a legal fight. He said he couldn't represent me, but he didn't refer me to you. He gave me the name of three other lawyers who he thought would be good."

"Then why are you calling me?"

"Honestly? Because he specifically told me not to hire you."

All doubts about Charlotte's veracity suddenly evaporated.

"How soon can we meet?" Jack asked.

Chapter 8

They met the following morning at Jack's office.

Jack Swyteck, P.A., was part of a neighborhood in transition, where historic residences were transforming into art studios, restaurants, and professional office space. Jack practiced out of a house dating back to the 1920s, ancient by Miami standards, built in the old Florida style with a coral-rock façade and a big covered porch that cried out for a rocking chair and whittling stick.

"Love your office," said Charlotte. "Funny, I had you pegged for a high-rise on Brickell Avenue, all glass and glitz."

"I like the sense of history here."

Lots of history. The previous owner was the Freedom Institute, where Jack had worked as a young attorney fresh out of law school. Four years of defending death-row inmates proved to be enough for Jack, so he struck out on his own as a sole practitioner. A decade later, when his mentor passed away and the Institute was on the brink of financial collapse, Jack came up with a plan to save it, which eventually meant buying the building. The Freedom Institute operated rent-free upstairs in the renovated bedrooms. Initially, Jack barely did well enough to fix the broken pipes and leaky roof, but things picked up. The original floors of Dade County pine were sanded and refinished. The high ceilings and crown moldings were restored. Bad fluorescent lighting, circa 1975, had been replaced in a total electrical update. The furnishings were upgraded with an eclectic mix of modern minimalist décor and period antiques.

"I tried to get Madeline to fix up our office like this," said Charlotte. "She wouldn't spend a dime. Clients would stop by, expecting the usual trappings of a successful lobbying firm. Instead, they got musty rooms cluttered with paper, files, and old bankers' boxes."

Jack led Charlotte to a sitting area near a stone fireplace. They were in what once was the dining room, seated in matching armchairs.

"Tell me something about yourself. Where'd you grow up?"

Charlotte Holmes was raised in Florida's Panhandle, aka "Southern Alabama," steeped in gun culture. Her father was an avid hunter. He had no sons and, by God, at least one of his five daughters was going to be a hunter. It fell to Charlotte. She owned a Davey Crickett .22 single-shot rifle before she was ten, and it became a way of life. Guns were purely sport for Charlotte, until she and her closest sister went off to college and roomed together at Florida State University. One night, Charlotte's sister didn't come home. They found her in the woods, half-naked and unconscious. A newspaper story the next day included a quote from a Tallahassee gun lobbyist: "These things wouldn't happen if these college girls would have the sense to protect themselves and learn to use a gun."

"I was furious," said Charlotte. "So I got in my car and went to see this big-mouth jerk named Madeline Chisel."

"Is that really how you met?"

"True story. It was my intention to tell her where to go. By the time I left her office, I was a fan."

"When did you start working for her?"

"A few years later. Right out of college, I went to work for a not-for-profit organization that helped victims of sexual assault. The more young women I met, the more

I came to believe that Madeline was right: women need to protect themselves, and anyone who would feel safer with a gun has every right to own one. I was about twenty-five when I reconnected with Madeline. By then she was the go-to gun lobbyist in the country. It was more work than she could handle. She offered me a job, and I took it on the spot."

"Did you like what you were doing?"

"Loved everything about it. I loved the work, loved being in the state capital, and firmly believed that we were on the right side of the Second Amendment argument. Madeline took me under her wing. By the time I was thirty, it was pretty clear to everyone that she was grooming me to follow in her footsteps when she retired."

"I take it that's no longer the plan."

"No. I resigned."

"Why?"

"I can't cast my electoral vote for Senator Stahl if I'm working for Madeline Chisel. It's not my intention to hurt or embarrass her. This is my decision, and I don't want anyone to get the impression that it has anything to do with Madeline."

"Have you told anyone in the Republican Party that you intend to vote for Stahl?"

"I think the White House got the drift when I dodged the meeting with President MacLeod on his victory tour through Florida."

"What about on the Democratic side? Have you told anyone 'I'm voting for Stahl?'"

"Not explicitly. But I'm sure they inferred as much when I called Mr. Kipner and said I was planning to vote my conscience."

"Why does your conscience tell you to vote for Stahl?"

"Why does that matter? From a legal standpoint, I mean."

"It probably doesn't, as long as this really is a matter of conscience. Let me ask it a different way. Are you voting for Senator Stahl because someone threatened you?"

"No."

"Are you voting for Stahl in exchange for money?"

"Of course not."

"Has anybody promised you anything in exchange for changing your vote?"

"No."

"As your lawyer, I'll have an easier time convincing people that there are no external influences, if I understand what's driving you."

"That makes sense. And I suppose at some point we

can get into all that. But none of it matters if I can't legally change my vote, does it?"

"That's true," said Jack.

"Then let's start the conversation there. I've been listening to the legal experts on television, just like everyone else. Some say members of the Electoral College are bound by party lines. Some say we're not. So I need a legal opinion. The bottom line is that Florida went Republican, even if it was only by eight thousand votes. As a Republican elector, am I legally bound to vote for the Republican candidate? Or can I vote for Senator Stahl?"

Jack recognized the importance of the issue and the potential ramifications, not just for Charlotte but for the country. He hoped he was being objective.

"I've been looking into this since the election, mostly out of curiosity. I was up late reading last night, after you called. I can explain my legal reasoning to you, but here's my bottom line: No, you are not bound to cast your vote for President MacLeod."

"Are you saying that because you voted for Senator Stahl?"

"No. I'm saying it because that's how I read the statute."

"Good."

"But here's the disclaimer. There are about a hundred

thousand members of the Florida Bar. Probably twenty thousand of them would agree or disagree with me without even bothering to read the statute. The only thing to inform their analysis would be whether they're a Republican or a Democrat."

"I see."

"But here's a piece of advice you'd get from any lawyer, regardless of party affiliation."

"What?"

"Stop talking about it. You've brought enough attention to yourself already. Don't tell another soul what you intend to do on December fourteenth."

"I heard about the elector in Michigan who got a death threat. But wasn't that from a Stahl supporter?"

"There are lunatics on both sides," said Jack. "We're only getting started."

Chapter 9

The press conference was at 1:00 p.m. Jack was standing at his client's side for the public announcement that Charlotte insisted on making, contrary to her lawyer's advice. But it was up to her, not Jack.

Media vans lined the street outside Hialeah Junior High School. Scores of reporters and camera crews encircled Charlotte and Jack, each jockeying for position and struggling to get a microphone close enough to pick up her words. It was a typical mid-November day in South Florida, warm enough for short sleeves, the sun shining so brightly that any reporters caught without sunglasses were squinting and shading their eyes.

"Good afternoon," Charlotte began, reading her prepared remarks. "My name is Charlotte Holmes, and I am a duly elected member of Florida's Electoral College."

The city of Hialeah was a crowded and in many places overcrowded immigrant community northwest of Miami. Its 90 percent Hispanic voting population had gone heavily for Senator Stahl in the general election, but that had nothing to do with Jack's selection of the fifty-year-old junior high school as the venue for Charlotte's announcement. Having lived in Miami all his life, Jack was one of the few Floridians who remembered that Hialeah Junior High School was nearly the site of Florida's first mass school shooting. Jack was himself a middle-schooler when a man named Carl Brown walked into a Hialeah gun shop, purchased two shotguns and a semi-automatic rifle, rode his bicycle six blocks to a welding shop that he claimed had overcharged him the day before, and methodically shot and killed eight employees at close range, wounding three others. He climbed back on his bike and was pedaling to Hialeah Junior High School with the announced purpose of "killing a lot of people" when an employee of the welding shop caught up with him and gunned him down.

It seemed like a fitting location for Charlotte's press conference, in light of the explanation she'd given Jack for changing her vote from MacLeod to Stahl.

"I was told that this public announcement of my intentions could be a dangerous move on my part," said Charlotte, still reading. "Many will label me a faithless elector. A few might resort to undemocratic methods to intimidate me. But I feel it's necessary to take that risk. My vote alone will not change the outcome of this election. Perhaps my words today will give other electors the courage to also vote their conscience."

Charlotte folded her script and tucked it away, her hand visibly shaking. "Thank you all very much."

It had lasted less than a minute. But the prepared remarks had been the easy part. A barrage of questions hit her from all directions, one of which seemed to cut through all the noise and demand a response.

"Charlotte, why are you changing your vote?"

Jack had been in agreement with Charlotte's decision not to explain "why" in her prepared remarks. If asked, however, her answer would mark the end of her career as a gun lobbyist, even if she hadn't already tendered her resignation to Madeline Chisel.

Charlotte's "evolution," as she'd called it, had begun with the Pulse nightclub shooting in Orlando. Forty-nine people dead. A year later it was the Parkland High School massacre. Seventeen students and teachers dead. In the next legislative session, hundreds of Parkland students marched on the capital to change the state's gun laws. Charlotte's job as lobbyist was to kill the proposed ban on "bump stocks"—devices that even the MacLeod administration opposed, because they made semi-automatic rifles perform more like fully automatic machine guns. The kids somehow won that battle. Their courage—and the horrific videos of the massacre in progress on their smartphones—made an impression on Charlotte. She would never turn her back on law-abiding gun owners. Truth be told, had that courageous employee at the Hialeah welding shop not owned a gun, no one would have chased down Carl Brown, shot him dead, and stopped him from carrying out his plan to massacre the students of Hialeah Junior High. But she'd lost her passion to get up every morning and sell the gun lobby's never-give-an-inch strategy. "Those Parkland kids changed me," she'd told Jack in the privacy of his office. "So I'm changing my electoral vote."

It had made perfect sense to her lawyer—which was why no one was more surprised than Jack by Charlotte's actual response to the media.

"I came here today thinking I had the perfect answer to that question," said Charlotte, reaching for her notes. Then she laid the paper aside. "But as I stand here now, I realize it's more complicated than a sound bite about any particular issue. It's about the media."

Jack tried not to look concerned in front of the cameras, but his pulse was pounding. His client was way off script.

"I'm not a journalist, but I learned this much from a J-school professor in college: the word *media* comes from a Latin term meaning 'intermediate'—which is a fancy-pants word for someone who comes between those who make news and the public that receives it. Intermediaries hold our leaders accountable for what they say. They help the public judge the truth of a politician's statements. President MacLeod hates intermediaries. He trashes the press. He tweets whatever he wants directly to the people, and his lies go out to tens of millions of Americans every day unmediated. With all due respect to hardworking reporters here today, you are becoming irrelevant as intermediaries. The new media is social media—which means that, by and large, people hear what they want to hear.

"So who will step up? Who will be the new intermediaries in the world without a functioning media?"

It was an interesting question, but the irony was not lost on Jack that his client was talking unmediated by her lawyer.

"When two-thirds of Americans believe their president is a habitual liar, and when he loses the nationwide popular election by more than five million votes, I believe it's time for the Electoral College to do its job. So, to answer your question, I'm not casting my vote for Senator Stahl because I disagree with the president on assault weapons or abortion or any other single issue. I'm changing my vote because the truth matters. That's my job. As intermediary."

"Thank you all for coming," Jack told the crowd, "there will be no further questions at this time."

Members of the media—the maligned intermediaries—were having none of it. The circle tightened around Charlotte, the questions kept coming, and Jack realized the flaw in his staged event: no clear escape route. The result was an awkward standoff in which reporters kept firing questions, Charlotte said nothing, and Jack kept thanking them all for coming as he pushed his way through the crowd. It was a slow and steady exit, like spilled milk heading for the edge of the tabletop, but finally they made it to Jack's car. Reporters continued to fire questions in machine-gun fashion even after Jack was behind the wheel and locked inside the vehicle with his client. Cameras captured the moment for the evening news as the car rolled out of the parking lot and pulled away.

"Don't ever blindside me like that again," Jack said sharply.

"I'm sorry," she said. "It just came out."

"It should have come out in my office first."

"I didn't lie to you. I did have a change of heart about the gun lobby."

"I don't doubt it. But this is why the law doesn't speak strictly in terms of 'the truth.' If I'm going to represent you, I need the whole truth."

She glanced out the window. "What will happen now?"

Jack kept his eyes on the road. His father's words at the "non-concession" speech on election night—"political Armageddon"—came to mind, but that wasn't Jack's concern.

"We focus on keeping you safe," said Jack.

Chapter 10

MacLeod's victory tour reached New Orleans that afternoon.

Charlotte Holmes's press conference was televised live, and the president watched with his chief strategist on Ground Force One, seeing most of it on the road through Mississippi. They'd decided not to stop in the Magnolia State, the official reason being that it didn't meet the new tour criteria of "battleground state." In truth, MacLeod was worried about turnout for any victory rallies, as party leaders were still steaming over the president's crack about "dumb southerners" on his last visit to the city of Jackson.

"Who is that lawyer of hers?" asked MacLeod. "Is that Governor Swyteck's son?"

"It is," said Teague.

"What a low-IQ, low-energy loser. By what authority does he think a woman from Leon County, Florida, can call me a liar and override the majority of registered voters in Florida?"

"It's called the Hamiltonian school, sir. Alexander Hamilton was of the view that the Electoral College has a constitutional duty to protect the voters from being fooled into electing a demagogue."

"Hamiltonian school, huh? You know what I call it?"

"No, sir."

"The deep state."

Teague blinked, confused. "Charlotte Holmes is the deep state?"

"No one benefits more from preserving the establishment than a paid lobbyist."

"Not everyone who is part of the establishment is part of the deep state."

"By definition, the deep state includes unelected, self-righteous, egotistical, elitist assholes who think it's their job to override the will of the American people and protect them from their elected president. That's exactly what Charlotte Holmes is doing by casting her electoral vote for Stahl."

Teague thought out loud for a moment. "The hijacking of the Electoral College as a political coup by the deep state. Interesting. That's a message that actually could play in Peoria."

"That's fine with me," said MacLeod, "as long as we continue to hammer away at Senator Harvey Milk Jr."

"Hashtag 'Deep State,'" said Teague. "That works for me."

"Lame," said MacLeod. "We need to go even harder and attack Stahl as a sexual deviant. I'm thinking a rhyme: Deep State, hashtag 'K-Y-Jellygate.'"

"Please, no."

"It's like Watergate, except—"

"I get it, sir. But don't tweet that. I'm begging you."

"We need to hit him hard, Oscar. And we need to hit back at Charlotte Holmes, too."

"Sir, our lawyers believe the White House should leave Ms. Holmes alone. It's best to let any action against the electors be handled on the state level."

"There has to be a price to pay for this kind of disloyalty. Politically speaking, there must be consequences."

"Consequences for whom, sir?"

"The man on the moon," MacLeod said, annoyed. "Come on, Oscar. Who puts forth the names of the Republican electors?"

"The State Executive Committee of each party nominates a slate of electors."

"Who approves the names?"

"Technically the voters do when they vote in the general election."

"No, before that. Who approves the slate as nominated by the parties?" It wasn't really a question; MacLeod was driving home his point.

"That would be the governor of Florida," said Teague.

"Exactly. So who's responsible if one of those electors goes rogue?"

Teague hesitated, clearly not ready to make the leap of logic that the president was suggesting. "I don't think you can blame the governor for this, sir."

"Watch me. Get him on the phone."

Teague retrieved the number. MacLeod gazed out the window, waiting, as his campaign manager dialed. Ground Force One typically avoided major intersections, but as they crossed St. Charles Avenue the president was able to catch a glimpse of the sixty-foot fluted column at Lee Circle. It rose pointlessly from the grassy center of the busy roundabout, no cauldron or monument atop its Doric-style capital, a completely unadorned column with no apparent purpose but to hold up the sky. The sixteen-foot statue of Robert E. Lee that had once topped the column, carefully positioned so that Lee would forever look north toward the enemy, was among the Confederate monuments removed by the city before MacLeod's first term.

"Pretty sad day in America when one of the greatest

generals who ever lived can't have a statue in his home state."

Teague had the governor on hold. "Lee was from Virginia, sir."

"I knew that. Why would you think I didn't know that?"

Teague didn't have a response, so flummoxed that he nearly disconnected the call as he put the Florida governor on speaker. MacLeod instinctively started talking in a southern accent, though not even the president was sure why.

"Gov-nuh, how y'all doin' down over there in Florida?"

Governor Terry Mulvane was an Iraq War veteran and former congressman who'd earned the president's endorsement in the Republican gubernatorial primary for being "tough on borders." Once elected, he also proved to be tough on corporations that poured pollutants into the Florida Everglades, a position that put his status as MacLeod's fair-haired boy in serious jeopardy.

"Fine, sir. How are you?"

"Not so good. I just watched the press conference for that traitor, Charlotte Holmes."

"I saw it as well."

"I'm very concerned about a domino effect. Stahl picks off one elector in Florida, and the next thing you know we lose another one in Ohio or Texas, and so on. They only need a handful to turn the election."

"I understand your concern, sir. We're on it."

"I don't want you to be 'on it.' I want you to fix it. These electors need to be made to understand that their actions have severe consequences—not only for themselves, but for all Republicans in their state. Do you understand what I'm saying?"

"I believe I do, sir."

"Good. We'll talk again tomorrow."

MacLeod said goodbye, and the call was over. He looked across the table at his chief strategist, who'd heard it all on speaker. MacLeod was a big believer in the power of collective responsibility; he hated it when the liberal media pointed out that so were the Nazis.

"There," MacLeod said smugly. "Problem solved."

"I'm not exactly sure what you expect the governor to do."

"I expect him to get out of the way and let his attorney general do what she does best. Charlotte Holmes is no match for Paulette Barrow. Now, let's you and me figure out how to hit back at Stahl," he said, reaching for his cell.

"Please don't tweet," said Teague.

"You're talking to the Twitter master."

"That's what you said about 'Sodom and Goliath.'"

"I hate auto-correct," he said, typing out another tweet. "Is the *y* capitalized in *K-Y*?"

Teague groaned. "Sir, this is exactly what Senator Stahl wants you to do. They're baiting you. The Democrats want you to say something so outrageous that it will push just enough Republican electors into his camp. Don't bite."

To his own surprise, MacLeod found himself persuaded. He deleted the draft tweet, laid his cell phone aside, and gazed out the window, searching. "There's a reason Stahl won't tell us who his lover is—a reason he vanished into thin air the minute this scandal broke."

"We don't know for sure it's a 'he.'"

"Oh, bullshit. I don't buy that crap about respecting the privacy of a woman who's fighting to save her marriage. Stahl is hiding something."

"Even if you're right, there isn't a voter in America who hasn't already heard the rumors. We worked that angle for two months on every available platform. I daresay we've milked the same-sex extramarital affair for all it's worth."

"You're dead wrong. It's still an abstraction. We need to put a face on the gay lover."

"We've been searching for two months, sir."

"Look harder!" he said firmly, then reeled in his anger. "He's out there. We didn't come this far to lose in the Electoral College. Find him before December fourteenth."

Chapter 11

Charlotte's flight landed in Tallahassee at sunset. She wasn't expecting a hero's welcome, but she could have done without the angry protestors waiting for her at the airport.

"Save us, Charlotte!" a man shouted sarcastically.

"Please!" shouted another. "Save us from ourselves!"

Security and other concerns permitted airports to restrict demonstrations in ways that would never fly, so to speak, at other public places, so the group that turned out against Charlotte was forced to stand behind a crowd-control barrier near the terminal exit. It was a tiny showing compared to her press conference earlier in the day, but Charlotte's every movement was being recorded on smartphones, which meant that the jeers and jabs of a few would look and sound like a nationwide movement when the videos went viral on social media. Jack had warned Charlotte that her words might be twisted to fit the president's conspiracy theories, so she wasn't surprised to see the "Deep State" signs in the hands of some demonstrators. But one sign really hurt—even more so because it was brandished by a teenage girl.

ELITIST BITCH!

The girl looked like any number of the friends and classmates Charlotte had grown up with in the Panhandle. In Florida's sliver of the South, where shops closed on Sunday morning for church, where teenagers couldn't help addressing a woman as "ma'am" even after she insisted that they stop doing it, the worst insult Charlotte could have imagined hurling at any woman was "elitist bitch." It made her want to run over to that girl and scream, "How is it 'elitist' to vote for the candidate who won by five million votes?" But that was MacLeod's political genius, the way he could label people and make it stick no matter what the facts were.

"Mal-colm! Mal-colm! Mal-colm!" the demonstrators shouted.

Charlotte hurried to the exit, thanking God that she

had no checked baggage, no need to endure further abuse while waiting at the carousel.

"Two-eleven Windermere Drive," she told the taxi driver, and off she went.

Charlotte drew a breath in the back seat, collecting herself, then checked her phone. The demonstration at the airport had been a love fest compared to the thrashing on the Internet. The headlines—"First Faithless Elector"—should have told her to avoid the mainstream media coverage of her press conference. She definitely shouldn't have read the political blogs. Reading the mostly mean-spirited comments to the blogs was utter insanity. Twitter put her over the edge. She was trending. At least she assumed it was her: #ElitistBitch. Charlotte had no idea how many thousands of people had to be tweeting at any point in time to elevate a hashtag to "trending" status. One was too many.

"Which house again?" the driver asked, as he steered onto Charlotte's street.

Charlotte was still torturing herself, staring at her phone. "Straight ahead. Right at the end of the cul-de-sac."

"The one where all those people are?"

Charlotte looked up from her phone and peered through the windshield. Dusk had turned to darkness during the ride from the airport. In the glow of the streetlamps, she saw what could only be described as a mob in the cul-de-sac, blocking the entrance to her driveway. It was at least double the size of the demonstration at the airport. The driver slowed the taxi to a crawl as they approached.

"You a Kardashian?"

"What? No."

A woman in the crowd pointed at the oncoming taxi, and even though Charlotte couldn't hear her exact words, the mob sprang into action in a collective "There she is!"

"You sure you want to get out here?" the driver asked.

The crowd rushed the car, forcing the driver to stop. It was like the airport, except that this mob was louder and more profane. "Elitist bitch" had morphed into the C-word, which made her cringe.

"Maybe you should come back later," said the driver.

Charlotte could hardly stand the idea of being chased away from her own home. But stepping out of the car would have been downright reckless, and calling the police would only have added gasoline to the flames. What these people clearly wanted was attention— except for the one standing by her mailbox, who was oddly calm, dressed in a camouflage jacket, the bill of a baseball cap casting a shadow over his face.

"Go or stay, lady?" asked the driver.

Charlotte glanced at the driver, then back at that guy by the mailbox, who seemed detached from the demonstration, as if there only to watch the crowd. Or her.

"Yes, let's go," she said.

Charlotte had unfinished business to deal with anyway. It was only six o'clock. Madeline Chisel would still be in her office.

"Take me downtown. Toward the Capitol."

The driver threw the taxi into reverse, did a quick three-point turn, and sped away from the cul-de-sac, but not before a raw egg splattered across the back window.

"Damn!" said the driver, accelerating even more.

"I'll pay for the car wash," said Charlotte.

"You sure you want to come back here tonight, ma'am?"

Charlotte was wondering the same thing, which also triggered second thoughts about going to see her old mentor. But after all that Madeline Chisel had done for her, Charlotte owed her something. An explanation. An apology. An opportunity to tell her to rot in hell like the ingrate she was.

They passed the Capitol and Charlotte directed the driver down the hill, to Madeline's office. Charlotte made good on her promised car wash, adding another ten bucks to the fare. The taxi pulled away with the remnants of dried egg smeared across the rear window. Charlotte crossed the street, wheeling her carry-on bag behind her. The lights were on in Madeline's office. Charlotte still had her key, but entering uninvited and sneaking up on a gun lobbyist was not a smart move. She rang the after-business-hours doorbell.

Charlotte waited on the street side of the glass door. She could see inside. Everything looked the same as the day she'd left. Lobbying was a multimillion-dollar business in Florida. The most profitable firms were full service, a dozen or more lobbyists under one corporate umbrella who pitched on behalf of anyone who'd write a check, from health care to the gaming industry. Madeline sometimes branched out and lobbied for something other than guns, but only if that other client's agenda was completely unrelated to or wholly aligned with the Second Amendment.

Charlotte rang the bell a second time. Madeline emerged from the back office, spotted Charlotte on the other side of the glass, and stopped. The office may have looked the same, but clearly everything had changed. Madeline walked slowly toward the door and, a bit like a gunfighter at high noon, stopped at the glass to look at Charlotte. It struck Charlotte how little Madeline had changed in the decade she'd known her. Five

feet tall and skinny as a rail, Madeline had a steeliness
in her gaze that could melt a glacier.

She turned the lock and let Charlotte in.

"I packed up your things," Madeline said without
emotion. "Wait here. I'll get them."

Charlotte waited as Madeline retreated to what used
to be Charlotte's office. She emerged with a cardboard
bankers' box filled with things left behind and handed it
to Charlotte. A framed photograph of her and Madeline
in happier times was at the top of the pile. It had been on
Charlotte's desk for nearly eight years.

"I'm sorry, Madeline."

"Don't be. I saw the change in you after Parkland."
She meant the South Florida high school shooting that
had killed seventeen. "A person can't do this work
if she doesn't have the passion. I knew it was only a
matter of time before you left."

"I meant about today. Changing my vote."

"Oh, that," she said, offering a hint of a smile. "Well,
what can I say? It's been a tough four years, trying to
maintain my own credibility with my cause linked to a
fool in the White House who doesn't know an ammunition clip from his tie clip."

"So you're okay with what I'm doing?"

"Hell no, girl. I'm not about to stand by and let you
hand the election to a man who will undo everything

I've accomplished over the last forty years. I'll play within the rules, like I always do, but rest assured: I didn't teach you *everything* I know. You won't beat the master."

Charlotte had seen Madeline in action. It was no idle threat. "Appreciate the warning."

"You're welcome. Oh, wait. Your Glock," she said, as she went to the gun safe behind the counter. "I took it from your desk and locked it up for you."

Charlotte normally kept it at her desk. A readily accessible handgun for all employees was Madeline's standard office policy.

"Thanks," said Charlotte, taking it. The pistol was in a conceal-carry waistband holster, the way Charlotte normally stored it.

"I'm guessing you're not carrying if you came from the airport."

"I'm not," said Charlotte.

"I play by the rules, but I'd venture to say you've pissed off some people who don't. You should carry at all times. I'm just sayin'."

Charlotte tucked the holstered weapon inside her waistband and clipped it to her belt. "I'll keep that in mind."

Chisel opened the door. Between the box of belongings from her office and the carry-on from her flight,

Charlotte had her arms full. She wasn't sure whether Madeline would have shaken her hand anyway.

"Good luck, Charlotte. And one last piece of advice. I wouldn't trust anyone if I were you. Not anyone."

It wasn't clear if Madeline meant the Stahl campaign, Jack Swyteck, or someone else. Charlotte took it at face value. "I can take care of myself," said Charlotte.

"I know you can."

Charlotte stepped out onto the sidewalk, went to the curb, and called for a ride.

Chapter 12

Jack stopped for a beer in Coconut Grove on his way home from work.

Once a Bohemian enclave for headshops and hippies, the Grove was a neighborhood struggling for identity, scarred by a decades-long war against development, gentrification, and the inevitable transition of bars and cafés to multimillion-dollar condos and high-end shopping. Cy's Place was a remnant of the old Grove, a jazz club owned by Theo Knight, Jack's best friend, bartender, therapist, confidant, and sometime investigator. Theo was a former client, a onetime gangbanger who easily could have ended up dead on the streets of Overtown or Liberty City. Instead, he landed on death row for a murder he didn't commit. Jack literally saved his life. With his civil settlement

from the state, Theo went on to open his own tavern—
Sparky's he'd called it, a play on words and double-
barreled flip of the bird to "Old Sparky," the nickname
for the electric chair he'd avoided. Sparky's had done
well enough to get him a second bar. Of course Theo
needed a second bar. After four years of living eight
feet away from death, Theo developed a simple credo:
"Anything worth doing is worth overdoing."

Jack climbed onto the barstool and glanced at the
television on the wall. "You ever watch anything but
ESPN in this place?"

Theo kept slicing lemons behind the bar, not even
looking up. "Would you rather watch that shit-stream
on AMATT Media?"

"AT—what?"

"A-M-A-T-T," said Theo, laying his cutting knife
aside. "Venezuela falling apart? So what. Children
starving in the Congo? Eh, who cares? Let's get straight
to Twitter. We are AMATT Media. All MacLeod. All
The Time."

Theo wiped the lemon juice from his fingers, grabbed
the remote, and changed the channel. The news coverage was transitioning from Jack's client, specifically, to
the never-ending battle of Stahl vs. MacLeod, generally.

"I actually did watch your press conference, if you're
wondering," said Theo.

"What did you think?"

"One glass of truth serum, coming up," said Theo, as he set up a draft in front of Jack.

"What does that mean?"

"A Tallahassee lobbyist fighting only for truth? Give me a break."

"You don't think it rang true?"

"That's funny. Truly."

Jack could have kept the truth-true-truly string alive, but it would only have led to tequila shots, Timothy Leary, the four hundred different kinds of truth discernible only through LSD, and, ultimately, no resolution to the red-paint-on-a-red-rose paradox. Jack changed the subject.

"You hear anything from Julia?"

Julia Rodriguez was the beautiful Salvadoran woman who had captured Theo's heart and then gone back to El Salvador. It was and wasn't her choice. She and her teenage daughter had come to Miami fleeing domestic violence and gang-related crime. Their petition for asylum was denied under the new policy announced by the MacLeod administration. Jack was with Theo at the detention center when he'd "proposed" a solution by proposing marriage. Julia was hours away from a one-way flight to Central America, but she had one question: "Would you ask if I wasn't about to be deported?" Theo had hesitated only for a moment, but it was a half second too long. He'd been miserable ever since.

"We talk on the phone," said Theo.

"When last?"

"A few days ago."

"Why don't you go down there and see her?"

A couple seated themselves on the other side of the U-shaped bar. Theo seized the opportunity to cut the conversation short. He wasn't one to talk about his feelings. Unless the feeling was hunger. Jack glanced at the newsfeed on his phone as Theo mixed cocktails. Jack's client appeared on the screen, and even though the sound was off, Jack could hear the sound bite in his head: Truth matters.

Theo returned and caught a glimpse of what Jack was watching. "The thing about the truth is that Jack Nicholson had it right in that movie with Tom Cruise. Most people can't handle it."

Jack laid his phone on the bar. "You don't really believe that."

"I can prove it. Try this one on for size: I didn't vote."

"What? You lost four years of freedom for something you didn't do! How could you not vote?"

"See. I knew you couldn't handle it. Actually, I did vote."

"Really?"

"Maybe. Maybe not. But now you can believe what you want to believe. Isn't that a lot easier to handle?"

Oddly enough, it was. But Jack wouldn't admit it.

Theo glanced toward the club entrance and smiled. "Well, here comes trouble."

Andie was holding Righley's hand as they passed the hostess stand. Righley broke free and ran to Jack, but the real purpose of the visit was soon evident.

"Can I play the piano, Uncle Theo?" she asked with excitement. "Please, please?"

Righley could have asked to burn the club down, and Theo would have said yes. Andie took the stool beside Jack at the bar, and they cozied up for a twenty-minute recital of "Twinkle, Twinkle Little Star." Theo got her started in the right key and then returned to his place behind the bar.

"Not to start trouble," said Theo, "but, Andie: What did you think of Charlotte Holmes and 'the truth matters'?"

"Sorry," she said. "Jack and I try not to talk about his cases."

"It's fine," said Jack. "Theo's not really asking about the case. It's something we all saw on the news."

She gave her husband a sobering look. "Jack, you're not going to like my take on it."

"I might surprise you. Let's hear it."

"Honestly, to me it sounded like she drank a bad batch of blue Kool Aid."

Theo laughed—too hard to suit Jack.

"What is that supposed to mean?" asked Jack.

"I'm not blaming Charlotte," said Andie. "It's what all people do when they suddenly change sides. What they say has a pious kernel of truth to it, but the message is really beside the point."

"It's not beside the point. Half the world calls our president the 'Lyin' King.'"

"Yes. But all politicians lie, and at least MacLeod's lies are contrary to verifiable facts. We know when he's lying. The same can't be said of Senator Stahl. He denies he had a gay lover. But is he lying, or is he telling the truth? Nobody knows, except for him and his lover. Potentially, that makes him more dangerous than MacLeod."

"It doesn't make him dangerous at all," said Jack. "Who cares if he's gay?"

"He does. And that's exactly what makes him so dangerous. If he's hiding something, he's vulnerable to blackmail. Not a good thing if you're president. That's the whole point of FBI background checks for public officials."

"So what is Charlotte supposed to do?" asked Jack.

"Wait for an FBI investigation before she casts her vote in the Electoral College?"

"Maybe that's not a bad idea."

"Now you sound like J. Edgar Hoover," said Jack.

"Better than sounding like the B-team on CNN."

"Whoa," said Theo.

Righley hit an off note on the piano, taking the twinkle out of the proverbial stars.

Jack took Andie's hand. "Sorry. I didn't mean to compare you to J. Edgar."

"I'm sorry, too," said Andie, and then she smiled. "You're at least as good as the B-team on MSNBC."

"Mommy, I need help!" Righley shouted from the piano.

Andie gave Jack a kiss, then climbed down from the barstool and went to Righley, leaving Jack and Theo alone at the bar.

Theo topped off Jack's beer glass. "Damn, dude. Now you know why I like to keep the TV tuned to ESPN."

"Bad?"

"Medium. A bartender sees it all. I can't count the number of dates I've watched blow up over this. It's like—*FOOD FIGHT!*—is the new political debate."

Jack smiled, then turned serious. "Andie's right, you know."

"About what?"

"If Senator Stahl is compromised, Charlotte is making a huge mistake."

"Does that worry you?"

Jack glanced at the television. AMATT Media continued, as yet another panel of experts dissected the latest MacLeod tweet. Had there been food on the set, it would have been flying.

"I'll tell you what worries me more."

"What?"

Jack looked down into his beer. "Right or wrong, my client may be in over her head."

Chapter 13

It was 7:00 a.m. in Singapore when Gwen Stahl woke to "breaking news" out of Florida. Her husband's vow to fight on to the Electoral College was gaining traction. Gwen nearly choked on her kaya toast when she saw the banner headline on CNN International: "'Truth Matters' to Stahl, Says Florida Elector."

"Except in his marriage," Gwen could have told them.

"Hi, Mommy," said Rachel.

Gwen grabbed the remote and switched off the television. This latest news update had yet to drift into the cesspool of sensationalism, but she couldn't take the risk. The whole world knew—Gwen had told everyone from her parents to the random passenger sitting next to her on the flight out of Miami—that insulating her nine-year-old daughter from salacious news coverage was the reason she'd agreed to leave the country. It just wasn't enough for the media to report on an "extramarital affair." It had to be, over and over again, "rumors of a same-sex extramarital affair."

"Good morning, pumpkin," she said, giving her daughter a hug.

Rachel took a seat and, with a glance from her mother, removed her elbows from the tabletop. Gwen served her the usual toast with kaya, a sort of jam made from coconut, egg, and pandan leaves. Rachel liked the hint of vanilla flavor.

"Can I call Daddy after breakfast?"

Singapore was twelve hours ahead of Miami. Evan hated being interrupted during dinner—unless the call was from someone other than his family. "Let's wait for him to call. It should be any minute."

Gwen went to the kitchen and poured herself another cup of kopi. A decent cup of coffee was one of the many things she missed in Singapore. Most Americans found kopi to be a thin and unremarkable brew, and drinking it required Gwen to rid her mind of the fact that it was made from partly digested coffee cherries eaten and defecated by the Asian palm civet. Gwen had become quite the expert at putting things out of her mind.

The phone rang, and Rachel sprang from her chair. "I'll get it!"

Gwen followed her to the living room. Rachel grabbed the phone from the coffee table and answered with excitement in her voice.

"Hi, Daddy!"

Gwen watched, trying to hide the sadness in her smile.

Rachel covered the phone and looked at her mother in a way that hit her like a glimpse into the teenage future. "Mom, privacy, please?"

Gwen wondered if the request had been prompted by something her father had said to her. Gwen shrugged it off, opened the sliding glass door, and stepped out onto the terrace.

The view from forty stories up was the best thing about their downtown Singapore apartment, though it reminded Gwen so much of Miami's storied financial district that it only made her homesick. It wasn't just the number of high-rises in such a small area—more than eighty buildings exceeded four hundred feet—that harked back to Miami's breathtaking beauty. It was the glimpses of blue-green sea through the fifty-story slits of airspace between buildings. The glimmer of chrome and glass in the tropical sun. The glisten of infinity pools atop towering hotels. Both cities even had man-made islands offshore, though that is where the similarity ended. The colorful Art Deco buildings of Miami Beach were built on sand dredged up by the Army Corps of Engineers. In Singapore, the man-made smear of mud offshore was home to the petrochemical industry, so crowded with spindly, cracking towers and squat oil-storage tanks that the landscape was a proverbial billboard of the biggest names in the business—BASF, ExxonMobil, Vopak, and more.

Gwen slid open the glass door and checked on Rachel.

"It's okay, Daddy," Rachel was saying into the phone. "I know, I know."

Gwen detected a hint of sadness in her little voice. She wanted to ask Rachel what was the matter, but the last time she'd interrupted a call from Evan it had triggered an across-the-globe argument over the to-be-defined boundaries of what was strictly between father and daughter and none of Mommy's business. Gwen stepped back onto the terrace.

Over the past few weeks, Gwen had done plenty of soul searching while sitting in the patio chair, taking in this view from the terrace. The FDLE had fully accommodated her request for a leave of absence so that she could travel with her husband's campaign. She understood that she wasn't the candidate, but as a trained psychiatrist who treated violent offenders in a psychiatric hospital, she'd thought someone might be curious about her views on mental health or treatment of the mentally ill. Right up to the convention, however, media interest was on the order of "Who designed your dress?" or "Which school will Rachel attend if the family moves to Washington?" It was awful. Or at least she'd thought it was awful—until after the convention, when the story broke, and Gwen longed for the good ol' mind-numbing days.

The glass door slid open. Rachel stepped out onto the terrace and sat in her mother's lap.

"Are you sad, pumpkin?"

"Yeah."

"Did you tell Daddy you miss your friends?"

"Uh-huh."

"What did he say?"

"He thinks maybe we can come back in January."

"January?"

"Maybe."

Gwen suppressed her anger. She and Rachel were absolutely not spending Christmas in Singapore alone, away from family and friends.

"I miss Nanny, too," said Rachel. "Nanny" had moved in to help with Rachel after Gwen returned to work. It had broken Rachel's heart to hear that Nanny had gone back to Colombia.

"Go get dressed, Rachel. Mommy needs to take care of something."

Rachel slid out of her mother's lap and left through the other sliding door that led directly to the master suite. Gwen dialed her husband on her cell phone.

"Hello, Gwen," he said in a flat tone.

"Apparently you don't take hints very well," she said. "Did you not get the message that Rachel misses her friends, her school—her life?"

"Now is not a good time for you to come back."

"And whose fault is that?"

"Can we not play the blame game, Gwen?"

"It's not about blame. It's about our daughter. I'm here because it was best to get away from . . . from everything. But it's been over two months now. That's long enough."

"Can you at least wait until the Electoral College vote?"

"No! That's three more weeks."

"Gwen, please. I wouldn't say this if it wasn't in everybody's best interest."

"By 'everybody' you mean your campaign."

"No. I mean you as well. It's getting very intense. My people tell me that MacLeod will pull out all the stops between now and December fourteenth to get to the bottom of who—well, you know the rumors as well as anyone."

"Ya think?"

"I'm just saying that if you come back before the Electoral College meets, they will pounce all over you."

Gwen considered it, but not for long. "None of this is my fault, Evan."

"I know it's not."

"Then deal with it. We're coming home. Be out of the house by Friday."

She hung up the phone, breathed out her anger, and then glanced out at the skyline that reminded her of home, wiping away the tear that was rolling down her cheek.

Chapter 14

Charlotte waited at the curb outside Madeline Chisel's office.

Services like Uber and Lyft were a crapshoot in a college town like Tallahassee, where drivers lined the back seats of their cars with protective towels that too often reeked of frat boys tossing their cookies. Charlotte took a chance, and the driver showed up in a shiny blue pickup truck, which made her smile. It was the closest she'd felt to home since returning from Miami. Her concealed-carry holster was uncomfortable when sitting, so she tucked it away in her box of belongings from Madeline, loaded the box and her carry-on in the small back seat of the extended cab, and climbed into the passenger seat.

"Nice truck, Tex," she said, feeling like she should literally be riding shotgun.

"How'd you know I was from Texas?"

With a jerk of her head Charlotte pointed out the tinted decal across the rear window: the Lone Star flag.

"Exhibit A," she said.

"Guilty as charged," he said, turning on the accent. Charlotte found it charming in a Matthew McConaughey kind of way, but her gaze carried past him, all the way across the street to the shadowy figure standing on the sidewalk just outside the glow of the streetlamp. The lighthearted moment was over, and Charlotte froze.

"You okay?" asked Tex.

It was that same guy again—the one she'd seen standing by her mailbox outside her house, wearing the same camouflage jacket and baseball cap. She was suddenly thinking of the death threats against the elector in Michigan.

"Just drive, okay?"

"Sure," he said.

Tex pulled away from the curb. They were quickly out of the business district, and Charlotte glanced several times over her shoulder as the avenue turned darker, more residential.

"What'd you do, rob a bank or something?" asked Tex.

"What? No. I just—"

"Somebody following you?"

Charlotte didn't answer.

"Boyfriend?" asked Tex, giving his V-8 a little more gas. "We can outrun him."

"No, nothing like that." Charlotte checked the speedometer. He was doing almost fifty in a thirty-mile-per-hour zone. "You don't have to speed."

Tex glanced over. "Hey, aren't you that lady who was on TV today," he said, pronouncing "TV" as if it were "Stevie."

Charlotte had no interest in that kind of celebrity. "What lady?"

He took another gander. "Yeah. That was you. No wonder you're lookin' over your shoulder. Woo-wee, you got folks pissed off."

Charlotte wasn't sure if it was on the "woo" or the "wee," but she smelled bourbon. "Have you been drinking?"

"Me? Nah."

"Could you slow down, please?"

"I just told ya, I ain't been drinkin'."

"You're speeding."

Tex just smiled and speed-dialed from the controls on his steering wheel. The LCD screen on the dashboard flashed the name "Jerry," and he answered on speaker. Tex shouted back much louder than necessary.

"Jerry! Guess who I got in the truck with me."

"No idea," his friend said.

"Lemme give you a hint. Hashtag 'Elitist Bitch.'"

Charlotte felt a chill. Were these guys at my house?

"You shittin' me?" said Jerry.

"Nope," he said, glancing at Charlotte. "Say hello to Jerry."

The smell of bourbon returned with Tex's hel-low. "Just stop the truck and let me out here," said Charlotte.

"That is her!" said Jerry.

"Told ya!"

"I'm dead serious," said Charlotte. "Stop the truck and let me out."

"What do you think, Jerry? Should I stop and let her out?"

"Hell no, dude. Do the world a favor and run your truck into a tree."

The men roared with laughter. "That'd make me a hero, wouldn't it?"

More laughter. "Yeah, it would," said Jerry.

Tex floored it, and his pickup lunged forward with so much thrust that Charlotte's head slammed against the headrest.

"Stop!" she shouted, but Tex wasn't listening. The truck came up quickly on the set of taillights ahead of them. Tex maneuvered around the slow-moving vehicle like a NASCAR driver, only to come upon a van pulling out of a gas station. Tex howled with excitement as he steered around it, tires squealing.

"Stop the damn truck!" Charlotte shouted.

"You still votin' for Stahl?"

"I said stop!"

"Got it up to eighty, Jerry. Still votin' for the homo!"

"Go to ninety! Make her change!"

Charlotte pulled her cell phone from her pocket. "I'm dialing nine-one-one."

"No, I'm on probation!"

Tex swung his arm and knocked the phone from her hands. It disappeared somewhere between the passenger seat and the console. Charlotte was digging for it when she noticed the sharp curve in the road ahead.

"Slow down!"

Tex veered left to make the turn, but his truck was going way too fast. A horn blasted as the pickup raced through the stop sign. Charlotte's heart was in her throat.

"Woo-wee!" shouted Tex.

The gun, thought Charlotte. She reached into the box behind her seat, tossing picture frames, pens, and

other supplies aside until she found what she was looking for. She pulled the pistol from the holster and aimed
it at Tex.

"Stop the truck! Now!"

Tex's eyes nearly popped from his head. He hit
the brakes so hard that Charlotte's gun flew from her
hand. Charlotte screamed, and Tex screamed even
louder. The truck swerved, and Tex's overcorrection
sent them skidding in circles, completely out of control. In the blur, Charlotte caught a glimpse of the
moon before the pickup ricocheted off a parked car
and spun in another direction. The air bag exploded in
Charlotte's face and then collapsed, but the pickup kept
skidding toward the guardrail at the end of the street.
It was like peering out from the center of a spiraling
tornado—spinning, swirling. The front end slammed
into the guardrail, and momentum carried the truck
right over the top. The pickup nearly rolled over but
righted itself and continued down the embankment.
Charlotte's arms flailed and her whole body jerked, her
head slamming forward and back against the headrest.
The passenger-side window exploded into glass pellets
that hit Charlotte's shoulder like buckshot. The skidding finally stopped, and the cabin tilted at a forty-five-
degree angle, as if the truck were struggling with all its
might not to roll over. The battle was lost. It was like

slow motion, the final tumble in the dryer, as the truck rolled onto its side and then came to rest on its roof.

Charlotte was hanging upside down, and the rush of blood to her head made her dizzy and disoriented. It was dark beyond the windshield, both headlights out. The dim glow of dashboard lights was enough to illuminate Tex suspended upside down from the driver seat beside her. His arms hung lifelessly toward the ground.

Charlotte smelled gasoline. "We have to get out!"

Tex didn't respond.

Charlotte had one hand on her seat belt, and with the other she held tightly to the door handle. The idea was to unbuckle and not land on her head, a victim of gravity, but she was only moderately successful. She landed on her shoulder, which sent a stinging pain all the way down her arm. She was looking up at Tex. A drop of blood from his mouth landed on Charlotte's forehead.

"Help!" she screamed, hoping that someone had seen the crash and was on the way.

Charlotte tried her door handle, but the passenger door was stuck. She reached across the inverted steering wheel and tried the driver's side, but it was stuck, too. The only way out was through the broken passenger-side window. She didn't want to leave Tex hanging like a side of beef, but if she unbuckled him in this unconscious state, he would probably break his neck.

Gotta get help.

Her mind was a fog, but she crawled toward the open window, the glass pellets crunching beneath her elbows. Adrenaline took her only so far. She was half in, half out of the cab when all strength seemed to leave her. She felt almost numb. She called out for help—"Somebody, please!"—but it was barely audible. Charlotte felt herself slipping away. The odor of gasoline gave way to the smell of fallen leaves in the woods around her. She could feel the cool earth beneath her shoulder blades, and for an instant she thought she could even see stars in the black sky above the canopy of the forest.

Then she felt a hand on her shoulder. A pair of hands. She struggled to keep her eyes open, and in the blur, she noticed that the hands were protruding from the sleeves of a jacket—a camouflage jacket, like the one she'd seen earlier, when she was being watched.

Then the night turned even darker.

Chapter 15

Jack took the early-morning flight out of Miami and was in Tallahassee by 8:30 a.m.

The phone call from his father had come after midnight, and, with aging parents, Jack's first thought was that it was the dreaded call in the middle of the night. It took him a moment to wake and realize what his father was saying, that it was Charlotte who was in the hospital. Even then, a "car accident" didn't compute. Charlotte's press conference had only escalated the death threats that electors around the country were getting from extremists on both sides. Jack had his doubts about an "accident."

Charlotte was at Tallahassee Memorial Hospital, one of the few Level II trauma centers available. It served a five-county area that included everyone from the governor to gator hunters, from college students to retirees, which meant that TMH saw more than its fair share of car crashes, boating accidents, hunting mishaps, overdoses, and other emergencies. The twenty-minute drive from the airport took Jack past Florida A&M University, Florida's first coeducational university, a distinction "earned" because state law once dictated that FSU serve white women and the University of Florida serve white men. So much had changed in Florida; so much had not.

"I'm here to see Charlotte Holmes," Jack told the ER receptionist. He started to explain his relationship to the patient, but the receptionist quickly recognized him from the press conference; in Tallahassee, public interest in politics extended well beyond the Capitol Complex.

"Ms. Holmes is resting in a recovery bay," she said.

Recovery bay. Jack had visited enough emergency rooms to know that it was code for "She's lying around doing nothing while we wait for one of the doctors to find the time to write a discharge order."

"'Recovery' sounds like a good thing," said Jack.

"Yes. It was a full house here last night. I'd be shocked if Ms. Holmes got any sleep before six, so I can't guarantee she's awake."

"I'd like to check on her," said Jack.

The receptionist printed a visitor badge and buzzed Jack through the automatic entry doors. The ER was one large room with a busy nursing station in the center and patient bays lining all four walls. Privacy curtains hung by chains from the ceiling. Some bays were open, others were closed, several with patients groaning from behind a pulled curtain. Jack found Charlotte in Bay No. 5 in the corner, plastic curtain parted. Her adjustable bed was in the upright position, forcing her to sit up. She seemed both surprised and glad to see her lawyer.

"How are you feeling?" Jack asked.

"Like I got hit by a truck. Literally."

Jack closed the privacy curtain so they could talk—not that it would stop their voices from traveling, but it would at least send passersby the message not to eavesdrop. Charlotte recounted what had happened and what she knew, which included good news about Tex, whose only injury was a lacerated tongue from his own bite, though he would need a good lawyer to explain his blood-alcohol level. Amazing, Jack thought, how it was always the drunk who walked away from a car crash.

"Have you talked to the police yet?" he asked.

"Yes. There was an officer here a little while ago."

"What did you tell him?"

"Her. Basically what I just told you. I also mentioned

that there's a man who seems to be watching me since I got back to Tallahassee."

"A stalker, you mean?"

"He was with the group of demonstrators outside my house when I got home from the airport. I'm pretty sure he was standing across the street when I left Madeline's office. And here's the creepy part: I think he pulled me out of the truck after the crash."

"Are you sure it was the same guy?" asked Jack.

"I didn't get a good look at the face, so I'm not a hundred percent sure. But how many people are there walking around wearing camouflage jackets and a baseball cap."

"What did the cop tell you?"

"She said somebody used my phone to text nine-one-one. I didn't even know you could reach nine-one-one by text."

"It's not everywhere, but the FCC is pushing for it."

"Still, why use my phone and *text*, no voice? And he left before the ambulance got there. Now, don't you think that's weird?"

"It's weird if it was the same guy in all three places: your house, across the street, and at the accident. But if it was just somebody who saw the truck careen down the hill, maybe he just didn't want to get involved."

"Why?"

"I don't know. Maybe he's an illegal alien. Maybe he was in a hurry. Maybe he was afraid you'd hire an ambulance-chasing lawyer to sue him for smearing your makeup when he pulled you away from the truck. Who knows what goes through people's heads?"

"I guess."

"Did you give the cops a description?"

"I really couldn't tell her much more than a camouflage jacket and cap. I didn't get the sense that she plans to do anything about it anyway."

"That's not surprising," said Jack. "Even when a victim can identify her stalker, it's sad how little the police can do."

The silhouette of a woman approached outside the curtain, and she appeared to be dressed in a business suit, not ER scrubs. Jack opened the curtain. It took him only a second to recognize the Florida attorney general, Paulette Barrow, who introduced the man with her as Josh Kutter, state attorney for Leon County. Two officers from the Florida Department of Law Enforcement were with them.

"I'm not familiar with criminal practice in Tallahassee," said Jack, "but sending out a team like this to interview the victim of a car accident can't be standard operating procedure. Are you here about the stalker she reported?"

"No, we have another concern." At the attorney general's direction, one of the FDLE officers handed Jack a clear plastic evidence bag. Inside was a handgun. "This was found at the scene," said Barrow. "Does this belong to you, Ms. Holmes?"

"Could you tell me why you want to know?" Jack asked.

Barrow ignored him. "Ms. Holmes, I can tell you that we checked, and this gun is registered in your name."

Jack's instincts told him to shut this down. "Sorry, General, but if you won't answer my questions, I can't let my client answer yours."

"Not sure what she has to hide," said Barrow.

"Ms. Holmes was nearly killed by some jerk who recognized her from television. She told the officer who interviewed her this morning that a stalker has been following her since she got home last night. Rather than show concern for the safety of a Florida elector who's clearly in danger," he said, his voice rising with incredulity, "you're here with the state attorney asking about a handgun? Something tells me you're not here to help her."

Barrow looked at Charlotte. "Let me ask you this, Ms. Holmes: Was the driver of that truck trying to kill you?"

"I don't think he was suicidal, if that's what you're asking. He was drunk and having fun with his buddy scaring the crap out of me."

"Rest assured, he's in plenty of trouble," said Barrow. "Now, about the gun."

"We're not answering questions about a gun," said Jack.

Barrow was plainly annoyed. "Can I see you for a minute in private, please?"

Jack agreed, but Charlotte wanted a word with him before he left. She waited for the law enforcement officers to step away and spoke in a soft voice. "I have a concealed-carry permit," she whispered. "If that's what this is about, there's no problem."

"Good to know," said Jack. He stepped away and followed Barrow and the state attorney around the busy nurses' station to a vacant examination room. The attorney general closed the door, but Jack could still see his client through the glass wall.

"I know you're just doing your job, but I choose to skip this dance," said the attorney general. "Ms. Holmes is going to be charged."

"Charged with what?"

"Illegal possession of armor-piercing ammunition. It's a felony under Florida statutes."

Cop-killer bullets. They were illegal in most states—even in Florida.

"Are you saying you found illegal ammunition in her concealed carry?"

"FDLE officers recovered an assortment of personal belongings that got tossed around inside the truck, including an ammo can with eight boxes of ammunition inside. Seven boxes of standard nine-millimeter identical to the ammunition in Ms. Holmes's Glock. And one box of nine-millimeter armor-piercing bullets."

"My client is a responsible gun owner. That ammunition can't be hers."

"Then how did it get in her ammo can?"

Jack couldn't say for certain until he spoke to his client, but this sure smelled like dirty politics. "By any chance would a felony conviction disqualify Ms. Holmes from serving in the Electoral College?"

Barrow took a step back, as if wounded by the insinuation. "Are you suggesting that someone planted illegal ammunition for political advantage?"

Jack had seen evidence planted in cases with far less than a presidential election at stake. "When do you plan to bring charges?" asked Jack.

"As soon as the state attorney can file the information."

The "information" was a formal criminal charge. In

Florida, indictment by a grand jury was required only in a capital case, and most criminal proceedings began with an information filed by the state attorney.

"This is a terrible political miscalculation on your part," said Jack. "There's no way to get a conviction on this charge before the Electoral College meets next month."

"It's a two-hour trial with one witness. I think our judicial system can handle it."

"I'll move to postpone it."

"Then it'll be up to the judge," said Barrow. "An elected judge who owes his or her job to voters who went overwhelmingly for President MacLeod. Good luck."

Jack wished he had a recording of this conversation, if only to explain to friends why this Swyteck had never ventured into politics. "Tell President MacLeod he isn't going to win this fight," said Jack. "Even if he does have the Florida attorney general in his ammo can."

Chapter 16

The state attorney didn't drive straight back to his office. He said goodbye to the attorney general in the parking lot outside the ER, and then, on his own, stopped to see Madeline Chisel.

Josh Kutter prided himself on being thorough and cautious. Two tours of duty in Iraq had taught him the bloody consequences of rushed and uninformed decision making. Under his leadership, the state attorney's office had a 90 percent conviction rate, due in part to a talented prosecutorial team, but also due to prudent decisions about which cases to prosecute. Under normal circumstances, he would probably defer to a junior prosecutor's judgment in a case built on possession of armor-piercing ammunition. These were not normal circumstances.

Chisel was seated behind an old oak desk. Kutter sat in the armchair, wondering if, hidden behind the front desk panel, there lurked a permanently mounted shotgun, loaded and aimed straight at his groin, just in case Madeline found herself in need of self-defense.

"Ms. Chisel, the driver involved in last night's accident told us that when he picked up Ms. Holmes outside your office, she had a box of belongings."

"Yes. I packed up her things from her desk."

"Did you pack any ammunition in that box?"

"There was an ammo can. We all keep a few hundred extra rounds at our desk. When you're a gun lobbyist, you have people all the time threatening to give you a taste of your own medicine. Somebody walks in here with a grudge and an AR-15, he's gonna regret it."

"Would it surprise you to hear that we found cop-killer ammunition in that ammo can?"

"After Charlotte said she's voting for Senator Stahl, nothing surprises me."

"You know it's illegal, right?"

"If by cop-killer ammo you mean a bullet with a steel inner core and a truncated cone that is designed for use in a handgun and to pierce body armor—then, yes, it's illegal. Unless you're a law enforcement officer."

"Impressive," said Kutter.

"I helped write the statute," said Chisel.

"Of course you did. But here's my question: Could you swear under oath that nobody touched that ammo can and swapped out lawful ammunition for cop-killer ammunition before Ms. Holmes walked out of this office with her box of belongings?"

"Are you asking if it's possible that somebody in this office could have gone into Charlotte's desk and made that swap?"

"Yes, I am."

"All I can do is tell the truth," said Madeline.

"That's all I want," said the prosecutor. "The truth."

Madeline leaned forward, resting on her forearms, eyes narrowing. "Are you sure about that, Mr. Kutter?"

President MacLeod was in what his White House staff called "volcanic mode."

"What do you mean the charge was never filed!" he shouted—screamed, actually.

The windows in the West Wing were bulletproof. When the president exploded like this, the better question was whether they were "MacLeod-proof." Fears were especially high when the eruptions coincided with his indoor putting practice on the White House carpet. Many a presidential club lay at the bottom of golf-course water hazards, and his staff had a running bet on how soon it would be until he sent one sailing across the Oval Office.

The president was still fuming as he lined up his next putt. His chief strategist took a step back, out of the president's line, and explained.

"The state attorney in Leon County decided that the case against Charlotte Holmes is not strong enough to move forward."

MacLeod smacked the little white ball so hard it ricocheted off the credenza and slammed into the historic Resolute Desk, no apologies offered to previous presidents who had taken such good care of it. He glared at Teague, his face red with anger. "Who the hell is the state attorney of Leon County to make that decision?"

Teague was flummoxed. "He—uh . . . frankly, sir, he would be the chief prosecuting officer that voters duly elected to oversee all criminal cases in the Second Judicial District of Florida."

MacLeod laid his golf club aside, went to his desk, and inspected the mark left by the errant putt. He was told that the nineteenth-century partner-style desk was a gift from Queen Victoria to then president Rutherford B. Hayes, made from the English oak timbers of the British Arctic exploration ship HMS *Resolute*. Nobody would notice another dent.

"Paulette Barrow assured you that the charge would be filed."

"She assured me that if she was the state attorney, she would file the charge. It would look very political if the attorney general were to override the local state attorney's decision not to prosecute."

"Then I'll call the little prick myself," he said.

"I wouldn't do that, sir."

"I want to know why this genius decided not to charge Charlotte Holmes."

"You can't just pick up the phone and bawl the guy out."

"Why not?"

"It's the same optics that made your lawyers put the kibosh on the victory tour. Whether it's face-to-face meetings with electors in battleground states or dressing down the Leon County state attorney, you can't be seen as strong-arming state officers to disrupt the Electoral College."

"But I'm right, am I not? Charlotte Holmes is dead in the water. Felony charge—boom. She's out of the Electoral College. The governor replaces her with someone who knows the definition of loyalty."

"My understanding is that the problem lies with our friend Madeline Chisel."

The president bristled. "That can't be. Madeline's a team player."

"The state attorney asked Madeline to sign an affidavit under oath that the ammunition she found in Ms. Holmes's desk in fact belonged to Charlotte Holmes. Madeline said she couldn't do that."

"What's her problem?"

"Too many people coming and going from her office. Clients, staff, FedEx, UPS, Postmates, janitors, housekeeping, the pest-control company, the guy who waters the plants, and on and on. Madeline couldn't swear under oath that no one went into Charlotte's office and planted the ammo before Madeline cleaned out that desk."

"Fine. Madeline swears now, the governor replaces Charlotte Holmes with a new elector, and then after the College votes for me on December fourteenth, Madeline can unswear. What's the problem?"

Teague grimaced. "It's under oath, sir."

MacLeod turned on his sissy voice. "Ith unduh oath, thir," he said, throwing in a few mocking gestures. Then he turned serious: "It's words on paper!"

"Tell that to Sir Thomas More," Teague muttered.

"Sir who?"

"Thomas More. Legal counselor to King Henry VIII. He was tried for treason and beheaded because he refused to swear an oath of supremacy recognizing the king as head of the Church of England. His famous last words were, 'The king's good servant, but God's first.' If you'd slogged through two years of religious studies in college like I did, you'd know who he is."

"I know who he is," said MacLeod, snarling. "You should have made it clear that you were talking about that Sir Thomas More."

"My apologies, Mr. President."

MacLeod sprang from his desk chair, crossed the room, and grabbed his golf club. Teague watched, his eyes wide with fright, as if the president might hit something—or someone. "'My apologies,' 'I'm sorry,' 'Excuse me, Mr. President,'" he said in a derisive tone. "Maybe King Henry had it right. It's time for heads to roll around here."

"Yes, sir. I have a few strategies in the works."

"I need something big. Really big."

"I can have a report to you in a couple of hours."

"One hour. We have to fix this. Today, Oscar!"

"Yes, sir."

The president took three deep breaths, in and out, the way his cardiologist had taught him. Then he assumed his putting stance, standing somewhat awkwardly over the ball, and lined up his shot.

"Sir Thomas More," he muttered. "What kind of idiot doesn't lie under oath to avoid a date with the executioner, anyway?"

He tapped the ball just right and sent it rolling toward the presidential seal, where it found the cup.

Chapter 17

On Friday morning, Jack and his client took a taxi to the courthouse for an emergency hearing.

"Walk straight into the building," said Jack, as their taxi stopped at the curb. "Don't stop, don't look at the TV cameras, and, most of all, ignore the hecklers who are trying to get a rise out of you."

"I'll try," said Charlotte.

A "never mind" e-mail had come from the state attorney late Thursday afternoon: "No criminal charges will be filed against Charlotte Holmes at this time." Jack was on his way to the Tallahassee airport, ready to fly home to his family, when his client had called to tell him that she was a named defendant—not in a criminal case, but in a civil action. "I've been sued by the state of Florida," she'd told him.

The battle lines were drawn, and Jack knew it would be anything but "civil."

"You ready?" Jack asked his client. A crowd of demonstrators was outside the building, shielded from the sun by neat rows of trees that canopied the brick courtyard.

"Ready," said Charlotte.

Jack was no stranger to angry mobs, once having been splattered with pig's blood on the courthouse steps to drive home the point that the victim's blood was as much on him as his client. This group of courthouse demonstrators, however, was evenly divided. Some cheered and applauded Charlotte as a hero, chanting "Five million matter!" It wasn't nearly enough to drown out those who felt very differently.

"We're praying for you, Charlotte!"

"Praying that you die before December fourteenth!"

It was hard not to feel threatened, even if it wasn't technically a death threat.

Jack and his client pushed through the crowd and funneled through the revolving door. The demonstrators stayed outside, but their partisan shouting could be heard through the glass, which made even the short delay of a security clearance seem interminable. Reporters fired questions as they crossed the lobby. Jack didn't use the words "no comment"—he never did—

but he limited his remarks to benign references to "justice" and the protection of his client's rights. He and Charlotte squeezed into an open elevator. The unwritten rule of crowded-elevator etiquette—silence—was broken by one especially persistent reporter who kept firing away until they reached the third floor. As they headed toward the courtroom, another set of elevator doors opened. Out stepped one lawyer after another. And another. And then another. It was like the proverbial stream of clowns piling out of a cramped Volkswagen Beetle, except that these were no clowns. They were Jack's opposition.

"The attorney general is here?" Charlotte whispered.

Jack had expected no less. Florida Attorney General Paulette Barrow had made a national splash as a prime-time speaker at the Republican National Convention. A win here could put her on the shortlist for MacLeod's second-term cabinet, possibly even U.S. attorney general. With her were senior members of her office and a host of other lawyers and advisors. The media immediately flocked to the attorney general. Jack and his client separated themselves from the circus and entered the courtroom.

The gallery was packed with spectators who'd arrived early enough to snag a seat. Some no doubt supported Charlotte, while others detested her; either way, they respected courtroom decorum and watched in silence as Jack and his client proceeded down the center aisle and took their place at the table for the defense on the other side of the rail. Seated right behind them, having staked out prime viewing seats, were lawyers for Senator Stahl and the Democratic Party. They weren't parties to the lawsuit, but they were certainly interested enough in the outcome to have lawyers at the ready. Lawyers for MacLeod and the Republican Party were similarly positioned behind the rail on the other side of the courtroom. A moment later the double doors in the back of the courtroom parted, and the attorney general began her journey down the center aisle, stopping to shake hands with everyone she knew or pretended to recognize.

"What does she think this is," Charlotte whispered, "the State of the Union Address?"

The question conjured up the perfect image in Jack's mind. Florida chooses its attorney general by statewide election, and at some point in the career of every elected AG, the transition from lawyer to politician became irreversible. Even courtroom appearances played out like staged political events. Jack was already thinking of ways to use that to his advantage.

Just as the attorney general and her team took their seats, a loud knock echoed through the courtroom, the door to Judge Lionel Martin's chambers swung open, and the bailiff called the courtroom to order.

"All rise!"

The silver-haired judge ascended to the bench as all watched in respectful silence. Judge Martin was the chief judge for the five-county area surrounding Tallahassee, a former trial lawyer who used to love trying cases in the old Gadsden County courthouse, because lawyers could hang out in the restroom and listen to jurors deliberating on the other side of the wall. Two decades on the bench had earned him the reputation of a tireless worker who took only one vacation a year, when he and half the Tallahassee bar crossed the state line to Thomasville, Georgia, for quail-hunting season. Judge Martin wished everyone a good morning, allowed counsel to announce their appearance for the record, and then laid down the law for both lawyers and spectators.

"Ladies and gentlemen, let's be honest: we have politicians and lunatics on both sides here today. And in some cases they are one and the same."

Jack liked him already.

"Now, let's be really honest," the judge continued. "Most folks love or hate the Electoral College based on which way it cuts for their candidate. But we're not here to decide if there should be an Electoral College.

That decision was made two hundred fifty years ago by the Founding Fathers. The only issue before this court today is this: Is Charlotte Holmes required by law to vote for Republican candidate Malcolm MacLeod when the Electoral College convenes on December the fourteenth?"

The judge looked at Jack, and then at the attorney general. "That's the long and short of it, Counsel. I want no grandstanding, no political speeches. General Barrow, let me hear the state of Florida's position first."

"Thank you, Judge," said Barrow, and as she approached the lectern, she shot a quick look at Charlotte that was anything but an innocent glance. Barrow was generally adored by men in Tallahassee but had a terrible reputation for the way she treated other women. The look Barrow had just thrown Jack's client seemed to say something on the order of "I am not your girlfriend."

"Your Honor," she began, "when you became a judge, you swore an oath to uphold your office. When I became attorney general, I swore an oath. When President MacLeod was inaugurated as president four years ago, he swore an oath. All of us are bound to uphold the oaths we have taken.

"Before Governor Mulvane certified Charlotte Holmes as one of twenty-nine Republican electors,

Ms. Holmes swore an oath. She swore that if Florida went Republican in the November election, she would vote for the Republican candidate at the meeting of the Electoral College. Does that oath mean anything? Not to Ms. Holmes. She has publicly announced her intention to vote for Senator Stahl. This court must order Ms. Holmes to uphold her oath and vote as she promised to vote. It's that simple."

The attorney general returned to her seat. Jack could scarcely hide his surprise. A legal argument devoid of self-serving political rhetoric was the last thing he'd expected from Barrow.

Judge Martin swung his gaze toward Jack. "Mr. Swyteck? What say you?"

Jack had prepared a lengthy presentation, having anticipated the need to rebut a host of incendiary arguments that the attorney general had chosen to ignore. Jack jettisoned the outline and responded in kind—short and to the point.

"Breach of oath is a crime under Florida law," said Jack. "As of this moment, no crime has been committed. If and when Ms. Holmes votes for Senator Stahl at the meeting of the Electoral College in December, she can be prosecuted for breaking her promise to vote for President MacLeod. She understands the consequences, and she is willing to accept them. The Florida

Legislature does not dictate how electors under the United States Constitution must vote. With all due respect, a Florida state court judge has no power to tell an elector how to vote. To borrow the attorney general's phrase, 'It's that simple.'"

Jack returned to his seat. Judge Martin leaned back in his leather chair, thinking, and then spoke.

"Every day in this courtroom, witnesses raise their right hand and swear an oath to tell the truth. Far too often, what follows is a stream of lies. Maybe I'm old-fashioned, but I'm troubled by a world in which a sworn oath means nothing."

"The state of Florida is equally troubled," said the attorney general, egging him on.

The judge leaned forward and looked straight at Jack. "Nonetheless, I believe Mr. Swyteck is right."

It took the attorney general a moment to untie her tongue. "Judge, this is a mockery. Ms. Holmes stated at her press conference that she can't vote for President MacLeod because, in her words, 'truth matters.' Doesn't an oath matter?"

"Your Honor, we don't live in a monarchy," said Jack. "In fact, we fought a war over that. It violates the Constitution for any state legislature to force a member of the Electoral College to swear an oath of allegiance to a specific candidate as a qualification for serving as an elector."

"Mr. Swyteck, I'm not going to try and read the minds of the Founding Fathers. And, General Barrow, the irony you point out is not lost on me. All I can do is follow the law." The judge then turned his gaze to Jack's client. "Ms. Holmes, breach of oath is a third-degree felony. You could go to jail. Proceed with your eyes wide open. But proceed—and vote—as you will."

Jack was shocked to get an immediate ruling from the bench, and, judging from the firmness of Charlotte's grip on his elbow, she was equally surprised.

"That's my decision," said the judge, taking the gavel in hand. "So unless the state of Florida has any other business before this court, we are—"

"There's one other matter," said Barrow, barely getting a word in before adjournment.

"What is it, General?" the judge asked.

"It's our position that, like all state officials, electors may be removed if they have committed misfeasance or malfeasance, or are otherwise unfit for office."

"Judge, there's no evidence of any misconduct by my client," said Jack.

"All we're asking for is an opportunity to present that evidence," said Barrow. "That's basic fairness."

"Judge, the attorney general is simply unhappy with the court's ruling and is flying by the seat of her pants to find a way around it."

"Mr. Swyteck, lawyers fly by the seat of their pants so often in this courtroom that I should hang an honorary pair of britches from the ceiling."

There were a few chuckles from the gallery, which the judge seemed to appreciate.

"For the record, I am not flying by the seat of my pants," said Barrow. "By accepting Mr. Swyteck's argument, this court has embraced Alexander Hamilton's view that, regardless of the results of the general election, it is the job of the Electoral College to protect the presidency from one who is unfit."

"Hamilton, huh. I must have slept through that part of the musical," the judge said, which drew more laughter.

"It wasn't in the musical," said Barrow. "It's in Federalist Papers, number Sixty-Eight. If electors are going to decide who's fit to be president, they themselves should be fit to hold office."

"What is the state of Florida asking me to do?" the judge asked.

"We request an immediate hearing to present evidence and call witnesses in support of our position that

Ms. Holmes should be removed as elector for good cause."

"Judge, I object—"

"Noted," said the judge, shutting Jack down. "But this court intends to be fair to both sides. If the attorney general wants a hearing, she can have a hearing. We will reconvene on Monday morning at nine a.m. Ms. Barrow, have your witnesses here and ready to testify."

At the risk of annoying the judge, Jack had to speak up. "Testify as to what? My client has a right to know what she's accused of doing."

"This isn't a criminal proceeding," said the judge. "She's accused of misfeasance and malfeasance."

"And unfitness for office," said Barrow, her reassertion of the "fitness" requirement making it clear that she had something in mind.

"Misfeasance, malfeasance, and unfitness," said the judge. "There you go, Mr. Swyteck. That's what your client is accused of. See y'all Monday morning. We're adjourned."

A crack of his gavel followed. On the bailiff's command, all rose and watched in silence as Judge Martin disappeared into his chambers. The paneled door closed with a thud, and the packed courtroom sprang into action. Some journalists raced from the courtroom to report the breaking news. Others rushed to the rail to get the reaction from counsel. They were calling for the attorney general, eager to hear her next move, but she stepped around the lectern and stopped at the defense table.

"Mr. Swyteck, I want you to know that the lines of communication are open between now and Monday morning, in case your client decides this fight isn't worth it."

"It's worth it," said Charlotte.

"No, it isn't," she said, technically addressing Jack, though her words were clearly for Charlotte's ears. "Every elector in the country will be watching this hearing, and when it's over, not a single one will decide that following your lead is worth it. That's not a threat; it's the nature of a fitness hearing. Even if you win, you lose."

Barrow turned and walked to the rail, where reporters were eager to speak to her, each elbowing out the other for the strategic spot.

"How am I unfit to be an elector?" Charlotte whispered. "What do they think they're going to do on Monday?"

"Character assassination," said Jack. "It's what Mac-Leod does best."

Chapter 18

Jack couldn't shake the crowd. Members of the media dogged them all the way out of the building, and the vibe in the courtyard outside the main entrance had gone decidedly hostile. Jack's guess was that the MacLeod campaign had bused in more bodies for the post-hearing demonstration. If their chant was any indication, the president's latest tweet had put out a new hashtag: "Unfit! Unfit! Unfit!"

Jack had reserved a town car for their getaway, but just getting to it was a struggle. He and Charlotte pushed their way to the curb and jumped into the back seat, the shouting still audible through closed doors. It was a bright day but the interior dimmed in what seemed like a partial eclipse of the sun, as demonstrators pressed their protest signs and posters against the car windows.

Several demonstrators raced across Monroe Street and jumped in their vehicles to follow. Leading a mob directly to Charlotte's house made no sense. All it took was one lunatic for Charlotte's worst fears to become reality, and it seemed fair to assume there was at least one out there, given the string of "hope you die" text messages flooding Charlotte's cell phone.

"Stop looking at those," Jack told her, as the car pulled away slowly from the curb. A line of cars and pickup trucks was forming behind them, engines running, an impromptu parade straight to Charlotte's residence. Jack needed a better exit strategy. The answer came in an unexpected text to Jack from the senator's lawyer, Matthew Kipner.

"Meet at Govs Club," the message read.

Jack hadn't planned on meeting with Kipner or anyone else from either campaign. But his suggestion made sense. The Governors Club was private, meaning no media and no demonstrators. Jack redirected the driver, and in just a few minutes they were safely inside.

The Governors Club was not the political "meet market" that was the bar at the Hotel Duval, but it was just a block away from the Capitol, which put it on anyone's list of Tallahassee's institutions of power and privilege. Brass chandeliers, fireplaces, and paneled walls of burled wood and exposed brick conjured up images of cigar-chomping power brokers. The reality, however, was that Florida's laws on open meetings and "government in the sunshine" made it risky for government officials to cut deals in a private club. It was better suited to private meetings, like the lawyer-to-lawyer discussion that Kipner wanted with Jack.

"Can I see you alone for a minute?" asked Kipner.

Charlotte was a club member, so she was comfortable by herself at the bar for a while. In fact, she seemed to relish the idea of time alone. Kipner led Jack into a back room, which struck Jack as the "belt and suspenders" approach to confidentiality, given that they were already in a private club. It was just the two lawyers in the company of a stuffed pheasant on the fireplace mantel.

"Your client is going through hell," said Kipner.

"No offense, but it's not because she's a huge fan of Senator Stahl. She believes in her position."

"It's only going to get worse. Starting Monday, this case is no longer about the intent of the Founding Fathers and the purpose of the Electoral College. MacLeod is a master of the personal smear campaign. Proving that Charlotte is 'unfit' to serve as an elector will be nothing less than a scorched-earth campaign."

"She knows that."

"But is she ready for it?"

"She will be."

"They will dig up everything in Charlotte's past."

"I have no way of knowing everything in her past," said Jack. "But I do know that not everything is admissible in a courtroom. We'll fight it one battle at a time."

Kipner was clearly not happy with Jack's position. "Legal victories don't matter from here on out. If they can't use it in the courtroom, any dirt they dig up will still be national news on television. They will besmirch her reputation and assassinate her character in every way possible, if for no other reason than to send a clear message to every other Republican elector in the nation: the law may allow you to vote for a Democrat on December fourteenth, but if you do, you will pay a terrible price."

Jack chose not to mention that the attorney general had explicitly confirmed as much. "I can't control what happens outside the courtroom."

"All I want to know is if your client is going to hang in there. Is she firm in her decision to vote for Senator Stahl? Or might we lose her?"

Jack didn't want to be flip, but trying to predict a client's actions in a situation like this was only slightly more scientific than using your kids' birth dates to "Pick 6." "I don't think there's any way to know until

Charlotte walks into the State Capitol on December fourteenth and votes."

"That's not very helpful."

"Here's what I can tell you. Charlotte is a fighter. If she backs down and votes for MacLeod, it won't be because the attorney general is too rough on her in the courtroom. She has other concerns. Her own personal safety being the biggest one."

"I'm sure we can find a loyal Democrat willing to pay for a bodyguard."

"You can't do that. If you provide anything of value to Charlotte, the attorney general will rush into court and accuse her of taking a bribe. You can't even pay Charlotte's cab fare to the courthouse."

"All right. If you want to play it that straight, that's your choice. Besides her personal safety, is there any other reason we might lose Charlotte's vote?"

"Yes, obviously. She could end up a convicted felon for breach of oath."

"That's not as bad as it sounds, though. Right?"

"I don't know what you mean."

"I spoke to a top-flight criminal defense lawyer about this. Just out of curiosity, of course. Breach of oath is a third-degree felony. With no criminal record, there's no chance your client will get jail time."

"That's true. Florida has a sentencing point system,

and there's no way her points will add up to jail time for breach of oath. But as a convicted felon, she can't be a lobbyist in Florida. I've seen it happen to lobbyists convicted of DUI. They're done in Tallahassee."

"She doesn't have to worry about that."

"Easy for you to say. She knows her career as a gun lobbyist is over, but she's an experienced lobbyist who can work for plenty of other industries. That door closes entirely if she's a convicted felon."

Kipner leaned forward in his chair, looking Jack in the eye. "A felony conviction precludes her from lobbying in Florida. Not in Washington. Hell, even Jack Abramoff registered to lobby after serving four years in prison. I'm sure someone as talented as Charlotte would find plenty of work after the election, even as a convicted felon."

Jack took a moment to react. Kipner was smart enough not to say "after the election if Stahl wins," but the implication was there. "I know you would never suggest anything improper, Matthew. But there are people who might construe what you just said as a promise of steady work after the election. A quid pro quo."

"You clearly misheard me, Jack. I'm not making any promises. I'm simply making an observation. You may choose to share that observation with your client. Or you may choose not to share it. It's totally up to you."

Jack had given him a wide-open opportunity to back away from the implication; Kipner chose not to, instead playing it way too cute for Jack's comfort level. "I need to check on Charlotte," Jack said, rising.

"We'll talk again soon," said Kipner.

"Actually, I think it's best if we don't talk again between now and December fourteenth."

"What? Come on, Jack, you're making way too much out of this."

Jack hesitated, not wanting to sound pious. But if Kipner wasn't going to let it go, then neither would Jack. "That's the funny thing about politics, isn't it," said Jack.

"What?"

"Nobody ever thinks they're the problem."

Jack glanced at the stuffed pheasant on the way out, glad the bird was without ears.

Charlotte waited at the bar while Jack was in the Pheasant Room. The lunch crowd filed into the club's dining room. Charlotte recognized at least a dozen fellow lobbyists, lawyers, and lawmakers who walked right past her. It was amazing how people she'd known for years could pretend not to see her. At least the bartender said hello, giving her the usual college-football razzing as he poured her a glass of chardonnay.

"How 'bout them Dawgs, Miss Charlotte," meaning his University of Georgia Bulldogs.

Like everyone who grew up in the Florida Panhandle, Charlotte was a die-hard fan of the Alabama Crimson Tide; like everyone from Georgia, Clem was a big talker until Alabama cleaned up in the SEC championship each December. But Charlotte loved chatting it up with him, and she loved the way he and all the Georgians called her "Miss Charlotte." And there were plenty of them in Tallahassee. A little-known fact among Floridians was that their state government was in large part run by Georgians who commuted to work every day from across the state line.

"This seat taken?"

Charlotte immediately recognized the voice, but she couldn't contain her surprise as Madeline Chisel climbed onto the barstool beside her.

"Am I not toxic to you?" asked Charlotte.

"At my age I find 'toxic' interesting."

Charlotte tasted her wine and smiled a little. "Is that supposed to make me feel better?"

Madeline smiled back, then turned serious. "Honey, you have really stepped in it this time."

"Paulette Barrow never could stand me," she said, a bit philosophical. "It's not like I'm losing a friend."

"Don't fool yourself into thinking the attorney general is calling the shots here."

"Is that what you came by to tell me?"

"No," said Madeline. "I wanted to thank you."

"For what?"

"Cop-killer bullets."

Charlotte knew exactly what she meant. "You don't have to thank me for that."

"You must've known it was me who put them in your ammo can. I was always the one who said that if someone busted into our office looking to pay back the gun lobbyists, he'd probably be wearing body armor."

Charlotte nodded. "Interesting thing is that my lawyer never doubted me for a second when I said they weren't mine. But he didn't point the finger at you. He thought it was somebody in law enforcement who planted illegal ammo at the scene."

"Typical defense lawyer reaction. They think all cops plant evidence and all prosecutors hide it."

"They are a suspicious breed," said Charlotte. "Defense lawyers, I mean."

"Look, the bottom line is that you knew it was me. You could have thrown me under the bus when Barrow tried to use it against you. You didn't. So I thank you."

"You're welcome."

"Gotta go," said Madeline, as she climbed down

from her barstool. "I'm meeting a client for lunch. But good luck to you."

"I think I'm going to need it," said Charlotte.

"You will," said Madeline. "But there's something you should keep in mind."

"What's that?"

"I owe you one, kiddo. Use it wisely."

Charlotte watched her old boss walk away and, for a minute, felt a little less lonely.

Jack and Charlotte ate lunch at the Governors Club and left around two o'clock. The town car had long since left, but it was a short walk to the hotel and Jack's rental car. The last time Charlotte had called for a ride she'd landed upside down in a ditch, so she seemed more than happy to accept Jack's offer to drive her home.

"Turn here," Charlotte told him.

Jack had been mostly honest in his talk with Kipner at the club. He did have a plan to keep Charlotte safe, and it was strictly between him and his client. Jack just hadn't shared it with her yet.

"It's the yellow house on the right," she said.

"I probably could have guessed," said Jack. Media vans were parked on the street, and a dozen or more reporters with their camera crews were waiting on the sidewalk. Jack slowed his rental car.

"Have your house key ready," said Jack. "We'll roll right past them and park in the driveway. Walk—don't run—inside. Answering questions at a media ambush never goes well. We'll hold a press conference later."

"What if they follow us to the door?"

"I'll take care of that."

A flock of reporters and cameramen hurried toward the moving car as Jack steered into the driveway. Jack drove slowly but didn't stop until he was beyond the mob, entirely on private property, and bumper to bumper with Charlotte's parked car. The demonstrators had apparently grown tired of waiting, but they hadn't left without parting remarks. Charlotte's entire car had been egged, a thin layer of goo baked onto the finish by the morning sun. Someone with a can of black spray paint had posted a welcome-home greeting on Charlotte's front door. The "Unfit" mantra seemed to be catching on.

"Go straight into the house," said Jack.

Charlotte took a deep breath and gave Jack a look that signaled she was ready. The car doors opened simultaneously. As coached, Charlotte walked at her normal pace to the front door. Jack went to the end of the driveway, each step drawing more intense questioning about the criminal charges, the election, and a jumble of other things that were no more than noise to Jack.

"My client needs time to herself," Jack announced to the media, as cameras rolled. "We will hold a press conference soon. Until then, please respect her privacy. Thank you for understanding."

Jack had nothing more to say, but it wasn't enough for this crowd. A barrage of questions followed him all the way to the front door, but the media respected the property line, no one stepping beyond Charlotte's mailbox near the end of her driveway.

Jack found his client in the TV room, half-submerged in the overstuffed couch. The white Bahamian shutters on the window were closed, though not quite all the way, the thin horizontal slats of sunshine the only light in the room.

"Is this what my life is going to be like until the meeting of the Electoral College?"

Running the gauntlet was taking a visible toll on his client. It seemed like an opportune time for Jack to pitch his "protection plan," but before he could say anything, a cacophony of shattering glass erupted in the kitchen. Charlotte jumped over the back of the couch to take cover.

"Get down!" she shouted, and Jack hit the floor.

Jack hadn't heard a gunshot, but Charlotte's reaction was on the level of a home invasion. Jack grabbed his cell phone and dialed 911, but Charlotte was already taking matters into her own hands. Jack was on the phone with the operator as Charlotte slid across the floor toward the closet, where he assumed she was going to hide. But instead of opening the closet door, she opened only the bottom panel of the three-panel door and retrieved a handgun, which the panel was constructed to conceal.

"What are you doing?" Jack asked her, but she ignored him. Charlotte rose to a crouch, standing only as tall as necessary. She gripped her firearm like a professional, the way Jack's wife was trained to respond, and quietly started toward the kitchen.

"Sir, what is your emergency?" asked the operator.

Jack told the operator what he knew, but he was more focused on what Charlotte was doing. With her back pressed against the wall, she glided out of the room.

"Is there an intruder in the house?" asked the operator.

"I don't know," Jack said into his phone. "We heard a window smash."

Charlotte disappeared down the hallway, leading with her handgun. Jack wished she would just stay put and wait for the cops, but that was like wishing he'd put his client-protection plan in place sooner. Pointless.

"Officers on the way," said the operator.

"The owner of the house is checking things out.

She's armed, so don't shoot *her*." He added a quick description of Charlotte and what she was wearing.

"Noted," said the dispatcher, and the call ended. Jack waited, hearing nothing from the kitchen. Then Charlotte called for him—"Jack, come here"—in a voice that conveyed no urgency. It seemed that the immediate emergency had passed. Still, Jack walked cautiously into the kitchen.

"Take a look at this," she said.

Charlotte was crouched over a blanket of glistening glass pellets on the floor. Something had flown through her bay window and shattered it to pieces. Charlotte pointed, directing Jack's focus toward a black handgun magazine. It had apparently skidded across the kitchen and come to rest by the icemaker.

"Somebody threw a magazine through the window?" asked Jack.

"If you threw a single round, it would bounce off the glass like a pebble. But a fifteen-round magazine will do the trick. If your aim is to send a message."

"How about *shooting* through the window? Doesn't that send the strongest message of all?"

"Not if your message is literally scratched onto the side of the magazine."

"Can you read it?"

Charlotte didn't want to get too close, and she definitely didn't want to touch it, knowing that this was a crime scene. She used her smartphone and zoomed in with the camera function. "'B-P-R-E-P apostrophe D.' Be prepared."

Jack thought for a moment but came up empty. "Does that mean anything to you?"

"The magazine holds nine-millimeter rounds," said Charlotte. "Nine by nineteen millimeter, to be exact."

"So?"

"So there's more than one way to refer to nine-by-nineteen ammo. Nine-mil Luger is one. Nine-mil para-bellum is another. No difference, really. Just parabellum is the name the first maker gave to a nine-millimeter bullet with the little extra powder that comes with a nineteen-millimeter casing."

Charlotte's clear implication was that "parabellum" was somehow significant. "I'm not following your point."

"The name 'parabellum' comes from Latin," said Charlotte. "*Si vis pacem, para bellum*. If you seek peace, prepare for war."

"So, whoever shattered your window with that magazine is telling you—"

"It's war," said Charlotte, finishing the thought for him.

Police sirens blared in the distance. Jack hoped that

the message was not intended to be taken literally, but this was a step beyond random threats from a crowd of demonstrators. It was definitely time to put his client-protection plan into action.

"Let me ask you something," said Jack.

"What?"

"How long would it take you to pack a suitcase?"

Chapter 19

It seemed counterintuitive, but Jack and Charlotte felt safer when their plane landed in Miami.

Charlotte had resisted leaving her home, telling Jack that, despite the allusion to war, "parabellum" ammunition wasn't actually military grade, which meant that whoever had scratched the message on the magazine and smashed her window didn't know much about guns or was being way too clever. Either way, Jack figured, Charlotte could still end up dead.

"Your friend is okay with me staying at his place?" she asked.

"Theo will be more than okay with you staying at his place," said Jack. "You'll be in the flat above his bar. Most people don't even know it exists. His uncle Cy used to live there."

"Cy, as in Cy's Place?"

"The one and only," said Jack.

It was after dark when they reached Coconut Grove. Once upon a time, an evening in the Grove would have meant streets and sidewalks packed with twenty-somethings and teens who pretended to be twenty-something cruising up and down Main Highway. Those days were gone. Now it was largely tourists in search of what the Grove once was, some of whom could be found standing in front of razed buildings, double-checking their outdated edition of *Fodor's* that had led them to another restaurant turned construction site. It was Theo's loyal following that kept Cy's Place alive—that, and the fact that finding another true jazz club in Miami was like trying to find the Copacabana in Fairbanks.

Jack and Charlotte parked and walked straight to the rear entrance. Theo met them by the outdoor stairwell in the alley. Jack made the introduction and Theo led them up to the apartment, with not so much as an arched eyebrow from Theo to acknowledge that Charlotte was an attractive brunette, around his age, and close enough to his type. It was very unlike Theo, which told Jack that he was still pining.

"My uncle Cy lived here for years, but the stairs got to be too much for him. Only one other person has stayed here."

"Who's that?" asked Charlotte.

Oh, God, here it comes, thought Jack. *Julia Rodriguez, the most perfect woman in the world, who was definitely THE ONE, but I was too stupid to realize it, and now she's gone back to El Salvador, and my life is ruined.*

"A friend of mine," said Theo.

Theo opened the door and stepped aside to let Jack and Charlotte enter. Jack smiled at his friend on his way inside. "Good answer," said Jack.

"I'm working at it," said Theo.

Cy's Place occupied one of the oldest addresses in Coconut Grove, a two-story brick structure that had "great bones" for a jazz club. The one-bedroom hovel directly above the club came with a prime view of the Dumpsters in the alley but was not without charm. Theo offered a quick tour of the old photos and jazz memorabilia that his uncle had left behind. The famous nightclubs of Overtown, where Cy used to play with the likes of Sam Cooke in his heyday, were a part of music history that was unknown even to most Miamians. Charlotte seemed interested, but once he got started, Theo could brag on his uncle all night long, and Jack had a lot of ground to cover with his client before they returned to Tallahassee for Monday's hearing.

"Dude, we only got till Sunday night," said Jack.

"Sorry," said Theo, then he smiled at Charlotte. "Next time."

"Sure. Next time," said Charlotte.

"Did you get everything on my list?" asked Jack.

Theo brought the paper bag from the kitchen counter, placed it on the table, and then began to empty it, starting with a phone.

"One disposable cell," he said.

They'd left Charlotte's smartphone in Tallahassee in case someone was tracking her by GPS. "Disposables aren't traceable," Jack told her. "But I still suggest you keep phone calls to a minimum."

"Understood," said Charlotte.

Theo removed a few other essentials from the bag and then laid out the last two items. The penultimate, a can of Mace, was one Jack had requested. The last was not.

"One semi-automatic pistol," said Theo. "Nine millimeter."

"You bought a gun?" said Jack.

"No. This one belongs to Uncle Cy. He wouldn't sleep up here without one, and neither would I. Especially if I had sixty-five million MacLeod voters out to kill me."

"There aren't sixty-five million people trying to kill her."

"Sixty-five million suspects," said Theo.

"Thanks," said Jack. "We weren't worried enough."

"Thank you, Theo," said Charlotte. She checked the gun. Theo handed her the magazine separately, and she loaded it.

"The kitchen is open till midnight," said Theo. "Just let me know if you get hungry."

"Thank you."

"I'll be tending bar all night. Happy to mix your favorite cocktail if you get bored."

Jack was happy to see Theo climbing his way out of the Julia Rodriguez pit of misery, but he needed to lay down some rules. "No going down to the bar. The point of this trip is for Charlotte to keep a low profile."

"Got it," said Theo.

"We'll add that to the 'next time' list," said Charlotte.

She and Jack thanked him, and Theo closed the door on the way out.

"Go ahead and unpack, and take thirty minutes to unwind," Jack said. "We have a lot to cover between now and Monday, so I'd like to get in a couple of hours of prep time tonight."

"Honestly, if I take time to myself, I'll check out mentally. Let's just start now and be done for the night."

"Fine by me," said Jack. They pulled up chairs at

the table, facing each other. Jack had his laptop open to take notes.

"Where do you want to start?" asked Charlotte.

"I'm sure MacLeod will have an army of investigators out all weekend digging up dirt. You and I need to go through everything you've ever done that could arguably bear on the question of your 'fitness' to be an elector."

"Do high school and college matter?"

Does a Supreme Court justice nominee "like beer"? Jack thought it, but he didn't say it. "Yes. High school and college matter."

"Well, if you want to go back that far, I can think of a few things."

"Let's hear them."

Charlotte shifted uncomfortably. "Not to alarm you, but you did say you wanted to go only a couple of hours tonight."

Jack paused but tried not to show his surprise. "That's fine. If we run over, we run over."

"All right, then," said Charlotte. And then she began.

Just around the bend from Cy's Place, closer to the Coconut Grove Marina, was the Mutiny Hotel. At the peak of the Grove's party reputation of the 1970s and

1980s, the hotel and its famous Mutiny Club once catered to everyone from the Bee Gees to the bad boys of the unbeatable Miami Hurricanes football team. In the heyday of the Cocaine Cowboys, it wasn't unusual for guests to pay cash and use an alias at check-in. Miami had changed since then. Somewhat.

"I'll need a credit card for incidentals," said the clerk behind the registration desk.

A couple of hundred-dollar bills slid across the countertop. "All I have is cash."

The clerk hesitated. "What's your name?"

"Ramos. Manny Ramos."

Ramos was an alias; Manny was a nickname.

The clerk took the money. "In the old days, Manny, no credit card meant a thousand-dollar security deposit for damages."

"I'm a quiet guest."

"Yeah, you look it. Need any help with your bag?"

"No, I got it."

Manny was no cheapskate, but tipping the bellman five bucks to wheel a small carry-on from the reception desk to the elevator seemed a bit ridiculous. The bag wasn't even full. Just a change of clothes. A camouflage jacket. And a baseball cap. Nothing more was needed. Charlotte Holmes had to be back in Tallahassee by Monday, which meant Manny did, too.

The elevator opened on the fifth floor. As requested, the room was on the west side of the building and had a balcony. The "Grove" view was less desirable than the east-facing water view, but this was no vacation. Manny needed to see all the way to Cy's Place.

Following Charlotte to Miami was a calculated risk. Media reports of Charlotte's broken kitchen window had traveled faster than a speeding bullet, so to speak. Initial reports had tagged the perpetrator as a political extremist, which put the number of potential suspects somewhere in the millions. Manny had no idea who it was, but this much was certain: police would be on even higher alert to spot anyone who might be following Florida's most famous elector. For Manny, the question was whether Charlotte had even noticed that she was being followed by someone wearing a camouflage jacket. The whole point of the jacket, after all, was to be noticed, not to blend in. The fact that the media had made no mention of it, however, had Manny thinking that Charlotte had not noticed. Or that she'd noticed and not told anyone. The latter would have been more like the Charlotte that Manny remembered.

I remember well.

Not all the memories were pleasant. One, in particular, was gnawing at Manny. As threats against Charlotte and other electors escalated, so increased the chance that reporters might do a deep dive to see if Charlotte had been in danger before. They might search old newspapers or other public documents. They might even search for court records. A search like that used to require a trip to the courthouse. Now all it took was a cell phone with Internet access.

Curious, Manny Googled "Escambia County circuit court records." Instantly, the clerk of the court's smiling face appeared on Manny's cell phone. Below the clerk's photo was a link to the electronic database for the westernmost county in the Florida Panhandle, which included Pensacola. Manny typed "Holmes" in the search box. A list of cases came up, some of them dating back twenty years or more. Only one pertained to Charlotte: *Holmes v. Lopez.*

Lopez was Manny's real surname.

Manny scrolled down to see what more was available to the public. The year included in the docket number indicated that the case was almost fifteen years old. Case status: closed. Assigned judge: Gibson. It was very basic information, none of which would be much use to an investigative reporter, or anyone else. An examination of the actual court filings—pleadings, motions, court orders, and the like—was the only way to determine what the case had been about. Manny clicked on the DOCKET link with trepidation, which brought welcome news.

"Docket sealed," the message read. "Docket entries available only upon court order."

Sealed. No record search, no matter how thorough, would turn up the petition filed by Charlotte's attorney. No one would find the order entered by the judge. No one would see the language telling Manny to stay at least five hundred feet from Charlotte Holmes.

Sealed. It was music to Manny's ears. Even if someone was diligent enough to search the archives of all sixty-seven of Florida's counties one by one, and even if they found the innocuous reference to an old case involving Charlotte Holmes, they'd get nothing.

Manny put the phone away, unzipped the overnight bag, and unpacked one camo jacket and one baseball cap.

Chapter 20

It was almost nine o'clock when Charlotte said good night to Jack. Their meeting could have gone longer, but Jack wanted to get home and see his family. They agreed to pick up where she'd left off in the morning.

It was nice of Theo to offer her a place to stay, but the apartment was frankly a little stuffy, and the thought of being cooped up like a prisoner until morning held no appeal. Charlotte showered, changed clothes, and was sitting in front of the bureau, combing her hair in the mirror, when she noticed the homemade card tucked into the frame. She laid her brush aside and opened it.

"Please, please, please come visit us!" the message read. The handwriting had the distinctive markings of a teenage girl, complete with big, loopy letters and the "i" dotted with a heart. A drawing on the inside panel also had an adolescent flair. It was a map of Florida and Central America separated by the blue-green expanse of the Gulf of Mexico and Caribbean Sea. A stick-figure man, presumably Theo, was standing in Miami. A woman and girl were in El Salvador. A jet was streaming southwest over Cuba and the Caribbean. "Fly Cheapo Airline!" the message continued. "Miss you already. Luv, Beatriz."

Charlotte returned the card to its place on the mirror. Her conversation with Jack hadn't been all business, and in the back-and-forth she'd learned more about him than Jack probably realized. Jack had mentioned that the "friend" who used to live in Cy's apartment was Theo's old girlfriend from El Salvador, Julia, whose teenage daughter had grown fond of Theo. Fond enough to want him to visit them in El Salvador.

It made Theo even more interesting to her.

Charlotte checked her makeup in the mirror and went to the kitchen. There was a bottle of tequila on the counter with two shot glasses. She didn't normally drink alone, but nothing about the previous two weeks was normal. She filled them both, belted one back, and enjoyed the head rush. It was quality tequila, not the rotgut she used to drink in those wild college days that her lawyer had just grilled her about. She downed the second shot and started downstairs, locking the door behind her.

The outdoor stairway in the alley ended just beyond the Dumpster, at the club's rear entrance. Charlotte heard a live band through the closed door. She opened it, and the music drew her down a narrow, dark hallway into the club. The old photographs of Little Harlem upstairs had put her in the proper frame of mind, and the tequila buzz made her even more receptive to the vibe of a jazz-loving crowd that oozed through Cy's Place. Old wood floors that creaked beneath her footfalls, redbrick walls, and period posters from jazz performances of another era made Charlotte think more of Harlem than Miami. Art Nouveau chandeliers cast just the right mood lighting. Crowded café tables fronted a small stage for live music. Theo was working both sides of the big U-shaped bar. Several barstools were open. She chose one on the far side of the bar. She recalled an old movie about a mobster who always took a seat from which he could see the door, just in case somebody came gunning for him. The strategy seemed to make sense in this life of hers that was making no sense.

Theo spotted her, smiled, and came over. "You escaped," he said.

"For a little while. Got any tequila?"

"Do I have any tequila," he said with a devil-ish smile. He poured her a shot. "You don't need any training wheels with that."

It was a line she'd heard from bartenders even before she was old enough to drink, but Charlotte played along. "Training wheels?"

"Lemon and salt," said Theo. "It's *añejo*. So smooth you can sip it if you want."

She smiled like a tequila virgin, no mention of the head start upstairs. But she took his advice and sipped.

"Does Jack know you're out and about?" he asked.

"No. And don't tell him. I appreciate all he's doing to keep me safe, but he's got me locked up like a prisoner."

Theo put a napkin under her shot glass. "Jack's at his best getting people out of jail."

"So I've heard." Charlotte didn't want to come off as nosy, but Jack had painted a pretty interesting picture of his friend's past, and this seemed like an opening. "Jack told me how you met."

"Yeah? What'd he tell you?"

"That you were on death row."

Theo poured a couple of drafts from the tap and placed them on a tray for the waitress, then turned back to Charlotte. "That was a very long time ago."

"How long?"

"Let me put it this way," said Theo. "You could

argue that a good number of people have landed on death row because they didn't finish high school. I think I'm the only one who didn't finish high school because he was on death row."

Charlotte felt his pain. To a point. "Did you kill a guy?"

"Not that guy."

"You killed someone else?"

Theo glanced toward the band, half laughing, then looked back at Charlotte. "You ever killed anybody?"

"I asked you first."

Theo laughed, but Charlotte didn't. Then she blinked. "Sorry," she said. "My lawyer just spent three hours picking apart every 'unfit' thing I've ever done in my life. I didn't mean to turn the tables on his best friend."

"No problem."

Charlotte drank more tequila, two sips. "So, did you?"

"Did I what?"

"Kill someone else?"

Theo poured himself a glass of water. "You're not going to let this go, are you?"

"I'm just asking."

"I've been in some 'him or me' situations. I'll leave it at that."

"Do you carry?"

"Nothing that a shot of penicillin won't clear up."

"I meant concealed carry, wise guy."

"Never in the bar," said Theo. "You didn't bring Uncle Cy's gun down here with you, did you? My club is a gun-free zone."

"I figured, so I left it upstairs," said Charlotte. "But what do you do if things get out of hand?"

"I got Carl."

"Who's Carl?"

Theo reached below for a baseball bat and placed it on top of the bar. "Yastrzemski."

Charlotte checked the barrel of the bat. The autograph looked like alphabet soup, but she took Theo's word for it that it spelled Yastrzemski. "Never heard of him."

"Then you're obviously no baseball fan."

"That's not true! I love baseball."

"Oh, yeah? Who's your favorite team?"

"The Blue Wahoos."

"Blue Wahoos? Sounds like a fruity cocktail that some underage girl would come in here and try to order."

"Bless your heart," she said, a southern woman's way of saying "get real." "The Blue Wahoo stadium in Pensacola is the best minor league park in all of baseball. How could anybody not love a team whose colors are

Blue Angel navy and Tin Roof tin? And by the way"—
bah the way—"where do you come off makin' fun of
the Blue Wahoos when you've got yourself a baseball
bat signed by a man named Carl Yazamatraz?"

"Yastrzemski."

Charlotte blushed. "Sorry. All this talk 'bout
Wahoos, Blue Angels, and tin roofs has my southern
accent comin' out in a big way."

"Could also be the tequila and not enough sleep."

"More likely the tequila."

"Don't worry about it," said Theo. "I love the
accent. Love the passion. But you still don't get a pass
for not knowing who Carl is."

"Tell me about him."

Theo leaned on the bar, resting on his forearms—
huge forearms, like the fishermen on the docks at
Pensacola Bay, where Charlotte's mother would take
her to buy snapper for supper.

"Twenty-three years with the Boston Red Sox," said
Theo. "Eighteen-time All Star. His jersey was retired,
so there will never be another number eight. Elected to
the Baseball Hall of Fame the first year he was on the
ballot."

"Well, what do you know? Carl and I have something in common. I was elected to the Electoral College
the first time I was on the ballot."

"There you go," said Theo.

Charlotte smiled awkwardly, then looked away. "Except nobody ever got killed for being elected to the Hall of Fame."

It was a mood killer, and Charlotte immediately regretted saying it.

"Really sorry you have to deal with that," said Theo.

"Thanks," she said, and she downed the rest of her "sipping" tequila.

Theo excused himself to help another customer. Charlotte shook off the effect of the shot; no matter how smooth, even the *añejo* had a kick. Tequila didn't usually make her sleepy, at least not right away, but she could feel herself running out of gas. If it hadn't been the worst week of her life, it was close. She was looking forward to a restful night with no demonstrators calling her an "elitist bitch," no crazy redneck driver to land her in the ER, no hateful text messages or crank calls, no parabellum ammunition flying through the kitchen window in a declaration of war. And no death threats—at least none she was aware of.

Charlotte climbed down from the barstool, which triggered another tequila head rush. She took a moment to steady herself. Theo was tending to other customers, and rather than wait for him to return, she decided to walk around to the other side of the U-shaped bar and say good night. She was a few steps away from the curve of the "U" when either her instinct or paranoia kicked in. She glanced at the entrance door: a couple leaving, two more couples coming—nothing unusual. She kept walking, but the sensation of being watched was palpable. She glanced toward the front of the club, through the plate-glass window with the painted-on CY'S PLACE in backward letters, and froze.

Standing outside the bar, on the other side of the glass, was someone wearing a camouflage jacket. And a baseball cap. Just like before—in Tallahassee. Charlotte froze. With the colored glow of neon bar lights reflecting off the window, it was impossible to make out the face, but she could almost feel the stare right back at her. It was enough to tap into Charlotte's fight-or-flight instinct: she chose fight. She wasn't carrying, so she grabbed the Yastrzemski bat from the bar and raced to the front door.

"Hey!" Theo shouted.

Charlotte kept going, weaving through customers and knocking a drink from one woman's hand as she rushed to the exit. Inertia carried her out the door and almost to the curb, but she fought to make a hard left turn and continued down the sidewalk.

"Stop!" she shouted, but the camouflage jacket was already halfway down the block. Charlotte gave chase.

"Charlotte!" Theo was running her down from behind

The camouflage jacket was pulling away from her. Charlotte reached inside herself to find another gear, but it wasn't there—not after three shots of tequila and everything else she'd been through. She was spent and could barely breathe. The sprint ended three blocks away from Cy's Place. Charlotte was hunched over with her hands on her knees, recovering, when Theo caught up to her.

"I don't know where you're going, but you can't take Carl."

She handed over the bat, struggling to get out a single word. "Okay."

"Charlotte, what gives?"

She caught her breath. "If I tell you, will you promise not to tell Jack?"

"Why don't you want to tell him?"

Charlotte gazed down the block, toward the forested end of the Grove, where century-old banyan trees and sprawling live oaks blocked out the moonlight, making a dark night even darker.

"Because Jack can't fix this."

"How do you know?"

Charlotte looked up at a former death-row inmate, who was at least a foot taller than her. "Because Jack would never hurt anyone."

Jack's phone rang on the nightstand. It was after midnight.

Andie was sound asleep, her head and torso on Jack's side of the bed, her legs and feet on hers. Andie's idea of sharing a mattress was a bit like their golden retriever's notion of sharing the couch. At least Andie didn't drool when she kissed him.

Jack grabbed the phone, jumped out of bed, and went into the master bathroom to take the call without waking his wife.

"Mr. Swyteck?"

Jack didn't recognize the woman's voice on the line, and it was filled with hesitation.

"Yes. Who is this?"

"Gwen Stahl."

Jack was suddenly wide awake. He hadn't seen or spoken to the senator's wife since a pre-convention fundraiser that his father had roped him into attending.

"I'm sorry for the late call, but I'm still on Singapore time. My daughter and I just got back to Miami today."

"It's fine. I was . . . up anyway," he lied.

"Uhm." More hesitation.

"Yes?" Jack asked.

She sighed, and Jack heard the crackle on the line. "I'd like to meet with your client. Please. If you would allow it."

Chapter 21

At 6:30 a.m. Jack's bedroom began to brighten, hinting at a new day. Jack had a severe case of "it doesn't feel like the weekend." He'd slept, but not well, having drifted in and out since the midnight phone call from Mrs. Stahl.

"Max, quiet," said Jack.

Jack's plan had been to sleep until eight, but his golden retriever had other ideas. Max was the most talkative dog Jack had ever known. Mornings especially. It was a throaty rumble that preceded the insertion of a big wet nose into Jack's ear and seemed to say, "Hey, Jack, I got a plan—let's jump in the pool and then go roll in the mud!" Eight years, and Max still didn't get it: mud first, pool second.

Jack rolled out of bed quietly, careful not to wake

his wife. Max happily followed him to the bathroom, the kitchen, the backyard for a pee—the dog, not Jack—and then back to the bedroom and into the walk-in closet. Not since the general election had Jack and Max started the day with a morning run to the beach and back. Judging from the excited tail wagging, Max in his endless optimism had somehow fooled himself into thinking that today was the day when life returned to situation normal: dogs rule. Jack hated to disappoint him.

"Sorry, pal," he said.

"I'm going with you," said Andie. She was seated on the edge of the bed, wiping the sleep from her eyes.

"The meeting is with my client, Gwen Stahl, and me."

"The three of you can meet in private. But your client is being stalked, and you have a family who would miss you if something crazy happened. Take advantage of the fact that your wife is an FBI agent."

The call from Gwen Stahl had been the first call after midnight. The second was from Jack to his client, who'd agreed to the meeting. The third was from Theo to Andie. Theo had promised Charlotte that he wouldn't tell Jack about the stalker who'd followed her to Miami, and Theo had kept his promise: he told only Andie.

"Abuela can watch Righley," said Jack. His grandmother was a fixture in the house on weekends, no limit to her love for her only grandchild.

"And I'll watch you," said Andie.

The meeting was set for 9:00 a.m. Jack chose a spot that minimized any chance of being sighted by the media. South Grove had the canopy of a rainforest, and tucked behind a stand of oaks and royal poinciana trees that lined Main Highway was an eighty-year-old house with yellow siding and bright blue shutters. It was Jack's old law office. The new tenant was a friend who, judging from the campaign poster that was still in the window, had not voted for President MacLeod.

Jack and Andie arrived first, and Charlotte was right behind them. She'd brought Theo with her, so apparently she'd forgiven him for breaking his promise to keep quiet about the Yastrzemski episode. Jack introduced his client to Andie, and Charlotte drew the obvious deduction.

"Looks like everybody's got a bodyguard these days," said Charlotte.

It suddenly occurred to Jack that with all the controversial clients he'd represented in his career, from a GITMO enemy combatant to an alleged white supremacist, never before had Andie felt the need to protect him. A lawsuit over the "peaceful" election of the president of the United States was the first.

The key to the office was beneath a potted bromeliad on the front step. The "bodyguards" waited outside, enough concealed firepower between the two of them to stop a charging rhinoceros.

"What do you think Mrs. Stahl wants?" asked Charlotte as they headed inside.

"She wouldn't tell me. Whatever she has to say, she wants to say it to you."

"Has she said anything to the media since all this talk of a gay lover started?"

"Not a word," said Jack. "Even the divorce petition her lawyer filed was bare-bones. 'The marriage is irretrievably broken.' No juicy details for the press."

Jack heard a car door slam outside the office window. Mrs. Stahl stepped away from her Mercedes and walked toward the building. She was alone, which surprised Jack, as presidential candidates and their wives were entitled to Secret Service protection. Andie showed the senator's wife inside, and the door closed.

"Nice to see you again, Jack," she said, shaking his hand.

Jack hadn't seen her since early summer, and with all the fund-raisers she and her husband had done in South Florida, he doubted that she even recalled meeting him. Jack introduced his client and led the women into the next room. Jack had almost forgotten how cramped his old office space was. The room directly behind the tiny reception area was the only one large enough for three people, as long as one of the three wasn't Theo.

"No Secret Service?" asked Jack, still curious about her traveling alone.

"It ended one week after the general election," she said. "That's the law. I presume it's because the meeting of the Electoral College is traditionally a nonevent."

Jack wondered if that was an additional reason Andie had insisted on coming this morning, her knowing something that he didn't. "It may be time to change the law," he said.

They took seats around a small glass-top table in what had always been a cozy room, though Jack's friend had added more feminine touches, right down to potted plants that were actually thriving, unlike the ones Jack used to kill on a regular basis by forgetting to water them. Mrs. Stahl insisted that they call her Gwen.

"Have you any idea why I asked for this meeting?" she asked.

"No," said Charlotte.

"Oh, let's be honest. Surely it's crossed your mind that a woman in my position might not be the senator's biggest fan."

"I understand," said Charlotte. "If I were married and my husband cheated on me, I don't think I'd be out encouraging Republican electors to jump ship and vote for him."

"I'm sure a lot of women would feel the same way," said Gwen. "But I've done a lot of thinking over the last few months, and this isn't about revenge."

"Then what is it?" asked Charlotte.

"Let's start with the political reality," Gwen said. "Millions of people lied in this election. They lied when they told pollsters, their friends, and maybe even themselves that sexual orientation didn't matter—and then they went into the voting booth, and it did matter. It's the rumors of a gay lover that killed my husband in the purple precincts and cost him the Electoral College. And before you ask—don't. I didn't come here to confirm or deny rumors."

"We weren't planning to ask," said Jack.

"Thank you. It's a private matter."

Jack left it at that—though his gut told him that Gwen was not the spouse who was "the last to know." If he had to guess, she knew. In fact, other than the proverbial two it takes to tango, she might well have been the only one who knew.

Charlotte cut to the chase: "Do you want me to vote for the senator, Mrs. Stahl?"

"Gwen," she said. "And, yes, I do."

"Why?"

"I wish I could tell you that I'm a patriot who is putting my personal pain aside for the good of the country. But that's not it. I'm here for just one reason. My daughter."

"My wife felt the same way," said Jack. "We have a daughter."

"You're reading too much into my words. This is not about the good of a future generation of women or anything like that."

"Then what is it?" asked Jack.

"We had a Colombian nanny who lived with us for years. She was like family. Under MacLeod's immigration policy, she couldn't get her visa renewed. So she left, and now she can't get back in. Rachel has been grieving ever since. If my husband wins, the nanny comes back. I'm sorry, but it's that selfish."

"Lots of families are in that situation," said Jack.

"Which is sad, but like I said, I'm not here for other families or for anyone else. After what I've been through, I'm here for Rachel. That's it."

Jack understood her bitterness, but he questioned whether this really was all about a Colombian nanny. Jack's read was that the senator's wounded wife was simply unwilling to look an unfaithful elector in the eye and say what she still believed in her heart was the truth about her unfaithful husband: he was a "better man" than Malcolm MacLeod.

Gwen gazed across the table at Charlotte, one woman to another. "I'm asking you to please hang in there."

Jack wasn't sure his client would promise anything, or if she still thought it was worth the threats and abuse she was taking.

Charlotte didn't answer right away, but finally she spoke. "Five million do matter," she said. "I'm not voting for MacLeod."

Chapter 22

Jack returned to Tallahassee Sunday afternoon with his client.

"Did you go to church today?" asked Charlotte.

It wasn't a totally random question. They were riding in a rental car to Charlotte's house, and they'd passed at least a dozen since leaving the airport.

"No. Did you?"

"I was under house arrest," she said, only half kidding. "Do you mind stopping for five minutes? I could use His help tomorrow."

The court hearing to determine Charlotte's "fitness" to serve as elector was less than eighteen hours away. If Attorney General Barrow held true to the hype over the weekend, the carpet bombing of Charlotte's character would last for days.

"Can't hurt to ask," said Jack.

Charlotte was a member of Tallahassee First Baptist Church, which came as no surprise to Jack. Any girl who'd grown up in the Panhandle had a transfer letter from her hometown pastor to gain membership wherever she went, even if her spiritual life was no longer in perfect order. The regular Sunday services had ended, but the doors remained unlocked until dark. Charlotte went inside, and Jack waited outside on a bench near the sidewalk. He was admiring the beauty of the old steeple when he realized that he'd visited this church before. Early in his death-penalty career, on the way to the Florida Supreme Court to ask for a last-minute stay of execution, Jack had actually popped in to pray that Governor Swyteck would stop signing death warrants. God wasn't listening that day. Or so it seemed.

"Hey, buddy. Got a cigarette?"

The man was wearing a hoodie and looked like he'd just rolled out of bed, even though it was nearly dinnertime. He was holding a cardboard sign that read: WILL WORK FOR MEDICAL MARIJUANA. Florida voters had made it legal in the previous presidential election, but a qualifying patient needed a licensed physician to get it. He gave the man a couple of bucks, which was all Jack had on him. The cashless society was a really shitty turn of events for panhandlers, though Jack surmised there was probably an app for that.

Five minutes passed, and Charlotte was still inside. Jack used the Watch Live TV app on his phone to see how President MacLeod was spending his Sabbath. He was at a rally in Texas. "What a sore loser that Senator Stahl is," the president told the crowd. "He did the whole fake media circuit this morning. *Face the Nation. Press the Meat.*" The crowd roared. "Sorry, I meant *Meet the Press.* Freudian slip."

Charlotte came out of nowhere. "What are you watching?"

Jack put his phone away. "A really bad movie, I think."

Jack had reserved a room in the hotel across the street from the courthouse and wanted Charlotte to do the same. But her legal bills were adding up, and paying for a hotel while her house sat empty was more than Charlotte could swallow, even if she was making herself an easier mark for the media, demonstrators, or worse. They drove to her place and did a final prep session in her family room. Jack ordered Chinese, and it arrived close enough to the dinner hour.

"Hungry?" asked Jack, as he laid out the cartons on the table.

Charlotte made a face, which Jack took to mean that, like most clients facing a court proceeding in the morning, she'd lost her appetite. She turned on the television.

"You should try not to watch the news," said Jack.

Charlotte either didn't hear him or pretended not to. One of the cable stations was replaying a snippet from a Democratic senator's "controversial interview" earlier in the day.

"I applaud Charlotte Holmes for breaking with all those Aunt Toms out there," said the senator, standing before a green-screen image of the Golden Gate Bridge.

"Aunt Toms?" asked the interviewer. "I've heard of Uncle Toms."

"Aunt Toms are to twenty-first-century women what Uncle Toms were to nineteenth-century slaves. They're the ones who know in their heart that President MacLeod isn't good for women. But their lives are way too cushy to worry about all the other women in this country who work real jobs for unequal pay."

Charlotte turned it off. Jack had seen her angry before, but this was an anger of a different sort.

"You okay?" asked Jack.

"My mother never had a paying job in her life," said Charlotte. "But she raised five daughters, kept our family from falling to pieces, and worked harder than any senator ever worked. I guarantee you she would have voted for Malcolm MacLeod over Senator Stahl if she were still alive. That doesn't make her an 'Aunt Tom.'"

If the senator from California was trying to move another wavering Republican elector into Senator Stahl's camp, her "Aunt Tom" speech wasn't doing the candidate any favors.

"Why do they keep saying things that make it impossible for any other elector to follow my lead? I swear, if a Republican gave a Democrat a ninety-yard head start in the hundred-yard dash, the Democrat would somehow make a wrong turn in the last ten yards and find a way to lose."

The party that never misses an opportunity to miss an opportunity was how Jack's father had once put it. "Charlotte, if you're having second thoughts about this fight, there are other options."

"Like what?"

"You could simply resign as an elector and say you can't in good conscience vote for MacLeod."

"This isn't a protest vote. I want it to matter. But why do it if MacLeod is going to win anyway?"

"I think you're the only one who can answer that," said Jack.

Charlotte groaned, as if her head were about to

explode, and went to the kitchen. She returned a minute later with her cell phone—not the disposable prepaid that Theo had given her, but her own cell, the one she'd left in Tallahassee to avoid being followed to Miami. She powered it on, and the phone chimed over and over again with a string of missed text messages. Jack watched her scrolling through them. Then she stopped, her expression tightening with concern.

"What's wrong?" asked Jack.

She handed him the cell, and Jack read the text message: "A promise is a promise."

Jack checked the sender's number and did a double take. "It's from Theo."

"What? Is this your friend's idea of a joke?"

Jack called Theo on his cell and put him on speaker so Charlotte could hear. "Theo, did you send any text messages to Charlotte—to her real phone, I mean, not the disposable."

"I don't even know her real cell number," said Theo.

"Then someone pirated your number and sent one to Charlotte."

"Shit. How?"

Jack thought about it. "Is your cell number on the Cy's Place Web site?"

"Yeah," said Theo. "Who uses a landline anymore?"

"There are spoof apps you can download to display

any number you want to the person you're calling. It's the same technology that robo-callers use to display a different number every time they call so you can't block their calls. Except in this case the caller didn't use a random number. He took yours from the bar's Web site."

"Why use my number to text Charlotte?"

"It's the stalker mentality. Could be his way of telling Charlotte that he knows she was in Miami this weekend, and he knows who she was staying with."

Jack's words gave everyone something to think about. Then Charlotte spoke.

"Do you think it's the same person who threw the gun magazine through my window?"

"I don't. I'm no criminal profiler, but I have a pretty good sense of when the m.o. fits and when it doesn't. Scratching letters on a gun magazine and hurling it through your kitchen window strikes me as the work of a dumbass who thinks he's clever. The spoof app shows some level of tech savvy. It's—"

"Scarier?"

"I don't know if that's the right word."

"'A promise is a promise' means I swore an oath to vote for MacLeod. Why send that text, unless you want me to know that breaking my promise will have consequences?"

"I agree. It's a threat."

"What should we do?"

"Call the police," said Jack.

"For what?" she said, scoffing. "They already know about the guy in the camo jacket. I told them in the ER. What did they do? Nothing. All they cared about was charging me with a crime for possession of armor-piercing ammunition."

"There are plenty of good cops at FDLE. My gut tells me that this text message and the broken window are unrelated, but FDLE has the professionals who can construct an actual psychological profile."

"Wonderful. A profile might narrow down the list of suspects from sixty-five million to—oh, I don't know, six million?"

"It's a start."

"You said it yourself: it's a threat. That's all the profiling I need."

Theo's voice came over the speaker. "Y'all want me to fly up there for a couple days? If nothing else, Jack, it might make your wife feel better."

"Good idea," said Jack. "All three of us will stay at the hotel."

"I'm not going to a hotel," said Charlotte.

"I'll pay for it," said Jack.

"It's not about the money. I refuse to be run out of my own house." She went to the closet where she kept her pistol.

"Charlotte, do not take this into your own hands," said Jack.

"Choosing to protect myself does not make me a vigilante."

Jack was in no mood for a gunfight. "We really need to be smart about this," he said, and then he dialed the police.

Senator Stahl waved to the media as he exited the Biltmore Hotel.

His wife had told him to be out of the house by Friday, and he'd met the deadline. He'd taken only a suitcase with him, and despite every effort not to make national news out of the fact that he was moving out, the media had followed him every inch of the way from his Coral Gables residence to the most historic hotel south of the Palm Beach Breakers. The Biltmore's classic Mediterranean style set the architectural tone for the "City Beautiful" for almost a century. The stories were equally enduring, some preserved in the "ghost tour" popular with tourists. The hotel's most famous "resident" was Thomas "Fats" Walsh, Al Capone's bodyguard, shot to death in the gambling suite on the "lucky" thirteenth floor. Some said his ghost still prowled the Biltmore's hallways.

Senator Stahl felt as if a few ghosts were following him all the way to his car.

"Senator, are you concerned that only one Republican elector is supporting you so far?"

"Not at all concerned. They will come." He smiled and waved as he got into his car. He always smiled. Even when he was lying.

Charlotte Holmes's announced defection should have started an avalanche. The senator had won by five million votes, yet MacLeod had somehow managed to convince all but one Republican elector and a good part of the country that his Democratic opponent was nothing but a "sore loser." Early in his first term MacLeod had once bragged that he could literally walk into an orphanage and rob the Sisters of Charity at gunpoint and not lose a single supporter. Democrats laughed, but as it turned out, no truer words had ever been spoken—at least not from the president's lips. How could anyone say the things MacLeod said and not only survive but thrive politically? "Press the meat." "Hashtag 'Sodom and Goliath.'"

What an ass.

Stahl waved again to reporters as he drove his car

out of the parking lot. He hoped they would follow, and a quick check in the rearview mirror confirmed that they had. He wasn't going far, but he drove slowly, careful not to lose a single journalist. He checked the mirror again and smiled. Coverage would be robust. He wanted coverage, far and wide.

The Stahl residence was less than five minutes from the hotel. He pulled into the driveway but took his time getting out of the car, allowing the media time to set up and position their camera crews. When he felt the moment was right, he climbed out of the car and walked not toward the house but directly to the lights and cameras at the end of his driveway. His intention was to keep the message short and powerful.

"As you all know, my wife, Gwen, and our daughter, Rachel, returned from Singapore on Friday. I'm happy to tell you that I'll be staying in my own house tonight. With my family. Thank you all very much."

His announcement elicited a flurry of questions, but the senator answered none of them. He turned away from the cameras and walked toward the house, smiling, inside and out.

Chapter 23

The courthouse elevator opened. Jack and Charlotte stepped into the commotion. Jack's gaze cut right through the crowd and fixed on the five men seated on a long oak bench in the hallway.

The third-floor lobby was packed with journalists and spectators who'd arrived too late for a seat inside Judge Martin's courtroom. But it was those five men—dressed in business suits and seated in contemplative silence, despite the swirl of pre-hearing excitement around them—who caught Jack's attention. They seemed to be sizing Jack up, the way ballplayers studied the opposing team's pitcher from their dugout. Jack had seen that look before. Witnesses for the government. They were taking stock of the lawyer who would cross-examine them.

"This is not good," Charlotte whispered, as she and Jack forged a path toward the courtroom entrance doors. It was a crack in her composure, and the hearing had not even started.

Jack and Charlotte had left the hotel before eight o'clock. Theo had walked with them. In his dark suit and sunglasses, he looked like a former NFL defensive end turned Secret Service agent—with an attitude. The walk to the courthouse should have taken five minutes. It took thirty-five. The number of demonstrators in the courtyard had doubled since Friday, but Jack's assessment was that his client was doing just fine—until she laid eyes on those five men in the lobby.

Jack made a quick detour, pulled Charlotte into the empty jury room, and closed the door. It was just the two of them standing at the end of a long rectangular table with twelve chairs.

"Do you know those men waiting outside the courtroom?" Jack asked.

"You could say that."

"Don't be coy. Who are they?"

"Two of them were state senators. The other three worked for legislators." She gave Jack their names and districts.

"Are either of the state senators still in office?"

"No. Florida has term limits."

"Why do you think they're here?"

"One of the former senators I dealt with professionally. The other four were personal."

"When you say 'personal'—"

"More than just friends," she said, which was clear enough, but she clarified anyway. "I was 'with' them."

"Were any of them married when you were with them?"

"No," she said firmly, and then she got angry. "Is that what this hearing is going to be about? Every man I've slept with since moving to Tallahassee?"

"Apparently that's what the attorney general has in mind."

"You have to stop this. The fact that I'm not a virgin has nothing to do with my 'fitness' to be an elector."

Jack checked the time. The hearing was still twenty minutes away. "You wait here. I'm going to take this up with the judge in his chambers and see if I can shut this down before Paulette Barrow turns this hearing into an X-rated circus."

He reached for the doorknob, then stopped. "Just to be clear, when you said you were with four of them, you didn't mean all at the same—"

"Jack, no!"

"Sorry," he said. "A lawyer has to ask."

Senator Stahl was standing in his foyer. The double entrance doors were mostly glass—half an inch thick—but the privacy wall and nine-foot hedge in front of the Stahl residence blocked his view of the street. He checked the display screen on the wall. Security cameras around the house and its perimeter transmitted a refreshed image every few seconds. He waited for the street view to cycle around and liked what he saw. Media vans galore.

"Time to go," he shouted down the hallway.

"I need a minute," his wife fired back from the bedroom.

Timing was key. His campaign had put out the word: photo-op at 9:00 a.m.

The senator pressed the OPEN button on the control panel. The wrought-iron gate at the end of the brick driveway swung open, which set the media in motion. Though no one crossed the invisible line and entered private property, a wall of excited journalists formed on the easement outside the pair of coral-rock entrance columns.

"We need to go now," he shouted again.

Mother and daughter emerged from the bedroom and hurried down the hallway. Rachel was dressed in her school uniform: red polo shirt, white tennis shoes, and blue shorts.

"Love those colors," he said, and then he gave his daughter a kiss on the forehead. "You look perfectly patriotic, honey."

There was no kiss between husband and wife.

"Ready, I guess," Gwen said.

The senator opened the door. His wife and daughter stepped out and stopped on the front stoop, standing side by side. The senator followed and closed the door. Then he took his place at Rachel's side. It was mother, daughter, father, in that order, with Rachel dressed in the colors of the American flag—all facing the media. The senator could barely contain his excitement.

"Now," he whispered.

Rachel clasped a hand of each parent.

"Hold it," said the senator, meaning the pose.

Cameras clicked at the end of the driveway, as dozens of photojournalists caught the money shot. The senator gave them all the time they needed, but after a minute or so, Rachel's hand was shaking in his, so he didn't push it any longer.

"Walk," he whispered.

Hand in hand, they headed down the walkway to the car in the driveway. The senator opened the rear door on the passenger side. His daughter climbed in, and her mother checked to make sure she was properly buckled. The senator closed the door and opened the front door for his wife.

And then they kissed.

It was brief but long enough to make sure the photographers got it. Gwen got into the car, and the senator closed the door for her. He walked around the back of the car, closer to the media, to the driver's side.

"Senator, are you and Mrs. Stahl back together?" a reporter shouted. Others fired questions to the same effect.

The senator smiled, as he climbed into the driver's seat, closed the door, and started the engine.

"Look happy," he said.

He put the car in reverse and backed out of the driveway, the entire Stahl family waving, as the senator's nine-year-old daughter made the most conspicuous return to elementary school in Florida history.

Jack sat across from the attorney general and her team of government lawyers. They were on opposite sides of a rectangular table that projected forward from Judge Martin's desk, lawyers and jurist in a T-shaped arrangement in the privacy of the judge's chambers. No media or spectators were present, but the judge wore his robe as in a court proceeding. A work of art that resembled something Jack and Andie might hang from their refrigerator was taped to the bookcase behind him: BEST GRANDPA, it read.

Jack was pleased to see the skeptical look on Judge Martin's face.

"I realize this is uncharted territory," said the judge, "trying to ascertain whether an elector is morally fit to serve as a member of the Electoral College. And I understand that 'fitness' can mean different things to different people. But I have not even the slightest interest in hearing the details of Ms. Holmes's love life."

"It's completely irrelevant," said Jack.

"Wrong," said the attorney general. "Ms. Holmes was a gun lobbyist. Two of these witnesses were state senators. The other three worked as the right-hand man to a state rep."

"So?"

"Trading sex for votes is wrong, and it bears directly on Ms. Holmes's fitness to serve as a member of the Electoral College. If she is willing to prostitute herself to gain votes as a lobbyist, what is she willing to take from someone else in exchange for changing her vote in the Electoral College?"

"Judge, there is no evidence that my client traded sex for votes," said Jack.

"Not yet," said Barrow. "The witnesses haven't testified."

The judge again looked skeptical. "Ms. Barrow, are you telling me with a straight face that each of these witnesses is going to take the stand and admit under oath that he traded votes for sexual favors—that he committed a felony?"

The attorney general squirmed. "I didn't say that."

"I didn't think so. Because if they admitted such things, I would order them cuffed on the spot and hauled off to the stockade."

"I understand."

"Well, let me make sure I understand," said the judge. "You want to put five men on the witness stand to say that they engaged in sexual relations with Ms. Holmes. They will deny that the relationship had any impact on any legislative votes. Ms. Holmes will deny that she traded sex for their legislative votes. And then you want me to infer the exact opposite. Do I have that right?"

"I think it's a reasonable inference," said Barrow. "Especially with respect to the three Democrats. Why else would a Democrat vote with the NRA to kill proposed legislation that Ms. Holmes was lobbying against? It's a quid pro quo."

The judge paused to consider the nuance. "I guess there's a kernel of plausibility to that argument. What do you say, Mr. Swyteck?"

"Judge, even Bernie Sanders voted against the Brady Bill. You can't generalize about Democrats on gun control. But even if you could, there's no reason to make this a public spectacle. My client will stipulate that she dated four of these men."

"She had sex with them," said Barrow.

"You're making her sound like a prostitute," said Jack.

"If the shoe fits . . ."

"Please, Ms. Barrow," the judge said.

Jack took a breath. "Your Honor, my client was in her twenties at the time. She dated several men over a period of five years. Four of these relationships became intimate."

"She had sex with state legislators and powerful members of legislative staff while she was lobbying for votes," said Barrow.

"That's false," said Jack. "At the time, she was working as a researcher. She was employed by a lobbying firm, but she wasn't lobbying anybody."

"That's splitting hairs," said Barrow.

"What about the fifth witness?" the judge asked. "Who is that?"

"Mr. Scoville," said Jack.

The judge did a double take. "The former chair of Senate appropriations?"

"Yes," said Barrow.

"My client denies any relationship with him whatever," said Jack.

The judge jotted a few notes on his yellow pad. "So you're willing to stipulate as to four witnesses—"

"That's not good enough," said the attorney general. "We are entitled to call all five witnesses live. We want—"

"You want to publicly embarrass a woman from Pensacola who is a respected member of the First Baptist Church." Jack didn't like playing that card, but when in Rome . . .

"Stop," the judge said. "Both of you. Here's what we're going to do. Ms. Barrow, you can call one witness live—Mr. Scoville. As to the remaining witnesses, the court will accept Mr. Swyteck's stipulation. They will not testify."

"That's highly prejudicial to the state's case," said Barrow.

"That's my ruling," said the judge. "See y'all at ten o'clock. Main courtroom."

Chapter 24

"The state of Florida calls Roger Scoville," said the attorney general.

The double doors in the rear of the courtroom opened, all eyes following the witness as he proceeded down the center aisle to swear the oath.

"I feel sick," Charlotte whispered.

Jack got it. This wasn't a jury trial, but had it been, the jurors would have looked at Scoville, looked at Charlotte, and asked themselves the same question: Why on earth would she sleep with him . . . other than to buy his vote?

"I do," said Scoville, affirming his sworn obligation to tell the truth, the whole truth, and nothing but.

Scoville settled into the chair, which took some maneuvering. His pear-shaped body spread even wider when he sat, which had been at the anatomical root of the press's beloved "Bootygate," a punster's handle for the government investigation into Scoville's "medical reason" for flying first class at taxpayers' expense while he was a legislator. He'd survived Bootygate Phase I. Rumors of a Bootygate Phase II—with "booty" taking its urban slang meaning—ended after Scoville announced that he would not run for reelection.

The attorney general approached the witness and began in a conversational tone, eliciting Scoville's description of a lifelong career in Florida politics. Distinguished himself in law school as editor in chief of the law review. Elected four times to the State House and twice to the Senate from central Florida, endorsed each time by the *Tampa Tribune* as "a powerful independent voice among Republicans." Served as chairman of the Senate Appropriations Committee.

"Your most recent position was what?" asked Barrow.

"I was chairman of the Florida Republican Party. I resigned after the midterm elections."

"Have you always been a Republican?"

"I was a registered Republican for twenty-nine years. I resigned from the party when I resigned as chairman."

"Why?"

220 · JAMES GRIPPANDO

"I don't consider Malcolm MacLeod a true Republican. At least not by Florida standards. To be clear: I didn't resign with the intention of supporting a Democrat."

The attorney general flipped the page on the notebook with more flair than necessary, as if to announce that the real testimony was about to begin.

"Mr. Scoville, in your decades of experience in Tallahassee, did you ever hear the term 'closer.'"

"Yes, I did."

"What is a closer?"

"A closer is one of the oldest tools in the lobbying profession."

"Let's break that down a little. A closer is a person who works in the private sector, right?"

"Yes. Someone who works for a lobbying firm. It's usually a very attractive woman. Though it can also be an attractive man, depending on who the target is."

"What do you mean by 'target'?"

"A target is a state legislator."

"Are all legislators a target?"

"No. Lobbyists target specific legislators who they believe can be persuaded to vote the way the lobbyist wants them to vote. A lobbyist might work on that target the entire legislative session."

"Does a closer have any role in that process?"

"She can. If it gets to the end of the closing weeks of the legislative session and the deal hasn't closed, so to speak."

"What does the closer do?"

He smiled, then quickly caught himself and resumed his courtroom expression. "Generally a closer will hang out in bars where legislators go to have a drink in the evening. Strike up a conversation. They might flirt a little."

"Anything else?"

"That depends on the closer. And the target."

"Have you ever heard of closers offering sexual favors?"

Jack saw where this was leading and objected. "Your Honor, rumors about what some unidentified closer might have said to an unidentified state legislator are clearly hearsay."

"Sustained."

"Let me ask it this way," said Barrow. "Has a closer ever offered you sexual favors in exchange for your vote on a piece of proposed legislation?"

"Objection."

"Ms. Barrow, stop beating around the bush," the judge said. "Ask the question that matters."

"Sorry," she said, but she really wasn't sorry at all. She stepped away from the podium and pointed at

Jack's client. "Did the defendant, Ms. Holmes, ever offer you sexual favors in exchange for your vote as a state legislator?"

Jack wanted to object, but the judge had already labeled it "the question that matters."

"She most certainly did," said Scoville.

"Did you accept her offer?"

"Of course not. That would be criminal."

The attorney general returned to the podium. "At this time, the state of Florida would ask to include in the record a stipulation that Ms. Holmes had sexual relations with the following state senators and legislative staff while she was employed by a registered lobbyist."

Jack could almost hear the journalists behind him scratching down the names as the attorney general announced each name. He rose, not at all liking the way this was playing out.

"Judge, so the record is clear, there is no stipulation that my client's personal relationship with any of these men had any impact on any legislative vote. In fact, Ms. Holmes vehemently denies that she ever offered anything, sexual favors or otherwise, to anyone in exchange for votes."

"Noted," said the judge. "The stipulation is accepted with those qualifications. Anything else, Ms. Barrow?"

"No, Your Honor," she said, smug as could be.

"The state of Florida requires nothing further of this witness."

Judge Martin glanced at the clock in the back of the courtroom. "Let's break. I know it's not exactly lunchtime, but I'm here to tell you that Super-Alpha-Omega-Prostate doesn't do the trick for me, so I gotta go. Literally. We'll resume with cross-examination at one-thirty," he said, ending it with a bang of his gavel. All rose, and as the judge disappeared into his chambers, the noise level in the courtroom approached that of a rock concert.

"Scoville is a liar," said Charlotte.

It was one of those rare attorney-client communications that Jack didn't care if the journalists on the other side of the rail overheard. But he could see in her eyes that Charlotte wasn't up for a walk back to the hotel and a media gauntlet.

"This way," he said, and they scooted out a side exit to the empty jury room. Jack closed the door, but several reporters were hanging in the hallway right outside. Jack took his client to the far end of the table by the whiteboard so that no one could eavesdrop.

"He's lying," Charlotte said again, her voice quaking.

"Okay," said Jack in a calming tone. "We get to take our shot on cross-examination. Let's walk through this. I want you to tell me everything he said that's false."

"Two big ones," she said. "First, I never offered any sexual favor to that pig."

"Did you ever flirt with him?"

"No way."

"Ever say anything that could be construed as . . . suggestive?"

"There's nothing. I could barely stand to be in the same room with him. Second—"

There was a knock on the door. Jack was inclined to ignore it, until the man announced who he was from the other side of the door: "It's Officer Frank Dalton."

With threats against his client escalating, Jack had formally requested that the Florida Department of Law Enforcement provide security for Charlotte. The FDLE's Capitol Police Division was the security detail for the executive and legislative branches. Dalton had promised to run Jack's request up the chain of command, all the way to the director of Capitol Police and the FDLE commissioner, if necessary. Jack took it as a good sign that Dalton had come in person to deliver the response. Jack invited him in and closed the door, silencing a barrage of questions from journalists in the hallway.

"Did you get an answer?" asked Jack.

"I did. I'm afraid the answer is no." He said "no" like a cow, a long moo with an "n."

"You can't offer her anything? No protection at all?"

"Ms. Holmes is one of twenty-nine electors in Florida. FDLE doesn't have the budget or the manpower to protect twenty-nine people, twenty-four-seven, from now till December fourteenth."

"We're not asking you to protect twenty-nine electors," said Jack. "We're asking you to protect the one who's been threatened."

The officer sighed. "They've all been threatened, Mr. Swyteck."

Charlotte sat up with concern. "They have?"

"Yep," said Dalton. "I can't give you details. But you got nutjobs on both sides of this dogfight, from alt-right to antifa, and everything in between."

"So there's nothing you can do to help me?" asked Charlotte.

"Have you tried the FBI?" he asked.

"My wife's an agent in the Miami field office," said Jack. "I asked, and she saw no basis for the FBI to get involved. I agree."

"Yeah," the officer said with a shrug, stretching out the "yeeeeah" almost as long as his opening "noooooo." Then he rose, as if his work were done, and shook hands with them. "Good luck to you, Ms. Holmes."

"Thanks. I guess," said Charlotte.

Dalton stepped out, triggering another burst of

questions from the journalists in the hallway, which ended with the closing of the door. Jack and Charlotte looked at each other.

"At least we have Theo," said Charlotte, only half-serious.

"There is that," said Jack. He went back to the table and checked his notepad, seeing where they'd left off before the officer's arrival. "So. Scoville lied when he said you offered him sexual favors."

"Flat-out lied," she said.

"Okay. Tell me what the second lie was."

"It's kind of more what he didn't say than what he said."

Jack wasn't sure what she meant. "All right. Tell me what he didn't say."

Chapter 25

Jack and Charlotte returned to the courtroom early, the bailiff having evicted them from the jury room for use in a criminal case. The attorney general and her team had yet to return from lunch, so Jack and his client were alone in Judge Martin's courtroom, seated at the defense table.

Various files and three-ring binders were arranged in front of Jack, exactly as he'd left things before the lunch break. Jack would attack Scoville's lies on cross-examination, and he wanted a fresh notepad to outline his key points. He reached toward his trial bag on the floor and stopped. Resting at the end of the table, beside one of his binders, was something he didn't recognize. It was a report of some kind. The word CONFIDENTIAL jumped out at him. Below it: FLORIDA

228 · JAMES GRIPPANDO

DEPARTMENT OF LAW ENFORCEMENT, PUBLIC CORRUP-
TION DIVISION, EXECUTIVE INVESTIGATION.

Jack stared at the cover page for a moment, the wheels
turning in his head. It had struck him as strange that
FDLE Officer Dalton had come to the courthouse in
person to deliver the bad news that the Capitol Police
could not provide protection for his client. Why not just
a phone call to tell him "Noooo"? Jack couldn't help
suspecting that Dalton's unnecessary visit was somehow connected to the magical appearance of the FDLE
investigative report. For the life of him, however, Jack
couldn't understand why Dalton would drop confidential information in his lap.

"Do you know how this got here?" he asked Charlotte.

She glanced at the cover page and shook her head.

Jack picked up the report, which was several dozen
pages in length. Beneath it was a one-page letter on
FDLE letterhead. It was addressed to the Office of the
Attorney General. Unlike the report, the letter was not
marked CONFIDENTIAL, so Jack went ahead and read it,
albeit to himself:

Dear General Barrow:
Enclosed please find the Department's final report
into the alleged sexual misconduct of Florida State
Senator Roger Scoville.

"Holy shit," said Jack, like a reflex.

"What is it?" asked Charlotte.

"Wait here," he said, as he rose from the table. Then he walked toward chambers, "confidential" report in hand.

President MacLeod sped through the second-floor residence like a racewalker, arms pumping but absolutely no bounce in his hips, as he hurried past the Truman Balcony and his shortcut to the master suite.

"Breathe," he told himself with each measured step. "Just breathe."

MacLeod had kept his composure as long as possible during a lunch meeting with the president of Chile in the Blue Room, the oval-shaped parlor on the first floor of the Executive Mansion. Communicating through translators was tedious enough under normal circumstances. It was anything but "normal" the way the president had excused himself every five minutes to get up from the table to use the restroom. The kitchen staff called it "First Lady's Revenge." Mrs. MacLeod put up with her husband's blatant infidelities of all sorts, from the wives of his own White House staff to campaign workers who were barely old enough to vote. But when the president pushed her too far— say, a personal friend of the First Lady—principles of proportionality called for nothing less than laxative-spiked lemonade.

MacLeod rushed into the master bathroom, dropped his pants, and planted himself on the commode, rocking back and forth to deal with the abdominal pain.

"Are you all right, Mr. President?" His chief of staff was on the other side of the closed bathroom door.

"I'm fine," he said, grunting.

"Your radio phone-in is thirty seconds to air."

Another groan. Watching the supposed reunion of the Stahl family earlier that morning had sent MacLeod into orbit. His press secretary had lined up a series of phone interviews with the top talk-radio shows to provide alternative facts.

"I'll do it from in here," said the president. He shuffled across the floor, his trousers still around his ankles, and opened the door a crack. His chief of staff handed him a headset. MacLeod closed the door, put on the headset, and then shuffled back to the toilet. The talk-radio producer was speaking into his ear. "On the air in five, four, three—"

The president flushed but remained on the toilet, just in case this episode of First Lady's Revenge had an Act II. The show's host welcomed several million listeners and introduced her "very special guest," going straight to the question of the day:

"Mr. President, what do you make of that display the Democrats put on at the Stahl residence this morning?"

MacLeod bit his lower lip, fighting through the cramps. "A total political stunt to make Republican electors feel more comfortable about changing their vote to Senator Stahl."

"And what about that kiss?"

"Can you say 'awkward'? I don't know if Stahl was trying to convince us that he loves his wife or likes women, but he failed on both counts, if you ask me."

The host laughed like a lackey, then turned serious. "To your point, Mr. President, I had one of my interns here at the studio do some research. If Senator Stahl is able to hijack the Electoral College, it turns out that he would not be this nation's first gay president."

"Is that so?"

"Most historians agree that James Buchanan, once regarded as the first 'bachelor' to live in the White House, was actually a homosexual."

"I actually did know that," said MacLeod with his usual assertiveness. "But there's an important difference between him and Senator Stahl."

"What's that, Mr. President?"

"James Buchanan didn't pretend to have a wife and didn't try to trick the American public into thinking that the nation will have a First Lady. So I warn my fellow Americans not to be fooled by what they saw on the news this morning. That façade will be over the day after the inauguration. The nation may not have its first gay president in Evan Stahl, but rest assured, Mrs. Stahl will be out of the picture, and we will definitely have a first 'First Homo' in the White House."

"That would be funny to my listeners," the host said with a grave delivery, "if it weren't so true."

The president grimaced. The laxative was still working overtime; Act II had begun.

"There you have it, friends," said the host. "Don't be fooled. Thank you very much, Mr. President."

"You're welcome."

The interview ended. The president yanked off the headset. First Lady's Revenge was more than living up to its name. MacLeod doubled over, emitting a cry of pain so loud that a pair of Secret Service agents burst into the bathroom, weapons drawn.

The courtroom was packed, but neither the judge nor the lawyers were in it. Jack and the attorney general were on opposite sides of the table, in chambers again to argue before Judge Martin.

Another attorney might have taken the position that

a "confidential" report found lying in a public court-room was no longer confidential. Some lawyers might have blown right past the "confidential" designation, devoured the report, and then sprung it on the witness in cross-examination, sending the courtroom into chaos. Jack knew better. Judge Martin was of the "handshake generation," a country lawyer at heart who longed for the days when a lawyer's word was his bond. Jack had seen many a lawyer from Miami—"My-amma"—play way too aggressively for the likes of Judge Martin, only to learn the hard way that "southern hospitality" could sometimes be summed up in just eight words: "You ain't from around here, are you, boy?"

"Mr. Swyteck, thank you very much for bringing this report to the court's attention."

"You're welcome, Judge."

"Ms. Barrow, did the FDLE issue this report to you?"

The attorney general cleared her throat. "What I'd like to know, Judge, is how Mr. Swyteck obtained a copy of the report."

"Maybe you didn't hear my question," said the judge. "Is this document authentic? Is this a copy of an actual report from the FDLE to you about allegations of Mr. Scoville's sexual misconduct?"

"Yes, but it's confidential. So I would really like to know how he got it."

"It was on my table when I returned from lunch."

"Oh, I'm sure," said Barrow. "Manna from heaven, is that it?"

"I'll state it under oath if I have to."

"Said the lawyer whose client scoffs at her oath," replied Barrow.

Jack ignored her but gave her points for style on that one. "Judge, I brought this to the court's attention because I believe it will be relevant to my cross-examination. But it was marked confidential, so I still haven't read it."

"Which is honorable of you," the judge said. "And let me just add that I have read it. It's relevant, all right. Wouldn't you agree, General Barrow?"

"Relevance isn't the issue. This report is part of a law enforcement investigation. Allowing Mr. Swyteck to use it to cross-examine Mr. Scoville could jeopardize that investigation."

"The state of Florida should have thought of that before you called Mr. Scoville to the witness stand."

Jack could hardly believe his ears. The judge was saying exactly what he was thinking. For a trial lawyer, life simply didn't get any better than that.

"Mr. Swyteck, I'm a slow reader," said the judge. "It took me thirty minutes to read the report. I'll give you twenty. Be back in my courtroom then, and we'll proceed with the cross-examination of Mr. Scoville."

Chapter 26

Jack approached the witness with the FDLE report in hand—with more ammunition than he needed, if the goal had been to indict Tallahassee as a cesspool of sex and abuse of power. That wasn't the goal. Jack's mission was to prove that Scoville had lied when he testified that Charlotte Holmes was up to her neck in that cesspool. He had to choose his ammunition wisely.

"Stress balls," said Jack. "They come in all shapes and sizes, don't they, Mr. Scoville?"

The judge sat up in his big leather chair. "I think I know what you're talking about, Counsel, but could we call them stress-*relief* balls?"

"Of course," said Jack, and then to the witness,

"People squeeze them to relieve stress. You've used them before, haven't you, Mr. Scoville?"

"On occasion."

"You kept a stress-relief ball on your desk when you were chairman of the Senate Appropriations Committee, did you not?"

"On my desk or around it, yes."

"Some stress-relief balls are made of foam rubber. Yours was made of gel contained by a rubber skin."

"So?"

"Some stress-relief balls are round," said Jack, and then he took a step closer, his voice taking on an edge. "Yours was in the shape of a woman's breast, was it not?"

He smiled, as if it were funny. "It was kind of a gag gift from some friends."

"A gag?" Jack opened the FDLE report. "Are you aware that seventeen women told the Florida Department of Law Enforcement that it was your practice to squeeze the breast-shaped stress-relief ball only when meeting with women in your office?"

"Whoever said that is a liar."

"All seventeen of them?"

"Yes. That's ridiculous."

Jack turned the page in the report. "During your

238 • JAMES GRIPPANDO

last legislative session, do you recall a meeting in your office with State Senator Amelia Suarez, who asked you to support her bill on sales tax exemptions for hurricane supplies?"

"I do recall that."

"And when Senator Suarez asked for your support, you—while squeezing your breast-shaped stress reliever—replied, 'What's in it for me?'"

"That's a lie."

The attorney general rose. "Judge, I object. You wouldn't let the state of Florida call just four witnesses to testify about their sexual relationship with Ms. Holmes. But now Mr. Swyteck wants to drag Mr. Scoville through seventeen meetings about stress balls?"

"Stress-*relief* balls," the judge said.

"Whatever. It's just not fair," said the attorney general.

"What's not fair," said Jack, "is Mr. Scoville's false accusation that my client offered sex in exchange for his vote."

"Excuse me," said Scoville from the witness stand. "Judge, I want it to be clear that she offered it, but I did not accept it."

"That's my point exactly," said Jack. "Your Honor, this report documents repeated instances of Mr. Scoville's abuse of his power and position by actively so-liciting sex from numerous women. If Ms. Holmes had ever offered sex for his vote—as he claims she did—Mr. Scoville would have immediately dropped his pants. And his stress ball."

"Stress-*relief* ball," the judge said.

"My apologies," said Jack. "If the court can indulge me for just ten minutes, I can demonstrate that the wit-ness is lying."

"I'll give you five minutes. But no more."

Jack quickly went to work, laying out the FDLE findings in machine-gun fashion. The strand of pearls he bought as a gift for a lobbyist, "joking" (or not) that she should visit his office sometime "wearing only the pearls." The monthly payments from his political committee to "consultants" with no political experi-ence, including a Hooters calendar girl and a *Playboy* "Miss Social." Unsolicited compliments about working out, losing weight, or "nice dress," coupled with the innuendo, "What do I get?"

"Mr. Swyteck, you have two minutes remaining," the judge announced.

Jack took the reminder—and then moved in for the kill.

"Mr. Scoville, let's focus on something you didn't say on direct examination. Something you left out."

"You need to be more specific than that," said Scoville.

"I'm talking about the first time Ms. Holmes visited your office as a lobbyist. She was twenty-eight years old."

"That would have been some years ago. I'm not sure I remember my first meeting with Ms. Holmes."

"Would it jog your memory if I told you that the first time Ms. Holmes was alone with you in your office was also the last time she was alone with you in your office?"

"No memory."

Jack checked his notes from his meeting with Charlotte in the empty jury room. "You don't recall saying, 'Madeline Chisel hired herself one hot assistant'?"

"I would never say anything so inappropriate."

"You don't recall squeezing your stress-relief ball and asking Ms. Holmes how 'firm' she was."

Scoville shifted uneasily in his chair, the way most witnesses did when confronted with details and specifics. "I can assure you that I was referring only to how firm she was in her position."

"Which is the same phony explanation you gave her when she got up and said she was leaving."

"I don't recall any of that."

"You followed her to the door, didn't you, Mr. Scoville?"

"It would be the polite thing to do, walking a guest to the door."

"And when Ms. Holmes tried to open the door, you held it closed."

"That's preposterous."

"You pressed your body against hers, pinning her against the wall."

"That's a lie."

"You placed your hand on her breast—"

"I did not!"

"You put your mouth to her ear and said: 'This is how things get done around here.'"

"Objection," said Barrow. "Judge, clearly Mr. Scoville denies that any of this happened, and there is absolutely no basis for these questions."

The judge looked confused. "Mr. Swyteck, is this in the FDLE report? Because I don't recall reading anything about Ms. Holmes in there."

"It's not in the report," said Jack.

"This entire line of questioning is improper," said Barrow. "It's out of left field with no basis in reality."

"This incident is very much a part of my client's reality," said Jack.

"But it's not in the FDLE report," said the judge.

"She chose not to report the assault," said Jack.

"Because it didn't happen," said the attorney general.

"Because like most young women in her position, Ms. Holmes felt powerless against a man in Mr. Scoville's position."

Barrow groaned. "Judge, now Mr. Swyteck is just testifying for his client."

"The objection is sustained," the judge said. "That's enough about this alleged incident for now. Mr. Swyteck, call your client to the stand as part of your case if she wants to tell her story."

"*Story* is a good word for it," said the attorney general.

"Ms. Barrow, please," said the judge.

Jack checked on his client with a quick glance. Charlotte had kept the senator's assault to herself for years. He wondered if she was up to the kind of ridicule she'd get from the attorney general on cross if he put her on the witness stand. Charlotte couldn't say if it had happened on a Monday or Friday, whether it had been morning or afternoon, or what bill she'd gone to the senator's office to discuss. She would fail on any number of little things that, to the interrogator, were just as memorable as the event itself—a man old enough to be her father pressing her against the wall, grabbing her breast, and telling her "this is how things get done." Jack wasn't sure he would put Charlotte through it. But they would make that decision later.

"I have just a couple more questions for Mr. Scoville," said Jack.

"Proceed," said the judge. "But let's wrap this up."

Jack retrieved the FDLE report. "Mr. Scoville, you were aware of the fact that the FDLE was investigating you for alleged incidents of sexual misconduct, were you not?"

"I may have heard something about it."

"May have? On page three of the report it states that FDLE officers interviewed you for forty minutes. Did that escape your memory?"

"No. We met."

"So, when you walked into this courtroom today, you knew you were under investigation by the FDLE, correct?"

"I guess that's true."

"You knew that the FDLE had issued a report to the attorney general, correct?"

"Yes, I knew that."

"It was also your understanding that this report was confidential—that no one would see it, unless the attorney general authorized its release."

"Objection."

"Overruled," said the judge.

"Yes," said Scoville. "That was my understanding."

"You were shocked that this report ended up being part of this public proceeding, were you not?"

"It—yes, I found it surprising."

"You were shocked because it was your understanding that if you testified against Charlotte Holmes, the attorney general would never authorize the release of this report."

"Objection!" the attorney general shouted. "The insinuation that I made some kind of quid pro quo arrangement for Mr. Scoville's testimony is outrageous."

"Sustained. Mr. Swyteck, time to wrap up."

"I'm finished with this witness," said Jack.

The attorney general rose. "Judge, I renew our objection to the use of the FDLE report, and, for the record, the state of Florida will be launching a full investigation into how this confidential report came into Mr. Swyteck's possession."

"Judge, I'll say it again for the third time: the report was sitting on my table when I returned to the courtroom after lunch."

"Someone had to put it there," said Barrow.

Jack glanced again at his client. Charlotte's chair was at an angle—enough of an angle so that with a slight turn of her head, her gaze carried toward the back of the courtroom. Jack followed her line of sight until it landed in the last row.

On Madeline Chisel.

It suddenly came clear. If anyone had the ability to make that report land on Jack's table, it was Chisel. He wondered if Officer Dalton knew what she was planning to do with it when he'd come to the courthouse, ostensibly to meet with Jack, and delivered it to her.

"Mr. Scoville, you are released," said the judge.

Scoville stepped down from the witness stand, walked in silence past the attorney general, and started down the center aisle. If there was any doubt in Jack's mind as to the source of the report, it was erased by the look Charlotte's mentor shot in Scoville's direction as he reached the exit doors and left the courtroom.

Jack took a seat beside his client.

"By any chance, did you call in a favor from your old mentor?" he asked beneath his breath.

"I only had one," she whispered.

Jack smiled with his eyes. "You made it a good one."

Chapter 27

"The state of Florida calls Megan Holmes," said the attorney general.

Jack glanced at his client. "Is that—"

"My sister," said Charlotte.

The double doors opened in the back of the courtroom. Megan entered, walked down the aisle, and passed three feet away from her sister on her way to the witness stand, never once making eye contact with Charlotte. Not a good sign.

"She hates me," Charlotte whispered.

Not good at all.

The bailiff swore in the witness, and Charlotte filled Jack's ear with the quick and dirty, as Megan took the stand. Since college, the sisters had seen each other only at major family events. At best, they'd tolerated each other. It all went back to a party one night, held off campus. Megan had left with the wrong people and ended up in the woods, alone and unconscious. Somehow it was Charlotte's fault.

"Are you the older sister of Charlotte Holmes?" the attorney general asked, moving quickly through Megan's background.

"Eleven months older."

"Ah, Irish twins," said Barrow, a little levity to put the witness at ease.

Megan seemed confused. "But . . . we're not Irish."

"She's just not smart," Charlotte whispered. Jack took it with a grain of salt, not ready to write off Megan as a dummy. She was a little rough on the edges, not as well-spoken or refined as Charlotte, but she was every bit as pretty as her sister, which left Jack no reason to believe that the luck of the genetic draw had left her any less intelligent.

"Would you describe your relationship with your sister Charlotte as a close one?" asked Barrow.

"Objection. May we have a sidebar?" Jack asked partly to prevent the witness from hearing, but mostly to keep it away from the media. The judge called them forward, and the lawyers huddled at the side of the judicial bench that was farthest from the witness stand.

Jack started. "Your Honor, I understand that the

issue in this hearing is my client's fitness to serve as an elector. But there has to be a limit as to what's relevant. Testimony from Megan Holmes as to how she feels about her younger sister is beyond the pale."

"That's not the purpose of her testimony," said Barrow.

"Sure sounds like it," said the judge. "You just asked if she and her sister were 'close.'"

"I asked that question only to be upfront with the court that these sisters do not get along. But that's not the point of her testimony."

"Then what is the point?" asked the judge.

"Charlotte Holmes stipulated to having sexual relations with four men who were either legislators or on legislative staff at the time of the relationships. The testimony of Megan Holmes will disprove Charlotte Holmes's claim that those sexual relationships had nothing to do with trading sex for votes."

"Judge, Charlotte and her sister have hardly spoken to each other in the last ten years. I don't see how Megan could have any insight into the nature of Charlotte's personal relationships."

"They're sisters," said Barrow, "and for a time they were roommates in college. Megan Holmes knows the defendant as well or better than anyone. We can listen to Mr. Swyteck argue all afternoon long, or we can give the witness a chance to be heard."

"The objection is overruled," the judge said. "If at the end of the day the court decides her testimony is entitled to no weight, I'll disregard it."

Jack accepted it, knowing that any hope the judge would disregard Megan's testimony was utter fantasy.

The attorney general returned to the lectern and continued her direct examination, breezing through more background before getting to the reason for the rift between the sisters.

"Ms. Holmes, pardon me for having to ask these questions. But I understand you were sexually assaulted when you were in college. Is that correct?"

"No, that's not correct."

Barrow walked to the projector and displayed an exhibit on the large screen. It was an article from the local paper of record, dating back to when Charlotte and her sister were in college. "Ms. Holmes, do you see the headline that reads, 'FSU Student Reports Sexual Assault'?"

"I see it."

"The article doesn't mention a name. Can you identify the 'student' referenced in this article?"

"It's me."

"Did you report to police that you were sexually assaulted?"

"No. Why would I, if I wasn't sexually assaulted?"

"Good question," said Barrow. "Did someone else report that you were sexually assaulted?"

"Yes," said Megan, her gaze drifting toward Charlotte. "My sister did."

"Why did she do that?"

"Objection," said Jack.

"Withdrawn," said Barrow. "Let's put this in context. Ms. Holmes, the night before this article appeared in the newspaper, who were you with?"

"My sister and me went to a getty."

"What's a 'getty'?"

"Before a party. A group of people getting ready to party."

"Getting drunk before you get to the party?"

"There's drinking. Not everybody gets drunk."

"Were you and your sister drunk before you left the getty?"

"I was. I don't know if Charlotte was or not. It's kind of hard to tell with her. She holds her liquor like nobody I've ever seen."

"Where did you and your sister go after the getty?"

"A party at someone's house. I don't remember whose. It was nothing special. Drinking, loud music, beer pong. All the things you'd expect around a bunch of college kids."

"Did you continue drinking at the party?"

"Yes. Some kind of punch."

"Did you leave the party with your sister?"

"No. She wanted to leave way too early. So she left without me."

"Who did you leave with?"

"Honestly, I don't know. I was very drunk. I remember getting into a pickup truck, riding in the truck, stopping somewhere. The next thing I remember is waking up in the hospital the next morning."

"How did you end up in the hospital?"

"All I know is what my sister told me."

The judge leaned forward to address the witness. "You can testify as to what the defendant told you," he said.

"Okay. So, Charlotte got worried when it was two o'clock in the morning and I wasn't back at our apartment. She called some friends who said I left the party before midnight. So she got in her car and went looking till she found me."

"How did she find you?"

"Same way I would have. Just check the usual spots people go to after parties. Pickup trucks are, you know . . . multipurpose vehicles."

A collective chuckle coursed through the courtroom, and the judge gaveled it down. "Order, please."

The prosecutor returned her focus to the exhibit on the screen. "The article states that the unidentified student was found 'partially clothed.' Is that accurate?"

"Again, all I know is from Charlotte. She said my jeans were missing. I was in my panties. She said she tried to wake me up, but I was blacked out. So she called nine-one-one."

"And when the police arrived, Charlotte Holmes told them that you had been sexually assaulted."

"Yes."

"Which was not the case?"

"No."

"She assumed you had been sexually assaulted, when you had not been sexually assaulted."

"Correct."

"Your sister jumped to the conclusion that this was a sexual assault, correct?"

"Objection," said Jack.

"Sustained. We get the point, Ms. Barrow," the judge said.

"Ms. Holmes, did you subsequently discover what really happened that night?"

"Yes," she said, sighing. "Two not very nice girls found me drunk on the couch at the party, walked me to their truck, dropped me off by the pond, stole my jeans, and left me there in my underwear. Ha-ha, very funny."

"This was the 'sexual assault' that your sister reported to police?"

"Yes. And for the rest of my college days, I was known as the Pink Panty Road Tripper. Thank you very much, Charlotte Holmes."

Jack rose, not sure what to say, but he felt the need to say something. "Judge, this doesn't bear any resemblance at all to the testimony Ms. Barrow promised in our sidebar. Obviously my client thought her sister had been sexually assaulted and acted accordingly. I don't see anything wrong with that."

"Your client falsely reported a sexual assault to make herself a hero at her sister's expense," said Barrow, glowering. "The only thing more reprehensible is the false accusation she's making against Mr. Scoville to cast herself as a victim."

"That's an outrageous accusation," said Jack.

"It's the truth," said Barrow.

Jack glanced at his client and then at the witness. True or not, it was clearly what Megan believed: Charlotte had embellished the story to cast herself as the hero who rescued her sister from sexual assault and got her to a hospital in time to save her life.

"I've heard enough," said the judge. "Ms. Barrow, you've made your point. But Mr. Swyteck also has a point. We're getting way too deep in the weeds. I agree with the state's premise that Charlotte Holmes is unfit to be an elector if, as a lobbyist, she offered sexual favors in exchange for legislative votes. I've heard nothing from this witness to support that premise."

"I'll get right to it," said Barrow.

"Please do," said the judge.

The attorney general stepped closer to the witness. "Ms. Holmes, I know this sounds tawdry, and I'm sorry about that. But your sister stipulated to having had a sexual relationship with four different men while she was a lobbyist."

"Objection," said Jack. "She was working as a researcher for a lobbying firm. She was not yet a registered lobbyist."

"Sustained."

"I stand corrected. Regardless, your sister and her lawyer claim that these relationships had nothing to do with her job. She claims that her sexual relationship with each of these men was purely personal."

"That's not true," said Megan.

Jack felt his client's fingernails in his forearm, but he was already on his feet. "Objection. Judge, as I mentioned at our sidebar, there has been almost no communication between my client and her sister since college. There is no basis for Megan Holmes to testify about the nature of her sister's personal relationships."

The judge rubbed his face, as if over the courtroom sex-capades. "This is not a jury trial, so let me just get to the nub of it," he said. Then to the witness: "Ms. Holmes, how do you know your sister's relationships were not simply a man and woman going out on a date and doing whatever it is people do after a date?"

"I know because my sister doesn't like men."

A collective gasp emerged from the gallery.

"Not that there's anything wrong with that," said the attorney general, smirking.

The judge pounded his gavel. "Counsel, in my chambers. Now!"

Chapter 28

Charlotte ordered room service for dinner and ate alone on the bed.

Judge Martin had delivered both sides a tongue-lashing in his chambers and then adjourned for the day. Charlotte hated that her sister's testimony would fester overnight, and Jack had argued nearly to his last breath that it was unfair to end the afternoon session on that note. But the judge was fed up. Charlotte would have to wait for her lawyer to clear things up when the hearing resumed in the morning.

President MacLeod's reaction was in the same news clip on every channel, a wisp of his dyed hair blowing in the breeze of the whirling propellers of Marine One.

"Charlotte Holmes said she couldn't vote for me because she cares about the truth," MacLeod said with a gleam in his eye. "Finally, the truth is out: she's the leader of the gay mob."

The gay mob. What next would come out of that man's mouth? Cement shoes by Gucci?

Her sister's support for President MacLeod had come as no surprise to Charlotte. All of her siblings supported MacLeod. Charlotte had supported him, too, until the president's five-million-vote deficit in the general election made it impossible for her to bear the weight of his lies. At bottom, though, Megan's courtroom performance wasn't about politics. It wasn't even about the Pink Panty Road Trip per se. It was a lifetime of Megan messing up and Charlotte cleaning up. Charlotte was the female version of Ferris Bueller; Megan was the older sister caught making out with Charlie Sheen in the police station—over and over again. Charlotte had tried to explain it to Jack, but she wasn't sure he got it. It was hard to relate if you were an only child, like Jack. When you were one of five, you just accepted the fact that, one day, one of them would stick it to you. Today had been that day. And unfortunately, it had been in front of the entire country.

There was a knock at the door. Charlotte climbed down from the bed, went to the door and checked the peephole. It was Theo, so she let him in.

"Jack's parents are at their house on the Gulf," he told her. "His stepmother's not doing so well, so he's going to see her."

"I'm sorry to hear that."

"Yeah, me, too. Anyway, he asked me to drive so he could work on the car ride. I just wanted to check on you before we left."

"I'm fine."

"You sure?"

"Positive. In fact, I'd be whistling Dixie and telling the world I've never been better, if not for hashtag 'Gay Mob.'"

"I heard."

"Everybody heard. But this, too, shall pass. I'm fine here in my room. Y'all go."

"Okay. It'll be close to midnight before we're back, but call if you need anything."

"It's a shame you have to turn around and come right back. You should visit during the day sometime. Beautiful."

"I might just do that," said Theo.

"Maybe when this is over, Jack can get his wife up here and we can all go. Beach all day. Great little cafés on the water. Gets nice and cool at night, so at sunset you knock back a few beers in the hot tub."

"I guess that would make it a . . . spa getty."

"Did you really just say that?"

"I don't think so. But, hey, if I did, it made you smile."

"A little," she said, the centimeter between her thumb and forefinger saying how little. "Thank you for trying."

"I'll see you later," he said.

They exchanged a smile. Charlotte let him out, closed the door, and turned the dead bolt.

"Spa getty?" she said, hoping that Theo wasn't kicking himself too hard over that effort. But then she realized that she was the one who'd embarrassed herself. *Oh, let's be couples and all go down to the beach like real heterosexuals. See? I do like men.*

Charlotte climbed back onto the bed. Her dinner was still warm, which was a problem, because it was a Greek salad. Some knucklehead in the kitchen had put the plate on a warmer in the room-service cart. Wilted lettuce. Yum. She reached for the phone to order ice cream. Chocolate. Two scoops. She had the room phone in hand when her cell vibrated on the nightstand.

A text message.

It was a number she didn't recognize, not a spoofed caller ID to trick her into thinking that the text was from "Theo Knight" or someone else in her contact list. Charlotte took it as the sender's arrogant way of signaling that he knew he had her attention—he knew she would read his message no matter what number it came from, no need for technological games.

And he was right. He did have her attention.

Charlotte lifted her cell from the nightstand and stared at the message bubble: "Clyde's. 10 p.m. Out front."

Clyde's was a popular bar on Adams Street. By itself, the designated meeting place was enough for Charlotte to hazard a guess as to the sender. Then the phone vibrated in her hand with a follow-up message from the same number.

"I dare you," it read, erasing all doubt in Charlotte's mind as to the sender's identity. He was serious. He wanted to meet. Tonight.

"You idiot" was all she could say.

Chapter 29

An hour into their drive from Tallahassee, Jack checked the time on the dashboard.

Most of the trip down I-10 had been in silence, with Theo behind the wheel and Jack working nonstop on his laptop in the passenger seat. Jack had known time to fly while deep in his thoughts, but never had he seen time stand still. They'd left the hotel around 6:30 p.m. Yet the clock was telling him that it was only 6:31 p.m. A vague recollection of high school physics crept into his mind, something about the slowing of time as objects approached the speed of light.

"How fast are you driving?" Jack asked.

"Faster than you would," said Theo.

Jack checked the upcoming exit sign and saw they were at Blountstown, population 3,500. Mystery solved.

Blountstown and everything west of the Apalachicola River was the reason networks never declared a winner in a Florida statewide election sooner than one hour after polls closed from Key West to Tallahassee. As if to make sure the "Southern Alabama" moniker stuck, the Florida Panhandle had been in the Central time zone for more than a century.

"So what's the story with Charlotte?" asked Theo.

Jack looked up from his computer screen. "The story?"

"What her sister said in court. That she doesn't like men."

"Oh, that," said Jack, closing his laptop. "She kissed a girl. When she was eighteen."

"Seriously? That's it?"

"That's it."

Theo snickered. Then he started laughing. Soon, he was laughing so hard that Jack thought he might crash the car.

"Can you get control of yourself, please?"

"I'm sorry," said Theo, wheezing with laughter. "She pulled a Katy Perry, kissed a girl when she was a teenager, and now she's the leader of the gay mob?"

Jack knew he wasn't laughing at Charlotte. It was one of his "gallows fits," as Jack called them, which were triggered by random episodes of institutionalized absurdity, unleashing the residual anger Theo harbored against a system that would put an innocent man on death row. It manifested itself in laughter, the way Theo—down to his final appeal, his head and ankles shaven for effective placement of Ol' Sparky's electrodes—had laughed out loud at the corrections officer who, in all sincerity, wanted to know if his last meal of fried chicken should be "extra crispy."

"I guess it's funny on some level," said Jack. He gazed out the passenger-side window. There was only darkness. "Except that sixty-five million voters believe it."

Jack squeezed in another hour of preparation for Megan's cross-examination, as Theo followed the moon toward the waterfront. At the end of a sandy road, well off the highway, was a tin-roofed cottage with the name SWYTECK on a sign hanging from a turtle-shaped mailbox. Harry had bought the place while a state legislator, when Jack was still in law school. It had survived dozens of hurricane seasons, having narrowly dodged disaster when Hurricane Michael chose to obliterate Mexico Beach to the east, sparing dozens of other beach towns that would have fared no better in a direct hit. A driveway of crushed seashells crackled as the car pulled up and stopped at the front porch. Jack inhaled the fresh gulf breeze as he climbed out of the passenger seat and stretched his legs. His father came out to greet them.

"Thanks for coming, son."

"Of course."

"And thank you for driving, Theo."

"No problem."

Harry invited them in, but Theo chose to wait outside, settling into a white wicker rocking chair on the porch. Years had passed since Governor Swyteck's signing of Theo's death warrant, but that kind of awkwardness never fully evaporated. This was a family matter, anyway.

"We won't be too long," said Jack, and then he followed his father into the cottage. Jack looked around. It felt familiar, but only because he knew his stepmother's tastes in decorating. He'd actually visited only twice before. Far from Miami in so many ways, geography the least of them, this cottage was all Harry and Agnes, nothing to remind anyone that Jack's biological mother had ever existed.

"I'll let Agnes know you're here."

Jack waited in the Florida room, which was cozy enough, decorated in the usual beach motif of driftwood, old fishing nets, and floral-patterned couch and armchairs. But he couldn't get comfortable.

To say Jack had a complicated relationship with his

stepmother was to say Gettysburg was a "disagreement." A psychiatrist might have said that Jack had been angry over the death of his birth mother, but he was too young to even know her before she died. The truth was that Agnes, at least when Jack had needed a mother most, was not a very good one. The darker truth was that she was a terrible alcoholic.

A doctor had once told Jack that, because of the way the brain is wired, nothing triggered memories like the sense of smell. For Jack, it was the smell of gin that triggered his worst childhood memories. It was hard to recall a moment when Agnes didn't reek of a spilled martini. The memory that had haunted him most was of the day he was looking for a hammer and nails to build a tree house in the yard. He'd gone into the garage to search his father's toolbox. In it, he found a crucifix, which seemed like a very unholy place to keep a religious artifact. He showed it to Agnes, and she went berserk. Not until Jack was older did he learn that it was the crucifix that had lain atop his mother's coffin, and that the toolbox in the garage was the only place Harry could hide it to keep his new wife from throwing it in the garbage or giving it away to the nearest Catholic church. It was the kind of crazy and spiteful thing she would do in her fits of jealousy, which were really about insecurity. In more than one of her drunk and tearful tirades, Jack had overheard Agnes shout that the real love of Harry Swyteck's life was dead and buried.

So it had caught Jack off guard when, after the adjournment of Charlotte's hearing, Harry had called to say, "Agnes would like to see you." His father didn't add any details. Jack hadn't asked for any. It was the Swyteck way of doing things: matters that a family should probably discuss and sort through were left to implication and inference. Jack simply got in the car and went, the assumption being that his stepmother hadn't asked to see him because she was feeling better.

"You can come back now, son."

His father was standing in the hallway outside the master bedroom. Jack rose and went to him. He was trying to keep his mind focused on how much better their relationship had gotten after the drinking had stopped. The fear was that Agnes would want to talk about the "bad old days," which Jack had simply left behind, never to speak of again, in keeping with Swyteck tradition.

"I'll be out here," his father said.

"You're not coming in?"

"No."

Jack drew a breath and entered the bedroom. The glow from the lamp was warm and soothing. The gentle sound of ocean waves kissing the beach were in the background, but it wasn't real. It was the purr of the relaxation machine on the nightstand.

"Come in, Jack."

He already was in, but he knew what she meant. Jack stepped closer to the bedside.

Agnes had aged ten years since summer. She wasn't a young woman, but seeing her like this was nonetheless out of step with the natural order of life. To the extent anyone could be prepared, Jack had been getting ready for a meeting like this with his *abuela*, not his stepmother.

"There's something I want to tell you," she said.

It was an oddly distant voice, made to feel even farther away with her head so deep in the pillow, her eyes sunk in their orbits.

"Okay," said Jack, and he could hear his own trepidation.

"Have you—"

She coughed once, and then again. The third cough was so deep that Jack almost ran to get his father.

"It's okay," she said. She paused to collect her strength. Her breathing returned to normal, and then she picked up where she'd left off. "Have you ever wondered," she asked slowly, looking up at Jack. She took another moment, then found the strength to finish the question: "Why you never had any brothers or sisters?"

Her words took Jack by surprise. It was true that Harry never had any children by his second wife, but Jack had never thought it was any of his business.

"Uhm" was all he could get out.

Agnes managed a tight smile. "Not the question you were expecting, I take it?"

"No. It wasn't."

"Have you? Wondered?"

"I—I probably have."

"Would you like to know?"

Jack hesitated. He honestly didn't have the answer. "If you would like to tell me," he said.

She smiled again, a little more noticeably. "Another Swyteck politician. God help us."

Agnes tried to sit up. Jack reached over to help her, but she started to cough again—deep, racking coughs so powerful that Jack feared she might break a rib.

"I'll get my dad," he said, but Harry was already on his way.

Jack's father crossed the room and hurried around to the other side of the bed, more responsive than Jack could ever imagine his father being. Agnes was in an uncontrollable coughing fit, emptying her lungs of fluids that would have disgusted even an experienced hospice nurse. Harry was unfazed by it. He just wiped away the globs of goo hanging from his hands, gently cleaned her mouth with a tissue, and then held her in his arms until she stopped trembling and felt safe.

Jack just watched. The way his father cared for Agnes, doing everything a human being could possibly do to calm and comfort her, and doing it as tenderly as a human being could do it, struck Jack as one of the kindest acts he'd ever witnessed. Harry Swyteck loved her. He loved this woman who was not Jack's mother, and he loved her with all his heart.

Agnes was the love of his life.

"Dad?"

Harry was whispering to his wife. He didn't seem to hear Jack.

"I'll wait outside," Jack said, and then he quietly left the room.

Chapter 30

Charlotte left her hotel room at 9:00 o'clock.

She'd thought about calling Jack to tell him about the text messages, but he would have insisted that she call the police, which would have been a mistake. The man who'd dared her to meet him at Clyde's at 10:00 p.m. was no stalker or political terrorist—at least not the last time she'd seen him. She took a screenshot of the text messages, just in case things had changed—in case he had changed. And she brought her Glock.

Charlotte exited the hotel through the restaurant to avoid any reporters who might be hanging around the hotel lobby. The night was cool enough for a light jacket, which afforded a more comfortable concealed-carry option. Charlotte's "Baby Glock" was holstered outside her waistband, which, without the cover of her jacket, would have been an illegal open carry. She was almost certain she wouldn't need it, but she was prepared.

Actually, Charlotte had been prepared all her life. Her father had made sure of it. Of the five Holmes girls, Charlotte had been closest to him, but even Charlotte had to admit that Dad was a bit over the top when it came to self-defense. Every Monday night, right after dinner, Mr. Holmes would take his girls to the garage for a dry-fire drill. He'd balance a penny atop the slide of an unloaded pistol, right behind the front sight. Any girl who could hold her aim at the wall for a count of five and squeeze the trigger without moving the penny didn't have to help her sisters clear the dinner table the rest of the week. Any girl who took his word for it that the gun wasn't loaded and didn't check for herself was an automatic loser. Charlotte made it all the way through high school without once clearing the table. Another reason for Megan to hate her.

The Uber driver met her a block away from the hotel, and Charlotte climbed into the back seat.

"There's bottled water if you want it," the driver said.

"No, thanks."

"Gum and mints, too."

"I'm good."

"If you need a phone charger, just ask."

Obviously a new driver fishing for five-star reviews. In a month, he'd be texting while driving, and his car would smell like a taco stand at 2:00 a.m.

Charlotte gazed out the window as they headed toward Clyde & Costello's, an eighteen-plus club that was popular with college students who were under twenty-one and without a fake ID. Charlotte had first visited Clyde's while still in high school, on one of her trips to FSU. It was the chosen destination—Clyde's—that had convinced Charlotte she was going to meet an old friend—one who had for some reason chosen to torment her with texts that weren't the least bit funny. And she was going to find out what the hell he was up to.

"You into younger men?" asked the driver.

There went his five-star rating. "What? No, I—"

"I didn't mean anything by it. Just, if you are, there are some other bars I could—"

"No. Thank you. I'm here to—oh, forget it."

Charlotte got out of the car, and the driver pulled away, leaving her on the brick sidewalk outside the club.

The bar scene in Tallahassee was notoriously slow on Monday nights. Clyde & Costello's was the exception. The line to get in extended halfway down Adams

Street, way beyond the green awning that ran the length of the old redbrick building. It was a queue of freshmen, or so it appeared to Charlotte; then again, since her thirtieth birthday, just about anyone under twenty-five looked like a college freshman. The Monday-night attraction, according to the poster in the window, was a rising star named Pressure, whose billing credits included "Winner of Best DJ Award" at the annual Bartenders Ball. Charlotte had never heard of him, but the Florida "electrocore" genre had been popular enough in her college days for Charlotte to recognize some of the festivals on Pressure's résumé, like EDC Orlando. It was more than music, however, that made Clyde's the go-to club on what, for most bars, was the deadest night of the week. It was also MMM.

Mandatory Make-Out Mondays.

It was exactly what it sounded like. Usually a young woman cut a glance at the cutie on the other side of the club, and the search for true love's kiss went from there. On a dare, Charlotte had kissed one of the servers—a woman. Later that same night, in a terrible lapse of judgment that came with underage drinking, she'd told her older sister Megan that she might do it again.

"I don't need to see your ID," the bouncer told her.

Between him and the Uber driver, this was getting annoying.

"I'm not going in," said Charlotte. The text message had told her to meet "out front." She stepped back from the club entrance and stood near the curb.

The line grew longer as the minutes passed. It was almost too chilly to sit outside, but the empty tables on the sidewalk were not weather related; MMM was more of an indoor sport. Charlotte pulled up a chair at one of the open tables and waited. She was about to check the time on her cell when she spotted a man on the other side of the street. A man who didn't look at all like the freshmen in the line outside Clyde's. He stopped. The glow of the streetlamp was enough for Charlotte to get a good look. He wasn't wearing a camouflage jacket, or the baseball cap that made it hard to see his face. It was exactly the man she'd expected.

Alberto Perez was smiling as he crossed the street and joined her at the table.

"You came," he said, grinning even wider.

"Yes, I came. What the hell is wrong with you, Alberto?"

Alberto was the friend who'd dared her to kiss a girl on Mandatory Make-Out Monday.

"Nothing's wrong with me," he said, confused.

"Why did you scare the crap out of me like this? I thought it was a psycho sending me death threats."

"Huh?"

"'A promise is a promise.' The text you spoofed to make it look like it came from my new friend Theo's number—what was that about?"

"Who's Theo? I didn't send anything like that."

Charlotte felt a chill, and it wasn't the night air. "You didn't?"

"No. The only messages from me said 'meet at Clyde's' and 'I dare you.' I read about Megan's testimony that you don't like men. I was the idiot who started that war between you and your sister by daring you to kiss a girl at Clyde's. I'm sorry if I scared you. I guess I could have put my name on the texts, but I was sure you'd know it was me. Clyde's? 'I dare you'? Who else would it be?"

"No one else," said Charlotte. "That's why I came."

"And I'm glad you came," said Alberto. "It's good to see you. It's been—I guess since college."

"Yeah. Sorry I'm so bad about keeping in touch."

"It works both ways," said Alberto. "I didn't even know you were a lobbyist until I saw your name in the news about the Electoral College. I'm a doctor, by the way."

"Wow, Alberto. Good for you."

"Yeah. Kind of ironic, isn't it? The guy who was everyone's biggest pain in the ass in college goes into pain management."

She laughed.

"The gun angle makes sense for you," Alberto said. "You must have been some kind of lobbyist to be Madeline Chisel's protégée."

"She trained me well."

"But no more guns?" he asked.

"I wouldn't say no more guns. Just no more gun lobbying."

"What's your new lobby agenda?"

"We'll see. I'm sitting out until after the Electoral College meets."

"Health care's big. I may have something for you." Alberto laid a flash drive on the table between them. "Take a look."

"What's that?"

"Your future."

Charlotte was suddenly uncomfortable. "I'm in the middle of a court hearing. This is no time to be sending me cryptic text messages and sliding flash drives across the table."

He nudged it closer to Charlotte. "Just take it."

She pushed it back. Alberto was always a bit of a schemer, and she honestly had no idea what he'd been up to since college. "Talk to me after the Electoral College meets."

He pushed it right back. "It's important that you see it now."

Charlotte didn't like his tone. "I don't want it now."

His voice took on a serious edge. Even a little scary. "Take it, Charlotte."

"Alberto, no. I said I don't want it."

A man approached their table. He was middle-aged and carrying the proverbial rubber tire around his waist, not at all like the younger crowd in line to enter Clyde's. "Hey, is this guy hassling you, lady?"

His voice was deep, which matched his frame. He was big, in the Paul Bunyan sense of the word, not particularly muscular but imposing nonetheless.

"Mind your own business," said Alberto.

"I wasn't talking to you," he said sharply. Then to Charlotte: "Is this man hassling you, ma'am?"

"It's okay," said Charlotte. "I can handle myself. But thank you."

The sound of her voice seemed to trigger a spark of recognition. "Hey, aren't you that elector lady in the news?"

It was exactly what she didn't want to hear. "You must have me confused with someone else."

"Yeah, it is you. Hey, I change my mind," he said to Perez. "You fuck with her all you want, pal."

"Go fuck yourself, pal," said Alberto.

The man started away, mocking Perez's accent in a cartoonish "Speedy Gonzalez" voice. "'Go foke yo-safe, señor.' Wetback."

It was all the provocation Alberto needed. He sprang from his chair and went after him.

The man turned on a dime, as if expecting Alberto's reaction. "Got fire in my pocket! Back off!"

Alberto didn't listen. He only charged harder.

The man reached into his pocket.

Charlotte pulled her Glock from her holster. "No!" she shouted, and in the same breath, she squeezed the trigger.

The man dropped to the sidewalk, and the crack of gunshot was like a starter's pistol, scattering the crowd in mass panic. Dozens of screaming college students broke ranks from the long line in front of Clyde's, running for their lives down Adams Street. The stampede sent tables and chairs flying, and the table slammed into Charlotte's knee, knocking her to the ground.

"Holy shit!" shouted Alberto.

Charlotte lowered her gun. The man hadn't moved.

"Oh—my—God," she said, her fractured voice quaking, her words barely audible in the hysteria all around her.

Chapter 31

Jack and Theo were just outside Tallahassee, headed back from the Gulf, when the call came from Charlotte.

"I'm in the back seat of a police car," she said.

Jack sat up in the passenger seat. "Stop talking and listen to me."

"I shot a man."

"I said stop talking."

"He's dead."

"Charlotte, stop right now."

Of course Jack had a slew of questions—who, why, how?—none of which any competent lawyer would want his client to answer on her cell from the back seat of a squad car. He stuck to the essentials.

"Are you hurt?"

"No. Well, my knee got banged up in the stampede. But I'm okay."

"Good. Listen to me carefully. Do not answer any questions from anyone."

"Okay."

"Don't turn over your cell phone if they ask for it."

"I already did. They gave it back."

Damn. "That's okay," Jack said, even if it wasn't. More than likely, every bit of data on her cell and cloud—photographs, text messages, contacts, call history—had already been downloaded under a broad interpretation of "consent."

"If they ask to see it again, or if they ask you anything at all, tell them you want to speak to your lawyer first."

"Okay."

"Now, tell me exactly where you are."

She did. "I'm on my way," Jack said. "Other than 'I want my lawyer,' don't say another word to anyone until I get there. Understood?"

"Yes," she said, and the call ended.

Jack had his second conversation of the night with Theo about the "speed of light," which cut the remaining travel time in half. Theo parked as close to Clyde's as possible and stayed with the car. Jack walked the rest of the way and stopped at the yellow police tape that closed off the street. A pair of perimeter-control officers stood on the business side of the tape. Portable transformers and crime-scene lights brightened the street in front of Clyde's. Outdoor tables and chairs were scattered about like lawn furniture after a windstorm, making it easy for Jack to envision the panic unleashed by the shooting. Farther down was the blue swirl of police beacons, and Jack assumed that his client was waiting inside one of the squad cars. Jack told the perimeter officers who he was. One of them radioed the detective in charge of the crime scene.

"Detective Dan Jenkins, FDLE," he said, as he approached the tape.

"Is Charlotte Holmes under arrest?" Jack asked.

"No," said the detective. "But I would like to ask her a few questions."

"Not before I've spoken to her."

"That's fine. But whether she talks or not, her gun stays with us. She gave it to us, and it's been tagged as evidence."

Jack didn't argue, though it appeared that his client had already said more than any lawyer would have liked. "Can you take me to her, please?"

"I'll bring her."

Jack called Theo while waiting and told him not to go anywhere. A minute later, Charlotte came into view in the company of Detective Jenkins, their shadows long in the bright portable lighting. Charlotte was limping, and when she stopped on the other side of the tape, she breathed out the pain, not to mention a good amount of stress and worry.

"Charlotte, let's go get an X-ray of that knee."

"I'm fine."

She didn't seem to get Jack's drift. "Charlotte," he said firmly. "Let's go."

Jack thanked the detective, and they exchanged business cards as Charlotte stepped beneath the tape. Jack offered a shoulder to lean on, but she insisted on walking under her own power. Theo was able to pull the car up a half block closer to shorten the walk. Jack had mentioned an X-ray just to get her away from the scene, but she was limping so badly that a trip to the ER probably made sense. She agreed. Jack got in the back seat with her so they could talk on the way. Charlotte explained everything, from Alberto's text messages to the rendezvous at Clyde's, from the crack of gunfire to the moments that followed—when she checked on the body.

"Are you sure the man you shot is not the same

guy you saw across the street from Madeline Chisel's office?" asked Jack.

"This guy is way bigger around the middle."

"Not the guy who pulled you out of the truck after the accident?"

"I don't think so. But I don't remember much about that, other than the camouflage jacket."

"Do you have any idea who he is?"

"I don't."

Jack would come down harder on her later, after the trauma of having shot and killed a man subsided. But every lawyer had his limit, and that bit about the customer always being right didn't apply to clients. "Why did you leave the hotel in the first place? How could anything good come of that?"

Charlotte apologized and then gave him the full background on Alberto.

"And where is this Alberto now?" asked Jack.

"His lawyer was on the scene even faster than you were. They left."

Jack was immediately suspicious, and he recognized the irony: the fact that Charlotte had left with her lawyer had surely struck the police as no less suspicious. Jack turned his questioning back to the shooting.

"Was the man coming at you when you shot him?"

"Not at me. The argument was between him and Alberto."

"Why did you shoot him?"

"I didn't want to. I had to."

"Why?"

Charlotte breathed deep, her tone more somber. "I thought he was going to shoot Alberto."

"Did he have a gun?"

"I think I saw a gun in his hand."

"What do you mean, you think?"

"When Alberto jumped up from the table, the guy said he had fire in his pocket. He reached into his pocket for something and—well, after that, it was a blur. I fired."

"Did you find a gun on the sidewalk?"

"It was a stampede. Tables were knocked over. People were falling on top of other people. Everything went flying. Alberto and I were trying not to get trampled to death."

"Was there a gun in his pocket?"

She glanced out the car window, then back at Jack. "I don't know."

"You didn't check his pocket before the police got there?"

"No. I took his pulse to see if he was alive." She

paused, and Jack could hear the lump in her throat. "There was nothing. He wasn't breathing. So I dialed nine-one-one."

They arrived at the hospital. Theo stopped the car, and the glow of the ER entrance signs bathed them in a rainbow of light. Jack could see in Charlotte's expression that the adrenaline was waning, taking her strength with it.

"What if it turns out he didn't have a gun?" asked Charlotte.

Jack looked into her eyes. Second-guessing wasn't what he'd expected from a gun lobbyist, but any combat veteran would attest to the world of difference between target shooting and firing on another human being at point-blank range.

"You did the best you could," he said.

"I . . . I shot him. What if I made a mistake?"

"It's not fair to torment yourself with what-if questions. Especially when you consider all you've been through in the last two weeks. Give your mind a rest."

"But a man is dead."

She seemed to be slipping into a bad place, and the only way Jack knew how to stop it was to stop talking about it. "Come on. Let's go check out that knee. Then we can have a conversation."

Jack climbed out, walked around to the other side of the car, and helped Charlotte out of the back seat. Together, they walked toward the emergency room entrance. This time, when Jack offered his arm, Charlotte accepted and leaned against him.

It had nothing to do with her knee.

Chapter 32

President MacLeod took the Florida attorney general's call at his table-like desk in the Treaty Room. On the wall behind him hung a portrait of Ulysses S. Grant, the former president seeming to watch over him. Alight in the distance, framed in a pair of windows that flanked the portrait, were the Washington Monument and Jefferson Memorial.

MacLeod didn't make regular use of the Treaty Room the way his predecessors had. Just a few doors down from the master suite, adjacent to the famous Lincoln Bedroom, it was perfect for quiet study and after-hours reflection. For MacLeod, it was simply too damn quiet. He liked the energy and controlled chaos of the West Wing, which he encouraged by leaving the doors to the Oval Office open late into the night, inviting an endless stream of high-level aides who came and went with praise, ideas, comments, and—if they were smart—still more praise for the man who fired staff on a weekly basis.

This after-hours call from the Florida attorney general had been flagged as "extremely private." The Treaty Room fit the bill.

"Good news, Mr. President," said Barrow. "The Leon County state attorney plans to bring criminal charges against Charlotte Holmes."

"Breach of oath?"

"No, sir. Second-degree murder."

The president gripped the phone with excitement. "That certainly ups the ante. What's this about?"

"It appears that Ms. Holmes arranged a meeting with two men at a Tallahassee nightclub. An altercation broke out, and she ended up shooting one of the men dead. Looks like a botched payoff."

"What makes you think this was a payoff?"

"FDLE obtained access to her cell phone and collected text messages. One of the texts was from an untraceable cell phone spoofing as another number. The message said 'A promise is a promise.' We take that to be code for 'A deal is a deal.'"

"As in a deal to support Senator Stahl? She sold her electoral vote?"

"Exactly."

MacLeod shot from his chair, so thrilled that he would have slapped a high-five with President Grant, had the eighteenth president actually been in the room. "Can you prove all this?"

"We have a nine-one-one recording of Ms. Holmes admitting that she shot him. Proving that this was a payoff will take some detective work. But we'll get there. We already have the text message about the promise—the deal."

"Excellent," said the president, settling back into his swivel chair. "Who's the dead guy?"

"His name is Logan Meyer. Basic troublemaker. A bunch of small-time arrests. We don't know what his role was in the payoff, but the fact that such a sketchy guy got involved makes for good atmospherics."

"Was he armed?"

"No report so far that he had a weapon."

"What about money?"

"Sir?"

"You said this was a botched payoff. Did money change hands?"

"Unfortunately, no money was recovered at the crime scene."

"What happened to it?"

"We don't know. Ms. Holmes won't tell us. I can

only presume that's why her lawyer won't let us talk to her."

A sour taste gathered in the back of the president's throat. "Would that be Low Jack?"

"Lojack?"

"No. Low Jack. Low-energy, low-IQ Jack Swyteck. The former governor's son."

"I don't see any reason why Ms. Holmes would replace him. It's my understanding that criminal defense law is his specialty. He did nothing but death penalty work for years."

"Will the state attorney seek the death penalty here?"

"There is no death penalty for second-degree murder."

"Ah, that's right. The death penalty is for breach of oath."

There was a pause on the line. "I'm sorry, sir. What?"

MacLeod chuckled professorially. "A little high-brow humor there, General. I guess you've never heard of Sir Thomas More? Executed for—uh, something to do with an oath."

"You never cease to amaze me, Mr. President. You are truly a Renaissance man."

"Don't you forget it." MacLeod swiveled in his chair, gazing out the window toward the Jefferson Memorial. "When do you plan to make the arrest?"

"The warrant will be issued tonight. I'll call Swyteck and extend the courtesy of allowing his client to voluntarily surrender in the morning. We're scheduled to continue the fitness hearing before Judge Martin at nine a.m. He's not technically the duty judge, but he has years of criminal experience on the bench. He can do the arraignment right there."

"What's the alternative?"

"Execute the warrant tonight and haul her off to the detention center in a squad car. She can be arraigned at the morning cattle call by A-V connection from the detention center, along with the DUIs, the armed robbers, and everybody else arrested in the last twenty-four hours."

"I say forget the courtesy. Let her spend the night in jail."

"That makes us look bad, Mr. President. Perceptions matter. Like you always say, when they go low, we go high."

"When did I say that?"

"Starting now. Plus, arraignment before Judge Martin is the surefire way to maximize media coverage.

Everyone is already planning to be in his courtroom for day two of the fitness hearing."

MacLeod smiled thinly. "You're lucky you're so damn good, General Barrow."

"I aim to please, Mr. President."

"Yes, you do."

Chapter 33

At 9:00 a.m. Jack and his client were in Judge Martin's courtroom. The judge was wearing his criminal-jurisdiction hat.

The phone call from General Barrow had come around midnight. Jack suspected an ulterior motive behind her proposed "voluntary surrender," but that was no reason to refuse what, on its face, appeared to be professional courtesy. By 7:00 a.m. Jack had a copy of the probable-cause affidavit in support of the arrest warrant, as well as the formal criminal information charging his client with homicide in the second degree. Jack had been expecting, at most, negligent homicide. The courtesies only went so far.

"Criminal case number twenty-dash-ninety-two,"

intoned the bailiff. "State of Florida versus Charlotte Lee Holmes."

"Truth matters!" a woman shouted from the back row. Jack had no idea which side she supported.

Judge Martin smacked his gavel. "There will be order in this courtroom."

Silence. It appeared to be an isolated outburst, not a coordinated protest.

An early press release from the Office of the Attorney General had unleashed a flood of tweets and other Internet chatter about Charlotte's alleged "electoral vote for sale," a botched payoff, and a dead bagman. Even before the shooting, Jack had expected demonstrations at day two of the fitness hearing, but news of Charlotte's criminal charges had drawn even larger crowds. Only a fraction of the people who'd flocked to the courthouse found a seat for Charlotte's arraignment. The media section was again at capacity, some determined reporters squeezing in sideways for a firsthand account.

Jack was at his client's side as they stood before the bench. The legal team for Senator Stahl was notably absent. They'd filled the first row of public seating for Charlotte the Faithless Elector. They were nowhere to be seen for Charlotte the Accused Murderer.

"Good morning, everyone," the judge said. "Ms.

Holmes, the purpose of this proceeding is to advise you of certain rights that you have, to inform you of the charges made against you under Florida law, and to determine under what conditions, if any, you might be released before trial. Do you understand?"

"Yes, Your Honor," said Charlotte.

"You have the right to remain silent," the judge said, and with the full recital of her Miranda rights, Jack saw a look of fear return to Charlotte's eyes.

"We'll waive the reading of the charges," said Jack. His client had read them before the hearing. A public reminder was unnecessary.

"Ms. Holmes, how do you plead?" the judge asked.

"Not guilty."

"So noted." The judge's gaze shifted to the other side of the courtroom. "General Barrow, what is the state of Florida's position on bail?"

"Judge, we wish to be reasonable wherever possible. I would point out that we didn't rush out to arrest Ms. Holmes and handcuff her at midnight. We allowed her to surrender voluntarily this morning."

"I appreciate that," the judge said. "Such gestures reflect well on you and the entire profession."

"Thank you," said Barrow. "We were comfortable with that arrangement only because the defendant's lawyer is in town to ensure her appearance in court. To be honest, we have no such comfort after Mr. Swyteck returns to Miami. We believe the defendant is a flight risk, and therefore the state of Florida opposes pretrial release."

Ulterior motive exposed. But Jack had prepared for it.

"My client has lived in northwest Florida her entire life, and in Leon County since she was eighteen years old. This is not about flight risk. The attorney general opposes bail for one reason. If Ms. Holmes is locked up, she can't attend the meeting of the Electoral College at the state capital on December fourteenth. By law, if she fails to show up, Florida's other Republican electors select her replacement. This is a political power play in response to her announced intention to cast her electoral vote for Democratic candidate Evan Stahl.

"In fact," Jack continued, "this entire criminal case is political. The allegation that my client sold her vote and that the words 'a promise is a promise' somehow mean 'a deal is a deal' is preposterous. Ms. Holmes was being threatened for breaking her alleged 'promise' to vote for President MacLeod. This unfortunate incident was clearly an act of self-defense."

"Save your speech, Counsel," the judge said.

Jack apologized, but it was worth the rebuke in open

court. His "speech" was mainly for the media, the press release he had yet to release.

"Bail is set at one hundred thousand dollars," the judge said. "The defendant shall surrender her passport to the clerk of the court and is prohibited from leaving the state of Florida. Anything else, Counsel?"

"Not in the criminal case," said the attorney general.

"Then this initial hearing is adjourned. Bailiff, call the civil case."

The bailiff complied, and the attorney general didn't miss a beat in transition. "Judge, we believe the homicide charge in the criminal case is dispositive of Ms. Holmes's unfitness to serve as an elector."

"Charges are just accusations," said Jack. "They aren't dispositive of anything."

"I agree," the judge said. "General Barrow, if you want me to remove Ms. Holmes as unfit to serve as an elector, you need to prove these allegations."

"Let me make sure I understand," said Barrow, though she looked more annoyed than confused. "To convince this court that Ms. Holmes is unfit to serve as elector, we have to prove in this civil case that Ms. Holmes committed murder in the second degree, as alleged in the criminal case. And you want us to do that before December fourteenth?"

"I don't want you to do anything," the judge said.

"I'm telling you that what you presented in court yesterday was a salacious circus. I wouldn't remove Ms. Holmes as 'unfit' to serve as dog catcher based on that record."

Jack liked the judge's assessment of the attorney general's "fitness" evidence so far. The rest was a problem. "Your Honor, the meeting of the Electoral College is less than three weeks away. My client can't be expected to defend murder charges in that time frame."

"Your client doesn't have to prove anything, Mr. Swyteck. And this is not the criminal trial. If the state of Florida chooses to pursue this civil action under the framework I've established, the defense gets a free look at the state's evidence at least six months before the criminal case goes to trial. Stop complaining."

Jack had never looked any horse in the mouth, and he wasn't about to start with a gift horse. "Understood," said Jack.

"General Barrow, how soon can you be ready to proceed with this additional proof of Ms. Holmes's unfitness to serve?"

She glanced down the table at the state attorney, who appeared to have no answer. "I'm not sure we can be ready before December fourteenth, Judge."

"That's unfortunate, because we start on Thursday morning. If you're not ready, the state of Florida's demand to remove Ms. Holmes as an unfit elector will be denied."

Barrow and the state attorney huddled at the end of the table and exchanged whispers, conferring. Then Barrow returned to the microphone and said, "We'll be ready."

"Good. I'm directing the lawyers to meet and exchange evidence no later than noon tomorrow. I want counsel to work out as many evidentiary objections as possible before the hearing. Understood?"

"Yes, Judge," the lawyers said in stereo.

"Very well. This court is in recess until nine o'clock Thursday morning," he said, and it was over with the crack of his gavel.

Chapter 34

President MacLeod was in the room that didn't exist. In the bed that didn't exist. Beneath the lights that didn't exist. If Ronald Reagan could deny the use of hair dye, Malcolm MacLeod could deny the existence of a state-of-the-art, Level 5 tanning bed in the Executive Mansion.

"I have General Barrow on the line," said Teague. Other than the president and First Lady, the president's chief strategist was the only person allowed in the tanning room. If there was such a thing as carcinogenic secondary tanning rays, Teague was a marked man.

"Put her on speaker," said MacLeod.

The president was flat on his back, wearing only a bath towel around his waist, his skin slathered in tanning lotion as thirty-six thousand watts of UVA high-pressure lamps did the work of the sun's rays. Protective goggles spared his retinas from UV damage, but they also gave him a permanent set of raccoon eyes that made deniability of the tanning bed less than plausible. Teague served as the president's eyes and switchboard operator.

"General Barrow," said MacLeod, energized by the warmth on his skin. "How's my favorite Florida blonde?"

"Just fine, sir."

"I hear Judge Martin gave you just two days to build a second-degree murder case. Can you do it?"

"The faster this case moves, the better," said Barrow. "And not just from the standpoint of the Electoral College. The longer this case drags on, the more it's going to unravel."

"What's the problem?"

"Logan Meyer is not, shall we say, an ideal victim."

"He's dead," said MacLeod. "Isn't that ideal enough?"

"Stand-your-ground cases can be tricky," said Barrow. "It turns out that Meyer has a history of insinuating himself into confrontational situations. Two years ago he got into an argument with a thirty-year-old man over a parking space. Meyer was on the winning side of stand your ground in that one. The man got out of his minivan, which Meyer took as an act of aggression, so he shot him dead. The bouncer at Clyde's told FDLE that Meyer has been hanging out outside the club lately, egging on drunk college boys to come at him. He says Meyer was itching for another stand-your-ground 'showdown.'"

"Charlotte Holmes's lawyer isn't going to put all that together in two days. That's a problem for the state attorney way down the road, if and when the criminal case goes to trial. All I need right now is for you to put on enough evidence for Judge Martin to boot Charlotte Holmes out of the Electoral College. Can you do that?"

"The short answer is yes," said Barrow. "But the real question is whether the removal of Charlotte Holmes is enough to keep you in the White House."

"I would hope that the Republican governor of Florida will replace her with a Republican elector who will vote for the Republican candidate."

Teague picked up on the attorney general's thought. "I believe General Barrow is asking if we're worried about any electors other than Charlotte Holmes."

"Are we?" asked MacLeod.

"Not specifically," said Teague. "Our real concern is that there might be a handful of sleepers out there who are lying low until the meeting of the Electoral College. They've seen how we went after Charlotte Holmes, and rather than put themselves through hell, they could just show up and vote for Senator Stahl. There's no requirement that an elector announce in advance of the meeting."

"I share Oscar's concern," said Barrow.

The president took a deep breath. It was suddenly feeling hotter beneath the tanning lights. "This shouldn't even be an issue. Just find the senator's boyfriend, and let's see how 'progressive' these electors are when we actually put a face on the First Homo."

"We're still looking, sir," said Teague.

MacLeod wiped the sweat from his brow. The bed was equipped with its own cooling system, but with the president's anger came perspiration, no matter what the ambient temperature—as anyone who'd mentioned "global warming" to him on a cold winter day could attest.

"Do you see what incompetence I have to put up with, Paulette? It's been since July, and we still can't find the boyfriend."

"The problem is we're not a hundred percent certain it's a man," said Teague.

"Of course it's a man. That kiss Senator Stahl gave his wife in that stunt in their driveway was a gay kiss if I ever saw one." There was no response, and MacLeod's eye guards made it impossible for him to see Teague's reaction. "Oscar, don't tell me you can't spot a gay kiss when you see one."

"Honestly, I appear to be challenged in that regard, sir."

The timer chimed, and the heat lamps switched off. The president removed his goggles and climbed out of the bed. Teague handed him a terry-cloth robe, which he put on.

"How do I look?" he asked, offering Teague his profile from both sides, chin out.

"Healthy as ever," said Teague.

He moved closer to the speakerphone. "General, I want you to crush it in that courtroom on Thursday. Your strategy of a botched payoff is the perfect one. If Mr. Meyer is the kind of guy who goes around looking for trouble, that fits the narrative. Tell me about the other guy. What's his name?"

"Alberto Perez."

"Good. A foreigner. Another sketchy guy."

"He's actually a second-generation Cuban-American from Miami. An M.D. No criminal record. Married five years to a woman named Heidi Bristol from Milford, Connecticut."

"Heidi Bristol from Milford? What the hell, Paulette? My base won't buy this theory if your bagman is married to a Daughter of the American Revolution."

"Things are never as they seem, Mr. President."

MacLeod smiled. "You see, Oscar? Do you see

why I love this woman? What do you have on him, General?"

"I'm told that Dr. Perez and his wife attended at least one major fund-raiser for Senator Stahl. By the end of the day I should have a photograph of the three of them together."

The president settled into the chair beside the tanning bed. "Beautiful. That is exactly what—wait a minute. I just had another thought. The dead guy was actually a hero," he said, adjusting the facts to fit the new narrative.

"But General Barrow just said he has a history of—"

"Don't interrupt, Oscar," said MacLeod. "Yes, now it's coming clear. A rich Democrat donor was in the act of buying an electoral vote just a few blocks away from the State Capitol. Charlotte Holmes shot the courageous American patriot who was trying to blow up the deal and save our democracy. Pardon me for a moment, but I think I'm about to ejaculate."

"You go right ahead, sir," said Barrow.

MacLeod took a deep breath, then released a full-throated groan in simulated climax. "I love it."

Chapter 35

Jack arrived at the Florida State Capitol late Tuesday afternoon. Barrow had asked for a meeting in her office, and if there was a way to resolve things before Thursday's hearing, Jack was all for it. But he wasn't optimistic.

"General Barrow will be with you shortly," the receptionist said, leaving Jack alone in a conference room adjacent to the attorney general's main office.

Jack looked around. It was white-glove clean. Not a scrap of paper on the table, not a stray paperclip on the credenza, not a volume out of place in the bookshelves. No sign of boxes, papers, exhibits, or any other form of "evidence" that the government planned to offer at the hearing and that required their discussion. Apparently, the general had something else on her mind.

The door opened. General Barrow entered alone, no entourage, which also struck Jack as odd. "Hello, Jack," she said with a politician's smile, her tone way too friendly.

Jack responded cordially and accepted the invitation to join her at the rectangular conference table. She took a seat at the head, rather than in the chair across from him, as if to signal that she was not the opposition, at least for purposes of this meeting.

"Jack, my friend, it is my assessment that this fitness hearing has taken enough of a toll on everyone. You, me, and most definitely Charlotte Holmes."

Jack agreed with that much, though calling him "friend" had put him on high alert. "What do you have in mind?"

"Let's work this out."

"When you say 'this,' you mean what? Strictly the hearing to determine my client's fitness to serve as elector?"

"No," she said, leveling her gaze, as if to say she really meant business. "I'm talking about the whole enchilada. Both the fitness hearing and the criminal charges."

"Shouldn't the state attorney be part of any discussion of the criminal charges?"

"He's on board," said Barrow. "Here's the deal.

Charlotte Holmes pleads to one count of aggravated assault. Five years probation. No prison time."

Jack did not respond right away. On one level, it was a generous offer to come down from second-degree murder with mandatory jail time to aggravated assault. On another level, it troubled him.

"Let me guess," said Jack. "Your deal is on one condition: my client has to enter her plea before the Electoral College meets on December fourteenth."

She smiled insincerely. "As always, Jack, you're one step ahead of me."

"Her guilty plea will make her a convicted felon— and therefore ineligible to serve as a Florida elector until she has served her sentence."

Another phony smile. "Two steps ahead. Bravo, Jack."

"I'll discuss it with my client," said Jack.

"I suggest you move quickly. There's a very short expiration date on this offer."

"How short?"

"Tomorrow at noon."

"That's the deadline Judge Martin gave you to show me the evidence you plan to offer at the hearing."

"Correct," said Barrow.

"That's a problem. Why should my client plead

guilty to assault before she even gets a hint as to the evidence against her?"

"Let me give you a quick preview," said Barrow. "Her gun. Her bullet. Does Ms. Holmes really want to roll the dice and argue that she was 'standing her ground' in the face of deadly force? After all, she did shoot an unarmed man."

Jack didn't flinch. "We believe the evidence will show that Mr. Meyer had a gun."

"That's not what you'll hear from the first responders," said Barrow.

"Perhaps his gun fell to the ground and got lost in the stampede of college students."

Barrow seemed to appreciate the way Jack didn't miss a beat. "Well played, Counselor. But that won't fly."

"Maybe it will, maybe it won't," said Jack. "But at the end of the day, it doesn't matter if Mr. Meyer did or didn't have a gun. He said he had fire in his pocket. My client thought she and her friend were up against deadly force. That's enough under the stand-your-ground statute."

Barrow chuckled. "Is that how you plan to advise your client, Jack? Turn down a generous offer of no jail time, because under one of the most controversial laws in Florida, you don't have to retreat—you can just go ahead and shoot an unarmed man, as long as you think he's got fire in his pocket?"

Jack didn't answer. He simply watched as the attorney general reached into her briefcase, removed a clear plastic evidence bag, and laid it on the table in front of Jack.

"What's that?" asked Jack.

"A flash drive," she said, stating the obvious. "We found it at the scene. Right by the overturned table where your client was sitting."

Charlotte had told him about the flash drive Dr. Perez had tried to give her. But there was no legal or strategic reason for Jack to educate the prosecution. "What's on it?"

"My tech experts at FDLE will tell us soon enough."

Barrow pushed away from the table and rose, signaling that the meeting was over.

Jack rose and walked with her to the door.

"Here's the bottom line," she said. "If it worries your client that she shot an unarmed man, she should take the deal. If your client is worried about what we might find on the flash drive, she should take the deal. If your client somehow grows balls as big as globes between now and noon tomorrow, I'll see you in court on Thursday morning." She opened the door. "I think that about covers it. Any questions?"

"I'll let you know our decision," said Jack.

The attorney general held the door, allowing Jack to show himself to the elevator.

"No," said Charlotte. "I won't plead guilty to a felony."

They were at the hotel restaurant, talking and having a late dinner alone in a private dining room. Theo had a bar to run in Coconut Grove and was on the evening flight to Miami, so it was just Jack and his client.

"General Barrow is offering no jail time," said Jack.

"I don't care. This is blatantly political."

Jack didn't disagree, but it was an oversimplification. "Let me explain a couple of things, Charlotte. You've been charged with second-degree murder. That means the prosecution doesn't have to prove premeditation the way it would in a first-degree murder case."

"I understand."

"And don't think that because the charge is murder in the second degree that this isn't serious. In Florida, any person who uses a firearm to commit second-degree murder gets a mandatory sentence of twenty-five years in prison. That's the law."

"I get it," said Charlotte. "But I didn't murder anyone. I thought he had a gun."

"General Barrow says he didn't."

She paused, clearly troubled by that bit of news.

"Why would that man say he had fire in his pocket if he didn't have one?"

Jack sprinkled black pepper on his parmesan-crusted chicken. "Could be like the skydiving instructor's video that went viral a few months ago."

"What are you talking about?"

"You never saw it? This guy taught skydiving for thirty years. One of his students was on her first solo jump, so the instructor fixed a camera on his helmet to record the moment. About halfway through the video, the student pops her parachute. But the instructor keeps falling. Then the camera starts jerking around every which way, in all these panicky motions, as the poor guy realizes that he jumped out of the airplane with no parachute."

Charlotte cringed. "That's an awful story, Jack. And what does it have to do with the fire in Mr. Meyer's pocket?"

"For the average person, strapping on a parachute—or holstering a concealed weapon—would be a big deal. But once you get used to it, you get careless. You don't realize it's not there till you need it."

"I guess that makes sense."

"I'll tell you what worries me more than Mr. Meyer not having a gun," said Jack.

"What?"

"They found the flash drive Dr. Perez was trying to give you. General Barrow said she doesn't know what's on it yet. FDLE is examining it. But I don't believe her. I think she knows. And she thinks you know."

"I have no idea what's on it. You'll have to ask Alberto."

"So far, Dr. Perez has shown no willingness to help. I had to call his office three times just to get his assistant to tell me the name of his lawyer. I've been psycho-calling her all day. No response. How many times have you called Alberto?"

"I'd say six or seven. Plus a few texts."

"Has he gotten back to you?"

Charlotte poked at her salad. "No. Honestly, I don't understand it."

"I do," said Jack, fully aware of what was going on. "His lawyer is telling him to stay away from you. At this point, you're the only one charged with a crime. Dr. Perez, I'm sure, would like to keep it that way. I'd give him the same advice, if I were his lawyer."

"Toxic Charlotte Holmes strikes again. Is that it?"

"The red meat in the biggest political dogfight in Florida history is now in the prosecutor's crosshairs on a murder charge. No lawyer would want his client to cozy up to you."

"Then just subpoena him, Jack. All we want from

Alberto is his testimony that Mr. Meyer threatened to shoot us, so I shot him first."

"I don't want to call Dr. Perez as a witness without knowing what was on that flash drive. I'm flying back to Miami tomorrow for the day to see my family. I'll drop in and see Dr. Perez's lawyer—ambush her, if I have to. I want to know what's going on."

"Now you sound straight out of an episode of *House of Cards*. What do you think is on it, the North Korean nuclear code?"

"No. But what do you think is on it?"

"All I can tell you is that Alberto offered to help me transition my lobbying business from guns to health care. Then he laid the flash drive on the table."

"So it was a business plan of some sort?"

"I don't know. I shut him down and told him to put it away. I had enough sense to know that three weeks before the meeting of the Electoral College was not the time to be negotiating business deals."

Charlotte seemed to have lost all interest in her salad. Jack could see that she was in need of a break. "I want you to sleep on this before I give General Barrow an answer to her offer," said Jack.

Charlotte laid her fork aside and rose. "Sleep sounds perfect. I'm too tired to eat, Jack. I'm going up to my room."

"Before you go, there's one more thing I'd like you to consider."

Charlotte indulged him, but without much enthusiasm. "Okay. Just one."

"Whether you hire me or somebody else, a criminal trial will probably cost you a hundred thousand dollars."

"You're a veritable fountain of good news tonight, Jack."

"Money matters," said Jack. "Andie's on a government salary, and our golden retriever has a real shot at the Ivy League. If he would just stop eating his homework."

That almost made her smile. "We'll talk tomorrow," she said, and she left Jack in the dining room.

Chapter 36

It was the end of the third quarter, and the Orlando Magic were hopelessly behind the New York Knicks. NBA fans often said that players dogged it for three quarters, and that the game didn't really start until the fourth quarter. Scoville was in no mood to test the theory. He left early, but he didn't go far. The real attraction of the Amway Center was literally on top of the arena, high above the hardwood.

One80 Skytop Lounge was a favorite late-night destination in Scoville's home district. The chrome, glass, and white-leather fixtures were standard for a high-end club, and Orlando had plenty of bars for late-night partying and dancing beneath colored lights. What set One80 apart was killer views of the city, whether from the indoor dance floor surrounded by walls of glass or from the terrace bar beneath the stars. One80 catered to the young and single crowd, but guys like Scoville made out all right, as long as they kept peeling off the Benjamins for bottles of Cîroc and Tito's that drew young women to their VIP table.

A waitress dressed in pink spandex brought another bottle of vodka on ice. One of the ladies who'd staked out a position at Scoville's VIP table put down her cell phone long enough to grab the bottle and top off her friends' cocktails on Scoville's dime. Another woman settled into the couch, leaving a comfortable distance between her and the older man.

"Why so glum?" she asked.

Scoville didn't immediately realize she was speaking to him. She was wearing a black skirt so tight that he wondered how she managed to cross her legs, but on second look, she wasn't as young as he'd thought. Probably mid-thirties: potentially within striking distance, even without the power advantage he exercised in Tallahassee.

"Tough week," he said, which was an understatement. After years of service to the people of Florida, his career was over. Charlotte Holmes and Jack Swyteck were not alone to blame. Paulette Barrow had let him down. The deal with the attorney general was exactly as Swyteck had described it on cross-examination: in exchange for his testimony against Charlotte Holmes, the FDLE report into Scoville's sexual misconduct would never see the light of day. There was no putting that genie back in the bottle.

"Buy me a drink and I'll let you tell me about it," she said.

It was nice that she asked, unlike the twenty-somethings who drank his liquor with no intention of showing him their pussies. Scoville poured a vodka on the rocks for each of them. Her name was Amanda, and as Scoville talked, Amanda listened, refilling his vodka several times. The bottle was nearly empty, and he was still talking.

"Damn, I'm sorry," he said. "I must have bored you to tears."

"Not at all," she said.

Scoville reached across the VIP table and snatched the bottle he'd purchased earlier for a couple of college chicks who were clearly a longshot—but, oh, what a threesome it would have been. He poured more vodka for himself and Amanda.

"I actually feel bad for you," she said. "Men don't

know how to act anymore. You can't tell a woman she looks like she lost weight. You can't tell her you like what she did with her hair. You can't pay the most basic compliment without being accused of harassment."

"Exactly!" said Scoville. "You totally get it."

"Hey, old man," said the college chick. "Give us our vodka back."

"Shut up, little girl," said Amanda. "Isn't it past your bedtime?"

The younger woman backed away. Scoville smiled. "I like you."

Amanda smiled back. "Let's go out on the terrace."

Scoville's knee made a popping noise as he pushed up from the couch. Amanda had to help him up. As they stepped into the night air, he felt dizzy. He was definitely feeling the vodka. The good buzz was becoming disorienting. He breathed in the night air and tried to hold himself together until they made it to the rail. He grabbed it tightly to stop the swirl of city lights in the distance.

"You okay?" asked Amanda.

"Yeah, sure. I'm fine." But he wasn't, and he was kicking himself. Amanda was his hottest pickup ever at One80, and he was too drunk to perform.

"I just love the view out here," she said.

It was beautiful, but only if you looked out toward the cityscape in the distance. In the near ground was the busy interstate.

"Did you know that I-4 is the deadliest interstate in America?" he asked.

"Is that so?"

"Annual fatality rate is one-point-two-five per mile."

Scoville had learned that while serving on a transportation task force, but he had no idea why he was repeating it now. A total mood killer. Why not also mention that he'd been standing at this very rail, watching from above, as emergency vehicles sped toward the deadly mass shooting at Pulse Night Club, less than a mile away? He was off his game, but Amanda seemed to find it amusing.

"You're cute," she said, smiling.

"You're gorgeous," he said, breathing out the word with such force that, had he been drinking whiskey instead of vodka, he might have bowled her over with the stench.

"Why don't we get out of this place?" she said.

"What do you have in mind?"

"Someplace quieter. There's a bar at my hotel. Would you walk me there?"

"It would be my pleasure," he said. *Prezzurr.*

She took his arm as they crossed the terrace. The

sliding glass door opened, and the dance music from inside hit him like a jolt of electricity. It had been playing all night, but it was suddenly more than his brain could process. They continued past the dance floor. The flashing lights became a blur. His gaze drifted toward a man and woman dancing near the DJ. Or maybe it was two women. He couldn't tell. It was impossible to focus. His hands felt numb. His knees were weak. A flash of hot and then cold ran from the base of his spine to the top of his head, and he suddenly felt himself falling. He reached for the nearest chair, which happened to be occupied.

"Hey, watch it!" the guy said.

"Sorry, so sorry," said Amanda, apologizing for her new friend.

"I don't know what's wrong with me," Scoville said.

Amanda took him by the arm and led him toward the elevator. The doors opened, she helped him inside, and they rode to the ground floor. Scoville wasn't feeling any better, but he tried hard not to show it.

"How far is your hotel?" he asked.

"Not far," she said.

The elevator doors opened and they exited the building to Church Street. The blast of cool air on the terrace had helped him earlier, but he got no such relief at street level. The whole experience was strange. Vodka didn't normally hit him this way. Maybe it was the beer and tequila-shot chasers at the basketball game, though he'd had only two. Or had it been three? Maybe that was the problem. He'd lost count.

"Should we call a cab?" he asked.

"Don't be silly," she said. "My hotel is right down the street."

They continued toward the overpass. Scoville glanced up at the streetlight, which seemed to have a strange glow around it, like a halo. He blinked hard, fighting off the illusion, and the halo went away. The rumble of cars on the interstate was above them. Graffiti covered the concrete support columns of the overpass. A puddle of fresh urine glistened near the cardboard house of a homeless guy. It was getting harder to walk, and Scoville finally realized they were heading uphill.

"You sure this is the way?"

"Just a little farther," she said.

Scoville kept putting one foot in front of the other, but his mind was losing its grip on his whereabouts. Something must have been in those drinks. It wouldn't have been the first time. Over spring break, a college chick had dissolved a synthetic drug of some sort in his drink just to get a laugh at the creepy old pervert's expense.

"Almost there," said Amanda, and then she stopped,

and his world stopped spinning. The sidewalk had led them up a ramp to an overpass, and the noisy interstate was directly below. A car sped past, traveling much faster than the normal traffic around the arena. Alcohol and drugs fogged his mind, but Scoville knew the area well enough to realize that they were at the interchange south of the arena, where an east-west cross street rose up and over the interstate. And they weren't actually on the sidewalk. The sidewalk was on the other side of the bridge, where a ten-foot chain-link fence kept pedestrians from falling or throwing things onto the interstate. Amanda had led him up the side with no protective fencing.

"Where the heck are—"

The words were still in the air as Amanda lowered her shoulder and drove it into his chest, knocking him backward and slamming his lumbar spine into the railing. Scoville reached for Amanda's hand, her dress, anything he might grab to stop from falling, but he got fistfuls of air. Momentum carried his upper body out over the rail, his arms flailing as he struggled to keep his feet on the sidewalk. His head rolled back so far that he could see the speeding cars and trucks on I-4 below him. He heard himself scream, which sent his mind racing. For a split second, it was as if he were outside his body and— witnessing his own body tumbling through the air.

Then, everything stopped. Amanda had grabbed him by the belt with both hands, and she was standing on his feet to anchor him to the sidewalk. Scoville was bent over backward like a gymnast, draped over the rail like a slice of microwave bacon, unable to do the single sit-up that was required to save his own life. Even in his impaired state, he fully comprehended the danger of the speeding traffic below him. If Amanda let go of his belt and stepped off the tops of his feet, he was a dead man.

"Help me up!" he shouted. Gravity had pulled his shirt toward his chin, exposing a belly that was dragging him down like a stage-curtain sandbag. Even his arms felt heavy, his hands reaching for the interstate below him.

"Please! Pull me up!"

The noise from the interstate was so loud that he could barely hear his own voice. The string of headlights was endless, but his line of sight—albeit inverted—was fixed on the oncoming eighteen-wheeler. It was just a few hundred yards away and closing quickly. Suddenly, Amanda yanked on his belt, jerking him forward in a jackknifed position. The strength of this woman shocked him, but she didn't pull him all the way up— just far enough to make eye contact as she peered down at him from the safe side of the rail.

"You're a lucky man, Senator."

Scoville didn't feel lucky. The blood was rushing to his brain, making him so dizzy that he felt anchored to the sidewalk no more, as if at any moment his feet might whip across the sky above him, as if to bicycle-kick the moon.

"Let me up, please!"

Scoville was too week, too dizzy, and too drunk to save himself. He imagined that he was falling again, directly into the path of oncoming headlights.

"You're lucky you're not worth killing," Amanda said, and with the strength of a trapeze artist, she jerked him forward, up and over the railing to safety. Scoville landed on the sidewalk and rolled onto his side. He was safe, but all the blood that had pooled in his brain was suddenly rushing in the other direction, making the night spin even faster.

"Don't you ever put your hands on Charlotte Holmes again," she said, adding a swift kick to the groin.

Scoville groaned like a wounded animal, but he didn't move. He lay in a heap on the sidewalk at the crest of the bridge, listening to the sound of Amanda's footfalls fade into the night and thanking God he was alive.

Chapter 37

Jack took the early flight from Tallahassee to Miami and was home in time to walk Righley to school. Max walked with them, which put Jack in the middle of a tug-of-war, pulled forward by a hard-charging golden retriever who seemed to think he was lead dog on an Iditarod sled, and pulled back by a five-year-old who wanted her daddy to take her to the beach.

"We don't have to tell Mommy," said Righley.

Jack nearly laughed out loud. Andie had one of those apps on her phone that told her where every member of her family was at every moment of the day. The adventures of Righley versus Mommy, Teenager Edition, were sure to be epic.

"We can't play hooky, honey."

They stopped at the traffic light, and Jack hit the

crosswalk button. It spoke back to them in the mechanical voice of Stephen Hawking and *The Theory of Everything*, even if it was just one word: "Wait."

As commanded, they stood at the curb. Jack made a couple of attempts to cheer Righley up, but she was still pouting about the beach. Dad jokes to the rescue.

"Righley, watch this. Mr. Crosswalk," Jack said, speaking to the pole. "Name a word that rhymes with 'gate.'"

"Wait."

That made her smile. "Cool! Do it again, Daddy!"

It was a one-trick joke, but Jack pulled another one out of the hat. "Mr. Crosswalk: What does Max lose when he goes on a diet?"

"Wait."

"Let me try! Mr. Crosswalk, what's my favorite color?"

"Wait."

"Hey! That wasn't nice!"

There was only so much a dad could do.

Jack got her to school on time, promised to take her to the beach on the weekend, and dropped Max off at the house. Then he drove to Coconut Grove to pick up Theo at Cy's Place. Jack knew better than to interview a potential witness alone, so Theo changed hats again, from bodyguard to investigator.

"Who's the witness?" asked Theo, as he climbed into the passenger seat. "Dr. Perez?"

"Nope," said Jack. "His wife."

The phone calls to the doctor's home number had gone unanswered until Heidi Bristol finally returned Jack's voice-mail message to tell him that her husband didn't live there any longer. The Perez residence was a few miles south of Cy's Place, along the waterfront. Theo fiddled with the radio for a few minutes, found the music he liked, and then was on to another subject.

"Anything more on Scoville?" asked Theo.

A state trooper had found the former Florida legislator drunk and passed out on a bridge, and the story went viral.

"No," said Jack. "Just another disgraced Florida politician."

"I think it was your cross-examination," said Theo. "You made him want to jump, except a guy like Scoville doesn't have the balls to do it."

"Stress-relief balls," said Jack.

The drive to Deering Bay Yacht & Country Club was down Old Cutler Road, a scenic highway that was once a nineteenth-century trail through the woods, stretching from a high-ground enclave on the bay to a fledgling settlement called Coconut Grove. Much of the

hardwood hammock was preserved, despite the influx
of multimillion-dollar estates, high-rise condominiums
with killer views of the Miami skyline, yacht-filled
marinas, and a golf course designed by Arnold Palmer.

The Perez-Bristol estate was on Deering Drive. The
housekeeper greeted Jack and Theo at the front door.
Jack acquainted himself with original works by Jackson
Pollock and Roy Lichtenstein in the wide corridor that
led to a paneled library in the back of the house. Heidi
Bristol was waiting near a set of tall French doors overlooking the golf course. Jack thanked her for taking
time to meet. They sat on the matching tufted leather
couches, facing each other, Jack and Theo on one side
of the cocktail table and Heidi on the other.

"I'm sorry for leaving so many messages," said Jack.
"I had no idea you and Dr. Perez were separated."

"We didn't broadcast it," she said.

"I do appreciate your help," said Jack.

"If you don't mind, I have some questions of my
own."

"Sure. I'll answer as best I can," said Jack.

She folded her arms and leveled a very serious gaze
in Jack's direction. "Mr. Swyteck, I had a loving husband for nine years. It was not without challenges. We
got married when he was in medical school. Trust me,
he was not always the nicest man during his internship

and residency. But we were happy. We had love in our marriage. Then something happened."

"I'm sorry."

Her eyes narrowed, and her gaze became a glare. "Was your client having an affair with my husband?"

The question caught him seriously off guard. "No. Not that I'm aware of."

"I have a right to know," she said firmly. "Alberto and I are separated, but we're still married. Seeing other people was not part of the arrangement."

"I would tell you if I knew," said Jack. "But it's my understanding that Ms. Holmes and your husband hadn't seen each other since college."

"Prior to this meeting at Clyde's on Monday night, you mean?"

"Yes."

"Where the two of them used to go to Make-Out Mondays?"

"Yes, when they were college kids. I don't think that's why they went there this time."

"No, of course not. It's all perfectly innocent that my husband makes a special trip from Miami to Tallahassee, five hundred miles, to see a beautiful woman like Charlotte Holmes. How silly of me. Why would I even be the least bit suspicious?"

"Mrs. Perez—"

"Ms. Bristol."

"Ms. Bristol, I truly believe you're reading too much into this meeting on Monday night. Have you spoken to your husband about this?"

"I would love to. But if you think he's bad about returning your calls, you should see how he ignores mine. And as of"—she checked her watch—"two hours ago, he's in Mexico City."

Jack bristled. "Your husband left the country?"

"Yes."

"How do you know he's in Mexico?"

"His office manager told me. Lourdes is very loyal to *el jefe*, but she can be a pretty good girlfriend to Mrs. Jefe, too."

She looked away, and Jack followed her gaze out the window. Across the fairway, a man nearly as old as Old Cutler Road itself was struggling to get out of a deep sand trap—to get himself out, not his ball.

Her gaze swung back to Jack. "This was a bad idea."

"Excuse me?"

"Meeting with you in hopes of hearing the truth about my husband was a bad idea," she said. "I'm very sorry you took the trouble to come all the way down here."

On her lead, Jack and Theo rose and followed her to the hallway, where they said goodbye. The housekeeper showed them out to the driveway. Across the street, a landscaper armed with a noisy blower was stirring up a blizzard of fallen leaves, sending them into the street, making them someone else's problem.

"What do you think?" Jack asked on the walk to his car.

"I think hell will freeze over before that old man in the sand trap finds his way out. They're gonna have to fucking bury him there."

"No, smart-ass. I was talking about Dr. Perez high-tailing it out of the country."

They got into the car. The doors closed, and Jack started the engine.

"Can you serve a subpoena in Mexico City?" asked Theo.

"Not one that I can enforce overnight," said Jack. "We can just forget about Dr. Perez as our star witness."

"Then here's what I think," said Theo.

Jack backed out of the driveway. "What?"

"Find out what's on that flash drive. Fast."

Chapter 38

G wen Stahl picked up her daughter from an after-school ballet class at the Miami Conservatory and drove straight home.

Gwen counted four photojournalists outside the front gate to her driveway. It was already dark, so how many more were hiding in the bushes she didn't know. All were looking for "the shot"—a telling look of anger or disgust between husband and wife—to prove that the kiss seen 'round the world had been a sham. The photographers watched her car pass, openly disappointed to see that it was just Gwen and her daughter inside.

The garage door opened automatically, and Gwen drove in faster than she should have, stopping just a few inches from the back wall. Rachel grabbed her book bag and jumped out of the car.

"I'll check the mail!" she shouted, and ran inside through the side door to the mud room. The mail was on the granite countertop, where the housekeeper always put it before leaving at four o'clock. Rachel was kneeling on a barstool, rummaging through the stack as Gwen entered the kitchen.

"Anything interesting?" asked Gwen.

"Nothing," said Rachel, and then she went through the stack again.

Rachel's first task after returning to Florida had been to send Nanny a letter in Colombia. Gwen had watched the same scene unfold every day since: Rachel running into the kitchen to check for a reply, only to find disappointment.

"International mail can be very slow," said Gwen, not knowing what else to say. "Do you have any homework, sweetie?"

"Just math."

Ironically, her school used the Singapore math curriculum. It was the one cool thing about their two-month hideaway on the other side of the world: Rachel was the only kid in her class to have learned Singapore math in Singapore, if only for a few weeks.

"Why don't you get your homework out of the way while I make dinner?"

THE BIG LIE · 335

"Okay." Rachel slung her book bag over her shoulder and climbed down from the barstool.

"Oh, and water the plants in the hallway, too, sweetie."

Rachel groaned the way any kid would about household chores. "Yes, master," she said, as she left the kitchen.

Gwen went to the refrigerator for a couple of chicken breasts. She was rinsing them off in the sink when her husband entered the room. "I didn't know you were home," she said.

He didn't answer, and then she noticed the cordless earbuds in each ear. His phone, as usual, was in his hand. He said something, speaking not to her but to whoever was on the line, as he grabbed a can of diet soda from the refrigerator. Gwen washed her hands and started chopping carrots. Evan ended his call. He was standing at the counter, drinking his soda.

"Will you be staying for dinner? I can grill another chicken breast."

The question snagged him from somewhere deep in his thoughts. "Uh, no. I have—things."

Evan checked his messages on his phone. Gwen kept chopping. Like old times.

She put down the knife. "I stopped by the hospital today to see about transitioning back to work."

Evan was still staring at his phone. "That's nice."

"Of course, I didn't make any promises. I told administration there's still a chance we could be moving to Washington."

Evan was typing furiously with his thumbs.

Gwen selected a tomato from the colander and started slicing. "The good news is that the behavioral health unit desperately needs help. Two clinical psychiatrists have quit since I started my leave of absence for the campaign. The director said I can start whenever the Electoral College issue sorts itself out."

No response from Evan.

Gwen put the tomato wedges in a salad bowl with the romaine. "I spent the rest of the afternoon with a bipolar ex-Marine who looks like a young Bradley Cooper. He was in his manic phase, so the sex was unbelievable."

Still no reaction.

Gwen seasoned the chicken breasts with a little salt and pepper. "I may go back again tomorrow. Do you have any condoms I can borrow?"

Evan looked up from his phone. "Huh?"

"Nothing," she said.

Rachel entered the room. "Mommy, what's this?"

Gwen turned. Rachel was standing on the other side of the kitchen counter. In one hand was the sprinkler she used to water the plants. In the other, squeezed between her thumb and forefinger, was something about the size of a thimble. It appeared to be made of brass.

"Let me see," said Gwen.

Rachel brought it to her. Evan turned his attention back to his e-mails as Gwen took a closer look. It was a spent ammunition casing. Just the casing. No bullet.

"Where'd you get this?" Gwen asked.

"I found it."

"Where?"

"In the planter outside my bedroom. Underneath the bromeliads."

"I don't know what that is, sweetheart. Evan?"

He looked up from his smartphone. "Hmm?"

Gwen stepped out from behind the sink and handed the brass casing to her husband. "What do you make of this?"

Chapter 39

Jack was back in court Thursday morning.

The continuation of Charlotte's hearing was still a civil proceeding, not a criminal trial, and the issue before Judge Martin hadn't changed: Was Charlotte Holmes "fit" to serve as a member of the Electoral College? But the case was no longer about Tallahassee's unofficial pastime, the alleged trading of sex for votes. A man was dead. His widow was in the courtroom, seated on the other side of the rail, directly behind the attorney general and her team of government lawyers. At the table beside Jack was an "unfaithful elector," now an accused killer. Although Charlotte's liberty was not yet at risk, the atmosphere was no less intense, as General Barrow wrapped up the testimony of witness number one, an FDLE ballistics expert.

"Sir, based on your examination, were you able to determine to a reasonable degree of scientific certainty whether or not the bullet removed from the victim's chest was fired from the pistol registered to one Charlotte Holmes?"

"Yes. It was fired from that gun."

No one disputed that it was Charlotte's gun, or that she'd pulled the trigger. But courtroom was theater, and in a case as politicized as this one, the attorney general needed an "Aha!" moment from each witness to feed the maw of social media, even if the drama wasn't real. With the precision timing of a Broadway choreographer, Barrow would pause after the well-rehearsed answer, as if waiting for the courtroom to reverberate with the *chong-chong* from *Law & Order*, the unmistakable two-note beat that was somewhere between the slamming of a jailhouse door and the banging of a wrench on a cast-iron pipe.

The Leon County medical examiner was next.

"Dr. Nelson, have you determined a cause of death?"

"Yes. A single gunshot wound to the chest, with perforation of the heart and lungs."

Chong-chong.

"Have you determined the manner of death?"

"Objection," said Jack, rising.

The judge looked confused. Or annoyed. Maybe both. "What's wrong with that question, Mr. Swyteck?"

In a shooting case, a medical examiner had only three choices when it came to the manner of death: homicide, suicide, or accident. Jack's only real "objection" was President MacLeod's inevitable tweet to five million followers that "Charlotte Holmes is 'guilty of homicide,' so said the medical examiner."

"It's important to point out that this is a case of justifiable homicide," said Jack. "As the evidence will show, Ms. Holmes is immune from prosecution under Florida's stand-your-ground statute."

The judge scowled. "It's also important to point out that when lawyers object in my courtroom, they'd better have a legally valid objection. Overruled. The witness may answer."

Dr. Nelson leaned forward to speak into the gooseneck microphone. "The manner of death was homicide."

Chong-chong.

Barrow used the final witness of the morning—the detective in charge of the crime scene—to drive home the point that the victim was unarmed. Theoretically, it didn't matter if Mr. Meyer had a weapon or not, as long as Charlotte thought he was going for a gun. But Judge Martin was only human, and the shooting of an unarmed man didn't sit well with anyone. Jack had to take some of the sting out of the detective's testimony that police found no gun on the victim or at the scene. Cross-examination was in order. Jack started with a photograph from the security camera outside Clyde's, which the attorney general had already put into evidence.

"Detective, this first image shows a line of people waiting outside the club. Can you confirm that it was taken before the shooting?"

"Yes," he said, and then he checked the time stamp in the corner. "Less than a minute before."

"You testified earlier that there were fifty-one people in this photograph, correct?"

"Yes. Not all identifiable, but around that number."

Jack showed him the next exhibit. Rather than continuous video, the security camera outside Clyde's was programmed to record a new fixed image every sixty seconds. "Look at this next image," said Jack. "Can you tell me what this is?"

"That's the same camera view outside the club, but a couple minutes later." The detective checked the time stamp. "Exactly two minutes later."

"How many people are in this photo?"

"Hard to say."

"It's hard to say because the crowd has scattered, correct?"

"Yes."

"It's pandemonium. People are running in every direction. Some have been knocked to the ground, right?"

"Yes."

"Outdoor tables and chairs are overturned on the sidewalk?"

"Yes."

"By the time the police arrived, all of these bystanders were gone. Is that right?"

"Yes."

"Did you follow up with any witness interviews?"

"Yes. We worked through local television and social media to ask anyone who had any information about the shooting to contact us for an interview."

"How many people had information and contacted the police?"

"Twelve."

"How many people had information and did not come forward?"

"Objection," said Barrow.

"Overruled," said the judge. "It's kind of a smart-alecky question, but Mr. Swyteck is entitled to make his points on cross-examination. The witness can answer, if he knows."

The detective shrugged. "There were at least three dozen other people in the photograph. How many of them had information, I don't know. But there was no reason for anyone not to contact us, if he or she had information."

"No reason?" said Jack. "Let's explore that. How many were afraid to come forward because they were under-age and didn't want the police to take their fake ID?"

"Objection."

"Overruled again. Answer if you know, Detective."

"I have no idea," he said.

"How many chose not to come forward because they didn't want a steady boyfriend or girlfriend to find out they went to Make-Out Monday with someone else?"

The detective waited for the attorney general to object, but she let it go. "I don't know," he said.

"How many had information and just didn't want to get involved?"

"I don't know."

Jack referred again to the post-shooting security photo. "Is that a storm drain at the curb outside Clyde's, Detective?"

He checked. "It looks like one."

"Did any of the fifty-plus people caught in this stampede accidentally kick a handgun into the storm drain?"

"I doubt it."

"Did you look in the storm drain?"

"No."

"Prior to the shooting, did any of these bystanders hear Mr. Meyer call Dr. Perez a 'wetback'?"

"In the case of the twelve witnesses we interviewed, none of them mentioned it."

"And with respect to the three dozen or more you didn't interview, the question was never asked. Correct?"

"Obviously."

"Prior to the shooting, did any of these bystanders hear Mr. Meyer say, quote, 'I got fire in my pocket'?"

Barrow jumped to her feet. "Judge, I move to strike this whole line of questioning. There is no evidence that Mr. Meyer uttered any racist slurs, or that he said anything about what was in his pocket."

The judge swung his gaze toward Jack. "Mr. Swyteck, do you intend to call a witness who can fill in that blank?"

Jack didn't answer. He meant no disrespect to the court, but something in the photograph had caught his eye—something he hadn't noticed earlier.

"Mr. Swyteck?" the judge pressed. "Do you have a witness who will testify that Mr. Meyer said, 'I got fire in my pocket'?"

Jack was still transfixed by his discovery in the photograph.

"Counsel?" said the judge, his tone sharpening.

Jack looked up from the photograph. "Sorry, Your Honor. I believe Dr. Perez will testify to that effect. Unfortunately, he's out of the country, so I'm not sure I can get him here in time."

"That's a problem," said the judge. "I can certainly understand why someone facing criminal charges would not want to testify on a rush-rush basis in a civil proceeding, before she's even had a chance to assess the evidence against her. It is certainly within Ms. Holmes's constitutional rights to remain silent. But unless someone testifies about this alleged altercation between Dr. Perez and Mr. Meyer that led to the shooting, it's not evidence in this hearing. Understood?"

"Understood," said Jack. He turned away from the witness and laid the photograph on the table. It was grainy, like most security-camera images, but Jack was pretty sure he was right: in the corner of the frozen-in-time hysteria outside of Clyde's, an island of calm in the swirl of panic, stood someone wearing a baseball cap and a camouflage jacket—like the "someone" Charlotte had seen among the demonstrators outside her house, across the street from Madeline Chisel's office, and on the sidewalk in front of Cy's Place—watching her.

"Do you have any further questions for this witness?" the judge asked.

Jack lifted his gaze from the photograph. "Nothing at this time, Your Honor."

"General Barrow, it's almost noon."

"Your Honor, there is just one piece of evidence I'd like to offer before the lunch break. Could I have just five minutes, please?"

The judge chuckled. "Five minutes? No offense, but it takes most lawyers longer than that just to sneeze."

She smiled, then turned serous. "This I can guarantee, Judge. At this time, the state of Florida offers the recording of the defendant's phone call to nine-one-one immediately after the shooting. It's two minutes and eleven seconds in length."

"Any objection?" asked the judge. "And this time, Mr. Swyteck, I mean a valid objection recognized under the law."

"No objection," said Jack.

"Very well," said the judge. "Let's hear it."

A techie on the attorney general's trial team queued up the audio recording and hit the PLAY button. The packed courtroom sat wrapped in silence. The speakers hissed from the ceiling above, as if waking from a slumber. After an audible beep, the dispatcher's voice followed.

"Nine-one-one," she said in a pleasant southern accent. "What is your emergency?"

The next voice was Charlotte's, and it was immediately clear why the attorney general was so eager to get her words into evidence.

"I shot a man!" said Charlotte, her recorded voice quaking. "I think he's dead."

Chapter 40

Jack didn't eat lunch. He was on a mission.

Dr. Perez's lawyer had managed to avoid him for days—until Jack put the world's greatest legal assistant on the case. Bonnie managed Jack's office like a pro, and it didn't hurt that she also had the tracking skills of a bounty hunter. Bonnie worked her contacts all morning and texted Jack the coordinates for the ambush: "Subject leaving his office at 11:55 for lunch at Wolfie's." Calling him "subject" was a bit much, but Jack had no reason to question the intelligence. He texted back a "thanks" emoji and made a quick plan with his client on their way out of the courtroom.

"Take the media down the elevator with you. I'm ducking out the back."

Charlotte played the Pied Piper, a dozen reporters in tow, and Jack made a clean getaway to the alley behind the courthouse. He had three minutes to get to College Avenue. No time to waste.

Harland Sands was one of nine hundred or so lawyers at "Kessler," a national law firm that formerly bore the name of Mr. Kessler and eight of his long-dead partners. It was a trendy mega-firm marketing strategy that didn't apply to the likes of Jack Swyteck, P.A.—the dropping of all but one surname from the masthead to become a one-word brand, the Big Law equivalent of Heinz or Bacardi. Some were reminded of the late George Carlin's comic routine about the paranoid sensation of walking through Sears and suddenly wondering, "Whoa, what ever happened to Roebuck?" Except that the more pertinent question had become, "Whoa, what ever happened to Sears?"

Kessler occupied the penthouse in Highpoint Center, a skyscraper by Tallahassee standards, even if its fifteen stories were well short of the Capitol Tower. As Jack entered the ground-floor lobby, his cell phone chimed with an update from Bonnie: "Getting in elevator now." Obviously her source was a Kessler insider.

Damn, she's good.

Jack watched and waited, as the blinking elevator

lights charted the "subject's" descent from the penthouse.

Jack was still assessing the damage done in Judge Martin's courtroom. The 911 recording had been a two-edged sword. Charlotte's admission was chilling. Had the call ended there, Jack would have been forced to put his own client on the witness stand to explain why she pulled the trigger. But the recording went on for another two minutes, and in between explaining where she was and answering the dispatcher's questions, Charlotte had managed to say the right thing: "He pulled a gun, so I shot him." Those eight words were now the heart of the case. They were either the honest-to-God truth, spoken by a woman who'd actually thought her life was in danger, or an after-the-fact story, made up by a reckless and trigger-happy shooter who'd killed an unarmed man without legal justification.

It was more important than ever that Jack speak to Dr. Perez's lawyer.

The elevator doors opened. Jack recognized Sands from the firm Web site, even if his online photo was well overdue for an update. He introduced himself, but Sands kept walking.

"I'm afraid I don't have time to talk."

Jack went with him, step for step. "I can walk and talk at the same time. How about you?"

Sands continued across the lobby and out the glass doors. Jack was right at his side.

"You didn't return my calls," said Jack. "I need your client to testify at the hearing."

"Dr. Perez is in Mexico."

"I'm sure Judge Martin will let us videoconference."

They stopped at the crosswalk. The afternoon sun glistened from the windshields of passing cars, an assault to the eyes. Sands put on his sunglasses. "My client is busy."

"Your client picked a fight with a man who said he had fire in his pocket. Charlotte Holmes had every reason to believe it was a life-or-death situation. That's all I need Dr. Perez to say."

The traffic light cycled to green. "He's very busy," said Sands, and he stepped down from the curb. Jack stayed with him as they crossed the street.

"Dr. Perez is my star witness."

"Your client is your star witness."

"She's charged with second-degree murder. It would be malpractice for me to put her on the stand in a civil hearing like this. You know that as well as I do."

Sands stopped. They were standing outside Wolfie's restaurant. "I can't help you, Mr. Swyteck. I'm sorry."

"Do me one favor," said Jack. "Take off your sunglasses."

Sands did, and Jack looked him straight in the eye: "Did General Barrow tell your client to leave the country until the hearing is over?"

Sands didn't blink. "No. I did." He tucked his sunglasses into his coat pocket. "Good luck to you."

A delivery truck pulled away from the curb, leaving Jack in a cloud of diesel fumes as Dr. Perez's lawyer turned and disappeared into the restaurant.

Alone in her hotel room was no place for Charlotte. The words that had reverberated throughout the courtroom echoed in her head. Jack had told her the case was about eight words, but for her it was a different eight. *I shot a man! I think he's dead.*

Jack had shown no reaction to her frantic 911 call. Nor had Judge Martin. The stenographer's fingers moved with no particular significance; Charlotte might as well have said, "I had coffee and a bagel for breakfast." The angst was inside her—driven home by the sniffle she'd heard from the other side of the courtroom, on the public-seating side of the rail, from Mrs. Meyer. A judge or jury might someday determine that the homicide was "justifiable," that her split-second decision to use deadly force had been "reasonable under the circumstances." That didn't mean Mr. Meyer deserved to die—at least not from his widow's perspective.

Solitary confinement in a hotel room triggered such thoughts. Charlotte hadn't touched the club sandwich from room service. She was staring at the wall, drowning in guilt, when the phone rang. She probably should have ignored it, but it felt like a reprieve. It was the front desk.

"Sorry to bother you, Ms. Holmes, but you have a visitor. She says it's extremely urgent that she speak to you."

"Who is it?"

"Her name is Heidi Bristol."

Charlotte immediately suspected a ruse by a reporter, someone using the name of Alberto's estranged wife to gain access to her. "Can you check her driver's license, please?"

Charlotte could hear the muffled exchange at the front desk. A moment later, the attendant was back on the line. "It is Heidi Bristol. Coral Gables, Florida."

There was more background noise, but Charlotte couldn't make it out.

"I'm sorry, Ms. Holmes," said the attendant. "Would you excuse me for just one second?"

Charlotte waited, getting more uncomfortable by the moment. Jack had told her about his meeting with Alberto's wife, and that she suspected "another woman."

The attendant's voice was back on the line. "Ms. Bristol wants you to meet her out by the swimming pool. She says she dares you."

Charlotte gripped the phone a little tighter. Apart from Jack, she'd told no one about Alberto's text—the "dare" that had lured her to the meeting at Clyde's. Not every fiber in her body was saying "meet this woman," but she found herself saying it anyway.

"Thank you," said Charlotte. "Tell Ms. Bristol that I will be there in five minutes."

Chapter 41

"The state of Florida rests its case," said the attorney general.

That after-lunch announcement in open court left many in the gallery scratching their heads, but Jack wasn't surprised. The government had established the essential elements of homicide in the second degree, especially in the context of a "fitness" hearing, where the criminal standard of proof—"beyond a reasonable doubt"—simply didn't apply. To prove that the shooting was justifiable, Jack would need more than a 911 recording with Charlotte's self-serving statement that "he had a gun." And even if Jack could prove up a defense, Barrow still had the right to rebuttal.

"Mr. Swyteck, you may call your first witness," said the judge.

Jack could feel the anticipation in the air. Everyone in the courtroom—most of all the attorney general—wanted to know if Jack would put Charlotte on the stand. Charlotte had been smart enough to invite her lawyer to the poolside meeting, however, making Jack's selection of witness number one a no-brainer.

"The defense calls Heidi Bristol," said Jack.

The doors opened in the rear of the courtroom, and there was head scratching anew in public seating, as the unexpected witness walked down the center aisle, stopped to swear the oath, and took a seat facing Jack. Stating one's name for the record was usually a formality, but this witness's use of her maiden name with no mention of "Perez" was noteworthy.

"Good morning, Ms. Bristol," said Jack.

"It's actually the afternoon."

It was a common affliction among trial lawyers, not knowing if it was day or night. Jack hoped this inauspicious start wasn't a sign of bad things to come. "You are married to Dr. Alberto Perez, correct?"

"Yes."

"How long have you been married?"

"Nine years. We've been separated the last couple of months."

"Without delving too deeply into personal details, why did you and your husband separate?"

"He told me there was someone else."

"Do you know who the 'someone else' is?"

"No. He didn't tell me."

"Did you do anything to find out?"

She took a breath. They had gone over this beforehand, but she wasn't the first witness to find the act of testifying in open court more daunting than expected. "I hired a private investigator," she said.

"When did you hire a PI?"

"Not right away. Frankly, I was numb for a while. Alberto moved out. I didn't do anything but get up in the morning and go through the motions. Then I found out he was taking a trip to Tallahassee. That's where he went to college. Call it a woman's intuition, but I got suspicious. Sure enough, I found out he was meeting with an old friend from school. A woman."

"Who was that old friend?"

"I didn't get the name beforehand. But as it turns out, it was Charlotte Holmes."

Jack should have anticipated the hateful glares that suddenly came from all corners of the courtroom and locked onto his client like a scarlet letter.

"What did you do then?"

"That's when I hired the investigator."

"Why?"

"That's a good question. Alberto had already told

me there was someone else. I guess I just needed to know if she was the one—this old friend from college."

"What did you find out?"

"It wasn't her."

"Your husband was not having an affair with Charlotte Holmes?"

"No. It was clear that this meeting at Clyde's was the first time they'd seen each other since college."

The hateful glares from the gallery changed to ones of puzzlement.

"Exactly how did that become clear to you, Ms. Bristol?"

"I heard their conversation."

"Were you seated near them at Clyde's?"

"No."

"Were you in Tallahassee?"

"No. I was in Coral Gables."

"Then how did you hear the conversation between your husband and Ms. Holmes?"

"I listened to a recording."

"Whoa!" said Barrow, rising.

"Is that an objection," the judge asked.

"You bet it is, Your Honor. May we have a sidebar? We've heard nothing about a recording until this very moment. This needs to be addressed outside the presence of the witness."

The judge agreed but went one better than a sidebar. "In my chambers."

The lawyers and the stenographer followed him out of the courtroom. The door closed with a thud, silencing the buzz of speculation that coursed through the gallery. The judge took a seat behind his desk. The lawyers remained standing. He addressed Jack first.

"Is this the way things are done in Miami, Mr. Swyteck? Trial by ambush?"

The dreaded slimy-lawyer syndrome. Any Miami lawyer who stepped out of Miami-Dade County was a suspected carrier. Jack had avoided it so far, having earned Judge Martin's praise for the "professional manner" in which he'd handled the confidential FDLE report on Senator Scoville. This audio recording required some explanation.

"Judge, our smartphones have microphones. We leave them on desks and tabletops wherever we go. It's a simple technological feat for a private investigator to control that microphone remotely and eavesdrop on our conversations."

Judge Martin was far from a techie, but he seemed intrigued. "So you're saying that Dr. Perez's phone picked up his entire conversation with Ms. Holmes while they were sitting outside Clyde's on the night of the shooting?"

"Not just his conversation with Ms. Holmes," said Jack. "Also his verbal altercation with Mr. Meyer. And the shooting."

"Are you asking me to allow Ms. Bristol to testify as to what she heard through this eavesdropping device?"

The attorney general jumped in. "I object on multiple grounds. Hearsay, reliability, to name a couple."

"We're not relying on Ms. Bristol's memory to reconstruct the events," said Jack. "We want the court to listen to the same recording she heard—the one made by her investigator."

"I object to that even more," said Barrow.

"You haven't even heard it," said Jack.

"Talk to me, not to each other," the judge told the lawyers. "Mr. Swyteck, how do we know this tape is authentic?"

"Ms. Bristol hired one of the top private investigators in Miami. Thirty years with the FBI. He knows how to make a recording. It's authentic."

"I still object," said Barrow. "I want to cross-examine this so-called recording expert."

The judge considered it. "Ms. Barrow makes a reasonable request. It's an important piece of evidence. Mr. Swyteck, how soon can you have this investigator in my courtroom?"

"He's in Miami. I can get him on an early-evening flight."

"I've done evening sessions before in nonjury cases. How does eight p.m. sound?"

"Good for me," said Jack.

The attorney general didn't answer. It was clear that this audio recording was the last thing she wanted.

"Ms. Barrow?" the judge prodded. "Eight p.m. is good?"

"Sure," she said. "I'll be ready."

Chapter 42

"Harder!" the president shouted into his desktop speakerphone. "When they hit us, we hit back twice as hard, Paulette!"

MacLeod was behind closed doors in the Oval Office, his senior strategist seated on the other side of the oak desk. Florida allowed television cameras in state court, and the president hadn't missed a minute of the Charlotte Holmes fitness hearing. He'd even controlled his urge to micromanage the attorney general's legal strategy—until the battle over Heidi Bristol's audio recording came up.

"We're doing our best," said Barrow.

MacLeod rolled his eyes, then glanced across his desk. "Oscar, tell the attorney general how I feel about people who 'do their best.'"

"They're losers," Teague said, but without sufficient emphasis.

"Losers!" shouted MacLeod, as he leaned into the speakerphone and used his thumb and index finger to make an "L" on his forehead, as if the attorney general could see it. "They're big . . . fat . . . losers!"

"Yes, sir," she said.

"And spice things up a little, will you? Your ratings are terrible. Below terrible. This is worse than the remake of *Knight Rider*, for Pete's sake."

"I'm not sure I understand the comparison, sir."

"You're right. I'm not being fair to the producers of *Knight Rider*. Nobody should have expected a remake to out-Hasselhoff the one and only David Hasselhoff. Let's put all comparisons aside: you suck! That's what I'm saying. Your show sucks!"

"But . . . this isn't a TV show."

"It's on TV, Paulette! Make it good TV."

"Yes, sir."

"And no more bad news out of Florida. I've heard enough."

"Yes, Mr. Pres—"

MacLeod cut her off before she could finish, ending the call with the push of a button. He sat back in his leather chair and groaned at the ceiling in his exasperation. Then he jackknifed into action, frantically rummaging through the mess of papers on his desktop.

"Where the hell is my phone?" he muttered.

Teague watched with trepidation. "You're not going to tweet, are you, sir?"

MacLeod shoved a stack of unread memos aside, knocking a few loose pages to the floor. Still no sight of his cell phone. "Somebody needs to salvage this shit show."

"You mean the hearing, sir? You want to tweet about the hearing in the middle of the hearing?"

The president paused long enough to fire off his signature look of contempt, which was usually reserved for members of the media. "You make it sound like a bad thing," he said, then continued searching through the mess. Beneath a foot-tall stack of magazine clippings—mostly articles about himself—he struck pay dirt.

"Ah, here it is," he said, but Teague grabbed it before he could.

MacLeod laid the magazine clippings aside and reached across the desktop. "Give it."

Teague tightened his grip on the cell. "No, sir."

The president cocked his head, not quite comprehending. "Excuse me?"

"You shouldn't tweet about the hearing until it's over."

"I'll tweet whenever I damn well want to tweet. Now, give me my phone."

Teague swallowed the lump in his throat. "No."

"Don't make me come over there and get it, Oscar."

The senior advisor didn't budge, except to lick his suddenly dry lips.

"You have five seconds to hand it over."

"I'm sorry, Mr. President. But this is for your own good."

"Five, four, three—"

Teague launched from his chair, about to make a run for it. MacLeod was even quicker, propelling himself out of his chair and around his desk and heading off his senior advisor before he could get a jump toward the exit. Teague reversed direction and raced around the other side of the desk, MacLeod in hot pursuit.

Then the president stopped.

Teague stopped.

They were at a standoff, breathing heavily but otherwise frozen in their tracks, having traded sides of the massive desk. Teague faked right, but the president didn't bite. The two men stared each other down. Teague clutched the smartphone as if it were the nuclear football. The president leaned forward, resting his fists on the desktop, his eyes narrowing as he spoke in a low, threatening voice.

"Do I need to call for Secret Service, Oscar?"

Teague slowly raised his arm, holding the smart-phone high above his head. "I'll smash it on the floor."

"You wouldn't dare."

"I will. I swear I will."

"I'm warning you, Oscar. All I have to do is shout out the safety word. You'll be dead where you stand before that cell phone hits the floor."

Teague stared back, silent but determined.

"Now, give me my phone," said MacLeod.

Teague didn't make a move, but the president could see him cracking. Teague was one of those people who always "did the best he could." A loser.

Teague let go of the phone. The president watched in horror as it dropped like a stone, hitting the corner of the desk with a crack before falling another three feet to the floor. MacLeod lunged to save it, but he was a split second too late. He gathered it up from the floor quickly, lovingly, as if a baby bird had fallen from its nest.

"You cracked the glass," he said with anger.

"I don't care."

"You'd better care."

"I don't. Because I quit." Teague said it without emotion; it was simply an assertion of fact.

"You can't quit."

"Yes, I can." He crossed the room with purpose, opened the door, and then stopped. "I quit," he said, making it official. Then he left the Oval Office.

The president hurried after him, but not to bring him back. Teague blew past several staffers as he continued down the hallway, and it was important for the president to set the record straight.

"That's right, go!" he shouted, loud enough for the entire West Wing to hear. "And in case you didn't hear me the first time, here it is again: You're fired!"

MacLeod turned and went back into the Oval Office, slamming the door behind him.

Chapter 43

Jack couldn't wait for Andie to retire from the FBI.

When Heidi Bristol's investigator said a thousand dollars, Jack thought he meant per day. It was actually a thousand dollars per hour, which was his standard expert witness fee for time spent testifying in court. By Jack's calculation, retired special agent Eugene Carson earned more in twenty minutes than active special agent Andie Henning took home for an honest day's work.

Carson's flight landed in Tallahassee around seven. Jack picked him up at the airport, and they did most of their prepping in the car ride to the courthouse. The hearing started promptly at 8:00 p.m. The courtroom was far less than full, the media apparently having gotten wind of the narrow and technical focus of the special evening session. In a rare display of humor, General Barrow made a wisecrack about the "lowest ratings of any show in the primetime slot." Judge Martin laughed; Jack did, too. It was the unwritten rule of courtroom humor: nothing was funny until the judge thought it was funny.

"Counsel, it's already late, and we all want to get home," said Judge Martin. "So let me expedite matters. I've read the witness's c.v. in detail. With over two decades in the tech unit of the FBI's Miami field office, Mr. Carson certainly qualifies as an expert in the area of electronic surveillance. You can skip the background questions, Mr. Swyteck, and get right to the heart of the matter."

Jack thanked him, choosing not to mention that, by shaving twenty minutes off Carson's testimony, the judge had just saved Jack enough money to buy everyone a steak dinner.

"Mr. Carson, when did Ms. Bristol hire you as her investigator?"

"Sometime before her husband—Dr. Perez—left town for what was supposed to be a business trip to Tallahassee."

From there, Jack took the witness step-by-step through the technological side of electronic surveillance. Over the next forty minutes, Carson demonstrated his expertise and, Jack had to admit, earned his pay. Carson was no egghead. He used plain English to help the judge grasp that it was one thing to eavesdrop on a conversation between two people on their telephones; it was quite another thing entirely to activate the microphone on a cell phone that was just resting on a table, apparently unused, and listen remotely to everything said between two people who thought they were in a private, face-to-face conversation.

Judge Martin was openly fascinated. "I saw this on TV and thought it was fake."

"No, sir," said the witness. "As long as the targeted cell phone has battery life, I can use the microphone to pick up everything said by anyone within range. In the case of this meeting outside Clyde's, we were able to pick up and record the conversation between Ms. Holmes and Dr. Perez, as well as the entire shouting match between Dr. Perez and the decedent, Mr. Meyer."

"I will listen to the recording with interest," the judge said. "Ms. Barrow, does the state of Florida have any cross-examination?"

"No," said Barrow, as she rose from her seat. "But we do have a motion to exclude this evidence in its entirety."

"On what basis?" the judge asked.

"This kind of electronic eavesdropping is illegal under Florida law."

"There's a quick answer to that," said Jack. "The law relied on by the attorney general doesn't apply here."

"That's wrong," said Barrow. "Just because you're married to a man doesn't mean you can hijack the microphone on his cell phone to spy on him."

"There's the rub," said Jack. "Dr. Perez didn't own this cell phone."

"Excuse me?" said Barrow.

"As I'm sure the court is aware, a lot of doctors choose to practice medicine without medical malpractice insurance. Dr. Perez is one of them. Like many of his colleagues, he protects his assets by putting virtually everything in the name of his wife. House, cars, boat, vacation home—even his cell. The phone Dr. Perez took to his meeting with Ms. Holmes technically belongs to his wife. Ms. Bristol can do whatever she wants with it."

Carson looked up at the judge from the witness chair. "I nail a lot of doctors this way."

The attorney general suddenly seemed smaller, as if deflating on the spot.

"I'll have a decision in the morning," said the judge. "See y'all at nine a.m."

Thursday night at Clyde's meant NFL football on the big-screen, draft beer on special, and tons of college students who wouldn't make it to their Friday-morning classes. Amanda was okay with beer and football, but classes at the university were a distant memory. She wasn't the oldest person in the bar, but she was in the over-thirty minority. She found an open barstool, ordered a draft, and told the bartender to let Andrew know that "Amanda says hey." Andrew was the manager, and Amanda was just a sophomore at FSU when he'd hired her to wait tables. She had little doubt that he was the oldest person in the bar.

"I'll tell him," said the bartender.

Amanda checked out the game on the big-screen while waiting. The team in black and silver was getting its butt kicked by the Tampa Bay Buccaneers. Amanda wondered if Scoville was at the Bucs' stadium. She guessed not. Probably still too scared to leave his apartment. He'd deserved what he'd gotten, and more. Talk about justifiable homicide.

The bartender set up her draft in a frosted glass. "This one's on Andrew. He'll be right out."

She smiled. "Thanks."

Clyde's hadn't changed much since her college days. Same exposed brick, same high tables, and same neon

lights. The table by the window was all too familiar.
Amanda had worked it three nights a week for almost
two years. So many nights. Thousands of customers.
They all seemed to run together—all but one. It had
been a Monday night. Make-Out Monday. Employees
weren't allowed to take part, but sometimes customers
got carried away.

Hi, I'm Charlotte. See that guy over there?

Sorry, girlfriend. I'm not going to kiss him.

Uhm, no. He dared me to kiss you.

"Manny!" said Andrew, all smiles as he reached over
the bar to give her a hug. Amanda had been his third
hire of the semester with the same name, so at Clyde's
she was always "Manny."

She hugged him back, and they told each other how
little they'd changed. The usual banter among old
friends followed, and before the small talk turned to
minutiae, Amanda segued to the point of her visit.

"I was so sorry to hear about the shooting."

"Nutty world, right?"

"I knew that girl in college. Charlotte Holmes."

"Funny, I've seen her here for drinks every now and
then with the business crowd. But I don't remember
her as a student."

"She came a few times. Then she stopped." Amanda
left it at that. But there was so much more.

"Her lawyer actually came by to interview me this afternoon."

Amanda already knew. Jack's sleuthing was the reason for her visit. "What did he want?"

"He thinks there's a missing gun."

Amanda drank her beer. "A missing gun?"

"The cops say Charlotte Holmes shot an unarmed man. Her lawyer thinks they just never found the gun."

"What does he want from you?"

"A name. Somebody who might have seen a weapon."

"If the guy had a gun, what does her lawyer think happened to it?"

"He thinks somebody picked it up in all the chaos. Why someone would do that, I have no idea."

"Huh," she said, keeping her thought to herself: maybe someone thought they were picking up Charlotte's gun—and doing her a favor.

"You never know," said Amanda, watching the beer bubbles rise in her glass. "Maybe it'll turn up."

Chapter 44

First thing Friday morning, Judge Martin announced his decision in chambers. Only the lawyers were present.

"I find the recording of the conversation and events in question to be both accurate and sufficiently reliable to be admissible as evidence. Mr. Swyteck, you may play it in the courtroom."

It was music to Jack's ears. Without having to put his client on the witness stand, the entire incident would play out in open court, from the "wetback" slur that had provoked Dr. Perez to the threatening words, "I got fire in my pocket." Jack thanked the judge and rose quickly, hoping to head off some other objection from the attorney general, but Barrow was not one to stop punching just because the proverbial bell had rung and the round was over.

"The state of Florida objects, Your Honor."

"I know you do," said the judge. "That's why the court was gracious enough to hold an after-hours hearing late last night."

"And we thank you for that, Judge. But just because the recording is accurate and reliable doesn't mean it's relevant."

The judge smiled, but it was a smile of amusement, not enjoyment. "Seriously, General? In a hearing to determine whether Ms. Holmes was justified in shooting Mr. Meyer, it's your position that the recording of events that immediately preceded the shooting is not relevant?"

"Not exactly," said Barrow. "The recording is several minutes in length. It's our position that most of the recording is irrelevant."

Jack spoke up. "Your Honor, clearly the attorney general would like to reduce the evidence in this case to two facts: Mr. Meyer was unarmed, and my client shot him. As this recording proves, there's much more to it."

"Not as much as Mr. Swyteck thinks," said Barrow. "Not under Florida's stand-your-ground statute."

"Exactly what are you getting at, Counselor?"

"We are lucky to have available to us one of the leading experts on stand your ground, former Orange County state attorney Robert Speer. As a prosecutor, Mr. Speer's office handled more stand-your-ground cases than any other jurisdiction. If the court will allow him to testify, it will be abundantly clear that anything more than sixty seconds before the shooting is completely irrelevant in a stand-your-ground case."

"Bobby Speer is here?" the judge said, and this time his smile was genuine. "How's that rascal doin'?"

Oh, shit, thought Jack.

"Fit as a fiddle, thank goodness. Just as important, I believe his testimony will be of great assistance to the court in deciding exactly how much of this recording is relevant to Ms. Holmes's rights under stand your ground."

"All of it is relevant," said Jack.

"Well, not so fast," the judge said. "Let's hear what Bobby has to say. I mean Mr. Speer."

No, you meant "Bobby," Jack thought, but he didn't say it.

Jack tried not to show too much disappointment as they entered the courtroom and he took his seat beside Charlotte at the table. He quietly explained to his client what had happened as Mr. Speer—Bobby—swore his oath and took his seat on the witness stand. Barrow moved quickly through the background questions, then Bobby began his pontification on stand your ground.

"I want to be clear on terminology," said Barrow. "Mr. Speer, could you briefly tell us your understanding of the difference between 'stand your ground' and 'self-defense'?"

"Sure," said Speer. "We've always had a right to protect ourselves when it reasonably appears that someone is threatening us with death or serious injury. What changed with stand your ground is the duty to retreat. It used to be that if you were somewhere other than your own home, and you could turn and run without a confrontation, you had that obligation. Now you don't have to back down. If someone comes at you anywhere, and that person means you harm, you can stand your ground."

"Thank you, sir. Now, let's take this step-by-step."

Barrow had a projector and slides with demonstrative drawings to aid in the presentation. This was one well-choreographed show.

"Slide one shows two people seated at a table on a sidewalk outside a bar. A third man approaches and asks, 'Excuse me, ma'am. Is that man bothering you?' My question is this: Does the fact that these people are in a public space affect stand your ground?"

"No. As long as you have a right to be at the place in question, you have the right to stand your ground. Everybody has the right to be on a public sidewalk."

"Does anyone have a right to shoot anyone at this point?"

"No. There's been no threat."

"Second slide," said Barrow, changing the image on the projection screen. "The man who is standing says, 'I have a gun in my pocket.' Does anyone have the right to shoot anyone at this point?"

"We're getting into a gray area. It's possible that the man or the woman at the table would feel threatened."

Jack liked that answer, but he knew that this presentation was far from over.

"Slide three," said Barrow. "The man who said he had a gun in his pocket turns away from the table and says, 'Stupid wetback.' With respect to the stand-your-ground rights of the man and woman at the table, are we still in the gray area, as you called it?"

"Objection," said Jack. "Doesn't that depend on whether the man is reaching for the gun in his pocket as he turns away?"

"Mr. Swyteck, that will make fine cross-examination," the judge said. "As an objection, overruled. You can answer, Bobby—uh, Mr. Speer."

"The man and woman at the table no longer have any stand-your-ground rights. The man is retreating. The threat has evaporated."

"Slide four," said Barrow. "The man at the table jumps up from his chair and goes after the other man who is in retreat. At this point, does anyone have the right to stand his or her ground?"

"Yes."

"Who?"

"The man who was retreating. He has the right to stand his ground against the man at the table who came after him."

"What about the woman at the table? Does she have the right to stand her ground?"

"No. The only aggressor at this point is the man who was with her at the table. And his aggression is not directed toward her."

"So if the woman pulls a gun and shoots—"

"Objection," said Jack, needing to throw a wrench into this juggernaut fast. "It sounds like General Barrow would like this witness to decide the entire case. The only purpose of this testimony is to determine which portion of the audio recording is relevant."

"That objection is sustained. General Barrow, please rephrase your question."

"Yes, Your Honor. Mr. Speer, as state attorney it

was your job to evaluate evidence and decide whether to charge someone with homicide, correct?"

"Yes."

"And in some cases you decided not to bring charges, because you determined that the shooter had a right to stand his or her ground."

"Many cases."

"In the situation I just laid out in these slides, how far back in time would you need to look in order to decide if the shooter—let's call her Ms. Holmes—had a right to stand her ground."

"Objection."

"Overruled. The witness may answer."

Speer's chest swelled, as if he suddenly had license to pontificate. "I've often said that the only relevant time frame in a stand-your-ground case is the final thirty to sixty seconds. Everything before that—the prelude, if you will—simply clouds the analysis."

"Move to strike as nonresponsive."

"Overruled. But do answer the question, Bobby." The judge didn't even bother with the corrective "Mr. Speer."

"In this situation, the critical point in time is when the man turns away. All the stuff before that is just flat-out immaterial."

"To be clear," Barrow continued, "does it matter

that the victim interrupted a private conversation between a man and a woman?"

"No."

"Does it matter that he hurled an inflammatory and
racist insult at the man seated at the table?"

"No."

"What does matter?"

"Everything that happened after he turned his back
and walked away. That's all that matters."

"Thank you, Mr. Speer. I have no further questions."

Jack rose, eager to make his point: what mattered
was that Mr. Meyer said he had "fire" in his pocket
and that Charlotte thought he was about to use it.

"Keep your seat, Mr. Swyteck," the judge said.

Jack hesitated, confused. But he did as directed.

"I find this all very interesting from an intellectual
standpoint," the judge continued. "I suppose some law
professor could write a thousand-page legal tome on
the question of whether Ms. Holmes had a legal right to
stand her ground against Mr. Meyer while Mr. Meyer
was standing his ground against Dr. Perez. It kind of
reminds me of an old Clint Eastwood western. I forget
the name of the movie. It's the one that ends with not
just two men in a high-noon showdown, but three of
them—mano a mano a mano, as it were. Maybe that's
where the world is headed. We can all just stand our

ground against other folks standing their ground until we're the last man—or woman—standing."

Jack rose respectfully. "Your Honor, I do have cross-examination."

"Keep your powder dry, Mr. Swyteck. Bobby—Mr. Speer—thank you kindly for the visit. Always good to see you. General Barrow, your objection on grounds of relevance is overruled. We are going to listen to that recording. The whole recording. Mr. Swyteck, if you please . . ."

Jack smiled to himself. Every so often, a ray of justice shone through a courtroom, reminding a lawyer why he went to law school.

"Thank you, Judge. Thank you very much."

Chapter 45

Jack felt momentum. Charlotte smelled blood.

"I want to testify," she said.

The recorded altercation had been played to a packed courtroom from start to finish, and the hearing was in recess for fifteen minutes. Jack and his client were down the hall, alone in an empty jury room. It had been Jack's intention to return to the courtroom after the break and announce, "The defense rests."

"We agreed that was a bad idea," said Jack.

"We've got our boot on General Barrow's neck. Let's finish her."

The metaphor seemed a bit brutal, but Jack reminded himself that nice girls from Pensacola grew up in Florida's largest military community.

"Let's keep our eye on the ball," said Jack. "This hearing is secondary. The most important thing is to convince the Leon County state attorney to drop the criminal charges against you. As things stand now, I believe I can do that."

"It can only help if we win this hearing."

"I never guarantee results," said Jack, "but I truly believe that the only shot General Barrow has at resurrecting this case is to shred you on cross-examination."

"What makes you think she'll shred me?"

"This hearing has always been political, but now it's political scorched earth. It's my view that no one who is the target of a politically motivated prosecution should testify under oath. Once you take the stand, the underlying charge becomes almost irrelevant. If your testimony doesn't fit the government's narrative, then the case is all about perjury, lying to officials, and obstruction of justice."

"Now you sound like President MacLeod's lawyer."

"Maybe he should have hired me."

Charlotte looked away, thinking. "If I choose not to testify, is the case over?"

"General Barrow has a right to put on rebuttal evidence."

"What if her rebuttal case is convincing?"

"Then we reevaluate."

"What does that mean?"

"This is a civil hearing. If we think there is a serious chance that Judge Martin will find you unfit to serve as an elector, you can resign before he rules. That leaves nothing for the judge to decide. The case will be moot."

"If I resign, the governor will appoint a replacement who will vote for MacLeod."

"True."

"You're okay with that?"

"My job is to protect you," said Jack, "not to get one candidate or the other elected."

"I don't want to resign. Not after coming this far."

"It would be a last resort."

"You really don't think I should testify?"

"While you're still facing criminal charges, it would be the worst decision you could make."

Charlotte breathed in and out. "Okay," she said. "Let's do it. Or should I say not do it?"

"General Barrow? Does the state of Florida have any rebuttal evidence?"

Jack had worried that the walk back to the courtroom was just long enough for Charlotte to change her mind, but his advice stuck. The announced decision to rest her case had surprised no one, least of all the attorney general. Jack did notice a hint of disappointment in Barrow's voice, however, as she rose in response to Judge Martin's question.

"The state of Florida calls FDLE officer Marcus Teller."

Teller worked in the tech unit of the Florida Department of Law Enforcement. Jack's initial impression was that General Barrow simply refused to give up her attack on the audio recording, and that she was bringing in a tech expert for another bite at the apple. He was wrong.

"Officer Teller, what was your role in the investigation into the shooting of Logan Meyer?"

"I was asked to examine a flash drive that investigators found at the crime scene."

The flash drive: Jack still didn't know what was on it. He was back to playing defense.

The attorney general laid the necessary groundwork, establishing that the flash drive was found on the table where Charlotte and Dr. Perez were seated. Then she got down to business.

"Did you find any data on the flash drive when you examined it?" asked Barrow.

"Yes."

"Did you encounter any difficulty examining that data?"

"Yes. It was encrypted."

"Were you able to break that encryption?"

"Yes. It took time, because the trick to decryption is to break encryption without deleting the contents of the decrypted file."

"Could you tell the court what you found?"

"I could, but it would be a lot easier to show it."

With the court's permission, the attorney general displayed an image on the projection screen for all in the courtroom to see. It appeared to be a code of some sort. A long code.

"What are we looking at?" asked Barrow.

"In a generic sense," said Teller, "this is a string of two hundred fifty-six numbers between zero and nine and letters between A and F."

"Were you able to determine the significance of these numbers and letters?"

"Yes. This is what is known as a bitcoin key."

Jack was familiar with it. His last case involving bitcoin was in defense of an American businessman accused of bribing a Venezuelan government official in violation of the Foreign Corrupt Practices Act.

"What is bitcoin?" asked Barrow.

"Bitcoin is a form of crypto-currency."

"How does crypto-currency differ from other forms of currency?"

"Objection," said Jack, just breaking the flow. "This witness is not an economist."

"Overruled. The witness can answer from a law enforcement point of view."

"In a word, bitcoin is a form of payment that has the added benefit of complete anonymity."

"Can you explain what you mean?" asked Barrow.

"Let's say I want to send you money by electronic payment. I can do a wire transfer from my bank account to your bank account. Obviously, there is a record of that transaction: sender, recipient, date, amount, and so forth."

"Is there a similar record with bitcoin?"

"No. In a bitcoin transaction, I park the crypto-currency at a bitcoin public address on the Internet. It's kind of like an e-mail address box, except that a bitcoin address is used only once. There's no way for an outsider to know who owns that address or how much bitcoin is parked there."

"Who can access the bitcoin at the bitcoin address?"

"The person who has the security key."

"So let's go back to the flash drive found on the table

where Ms. Holmes was seated with Dr. Perez. The only thing on that flash drive was what?"

"A unique two-hundred-fifty-six-bit security key."

"What does a security key allow the holder to do?"

"Every key has a mate. In bitcoin parlance, the mate is a bitcoin address where bitcoin is parked. The person who has the bitcoin key takes the bitcoin. If it helps, think of the two-hundred-fifty-six-bit key as a key to a safe full of money."

"In other words, handing someone a flash drive with a two-hundred-fifty-six-bit key is like handing her the key to a safe."

Jack objected, but again he was overruled.

"Correct," said the witness.

"Thank you. I have no further questions." The attorney general stepped away from the podium. "Your witness," she said to Jack on her way back to her seat at the government table.

Jack had to be careful. The audio recording made it clear that Dr. Perez was trying to give her something, but there was no evidence it was the flash drive. Jack didn't want to fill in the missing blank by overreaching on cross-examination.

Jack rose and, while standing at his table, read from his notes. "'Like giving someone a key to a safe,'" said

Jack, repeating the witness's words. "That was your testimony?"

"Yes."

Jack laid his yellow notepad aside, approached the witness, and stopped. "Sticking with your analogy: You don't know where the safe is, do you?"

The officer's body language screamed pushback. "I don't understand the question."

"The security key can access a bitcoin address, but you have no idea what that bitcoin address is, do you, Officer Teller?"

"We don't know the address."

"Nothing on that flash drive tells you how to find that address."

The witness thought about it, then conceded. "That's true."

"So giving someone that flash drive is like giving him the key to a safe, but not telling him where the safe is. Right?"

"In a way, I suppose."

"And the bitcoin address tied to that key could be anywhere in cyberspace. Or, to put it another away, the safe could be anywhere in the world. Correct?"

"Theoretically, that's correct."

Jack pointed to the image on the screen. "That

series of two hundred fifty-six bits—the bitcoin security key—has zero value unless you know the bitcoin address; the mate to the key, as you put it. Isn't that right, Officer?"

The witness shifted his weight, searching for a way around Jack's point. "I'm not sure."

Jack pointed to the screen. "How much would you pay for those two hundred and fifty-six numbers and letters floating around in cyberspace if there was no bitcoin address linked to them?"

"Objection. Harassing."

Jack turned and faced the judge. "Your Honor, I'm being earnest about this. The clear implication of this witness's testimony is that Dr. Perez was trying to bribe my client. You can't bribe someone if there's nothing of value."

"Overruled."

The witness paused, then answered. "As I said— theoretically, you're correct."

"Let's talk less theoretically," said Jack. "Can you point to any evidence that my client, Ms. Holmes, ever received the flash drive?"

"It was found on the table where she was seated."

"That wasn't my question. Were her fingerprints on the flash drive?"

"I don't know. That's not my job."

"Fair enough. Fingerprints aside: Do you have any evidence whatsoever that Ms. Holmes ever laid a finger on that flash drive?"

"I do not."

"Do you have any evidence that Ms. Holmes received the two-hundred-fifty-six-bit security key from any other source?"

"No."

"Do you have any evidence that Ms. Holmes had knowledge of the bitcoin address connected to that key?"

"I do not."

"Do you even know if that bitcoin address holds any bitcoin?"

"I would assume it does."

"I'm not interested in your assumptions."

"Then—I don't know."

"So we have a key that my client never received. The key opens a safe at some unknown location. And that safe may or may not have anything of value in it. Is that about the size of things?"

"Objection. Compound question. Argumentative."

"Sustained," said the judge. "But I take your point, Mr. Swyteck."

"Thank you. That's all I have for now." Jack returned to his seat at the table and looked his client straight in the eye.

"Good work," she whispered.

"We need to talk," he whispered back.

Chapter 46

Court recessed for lunch. Jack and his client retreated to their hotel, dogged by a re-energized media. Reporters followed them out of the courthouse, across the street, and all the way through the hotel lobby, firing off the same question that Jack wanted answered. He waited until he was alone with his client and behind closed doors before asking it.

"Do you know where the safe is?"

They were standing in a ballroom big enough for two hundred guests. It was just the two of them.

"The what?"

"Don't go Officer Teller–dumb on me," said Jack. "The bitcoin address that matches the key. Do you know it?"

"No, Jack. I don't know anything about bitcoin, the

address, the key. I didn't go to Clyde's to get anything from Alberto. You heard the audio recording. When he pulled out the flash drive, I didn't even want to know what was on it. I told him to put it away."

The audio: they had that much working in their favor.

A dozen ballroom tables, each with twelve Chiavari chairs in wedding-reception white and gold, dotted the cavernous room. Charlotte went to the nearest one and took a seat, alone, looking a bit like a jilted bride. "Does this change your view on whether I should testify at this hearing?"

"No. We can't do anything in this hearing that might hurt you later in a criminal trial. It would be suicide for you to testify before we know what Dr. Perez is going to say. He's obviously a scumbag. We can't give him the chance to come back in six months for the criminal trial and bury you by shaping his testimony in response to yours."

"No wonder he's in Mexico, if he was trying to pay me to vote for Senator Stahl."

Jack joined her at the table, leveling his gaze. "Has anyone else tried to pay you to vote for Stahl?"

"No!"

"Why would Dr. Perez think your vote was for sale?"

"Maybe he thought I was wavering in my decision."

"Why would he think that?"

"Oh, I don't know," she said, a tad sarcastic. "Maybe I'm overly sensitive, but I've been stalked, threatened, harassed, and ridiculed on a daily basis. I can't go back to my house, I can't go back to my job, I've been publicly portrayed as a slut who trades legislative votes for sex, and the attorney general of Florida says I'm a cold-blooded killer with an itchy trigger finger. If you were counting on me to breach my electoral oath and vote for Senator Stahl, wouldn't you be wondering just how much I can take?"

"Yes, I would," said Jack. "But that's not really the question, is it?"

"What is the question?"

"Why is Dr. Perez counting on you being a faithless elector? To put a finer point on it, why was it so important to him that he tried to bribe you to make sure you voted for Senator Stahl?"

Charlotte shook her head, coming up empty. "I have no idea."

"Your ratings are way up, Paulette."

President MacLeod was alone in the Oval Office. He had the Florida attorney general on speaker. His new cell phone, encased in a military-grade shock-proof case, lay on the desktop.

"Thank you, sir," said the attorney general. "It only gets better."

"Better is not what I'm after," he said in a serious tone. "Finish it."

Chapter 47

The lunch break was over. The government's first rebuttal witness had done little damage, so Jack expected another.

General Barrow rose to make her announcement. "At this time, the state of Florida recalls Heidi Bristol. Your Honor, since Ms. Bristol was a witness for the defense, I respectfully request permission to treat her as an adverse witness."

In courtroom parlance, she wanted to proceed in cross-examination format, as opposed to a simple Q&A. Jack had no objection. In fact, it was a relief to hear that the government still considered the doctor's wife "adverse." Jack had seen witnesses flip in midtrial before.

"Permission granted," said the judge.

The door opened in the rear of the courtroom, and Heidi Bristol retraced her steps down the center aisle to the witness stand. The judge reminded her that she was still under oath. As she settled into her chair, she glanced in Jack's direction, and Jack read her brief eye contact as another positive signal that she wouldn't go out of her way to hurt Charlotte. But the attorney general was running out of rebuttal witnesses, and the tension in the courtroom reflected a general consensus that Ms. Bristol was in for an unpleasant ride.

Barrow stepped to the podium, and the first exhibit flashed immediately on the projection screen: a photograph.

"Ms. Bristol, do you recognize the people in this picture?"

The witness hesitated, but not because the image was unfamiliar. She seemed to be wondering where the attorney general was headed with this image. So was Jack.

"That's me, of course, on the left," she said. "I'm with my husband and Senator Evan Stahl."

Jack looked at it carefully. It was like hundreds, if not thousands, of photographs he'd seen over the years of smiling couples posing with his father, usually inscribed with the obligatory "Thanks for your support!"

"When was this picture taken?" asked Barrow.

"June, I believe. During the campaign, before my husband and I separated."

"Where was this picture taken?"

"At our house in Coral Gables. Out by our swimming pool."

"Was Senator Stahl a guest at your home?"

"I suppose you would call him a guest. But this was not a social visit. It was a fund-raiser for the Stahl presidential campaign."

Jack glanced in the direction of the media section of public seating. Interest was quickly rising, as the point of this photograph became clear.

"Were you a host of the Stahl-for-president fund-raiser?" asked Barrow.

"My husband was."

"How many people attended this event?"

"Two hundred or more. We have a big house."

"How much money did Dr. Perez raise for the Stahl campaign?"

"I can't say exactly. I do know there's a limit on how much each person can contribute."

"Did this event raise more than fifty thousand dollars?"

She paused to do the math in her head. "I would say yes."

"More than a hundred thousand dollars?"

"Probably. Some people showed up with more than one check. One from them, one from their son, one from their daughter."

"One from their dead aunt Lilly."

"Objection," said Jack.

"Withdrawn," said Barrow. "Ms. Bristol, what does your husband stand to gain if Senator Stahl wins the Electoral College vote on December fourteenth?"

Jack objected again, but the attorney general fired back. "Your Honor, we've already put into evidence the flash drive that contains a bitcoin security key. The state of Florida intends to prove that Dr. Perez met with Ms. Holmes to buy her electoral vote. I have a right to know what he stands to gain from a faithless elector who can deliver a Stahl victory."

"Overruled. If the witness is aware of something her husband stands to gain, she can tell us."

"I'm not aware of anything," she said.

"Fine," said Barrow. "Let's talk more about the timing of the fund-raiser. You said it was before you and your husband separated?"

"Right."

Barrow retrieved a transcript. "Ms. Bristol, I want to read a snippet of yesterday's testimony. Mr. Swyteck asked you this question: 'Without delving too deeply into personal details, why did you and your husband separate?' Your answer was as follows: 'He told me there was someone else.'"

Barrow laid the transcript aside. "You later concluded that the 'someone else' was not Charlotte Holmes, correct?"

"That's correct."

"Your husband never told you that he was having an affair with Charlotte Holmes, true?"

"Never. That was an incorrect assumption on my part."

"Dr. Perez told you that he was seeing 'someone else.' That was your testimony yesterday, and your testimony is the same today. Correct?"

"Yes."

"'Someone else.' Those were your husband's words?"

"Yes. His words."

"Your husband didn't say he was having an affair with Charlotte Holmes, Charlize Theron, or any other woman. Did he?"

"No. He said it was someone else. I think I've made that clear."

"Abundantly clear," the judge added, groaning.

Barrow stepped toward the projection screen, referring again to the exhibit on display, the threesome blown up larger than life. "Ms. Bristol, in this photograph of you, your husband, and Senator Stahl, who is standing closer to Senator Stahl? You or your husband?"

She glanced at the photograph, then back at the attorney general. "My husband is closer."

"Who does Senator Stahl have his arm around? You or your husband?"

She hesitated, her eyes narrowing. "What are you implying?"

Barrow turned to address the judge. "Would the court please direct the witness to answer the question?"

"Please don't argue with counsel, Ms. Bristol."

"I'm sorry," she said. "What was the question?"

Barrow's voice took on an edge. "Let me ask it this way: Does Senator Stahl have his arm around you?"

"No."

"Does he have his arm around your husband?"

Again she glanced at the photograph on display. "Yes. But that's to be expected. I didn't know Senator Stahl. He and my husband were friends."

"Did your husband and Senator Stahl spend time together without you?"

"Yes. Of course."

"Did your husband ever take Senator Stahl on his fishing boat?"

"Sure. My husband took a lot of his friends fishing."

"On those occasions when your husband took Senator Stahl on his fishing boat, can you swear for a fact that they did nothing but fish?"

A rumble from the gallery nearly drowned out Jack's objection, so he restated it: "Your Honor, I really thought we had moved beyond the campaign innuendos."

"Mr. Swyteck, if that's an objection, it's overruled. Ms. Bristol, the attorney general is simply asking if you can testify under oath as to what your husband and Senator Stahl were doing every minute of every hour they spent together on the fishing boat."

"No, of course not. But it's a fishing boat. They went fishing."

Barrow took a step closer, a control tactic, as if to step on the figurative tail of a squirming witness. "I would like an honest answer, Ms. Bristol: Did your husband and Senator Stahl ever come home from a fishing trip without any fish?"

Jack was on his feet. "Judge, I have to object. Campaign rumors are no basis for cross-examination."

"Overruled. The witness may answer."

She clearly didn't want to. "I'm sorry. What was the question?"

Barrow repeated it. The witness wrung her hands.

"I don't know. I'm sure there were times they didn't catch anything. Fish aren't always biting. But I know what you're suggesting, and it just isn't right. It isn't right at all."

Right or wrong, the implication lingered. The attorney general slowly walked back to her table, but she remained standing. "Just a couple more questions, Ms. Bristol. And please listen carefully. Did your husband meet with Electoral College member Charlotte Holmes, his old college friend, at the request of presidential candidate Evan Stahl—his lover?"

"Objection."

"Sustained. Strike those last two words—'his lover'—and the witness may answer."

Barrow seemed satisfied with the judge's edits. "How about it, Ms. Bristol? Did your husband meet with Charlotte Holmes at the request of Senator Stahl? And please remember that you are under oath."

Her glare could have burned a hole through the attorney general. "How would I know? Ask my husband."

"Where is your husband now, Ms. Bristol?"

"I believe he's in Mexico."

"Did Senator Stahl send him there?"

Jack objected, and he was again overruled.

"I don't know," said the witness.

"We would have to ask him. Isn't that right, Ms. Bristol?"

"I suppose."

Barrow turned and faced the judge. "Your Honor, it is now abundantly clear that Dr. Perez is an absolutely critical witness. Why did he bring the flash drive with a bitcoin address to the meeting? Why did he arrange the meeting in the first place? What was his relationship with candidate Evan Stahl? The state of Florida is on the verge of demonstrating that Ms. Holmes's decision to breach her oath as elector and to cast her ballot for Senator Stahl has nothing to do with 'truth' or her conscience. This is an illegal and corrupt political power play that reaches all the way up to Senator Stahl, himself."

"What are you asking this court to do, General Barrow?"

"Give us time to bring Dr. Perez to this courtroom from Mexico."

Jack rose. "Your Honor, this has gone on long enough. This all started with a simple question: Can an elector exercise her own judgment and vote as she sees fit at the meeting of the Electoral College, or is she bound by oath to vote strictly along party lines? The court decided that issue against the state of Florida. Since then, it has been one outrageous allegation after another to attack my client's moral fitness, from sexual misconduct to homicide. This afternoon General Barrow added bribery to the list of malicious accusations. We ask the court to decide the issue today and put an end to it."

"We all want this to end," the judge said. "But this is an important issue with obvious national implications. The meeting of the Electoral College is not until December fourteenth. I don't see the harm in a short continuance."

"I mean no disrespect," said Jack, "but this court was of the opposite view when the defense asked for time to bring Dr. Perez to this courtroom."

"Apples and oranges, Mr. Swyteck. At that juncture, I saw no point giving the defense more time when the government's case was so weak that no defense was needed." The judge swung his gaze toward the other side of the courtroom. "In other words, General Barrow, I'm giving you one last chance to meet your legal burden and prove your case. How much time do you need?"

She quickly conferred with the other lawyers at her table, then answered. "Could we have one week?"

"Granted. Ms. Bristol, you may step down before we adjourn. I would ask that the media show some restraint and not smother the witness when she leaves the courtroom."

Heidi Bristol moved with trepidation as she passed between the tables for the government and the defense, continued through the gate at the rail, and walked down the center aisle. Jack had seen inmates walk down death row with less dread. Several reporters sprang from their seats as she passed, ignoring the judge's admonition and following her out to the lobby.

"Nobody move," the judge said firmly, freezing several reporters in their tracks, as the witness exited through the double doors in the back of the courtroom.

"The state of Florida has until next Friday to bring Dr. Perez into this courtroom voluntarily or through other lawful means. He will be the final rebuttal witness. Until then, this hearing is adjourned," he said with a crack of the gavel.

"All rise!"

Judge Martin stepped down from the bench. Lawyers and spectators watched in silence as he exited to his chambers, and the entire courtroom sprang into action as the heavy paneled door closed with a thud. Some reporters resumed their pursuit of Heidi Bristol, while others rushed to the rail, firing questions at Charlotte.

"Was Dr. Perez the senator's lover?"

"Ms. Holmes, did you know about the same-sex affair?"

"How much did they pay to keep you quiet about it?"

Jack shielded his client from the onslaught, pushing through the crowd as he led the way to the exit.

Chapter 48

Senator Stahl got in his car and drove. The media would be all over his neighborhood in minutes, and he needed to sharpen his legal strategy. He called his lawyer from the road to tell him he was heading downtown. Matthew Kipner agreed to meet, but not at his law office.

"I want to see the boat," his lawyer said.

"What for?"

There was a familiar silence on the line—familiar in the sense that Kipner always paused before he got tough with his client. "Senator, if it's going to be my job to paint you as a fisherman, I want to see an actual fishing boat."

Stahl agreed. He made a quick turn off the highway,

and fifteen minutes later reached Coconut Grove Marina.

A late-afternoon breeze blew in from the bay, and the senator's ears tingled from the steady ping of halyards slapping against the tall, barren masts of countless sailboats. Motorboats and yachts of every size and description slept silently in their slips. A party boat rumbled up the channel at "slow-wake" speed. It had the earmarks of a bachelor party: loud music blaring from the oversized speakers, young men drinking beers from their college fraternity cozies, and beautiful women in bikinis dancing on the bow. The senator was suddenly reminded of another Democrat's presidential bid derailed by boat. Stahl had been a boy at the time, and it seemed quaint by twenty-first-century standards that, once upon a time, a single photograph of a married candidate and an attractive young woman in a bathing suit could end a presidential campaign. It probably hadn't helped that they were on a boat named *Monkey Business*.

Stahl met his lawyer at the end of the long, floating pier, where they boarded a forty-six-foot Hatteras Convertible.

"My floating man cave," said Stahl. He unlocked the door to the main cabin and showed his lawyer inside. For a career politician, Senator Stahl did not lack for expensive toys. His yacht, though more than two decades old, had all the bells and whistles. It was technically a fishing boat, but the senator had rigged the salon for entertainment, complete with club chairs, a wet bar, handcrafted teak cabinetry, and a flat-screen television.

"Any fishing gear?" asked Kipner.

"You betcha," he said. It was an expression he'd never used, which drew a curious look from his lawyer, who was probably wondering why the senator from Florida was suddenly talking like Hubert Humphrey, Walter Mondale, or someone else from "Minnes-ohhh-ta."

Stahl opened the locker and showed him the rods and reels.

"What do you use for bait to catch dolphin?" asked Kipner.

"Live shrimp."

"Marlin?"

"Live shrimp."

"Snapper?"

"Live shrimp."

It was a test, and his lawyer seemed to be looking for the more nuanced responses of a true angler.

"Look, I'm not the world's greatest fisherman," said Stahl. "But this is a fishing boat, and I've caught fish. I have pictures to prove it."

"That's good. You'll need them."

Stahl took a seat in one of the leather captain's chairs. Kipner took the other one, and they gazed at each other from opposite sides of the old wooden wheel of a ship that had been turned into a round, glass-top table. The lawyer broke the silence.

"This alleged conspiracy to bribe Charlotte Holmes will almost certainly go away if you lose the Electoral College vote."

"I don't plan to lose. We only have to flip five Republican electors. Four, if we keep Charlotte Holmes."

"Did you know that Dr. Perez was going to meet with her?"

"No."

"Do you know anything about a flash drive or a bitcoin payment?"

"Not a thing."

"If you do, please tell me now. Because if you win—if somehow you flip five Republican electors on December fourteenth—this will dog you from day one in the White House. Republicans will call for a special counsel."

"Isn't that just the way it is anymore?"

"The way what is?"

"Special counsel," said Stahl, rising from his chair. He opened the bar and poured himself a scotch, neat.

"We should just put it right on the ballot. Page one. 'Please select one candidate for the office of president of the United States.' Page two. 'Please select one candidate for the office of special counsel.' Let's save ourselves the time and aggravation of figuring out who the special counsel will be. We hold a general election to elect the members of the Electoral College who elect the president, and on the same ballot we elect a special counsel to undo the election. Because this idea of waiting four years for voters to correct their mistake—well, that went out of style with feather quills and horsehair wigs."

"This isn't a joke, Evan."

He tasted his scotch, then dropped the sarcasm. "Should we reach out to Swyteck?"

"We? No way. Me? Yes."

"Do you want me to hold off on my press conference until after you speak to him lawyer to lawyer?"

"When do you want to do your press conference?"

"As soon as possible."

"Are you going to name her by name?"

"Who?"

"The woman you had an affair with?"

It was the closest his lawyer had ever come to asking the sixty-four-thousand-dollar question: Man or woman? Stahl walked to the window, turning his back to Kipner. The sun was a sliver on the cloudless horizon, setting the marina aglow. In this glorious natural light, a bridal portrait on the waterfront was a photographer's "money shot"—the kind of lighting Gwen had prayed for but didn't get for their wedding reception at the Coral Reef Yacht Club. The senator could hardly believe that it was going on seventeen years. No, eighteen. It seemed like another lifetime.

"I can't do that," he said.

"None of this would have happened if you had nipped it in the bud," said Kipner. "The minute MacLeod put it out there that 'she' was a 'he,' you should have named the other woman. What's the deal, Evan? Why can't you name her? Is she the wife of a close friend?"

Stahl didn't answer.

"A friend of your wife?"

Stahl downed more scotch, then turned away from the window and faced his lawyer. "I just can't," he said.

Chapter 49

Jack made one more attempt to push through the politics. He reached the Leon County state attorney's office a few minutes before six o'clock. Josh Kutter never missed a Friday happy hour, and he was on his way out when Jack announced himself to the receptionist. Jack promised to be quick, and Kutter gave him fifteen minutes.

"But only because I like your father," he said, only half kidding as he led Jack back to his office.

Jack saw it as a waste of time trying to convince the attorney general to drop her civil lawsuit to remove Charlotte from the Electoral College as "unfit" to serve. The criminal charge, Jack hoped, was a different matter. Ultimately, the decision to prosecute Charlotte for homicide or to dismiss the charge based on stand your ground was in the hands of the Leon County State Attorney. Jack began his pitch with the criminal defense lawyer's mantra:

"Beyond a reasonable doubt," said Jack, invoking the highest standard of proof in American jurisprudence. "General Barrow is lucky she doesn't have to meet that standard in the fitness hearing. If she did, Judge Martin would have thrown the case out already."

"I take your point," said Kutter. "But this case is much simpler than you think. My position is that stand your ground just doesn't apply here."

"It's textbook," said Jack. "Mr. Meyer threatened to use the 'fire' in his pocket, and Charlotte Holmes thought he was going for his gun. If there's a criminal trial, I'll put her on the stand to say exactly that. The law doesn't require her to turn and run. She stood her ground, unless you accept General Barrow's myopic argument that the only thing that matters is the final seconds before the shot."

"To me, the key is what happened before Mr. Meyer even arrived."

Jack assumed he was talking about the flash drive. "The only charge against my client is second-degree homicide. The flash drive has nothing to do with the shooting."

"The bribery and the homicide go hand in hand."

"Whoa," said Jack. "Let's back up. First, there was no bribery. My client didn't go to the meeting to accept a bribe. She had no idea what was on the flash drive, and when Dr. Perez offered her the flash drive she refused to accept it."

"I have reason to believe that Dr. Perez will cooperate and testify that he met with Ms. Holmes to buy her vote."

Jack couldn't tell if the prosecutor was bluffing or not. "I can't stop Dr. Perez from lying to save his skin. But his lie about a bribe doesn't change the fact that Charlotte Holmes had a legal right to stand her ground against Mr. Meyer and his threats."

"Are you asking me to drop the homicide charge before I've even heard from Dr. Perez?"

"Yes—because there's no story Dr. Perez can craft about bribery that will turn my client into a murderer."

"You're ignoring the most important language in the statute," said Kutter. He reached for the book of Florida statutes on the credenza behind his desk and flipped to the stand-your-ground provision. "A person using deadly force 'does not have a duty to retreat and has the right to stand his or her ground if he or she is not engaged in a criminal activity.' Plain as day," he said, closing the book. "You have no right to stand your ground while you are engaged in a criminal activity."

Jack was aware of the exception. "The legislature put that language in the statute to prevent drug dealers from shooting their customers."

"That's not the way I read it. If Charlotte Holmes was in the process of accepting a bribe, she was engaged in a criminal activity at the time of the shooting. Stand your ground does not apply."

"You're going out of your way to reach an unjust result."

"Please, Jack. Don't accuse me of playing politics. I've done my best to stay out of this shit storm."

"My point is that my client didn't go to this meeting intending to hurt anyone. She was stalked and harassed for weeks. The police were no help. The gun she carried was purely for protection, and a situation arose where she needed to protect herself."

"That's why the charge is homicide in the second degree. I'm being more than fair." He set the statute book back on the credenza. "Look, I'll be honest with you: I don't like stand your ground. In a civilized society, a person's first instinct should be to de-escalate a situation, not pull out a gun and start shooting. That's how we end up with cases like this, where a guy who doesn't have a gun says something stupid—'I got fire in my pocket'—and he ends up dead."

"Do you really believe Mr. Meyer was unarmed?"

"No gun was found."

"I checked with the Department of Agriculture," said Jack. "Meyer had a concealed-carry license."

"So? Not everyone carries all the time."

"He had a license to carry. He made a racial slur, baiting Dr. Perez to come at him. He said, 'I got fire in my pocket.' Charlotte Holmes saw him reaching for his gun. But no gun was found at the crime scene. It doesn't add up to me."

"Are you suggesting that someone in law enforcement made that gun disappear?"

"In the middle of a partisan lawsuit to get my client disqualified from serving as an elector, a gun gone missing strikes me as politically expedient."

"If you came here to threaten me with allegations of police misconduct, you made a very bad miscalculation."

"If you're vouching for every MacLeod supporter in that crowd of hysteria outside Clyde's immediately after the shooting, the miscalculation may be yours."

"We'll see," he said, checking his watch. "My Jameson and water beckons."

422 • JAMES GRIPPANDO

Kutter rose, and Jack walked with him to the door. Jack started out, but the state attorney stopped him.

"Jack, let's not get hung up on did Mr. Meyer have a gun or didn't he. I've listened to the audio recording. If your client was not there to receive a bribe, she was not engaged in criminal activity. If there was no criminal activity, she had a right to stand her ground, whether I like it or not. The homicide charge goes away."

"That's good to know."

"I had no legal or ethical obligation to throw you that bone."

"Understood."

"But, like I said: I do like your old man. Say hello to him for me."

Jack smiled more on the inside than out. "Thanks. I will."

The lighting of the national Christmas tree on the Ellipse south of the White House was that evening. President MacLeod and the First Lady graced the dais, seated behind the podium for the musical portion of the program. As the St. Thomas Episcopal Parish Children's Chorus sang "Christmas Time Is Here," the jazz hit written for *A Charlie Brown Christmas* in 1965, the president fired off another tweet:

"Senator Stahl sends boyfriend to buy a Florida Elector. TREASON!"

The fake news would skewer him for working social media in the middle of a holiday tradition, but he didn't care. The media never treated him fairly. If a Democrat invoked an inflammatory anti-Semitic stereotype, it was merely "a trope." If MacLeod said "Merry Christmas" instead of "happy holidays," it was a dog whistle for white-supremacist hate speech. So dishonest.

He tucked his smartphone into the pocket of his overcoat and, when the music stopped, stepped up to the podium.

Although the First Amendment required the separation of church and state, the national Christmas tree and the nearby national menorah had survived constitutional challenges as "secular symbols" for purposes of the Establishment Clause. It was a chilly night, and apart from the sea of glowing smartphones in RECORD mode, the principal sign of life in a crowd shrouded in darkness was the sporadic steaming of breath into puffs of conversation. Attendance at the ceremony was by national lottery, and each year twenty thousand lucky winners had a folding chair waiting on the lawn. Not every winner came, no matter who was president. MacLeod's first-term average was about eight thousand no-shows, which his press secretary declared was the fewest empty chairs at any tree lighting since Calvin Coolidge began the tradition in 1923. No explanation was given as to how that historical fact was ascertained, and some questioned its veracity, given that official White House photographs show no chairs, let alone empty chairs, at the 1923 ceremony.

"I want to thank all of the talented people who contributed to this year's America Celebrates display," MacLeod said, referring to the smaller trees surrounding the thirty-foot blue spruce that was the national Christmas tree. "Christmas trees from our states, territories, and the District of Columbia are decorated to symbolize the history, heritage, and culture of our great land. Each Christmas tree includes one-of-a-kind ornaments made by creative Americans, mostly children."

MacLeod paused. He'd promised the First Lady that he would stick to the script, but he couldn't ignore the ongoing effort to steal his Electoral College victory. He suddenly found himself way off track, going state by state to praise the artistry of each ornament—but only the states that he'd won in the general election.

"Alabama. What a beautiful ornament from the art class at Hewitt-Trussville Middle School outside of Birmingham. I won Alabama by over six hundred thousand votes. Arkansas. Don't miss the Razorback ornament. Sixty percent of Arkansans voted for me." And on he went, skipping over the blue states, spiraling into campaign-rally mode—Georgia, Idaho, Indiana; state, ornament, and margin of victory.

"Love, love, love the Hoosier ornaments from Oakwood Junior High in Indianapolis—uh, excuse me, that would be 'Native-American-apolis' for any Democrats out there."

The First Lady could take no more. "Malcolm," she said through clenched teeth, "time to light the tree."

MacLeod had no appetite for another overdose of laxatives in his pudding or lemonade, another round with First Lady's Revenge. He sped things up, racing through Tennessee, Texas, and Utah to get to the big finish, "Wyoming, a landslide sixty-seven percent of the vote!" It left him so out of breath that he had to truncate the traditional "backward from ten" countdown:

"Three, two, one!"

The First Lady pushed the button, and some 75,000 colored LED lights brightened the night sky. As the Navy Band played "Joy to World," the president stepped back to admire gold and silver stars and ribbons, icicle lights, and a sparkling heirloom tree topper. Beautiful, but it was MacLeod's personal

426 · JAMES GRIPPANDO

opinion that the tree looked better on television. Being there made it obvious that the tree had nothing hanging from its limbs; the tree was actually tented, with decorations draped over the branches like a giant wigwam in order to prevent damage to a living tree that stood on the Ellipse year-round.

A post-lighting speech was not part of the program, but when the Navy Band paused between songs, the president returned to the podium, and the band instinctively deferred.

"One last sentiment," he told the crowd. With his impromptu launch into a state-by-state victory tour, he'd forgotten to deliver his prepared remarks. "The lighting of the national Christmas tree marks the beginning of our beautiful Pageant of Peace, a tradition started by the great Republican president Dwight D. Eisenhower. The Pageant of Peace was intended to echo the words of the angels during the Annunciation to the shepherds, as found in the Authorized King James Version of the New Testament. 'Glory to God in the highest . . .'"

MacLeod looked beyond the crowd, gazing toward the south portico of the White House, where, he was certain, Senator Stahl and his queer-as-a-three-dollar-bill Dr. McDreamy would never live.

"'And on earth peace, goodwill toward men.'"

Real men, he said to himself, giving a presidential twist to the holiday blessing.

"Merry Christmas to all."

The president and First Lady stepped down from the dais, waving to the crowd as they walked toward the exit.

Chapter 50

The call came Friday evening, while Jack was on his way to the airport to catch his flight to Miami. It was from his father.

"You should come now, son. This will be goodbye."

Jack headed for the Gulf Coast, and in about an hour he reached the Swyteck home-turned-hospice in the resort town of Seaside. His father greeted him at the door with an embrace. There were few words, which was the Swyteck way, but the expression on his father's face said it all. Agnes probably wouldn't make it till morning. Harry disappeared into the bedroom and brought the homecare nurse into the hallway with him. Jack went inside, alone.

Jack wasn't sure he wanted to finish the conversation they'd started on his previous visit. A proper goodbye,

THE BIG LIE · 429

however, was the right thing to do. Agnes seemed to rally as he approached the bed, and she even managed to sit up a bit in her weakened condition.

"How's your father doing?" she asked.

Not the question Jack had expected, but the focus of her concern said something about those two. "I think he'll be okay," said Jack.

A hint of a smile was in her eyes. "I know he will."

They sat in silence for a moment. Agnes turned her head, her gaze landing on the collection of framed photographs on the table beside her bed. It was a pictorial timeline, the story of Harry and Agnes in color and in fading black and white. One photo that Jack had never seen before was a portrait of the three of them: Harry, his new wife, and Jack as a preschooler.

Agnes drew a deep breath, and her gaze drifted back to Jack. "You know, Jack," she began softly. "People were talking about your father being governor before your father even thought about being governor. I remember his first campaign for State Senate. We walked for days on end, literally knocking on doors and asking for votes. He was so impressive. I was impressed."

"He was a skilled politician," said Jack.

"No, I meant as a man. I was so impressed with Harry Swyteck, the man."

"Were you dating at this time?"

"Not yet. Your father was a widower, and I fig-ured he'd ask when he was ready. But he never asked while he was campaigning. Then he won the election. I thought he'd ask then. But he didn't. And then it came time for him to leave for Tallahassee for his first legis-lative session, and he still didn't ask. So I just figured we would be great friends, and that would be that."

"How did you end up together?"

"Well, I took it as a pretty positive sign when, in-stead of asking me out on a date, he asked me to look after you while he was in Tallahassee."

"Lucky you," said Jack, kidding.

"You were precious, and I was a good mother. Or practice mother, I guess you'd call it. I really was."

"I don't doubt that," said Jack, even though he had reason to.

"When the session ended, he came back to Miami. We dated a little, but we knew we were already in love. We wrote to each other almost every day while he was away. Your father wrote such beautiful letters," she said wistfully. "We didn't wait long after he was back. We got married."

"Sounds kind of magical," said Jack.

"It was. It really was." Her eyes brightened for a moment, and then clouded. "But the following spring, it was time for him to go back to Tallahassee. You were just starting kindergarten. We agreed that moving you in and out of schools for each legislative session wasn't the best thing for you. Harry would be gone for weeks at a time. I stayed back in Miami with you."

Jack had his own memories of those long stints alone with Agnes, and they were not pleasant. But this was her story, not his, and so he just listened.

"I was friends with the wives of other state representatives. I wasn't so keen on being away from your father for so long, but they explained the rules to me. We were the proper ladies who were supposed to smile and support the opposition of southern Democrats to the Equal Rights Amendment. We were exactly what was meant by the old saying, 'Behind every successful man, there's a good woman.' And all of us 'good women' understood that the home district was for the wife; Tallahassee was for the mistress."

Jack couldn't believe what he was hearing, and he felt some resentment that she felt the need to tell him.

"Are you saying that my father—"

"No, no. Harry would never. It was my own insecurity."

Jack was relieved, but he again reminded himself that this was her story, and the point of it surely wasn't to tell him something that he already knew—that his father would never cheat on his wife. "Was it Dad who made you so insecure?"

"No. It was your mother."

"What?"

"Oh, come on, Jack. I'd seen the photos. I wasn't nearly as pretty as your mother. And I was older than your father. He was the hotshot young politician. The thought of him being in Tallahassee with so many pretty and younger women was—well, it was more than I could handle. I'd already divorced one man who'd done that to me."

Jack had been unaware. "I'm sorry" was all he could say.

"I'm the one who's sorry, Jack. I coped with it by drinking. You paid the price."

The deepest wounds between Jack and his step-mother were inflicted when his father was away during the legislative session and Jack was home alone with Agnes. The wives of other state representatives may have been willing to put up with the "other woman" in Tallahassee, but Agnes had no room for the "other wife" in Miami, ridding their house of all memories of Jack's mother. The crucifix from the casket that Harry hid in the toolbox. A photograph in Jack's bedroom that mysteriously disappeared after a particularly loud argument between Harry and Agnes.

"I told your father that I would leave him if he ever cheated on me."

"I'm sure he respected that."

"Just listen. The way I was thinking in those days deserved no respect." She swallowed hard, then continued. "Having a baby with your father would have made it impossible for me to leave. Or at least that's the way I saw it back then. What man would want a twice-divorced woman who had a child and who drank too much? Isn't that a terrible way to think?"

Jack didn't answer.

"My doctor said I would probably never get pregnant if I didn't stop drinking so much. In my own alcoholic mind I twisted that around completely and told your father I drank because the doctor said I couldn't get pregnant."

Jack wished she would stop punishing herself, but she was determined.

"By the time your father and I worked through my problems—my drinking problem—I actually couldn't get pregnant. They didn't have the kind of fertility drugs they have now. I drank my way through my childbearing years, and your father stuck by me, because I lied and told him I drank because I couldn't have children. Poetic justice, you might call it."

Jack suddenly realized where the story was headed. Agnes took a deep breath and made her point explicit.

"That's why you never had any brothers or sisters, Jack."

There it was: the end of the unfinished story. Jack didn't know how to respond.

"I thought you deserved to know that," said Agnes. She extended her hand, slowly sliding it toward him atop the comforter. She wanted him to take it.

Jack wondered why she thought it was so important to explain why he was an only child, but he didn't question it. He held her hand.

"There's something you should know, too," he said.

Jack was glad to have something to say, even if it was something he hadn't known very long. The realization had just come to him on his previous visit to Seaside, when he'd witnessed Harry caring for her so lovingly in a moment of need. A man who, if not for Agnes, couldn't have managed to get out of the house with his hair combed and tie straight was more attentive than any caregiver could possibly have been, more devoted than any husband Jack had ever known.

The words did not come easy, because Jack knew what they would mean in the greater scheme of things.

Jack knew that the gravesite beside Ana Maria Swyteck in St. Hugh's cemetery would be forever empty—that one of the side-by-side plots Harry had purchased before finding love again would go unused. But Agnes was a good woman. She'd stumbled, probably at a time when Jack had needed her most, but Righley's entry into the world had given Jack an appreciation of just how hard it was to be a parent even under the best of circumstances. Agnes deserved to hear the truth, and she deserved to be called the special word Jack had never called her.

"You are the love of Harry Swyteck's life. I hope you know that . . . Mom."

She squeezed Jack's hand, however weakly, and a smile creased her lips.

Jack wasn't sure who had needed this more, her or him. But he knew one thing for certain.

He would remain there at her bedside, holding her hand, as long as Agnes wanted.

Chapter 51

The moonless night was to Amanda's advantage.

Clyde's closed at midnight, but Amanda waited until 2:00 a.m., when all the bars in Tallahassee were closed. Then Amanda drove downtown. The sidewalks were empty. The storefronts were dark. Amanda checked her speedometer. She was minding the speed limit, but not driving so slowly that police might mistake her for a drunk on the road in the wee hours of the morning.

Amanda—"Manny"—had been thinking about the visit with her old boss. That Andrew had no memory of Charlotte coming to Clyde's as a student was not surprising. In a city of eight colleges and universities, no bar manager could keep track of every college-aged patron who walked through the door. At the time, however, Amanda had thought the whole world had noticed when Charlotte stopped coming to Clyde's. Probably because, to Amanda, it was her whole world.

The first kiss had been on a dare. Not the second. And not what followed. Amanda understood that nice girls born again in the First Baptist Church of Pensacola didn't bring a girlfriend home from college to meet the parents. So they flew under the radar. Still, it hurt that, to Charlotte's friends, Amanda was nothing more than "that chick Charlotte kissed on a dare." Nobody had been more obnoxious about it than the guy who'd put the dare to her. Amanda had forgotten his name—Alberto Perez—until the hearing in Judge Martin's courtroom brought it all back to life. In hindsight, maybe he was so homophobic because he was in the closet. Or maybe he was simply the jerk she'd always thought he was.

Amanda stopped at the red flashing traffic light, and then turned on Adams Street. Clyde's was a block away.

Millions of Americans had watched the Charlotte Holmes fitness hearings on livestream over the Internet. None had watched with the interest of Amanda.

Common sense dictated that the disappearance of a murder weapon would make it harder to convict an accused killer. Not until the hearing before Judge Martin, however, did Amanda realize that it wasn't Charlotte's handgun that she'd found on the sidewalk outside Clyde's and that had "gone missing." That gun belonged to the dead man, and in a classic case of unintended consequences, the missing handgun didn't make it harder to convict Charlotte; it actually made Charlotte's defense more difficult to prove. It was human nature to be uneasy about the shooting of an unarmed man. Charlotte's lawyer had gone to great lengths to suggest that Mr. Meyer was in fact armed, and that police had simply failed to find his gun.

"Did any of the fifty-plus people caught in this stampede accidentally kick a handgun into the storm drain?"

"I doubt it."

"Did you look in the storm drain?"

"No."

Amanda slowed her car as she approached Clyde's. It was important that there be no witness. The street was empty. No cars were ahead of her, and a quick check of the rearview mirror confirmed none behind. She reached into her purse and grabbed the gun. The driving gloves would ensure no fingerprints. She stopped the car, but only for a second, and opened her door a foot or so. She pitched the gun into the storm drain, quickly closed the door, and drove away.

Problem solved.

When the police followed up on the soon-to-arrive anonymous tip, they'd find the dead man's gun. They'd know that the man Charlotte had shot was not un-armed.

Jack called Andie to tell her that Agnes had passed. They agreed that Righley should stay home with Abuela.

Morning flights from Miami were booked, so Theo and Andie shared the ten-hour drive through the night, arriving in Seaside just around 9:00 a.m. Harry trusted his former campaign manager to notify the long list of friends who should know, and word spread quickly on social media. Condolences poured in all morning, and by noon they had more flower arrangements than places to put them.

Senator Stahl and his wife arrived after lunch-time, which was a surprise. Jack had overheard his father's end of their phone conversation earlier that morning. Harry had been clear that it really wasn't necessary for the senator to stop by the house. Apparently, Harry should have just come right out and said that he didn't want the senator turning Agnes's death into a diversion from the roiling political scandal of a same-sex affair.

"Can I speak to you in private, Jack?" the senator's wife asked.

Harry and Senator Stahl were in the Florida room with several Seaside neighbors who had stopped by the cottage. Jack led Gwen out the back door for a walk toward the beach. They followed a wooden-plank path that meandered through sand dunes and sea oats. Seagulls hovered in a cloudless blue sky. They seemed almost stationary, like nature's helicopters, their white wings spread at the perfect angle to let the breeze do all the work.

"I'm so sorry to intrude on your family," said Gwen. "I told Evan this was not our place."

"It's fine," said Jack.

A sea crab scurried across the path. Gwen paused to avoid stepping on it, then continued.

"I wanted to ask you about the rest of Charlotte's court hearing. Is it possible I could be called as a witness again?"

"Do you want to be?"

"No," she said with a nervous chuckle, and then more firmly: "No."

"I have no plans to put you back on the stand."

"What about the attorney general? Might she?"

"I wish I could tell you one way or the other. Unfortunately, General Barrow seems to change the theory of her case every time we step into the courthouse."

Gwen stopped. The sound of the surf grew louder. The beach was just on the other side of the last line of sea oats.

"How do you think I did on the witness stand?"

"You did fine," said Jack.

"I'm serious. Give me a letter grade."

"When I questioned you, I give you an A."

"You know that's not what I'm asking. What grade do you give me under fire from General Barrow? Be honest."

"I don't know. A solid B, I'd say."

"And I'd say you're wrong." She started walking again. Jack went with her.

"You're being too hard on yourself, Gwen."

She flashed a clever smile. "You misunderstand. I give myself an A-plus for the way I matched up against the attorney general. Things could have gone so much worse."

"I hear you. Things can always go worse."

They stopped where the dunes ended and the end-less white strip of sugar-like beachfront began. "I mean so much worse."

Her expression alone was enough to pique Jack's concern. "Worse for whom?"

"Everybody. General Barrow didn't really ask the right questions the first time she had me. I'm afraid she will, if she gets a second chance."

"Is there something specific I should know about?"

"No," she said. "This is something no one should know about."

"Exactly what are you telling me, Gwen?"

Her expression turned very serious. "I'm giving you a little advice: do whatever it takes to keep me out of that courtroom."

She let her words settle on Jack, but her expression invited no follow-up question from him. Then she turned and started back down the path toward the cottage.

Jack's gaze shifted offshore, where surfers in wet suits negotiated the whitecaps. Pundits the world over had their opinions as to why Gwen Stahl had left her husband and gone to Singapore, and Jack had wondered what was really behind her decision to yank her daughter out of school and go into seclusion halfway around the world. A wife angered and embarrassed by an unfaithful husband? A mother trying to protect her preteen daughter from salacious media coverage? Or something else?

Jack let the senator's wife go on ahead of him before starting back to the cottage, alone.

Chapter 52

Nonstop visitors and the parade of consolation continued throughout the day. Jack wasn't looking for an excuse to leave the beach house, but late that afternoon one landed in his ear. Bonnie called from his office in Miami. His reliable assistant had been searching government records online for two days and had a breakthrough.

"I found a name for you," said Bonnie.

Jack was relaxing on the front porch in a white wicker love seat, with Andie in his arms. He really didn't want to get up, but Bonnie had a voice like a bugle when she was bursting with pride from a "mission accomplished," and Andie had the ears of an FBI agent even when she wasn't on duty. He went to the other side of the porch. "Tell me," he said into the phone.

"All lobbyists have to include a list of clients on their registration forms," said Bonnie. "I checked every registration filed this year. Not a single one lists Alberto Perez, M.D., as a client."

Jack had hoped otherwise. The idea had come to him after listening to the audio recording of Charlotte's conversation with Dr. Perez. Right before offering her the flash drive, the doctor had suggested that Charlotte could have a future as a lobbyist in the health care field. Jack wondered if Dr. Perez was already working with another lobbyist.

"Now for the good news," said Bonnie. "I focused on lobbyists who work in the health care field and made a list of all their corporate clients. Then I went through the secretary of state's business records and got the names of all the corporate officers. And, voilà."

"Voilà, what?"

"I found a lobbyist named George Carpenter who lists a certain limited liability company as a client. And the managing director of that certain LLC is Dr. Alberto Perez."

"That's fabulous work, Bonnie."

"That's not the best part. Wait till you hear the name of the LLC that Dr. Perez manages."

"What is it?"

"Guess."

"Bonnie, I can't possibly guess."

"It starts with the letter 'C,' and you smoke it."

"I don't know. Crawfish?"

"Not that kind of smoking. It's cannabis."

"What?"

"Cannabis Solutions of Florida, LLC. That's the name of Dr. Perez's company."

Jack was glad he'd stepped away from Andie to take the call. He asked Bonnie to set up a meeting with Carpenter that afternoon, thanked her for the good work, and ended the call. Then he walked back to the love seat. Andie knew what he was going to say before he said it.

"It's okay," she said. "I can look after your dad."

"You don't mind?"

"No. Just take Theo with you. He's like a crawfish out of water here."

Sometimes Jack wondered if she had bionic ears. He gave her a kiss, and ten minutes later Jack was on the road with Theo. Carpenter had agreed to meet, which was no surprise to Jack, as it was another of Bonnie's gifts that no one ever said no to her. Even better, Jack didn't have to go all the way to Tallahassee. Carpenter's son played varsity basketball, and his first away game of the season was that afternoon at Wewahitchka High School, midway between Seaside and Tallahassee, somewhere between Dead Lakes Recreation Area and Tate's Hell State Forest.

"What's up with these names?" asked Theo.

"Wewahitchka is Native American."

"I'm talking about the ones you can pronounce. Tate's Hell. Dead Lake. Why don't they just call it 'Don't-fucking-come-here-ville'?"

"A cannabis plant by any other name . . . ," he said, though he was pretty sure the literary allusion was lost on his friend.

It was late in the fourth quarter when they reached the high school gymnasium. The Wewahitchka Gators lost on a buzzer beater, which made the home team sad, but it was Carpenter's son who'd hit the game winner, so Dad was in a particularly good mood. Jack gave him a few minutes for hugs and pictures with his son, and then they found a concrete patio table in the courtyard outside the gym where they could talk in private.

Jack already knew a thing or two about growing pot, and not just because he'd gone to college in Gainesville. Four years had passed since the previous general election when, in addition to sending MacLeod to Washington for his first term, Florida voters approved an amendment to the State Constitution to legalize medical marijuana. The fact that Florida's tropical climate was ideal for cultivation of marijuana had many an entrepreneur envisioning fields of cannabis as endless as the amber waves of grain and piles of cash as high as the purple mountains' majesty. But the movement hit a roadblock.

"Cannabis is Florida's next multibillion-dollar industry," said Carpenter. "If we can get Tallahassee to move on it."

"There's already a constitutional amendment," said Jack.

"Words on paper," said Carpenter. "Medical marijuana is legal in Florida if it is grown, processed, and sold in the state. Since the amendment passed, the Department of Health has issued, on average, two or three licenses a year. You know how many facilities are up and running? Less than half that many. That's supposed to serve the needs of over twenty million people."

"So if I want a license in Florida, what do I do?"

"Two options. First, you can buy it from one of the lucky guys who got one. That'll set you back about a hundred million."

"Just for the license?"

"Right."

"What's my other option?"

"Lobbying works. Hire me."

"Is that what Dr. Perez did?"

"He's one of many, but he was among the first. Dr. Perez is a pain management specialist. He saw firsthand how addiction to opioids ruined people's lives. He's also a smart businessman who recognized the profit potential a lot sooner than the Johnny-come-latelies."

"Do you know why he was talking to Charlotte Holmes?"

"Not specifically. But it's not unusual for clients to have more than one lobbyist."

"Why would Dr. Perez want to hire Charlotte Holmes?"

"My understanding is that he and Charlotte Holmes are old friends. She also just got cut loose from Madeline Chisel. Maybe Dr. Perez thought she could do for legalized marijuana what she and Madeline did for the NRA."

Carpenter's son caught his father's attention from across the courtyard. "I think LeBron James is ready to go home," said Carpenter, rising.

Jack thanked him as they shook hands, and Carpenter offered to talk again if they wanted to visit his office in Tallahassee. Jack and Theo stood and watched as Carpenter walked away with his arm around his son.

"Nice enough guy," said Theo. "Pretty helpful."

"Not that helpful," said Jack. "He skated right over the biggest bump in the road to legalized marijuana: Malcolm MacLeod."

"Isn't this up to the state governments?"

"The MacLeod administration took a firm stand against legalization and vowed to enforce federal narcotics laws even in states that have legalized marijuana. Legalized pot on a state level is meaningless if the Justice Department still prosecutes growers and distributors under federal law."

"So when Mr. Carpenter said that Dr. Perez approached Charlotte Holmes because he needed another state lobbyist in Tallahassee, that's bullshit?"

"Totally," said Jack. "What legalized pot needs is a president who is friendly to legalized pot."

"What's Senator Stahl's position on legalized marijuana?"

"What do you think?" asked Jack.

"So when Perez pulled out the flash drive and put the bitcoin key on the table, that wasn't a lobbyist's retainer fee."

"Nope," said Jack. "More like a down payment on her electoral vote."

Chapter 53

Charlotte drove two hundred miles to Pensacola to see Megan.

A good sister-to-sister conversation had been in order since her snarky "doesn't like men" testimony at the hearing. After considerable persistence on Charlotte's part, Megan had finally agreed to a lunch meeting. Charlotte chose the Oar House, because she wanted to be near the water, and the Oar House had outdoor tables for dockside dining. Charlotte was already seated and drinking her second sweet tea, waiting for Megan to arrive, when the text message popped up on her cell.

"I can't make it" was all it said.

No "Sorry, sis." No explanation.

Megan did that kind of thing.

Charlotte made the most of it. She ordered the fried

blue crab claws with coleslaw and ate alone in the shade of a big blue umbrella.

Things had not been right between Charlotte and her sister for years. The "Pink Panty Road Trip" was just the tip of the iceberg. Charlotte couldn't say for sure if Megan truly believed that her sister would have called the police—to find Megan passed out in her underwear—just to make herself look like a hero. One thing was certain: Megan resented the fact that she was always "the screwup" and Charlotte was Mom and Dad's favorite. Charlotte remained Dad's favorite until the day he died. Not so with Mom. It was a few months after the kiss-on-a-dare at Clyde's when everything had changed. Charlotte sat her mother down to tell her about the new friend she'd made and the feelings she was having. Big mistake.

"It would hurt less if you told me you'd slept with every boy at school."

Her mother had cried for a week, and not just in front of Charlotte. Everyone in the family knew that Charlotte had broken Mom's heart in some unspeakable way. Megan had decided to make it her business, got the truth out of their mother, and took it straight to Charlotte. Boy, did Megan take it to her. The slap across the face had split Charlotte's lip, leaving it so swollen that it physically hurt to speak when she met with Amanda to tell her where things stood between them. Charlotte was just a teenager.

"I can't believe that bitch did this to you."

Amanda reached for her hand, but Charlotte pulled away.

Charlotte tried to explain that it wasn't just Megan giving her "what for" and then moving on. Amanda was from Miami; Pensacola wasn't Miami. Charlotte had taken ten years off her mother's life, and there would be no forgiveness of this sin.

"I can't do this, Amanda."

Amanda had given her a hundred reasons why they had to fight through this and why it would be worth it. But Charlotte had made up her mind. Or someone else had made up her mind for her. It was not without tears, but Amanda accepted the decision.

"You can do this if you want, Charlotte. But either way, no one will ever hurt you again." She planted a kiss near the cut on Charlotte's lip, then whispered the last words between them:

"That's a promise."

Charlotte dropped her crab claw right onto the picnic table. She dug her cell phone out of her purse and quickly scrolled through her photo library to find the screenshot she'd snapped of a text message. She was looking for the spoofed message from Theo's number, the one that she'd taken as a warning to remind her of the oath she had sworn as an elector. The same message that, later, the attorney general had twisted to mean that Charlotte had sold her electoral vote, and that "a deal was a deal." The image came up on her screen, and the memory of Amanda's words gave it an entirely different meaning.

"A promise is a promise."

Charlotte stared at the message for a moment, then laid her phone aside in disbelief.

"Oh, my God," she whispered. "Amanda."

Charlotte attacked her cell phone with both thumbs, starting with an Internet search of Amanda's full name. The top news story was almost five years old, about a Miami woman who became one of the first female soldiers to enter combat training at Fort Benning. It wasn't directly about Amanda, but she was mentioned in the story as an example of "another Miami woman" who, before the repeal of the Department of Defense Direct Combat Exclusion Rule, had been part of the de facto integration of women into frontline combat, the military police. Charlotte felt a rush of pride but quickly moved on to the next listing: a social-media address. She sent a friend request with a message:

"I need to see you."

She didn't know when Amanda would see it or if she would respond, but she felt the urgent need to get on the road. She left more than enough money on the table to cover her bill and a tip, grabbed her purse, and headed for her car, anxious to get back to Tallahassee.

Chapter 54

Jack and Theo returned to a quiet beach house. Andie had proved quite effective at telling visitors to back off and leave Harry alone for a while. Jack found his wife and father alone, playing chess in the Florida room. Harry had nothing left on the board but his king and a couple of pawns.

"Your wife's a chess machine," said Harry.

"Actually, I've never played before," said Andie. Harry's jaw dropped, but she quickly came clean. "Gotcha."

The game ended with Harry's surrender, and Jack invited Andie to take a walk with him. She grabbed her coat, Jack took her hand, and they headed down the sandy road in the cool night air. A sliver of a moon hung over the tree line. Jack never shared specifics about his cases, but that didn't stop him from picking her brain every now and then.

"What can I learn from an FBI agent about legalized marijuana?"

"What do you want to know?"

"There's a dark side to everything, right?"

"Not Righley."

Jack smiled. He missed their little munchkin. "True. But more to the point: just because you call it 'medical' marijuana doesn't change the fact that you're growing and selling one of the most profitable recreational drugs in the history of the universe. There has to be a dark side."

"No question," Andie said. "No surprises here. It's the cartels. Cuban, Chinese, Mexican. They were all smart enough to realize that profits on imported pot would shrink as more states warmed up to legalization. The import market has shifted to harder drugs, like heroin. And the marijuana market is moving from imported product to cannabis grown north of the border."

"Homegrown, you mean?"

"Not literally in homes. They cultivate in states where it's legal to grow a limited number of plants for personal or medical use, but these narcos come up with all kinds of schemes to grow massive quantities way above the limit. Then, like any other drug dealer, they distribute it to states where marijuana is still illegal and sell it at market rates."

Jack wanted to ask how a pain-management physician like Perez might be connected to one of these narco operations, but he had to be careful about getting too close to the facts of his own case when talking to Andie while she was wearing her FBI hat. The fact that South Florida pill mills led the nation in the overprescription of opioids, however, gave Jack some clue.

"How established is this business in Florida?" he asked, keeping it general.

"You'll have to talk to someone in DEA. But the risk analysis for the narcos is a no-brainer. They can use the old business model and rely on illegals to transport foreign-grown marijuana and hope the mules don't get caught at the border. Or they can use illegals who are already in the U.S. to cultivate thousands of plants on land that's licensed to grow a few dozen plants a year, and probably never get caught. Who's going to blow the whistle? The illegal farmhands who are spreading the fertilizer?"

"Thanks," said Jack. "That was helpful."

They continued down the road, and then at Andie's insistence, they stopped. She wanted to face him squarely to put her question. "Did this come up in your case for Charlotte Holmes?"

"Sorry, honey. You know I can't—"

"I know, you can't talk about it. But listen to me, Jack. These narcos are just as ruthless in their U.S. operations as they are outside the U.S. It would worry me less if you were defending a serial killer on death row. Please be careful."

"Okay," said Jack. "I will."

Dr. Perez was sweating through his shirt. He shouldn't have been. The apartment came with a Savant home-automation and climate-control system that maintained the indoor air temperature at seventy-one degrees Fahrenheit and, more important, kept out the smog. Like all luxury residences in Mexico City's Federal District, this seventeenth-story gem with wraparound views of the city and mountains also came with state-of-the-art security and twenty-four-hour guards.

No security system, however, could keep out the deputies sent by the apartment's owner.

"Mr. Ortega wants to see you," the man at the door announced in Spanish. He said his name was Cesar, which didn't mean anything to Perez. He had two other men with him. They were all business, the kind of business that made Perez nervous—and sweaty.

Perez had met Ortega only once, and that was in Miami. His accountant had made the introduction at yet another Ortega penthouse, and it was even more exquisite than the one Perez was using in Mexico City. On the terrace overlooking the Miami River, the three men had worked out the terms of their arrangement. Perez brought to the table his network of "cooperating physicians" from the halcyon days of Florida pill mills. With the exception of one or two who were still in jail, those same docs would be on the ground floor of a business built on a Florida appellate court ruling that patients had a constitutional right to grow their own medical marijuana. Each doc would write a bogus script to five "patients"—handpicked by Ortega or his deputies—to grow a "limited amount" of cannabis for "personal medical use." With just average growing skills, those five patients could grow about five hundred plants every ninety days. A plant typically produced a pound of marijuana, which could sell in the illegal market for about four grand per pound. The Miami meeting had been about Dr. Perez's cut of the $8 million in annual revenue generated by each cooperating doc under his umbrella.

The point of the Mexico City meeting was not so clear.

"What does he want to see me about?" asked Perez.

Cesar stepped into the foyer. His wingmen followed. "He wants to renegotiate."

Perez assumed he meant the revenue split. "Why?"

"Because you fucked up."

Perez felt like he'd been punched in the chest. Hiring a lobbyist to push Tallahassee bureaucrats to issue more cultivation licenses had been a smart move on his part. Trying to bribe his old friend Charlotte to put a marijuana-friendly president in the White House was the dumbest thing he'd ever done. And now there would be consequences.

"I don't think a meeting is necessary," Perez said nervously.

Cesar tugged at his jacket just hard enough to reveal the outline of a pistol just behind the breast pocket. "Mr. Ortega wants to meet."

Perez glanced at the other two men, then back at Cesar. "I'll get my coat."

He didn't need a coat. He needed a plan. This unexpected visit from Ortega's men had all the markings of a one-way trip to nowhere, and a seventeenth-floor apartment didn't offer many escape routes.

"I'll go with you," Cesar said, and he followed Perez to the bedroom.

Perez went to the closet and found a jacket. His cell phone was charging on the dresser. A call to his accountant, the man who'd introduced him to Ortega, might save his life. Or maybe sometime during the car ride to wherever they were going he could send an emergency text to put a stop to this insanity. He walked to the dresser and reached for his cell.

"Leave it," Cesar said.

"But—"

"No phone," he said firmly.

Perez wondered if he'd seen the news accounts of journalist Jamal Khashoggi's iPhone recording of his own murder, which had exposed the dirty work of a Saudi-sponsored hit squad in Turkey.

"Let's go," he said, and Perez followed him back to the foyer. Cesar led the way, followed by Perez, with the two other men trailing behind him like the Secret Service, narco-style. Cesar had his own passkey to the apartment's private elevator, as if to validate his direct nexus to Ortega. Perez was starting to feel nauseous. The elevator opened directly to the main lobby, and a sedan was parked right outside the front door. One of Cesar's men opened the rear door on the passenger side and climbed in. Cesar directed Perez to sit in the middle, and the other man got in last. Cesar drove, with Perez sandwiched between two goons in the back seat. He supposed that it was better than being bound, gagged, and stuffed in the trunk, but it was hard to feel good about anything at the moment.

"How far is it to Mr. Ortega's place?" he asked.

"Shut up," said Cesar.

Perez sank back into the seat. His options were narrowing. He could take this ride to its unhappy ending, or he could figure his way out of a very bad situation. He was a bright guy. Top ten percent of his medical school class. Smart enough to marry a rich woman to put him through med school. Talking his way out of trouble wasn't a realistic strategy with these blockheads. The guy on his left had a neck like a bull, and probably the brain of one, too. The other smelled like the sticky floor of a college bar on dollar-a-shot night. The whiskey stench was overpowering. Each bump in the road set his head in motion like a bobblehead doll. He was hungover, no doubt about it, and barely awake. And the stink. Perez wished Mr. Whiskey-Breath would open the window—or, even better, the door.

The door. The sedan had power locks, and Perez had no recollection of the distinct sound of those locks engaging. Could the doors be unlocked?

It was decision time. They were still inside the city, and Cesar was focused on negotiating his way through urban traffic. Perez craned his neck for a glimpse of the dashboard: forty kilometers per hour. Around twenty-five miles per hour, but his clinic had managed the chronic pain of patients who'd merely fallen out of bed, so he knew it would hurt like hell to hit the pavement at any speed. He might even break a few bones or hit his head and kill himself. But it was better than a drill bit powering through one ear and out the other—or whatever execution method Cesar fancied.

They were on Avenida Paseo de la Reforma, a wide and historic artery that cut a diagonal path through nine miles of countless neighborhoods. Perez had traveled on it many times, but they were farther north than he'd ever been before, heading through barrios unfamiliar to him. He lived by the handy rule of thumb for infrequent visitors to Mexico City: "Stay safe, stay south." If the road to Señor Ortega's residence really did lead north, it seemed to Perez that it should have taken them farther west, to the Colonial Californiano–style estates of Lomas de Chapultepec or to the trendy apartments of Polanco. The north side of the city was famous for its street markets, *los tianguis*, where shoppers bargained for cheap clothes, foodstuffs, and electronics—"*que se cayeron del camión*," a colloquialism for things that "fell off the truck." *Los tianguis* at Tepito, La Lagunilla, and Nezahualcóyotl had their dark side as well, drawing not only adventure seekers but hard-core criminals dealing in everything from drugs and illegal weapons to endangered species and sex slaves. The most notorious streets were downright lawless, especially at night. Perez didn't have the luxury of choosing the perfect location for his exit. Time and daylight were running out. Whiskey-Breath was at most half-awake, fighting off too much drink, his day likely having started with breakfast shots. Perez watched him out of the corner of his eye and waited until the moment was right: eyelids heavy, chin on his chest, his breathing deep. And then he launched.

Perez was no athlete, but the adrenaline propelled him from the rear seat like an Olympic sprinter from the starting blocks. Before Whiskey-Breath could react, Perez reached across his lap, yanked the door handle, and pushed open the door. They were midway through a multilane roundabout, and with traffic flowing like a giant wheel around a granite monument at the axis, the centrifugal force created by the sedan's circular path added to Perez's momentum, carrying him through his captor, not over him. The two men catapulted from the vehicle like human cannon balls. Perez heard bones cracking as they hit the pavement, but the bones weren't his. Whiskey-Breath took the brunt of the landing and cushioned Perez's fall. Perez kept rolling toward the perimeter, finding daylight between bumpers like an urban cat with nine lives. It was a blur, but to his amazement, he was alive and fully conscious as he rolled up the curb and onto the sidewalk. Whiskey-Breath lay motionless on the pavement until a delivery truck ran over him, crushing his torso like roadkill beneath a set of double rear tires. Horns blared and traffic screeched to a halt. Perez picked himself up from the sidewalk, as a string of cars collided in a bumper-to-bumper chain reaction that led all the way to Cesar's sedan.

Perez didn't wait for Cesar to give chase. He turned and ran, but he had no idea where he was headed. He simply knew he had to hide. If a narco-style execution hadn't been Cesar's plan all along, then turning Whiskey-Breath into a human pancake had certainly marked Perez for an unpleasant death. He'd seen Mexican newspaper accounts of charred and headless bodies found on the side of the road, the narcos liking to roast their victims alive by placing a rubber tire around the neck and setting it afire.

Perez took the first street off the roundabout, racing past a few pedestrians who seemed to be in a hurry to be off the sidewalk before dark. Street vendors were packing up unsold merchandise, closing down for the night, and the trash that littered the pavement was the only sign of bargain hunters by the thousands who had gone home. He ran past a Laundromat, a small grocery store, and a *farmacia*—all closed. Most of the brightly painted shops were no wider than a box truck, and shopkeepers had already secured their storefronts for the night with burglar bars and steel roll-down doors. There was a gathering of a dozen or more men and women at the end of the block. Perez ran toward them, intending to ask for help. But as he approached, he noticed the makeshift altar surrounded by a ring of votive candles, the sacrificial offerings of cigarettes and tequila spread across the sidewalk, and, at the center of it all, the three-foot statue of the Santa Muerte. Perez sprinted right past it. The "Saint of Death" was an occult figure depicted in everything from statues to tattoos as a scythe-toting skeleton with flowing dark hair and a toothy grin, often dressed in a bridal gown. Perez knew from his recent business acquaintances that the Santa Muerte was not only the patron saint of Tepito, the most dangerous barrio in Mexico City, but also of Mexican narcos, who appreciated her tolerance of vice.

Gotta get out of here.

Still running, Perez spotted a coffee shop at the end of the block. It appeared to be open. Many of the coffee shops he'd been to in Mexico City were also Internet cafés with phone service. He ducked inside, his heart nearly exploding with excitement to see that this coffee shop was no exception.

"*Estamos cerrados,*" said the man behind the counter. We're closed.

Perez ignored him and hurried to one of the *casetas* in the back. It was like a phone booth but less private; like most *casetas* in the city, this one didn't have a closed top. Privacy was the least of his concerns. Perez entered his credit card information from memory. Then he put on the headset and dialed his accountant's cell number. He got a recorded message: "The voice-mail box for the number you have dialed is full. Please try again later. Goodbye."

"Shit!"

This was no situation for e-mail; Cesar might burst into the café at any moment, gun drawn. Perez wanted to dial his accountant at home, but it was unlisted, and he couldn't remember the number. It was on speed dial on his cell phone, which was sitting on the dresser in the apartment. At that moment, he hated himself for not having backed up his contact list to the Cloud. He couldn't remember any numbers, except one: his home number. Technically, his old home number. His wife's home number. Heidi was his last hope.

"We're closed," the attendant shouted again, and he turned off the fluorescent lights.

Perez dialed anyway, bathed in the glow of the display screen as he listened to the lonely pulse of a ringing phone overseas. Once. Twice. She answered, and he truly had never been happier to hear his wife's voice.

"Heidi, you have to help me!"

"Alberto?"

"Yes," he said with urgency. "I'm in Mexico City, and I've run into some trouble. An emergency."

"What kind of emergency?"

Alberto had told his wife nothing about his marijuana business, and he intended to keep her in the dark. "That's not important."

"What do you mean it's not important? Alberto, are you okay?"

"I'll be fine if you just listen to me. I need you to call my accountant, Harvey Tomlin."

"Your accountant? Alberto, I'm heading out to dinner. You call me from Mexico City on a Saturday night and want me to track down your accountant? I'm not your secretary."

"Heidi, please."

"Don't 'Heidi please' me. Why is it so urgent for me to call your accountant, anyway? Are you hiding assets and gearing up for divorce? Is that what this is about? Does Mr. Tomlin have some papers for the wife to sign?"

"No, it's not anything like that! It's a legitimate emergency."

"Then call the police."

"No! We can't call the police."

"Why not?"

He hesitated—why not?—and came up with the answer. "Because the police are corrupt down here. And this is not the kind of emergency the police can help me with."

"Fine. If your emergency is such a big secret, then call your boyfriend. He has lots of friends who can help you, I'm sure."

"Senator Stahl is not my boyfriend!"

"Then find a new one. Goodbye, Alberto."

She hung up. She actually hung up.

"Heidi, you fucking bitch!"

Chapter 55

Charlotte pulled her car into her driveway, turned off the engine, and immediately reached for her cell. She'd resisted the urge to check her Instagram account while driving back from Pensacola, but her curiosity could no longer be contained. She launched the app, and her screen told the story. Amanda had accepted her friend request. Charlotte's message—"I need to see you"—was marked SEEN.

But there was no reply.

It made Charlotte wonder. Could Amanda have "seen" but not read it? Did she read the message and then get pulled away to something else before she could respond? Charlotte had no way of knowing.

She was about to put her thumbs to work and access all

of the personal information at her disposal as Amanda's newest virtual "friend." Then she stopped. Since her realization that the "promise is a promise" text message had come from Amanda, Charlotte's feelings had run the gamut. The fact that an old friend with a military background had stepped up to protect her was in some ways flattering. The politically motivated threats against Charlotte as a faithless elector had made national news, so anyone—Amanda included—simply had to read the headlines to learn that Charlotte was in danger and needed help. But she wished Amanda had just reached out and asked, "Hey, is there anything I can do?" Instead, Amanda had acted less like a friend and more like a stalker. Charlotte was owed an explanation—but with her thumbs at the ready, poised to scroll through Amanda's every social-media post, it suddenly occurred to Charlotte that the shoe was arguably on the other foot.

We're all stalkers. Every single one of us.

Charlotte tucked her phone inside her purse, climbed out of the car, and started toward the front door. With each step, the second-guessing escalated. She'd selected the words in the message carefully— nothing accusatory, which would have only pushed Amanda away; just something catchy enough to make her want to respond. But in hindsight, maybe a better message would have said, "We should meet," not "I need to see you."

"Need" was such a loaded word.

The porch light was off, but she found the lock in the darkness, turned her key, opened the front door, and stepped inside. She flipped the two switches on the wall. The porch light went on, but the lamp in the living room was still dark. She closed the door and set the chain lock, then crossed the dark room to the lamp and turned the switch. Nothing. One possibility was that she'd unplugged the lamp for the vacuum cleaner and forgotten to replug it, but with her life turned upside down, she honestly couldn't remember the last time she'd vacuumed. A chill came over her, and she had the unsettling sensation that she was not alone in the house.

"Amanda?" she said with trepidation.

There was no answer, but the sensation did not subside. Charlotte was carrying, but as she reached for her weapon, she felt the pressure of a cold metal gun barrel at the back of her head.

"Don't move."

It wasn't Amanda's voice. It was a man's. He sounded Hispanic.

"What do you want?" asked Charlotte.

"Raise your hands up over your head. Very slowly."

Charlotte complied, and another man emerged from the kitchen. He searched her from head to toe for a weapon, taking the opportunity to grope her every private place. Her Baby Glock was in the holster around her ribs. After getting a handful of her breast, the man found the gun and took it.

"My jewelry is in a box on the dresser in the bedroom," said Charlotte. "There's some cash in the top drawer. Take whatever you want."

She felt the gun press harder against the back of her head.

"We will," the man said, but he showed no interest in her cash or jewelry. He led her to the TV room adjacent to her living room and directed her to sit on the couch. The room had one window, and the man went to it and closed the slats on the Bahamian shutters. The other man went to the kitchen, and Charlotte could hear him talking in Spanish on his cell phone. The light switched on, and the man who spoke English pulled up a chair. He sat on it cowboy style, his legs straddling the seat and his forearms resting atop the chair back. The gun was aimed at her face.

"Who's your friend talking to?" asked Charlotte.

THE BIG LIE · 475

"The boss."

"What are they talking about?"

"You."

"What about me?"

"Whether you should live or die."

"I vote live."

"It's not up to you."

Charlotte's "vote" had been a nervous reaction, the way some people laughed when they were supposed to cry. This guy spoke of life and death with no more emotion than the average person's sandwich order.

"There's no reason to kill me."

"That depends."

"On what?"

"On how much Dr. Perez told you."

"Told me about what?"

An evil smile creased his lips. "Well, if I told you, then it wouldn't matter what Dr. Perez told you, would it? I would have to kill you."

"Dr. Perez didn't tell me anything," said Charlotte.

"That may be. We'll know soon."

"How?"

"Dr. Perez will tell us everything he told you," he said.

"What if he lies?"

The man's smile faded. "Believe me," he said in a deeply serious tone, "Dr. Perez will be in no position to lie."

The doorbell rang. For the first time, Charlotte saw a look of concern on her captor's face. The kitchen went silent, and the man on the phone quickly entered the TV room, cell phone in hand.

"*Tranquilo!*" he said in a harsh whisper, which Charlotte assumed meant "quiet."

"Are you expecting anyone?" the man with the gun whispered.

Amanda? Charlotte wondered. "No," she said.

"*Tranquilo!*" the other man said, this time even more harshly.

They waited in silence, and after a few seconds, the doorbell rang again.

Jack was in the Florida room with his father, reviewing the plans for Agnes's memorial service. Everything was settled, so there was no work to be done. His stepmother had been sick longer than Jack had known, and Harry and Agnes had used the time to take care of every arrangement and plan out every detail.

Jack's cell rang. He didn't recognize the number, but it was the "305" Miami area code, so he took the call. It was Heidi Bristol.

"Jack, I'm so sorry to bother you."

"No problem. What's up?"

"I—I don't know," she said, and Jack noticed the quake in her voice. "Something very weird is going on with Alberto."

Chapter 56

Amanda waited at the front door, wondering if she should ring the bell a third time. A light was on inside, but the window shutters were closed, making it impossible to see if anyone was home. Charlotte's car was in the driveway. Either Charlotte was out with a friend who'd picked her up, or Charlotte had changed her mind since reaching out to Amanda on Instagram: she didn't need to see Amanda.

The friend request with Charlotte's message—especially the message—had sent Amanda's heart soaring. Amanda hated the way things had ended between them in college, but she'd accepted it. No calls, texts, e-mails, snail mail, or communications of any kind. Stay at least five hundred feet away from Charlotte, her residence, her place of work or schooling, and her vehicle. Those were the terms of the permanent restraining order, and Amanda had strictly adhered to that order for years. She hadn't even bothered to appear in court to oppose the petition. Her view was that if Charlotte needed to go to such ridiculous lengths to deny who she was, or at least one side of her bisexual self, so be it. What chance did a lesbian Latina from Miami have before a Pensacola judge, anyway? He would have thrown her in jail before siding with Amanda. She'd put Charlotte behind her and moved on—until her picture was popping up in the news every day. Seeing Charlotte's face, and knowing that she was in danger, resurrected so many feelings and memories for Amanda.

But even after deciding that "a promise is a promise"—that she would stop even political nuts from hurting Charlotte—Amanda had done her best to comply with the order. It was, after all, "permanent." She'd sent only the one text, and with the spoof app, there was no proof that it had come from her own cell number. She didn't even send an electronic response to Charlotte's Instagram message. And except for pulling Charlotte from the pickup truck that had sailed off the road, Amanda had maintained the required distance. Only when Charlotte invited her—"I need to see you"—did Amanda show up at her front door.

With flowers.

And she was feeling pretty stupid about that.

Amanda turned away, started down the porch steps, and then stopped. She heard a noise from inside the house, and it sounded like someone removing the chain lock. A moment later the dead bolt turned, and the door swung open. But there was no one there. Amanda peered inside from where she stood, but the living room was dark, and the glow of the porch light only reached so far.

"Charlotte?"

There was no answer. The door remained open.

Amanda took one step closer to the opening and stopped. "Charlotte, I'm sorry. I know it probably feels like I've been messing with you, but I can explain. Please, don't—"

A blow from behind knocked every bit of air from her lungs. Flowers flew into the air, and Amanda staggered forward, driven by the force of an attacker who had lowered his shoulder, launched his body, and sent his full weight into her spine. Amanda tumbled through the doorway, the door slammed behind her, and the man who'd been standing behind the open door landed on top of her, pinning her to the floor. Amanda was on her stomach, he was sitting on her kidneys, and his enormous hand pressed down on her right cheekbone, shoving the other side of her face against the carpet.

"Don't hurt me!" Amanda pleaded.

"Quiet!" the man said in English.

A light switched on in the hallway. Amanda couldn't turn her head, but with a shift of her eyes she glanced up and saw Charlotte standing there, her expression taut with fear. Another man was holding a gun to her head. A third man—the lookout who'd pushed Amanda through the doorway—entered the house through the back door and hurried into the living room from the kitchen. He spoke in Spanish, which Amanda understood perfectly.

"I checked her car and went around the whole house," the lookout said. "She's alone."

The man on top of Amanda spoke in English—good English, albeit with a Hispanic accent. "What's your name?"

She chose not to lie. "Amanda."

"Nice to meet you, Amanda. Things will go much better if we get on a first-name basis. What do you want to call me?"

Asshole. But she didn't say it.

"Call me Paco." He picked up one of the flowers that had scattered across the floor. "Tell me, Amanda. What's up with the roses?"

Amanda didn't answer. Paco looked at Charlotte, but she, too, was silent.

"Are you two . . . you know?"

Neither woman answered.

Paco smiled knowingly. "Well, *agradecimiento a mi Santa Muerte*," he said, giving thanks to the holy mother of death. "The night just got a whole lot more interesting, ladies."

Chapter 57

Jack flew out of Northwest Florida Beaches International Airport on the last nonstop of the day to Miami. Andie and Theo were with him. Jack's father had tired of being asked how he was doing and insisted that Andie get back home to his granddaughter. She took a taxi to Key Biscayne. Jack and Theo left separately. Even with the one-hour time difference between the Panhandle and the rest of Florida, they were on Miami Beach before Dr. Perez's accountant returned from dinner with his wife.

The Tomlins lived in a waterfront high-rise. It turned out that Theo and the security guard had grown up two blocks away from each other in the Grove ghetto, before Theo had gone to prison. He even remembered Theo's older brother from the glory days of the Grove Lords. It came as no surprise when Theo told him that Tatum

Knight, like most of the old gangbangers from the 'hood, was long since dead. With the guard's permission, Jack and Theo waited in the lobby. They watched through the glass entrance doors as the accountant left his Bentley with the valet attendant, and they rose from the white leather couch as the couple entered the lobby. Tomlin was middle-aged and way too portly to be wearing an Armani slim-fit suit. The young woman on his arm, a walking advertisement for breast-augmentation surgery, was without question the trophy wife.

Jack introduced himself, then cut to it: "Can I speak to you about Dr. Alberto Perez, please? It's extremely important."

Tomlin sent his wife upstairs in the elevator, and Jack took note of the fact that he didn't ask "What's this about" in front of her. The men gathered around a chrome-and-glass table at the other end of the lobby, in relative privacy behind a pair of polished granite columns and a replica of the *Venus de Milo*, which was every bit as tall as the six-foot-eight-inch original Jack had seen in the Louvre.

"Damn near the total WNBA package," said Theo. "Too bad about the wingspan."

Jack could only wonder what Theo's lectures in art history must have been like at Florida State Prison.

"How do you know Dr. Perez?" asked Tomlin.

Surely he knew that Jack was Charlotte's lawyer—anyone who watched the news did—so Jack skipped ahead. "I know his wife," said Jack, and then he told him about the urgent phone call from Heidi Bristol.

"Hmm," said Tomlin.

Jack waited for more, but "Hmm" was the totality of Tomlin's response.

"Do you know what he's doing in Mexico City?"

"No."

Again Jack waited, but Tomlin had nothing to add. Jack had prepared hundreds of witnesses for depositions over the years, trying to teach them to give a yes-or-no answer whenever possible and to volunteer not the slightest information to the opposing lawyer. They usually ran their mouths anyway. Tomlin was a pro, and this wasn't even a deposition.

"Do you know where's he's staying in Mexico City?" asked Jack.

"No."

"Do you know who he went there to see?"

"No."

"Do you have any idea why Dr. Perez would phone his estranged wife from a *caseta* and tell her that he needs to reach you—that it's an emergency?"

"No."

"Do have any reason to think he might be in danger?"

"No. Do you?"

It was better than a flat "no," but not much. "His wife found the call from Alberto very strange," said Jack.

"Alberto is a strange guy."

"How so?"

Tomlin paused, as if to measure his words, and then reerected the stone wall. "I couldn't tell you. The truth is, I haven't seen Alberto in at least two years. Maybe longer."

"Alberto told his wife that you're his accountant."

"I was," said Tomlin. "But as I just told you: I haven't seen the guy in years. Sorry, gentlemen," he said, rising. "I can't help you. Have a good night."

It was an abrupt ending to a very short meeting. Tomlin went to the elevator. Theo swung by the security desk to have one more laugh with his new homeboy before leaving. Then Jack and Theo exited the lobby, briefly turning blue as they walked in the glow of the lighted fountain outside the building.

"'Haven't seen him in years,'" said Theo in his white-man voice. "What bullshit."

"I Googled him on the plane," said Jack. "Pulled up

a few photographs. Dr. Perez and his accountant were in the same box for the Super Bowl last February."

"You should've shoved that in his face."

"Yeah, you're right," said Jack. "I'm sure he would've cracked on the spot and immediately turned into a font of information."

They continued through the visitors' lot to Jack's car and got inside.

"Whaddaya gonna do now?" asked Theo.

Jack started the engine. "Go home, give Righley a hug and a kiss, and then crawl in bed with Andie."

"Damn," said Theo, buckling his seat belt. "That's what I was gonna do."

This time, the doctor rode in the trunk.

The Internet café in Tepito had turned out to be a death trap, not a godsend. Of course an American running for his life in one of the most dangerous parts of Mexico City would seek out the nearest phone. Tepito was Cesar's territory, and when he showed up at the café, the shop owner addressed him by name and led him straight to "the American." Cesar cornered his prey in the *caseta* and could have easily emptied his pistol and left Perez in a pool of blood. Instead, he and his surviving goon took the doctor at gunpoint to the car. The tail end of the sedan was smashed from the chain-reaction collision at the roundabout, but Cesar pried open the trunk, stuffed Perez inside, and tied his hands behind his back. The trunk latch was broken, so he tied the lid shut with the leftover rope. The lid rattled at each pothole, and the sporadic glow of streetlamps and head-lights from other cars shone through the openings. At least Perez could breathe. For a time.

Perez lay with his head against the wheel well, lis-tening to the hum of the engine and the whine of the pavement. The car stopped, and a red glow through the openings in the damaged trunk told him that they were at a traffic light. He heard tires squeal in the distance, maybe from the next block, and he thought he heard a gunshot from somewhere, but perhaps it was just his mind playing tricks. The glow changed from red to green, and the car started moving again. A sudden turn sent Perez rolling off his hip and onto his back. The steady whine of the pavement gave way to the crunch of gravel beneath tires. The car stopped again. The engine went silent. A car door opened, and then another. They slammed shut in quick succession, like the racking of a shotgun, and the scratchy chorus of men's footfalls on loose gravel stopped directly behind the trunk. He heard a serrated knife cutting through rope, and the lid squeaked open. The Mexi-cans were staring down at him.

"Get out," said Cesar.

With his hands tied behind his back, Perez was having trouble. Cesar's sidekick grabbed him by the arm and dragged him out of the trunk like a dead animal. A sharp hunk of twisted metal tore through his sleeve and sliced open his arm as Perez tumbled over the damaged rear bumper and hit the ground hard, landing on his knees. He wasn't sure which hurt more, his arm or his knees, but he fought through it to size up the situation. Towers of flattened vehicles surrounded them, one compressed hunk of metal stacked on top of the other. Cesar, his sidekick, Cesar's car, and the walls of junk vehicles all around them were bathed in the eerie yellow glow of sodium-vapor security lights. The thought of what a trip to the junkyard could mean for his immediate future had him praying for a quick bullet to the back of the head.

"This isn't necessary," he said, his voice quaking.

"I'll decide that," came the voice from the darkness.

Perez's head turned, and he saw Señor Ortega step toward him. Ortega was dressed in a designer suit, white shirt, and silk necktie, the salt-and-pepper stubble on his broad face groomed to the perfect five o'clock shadow. It was apparent that this rendezvous at the junkyard was important enough to draw Ortega away from a social engagement.

Perez had never begged for his life before, but he was not above it. He was already on his knees. "Please, Señor Ortega. Don't do this."

"Did you share my name with Charlotte Holmes?" asked Ortega.

"No!"

"What about Harvey Tomlin? Did you give his name to Ms. Holmes?"

"Absolutely not, Señor Ortega. I swear I didn't."

"To your wife?" he asked, but his tone was more like an accusation than a question. "Did you give Harvey Tomlin's name to your wife?"

Perez hesitated. With the open top, the *caseta* at the Internet café was not private. The attendant could have easily overheard his conversation with Heidi—and Perez knew whose side the attendant was on.

"I called her. But I didn't tell her any—" He stopped himself. The anger in Ortega's eyes told him that his answer didn't matter. All the doctor could do was brace himself.

"Cesar," he said, barking out the order. "*La goma.*"

Perez could barely breathe.

Cesar walked around the sedan toward the tower of flattened vehicles. The other man went to the trunk, retrieved a box, and opened it. Inside were glass votives with candles. He removed four and placed them on the ground in front of Perez. Then he took a rubber hose from the box, shoved one end down the sedan's gas tank, and siphoned out enough to soak the doctor's head. It stung his eyes, but he was already crying.

Cesar returned with an old radial tire—just the tire, no rim.

"Just your size, Doctor," he said, as he placed the tire—*la goma*—around Perez's neck.

The doctor was blinded by the gasoline, and the combined odor of spilled fuel and road-worn rubber was making him sick.

"Please, I'm begging you. Please, don't light the candles!"

"We won't," Ortega replied. "You will."

And the last thing the doctor heard was the striking of a match, the roar of a tire engulfed in flames, and the sound of his own screams trapped in the inferno.

Chapter 58

Charlotte and Amanda were in the TV room, seated side by side on the floor with their wrists bound, backs against the wall, and knees drawn up to their chests. Charlotte normally kept the room divider between the kitchen and TV room closed, but Paco had the sliding-track panels open to create one large room. It made it easier to keep an eye on the prisoners while the men sat around the granite-topped island doing shots of whatever firewater they could find in Charlotte's liquor cabinet.

"The more they drink, the more I worry," Charlotte said under her breath.

Paco climbed down from his barstool and crossed the room toward the women. He removed the pistol from his belt so that he could squat down and speak to them at eye level, holding the weapon loosely as he spoke, using it casually to punctuate his hand gestures.

"I need to know something," he said.

The stupid grin on his face was concerning enough, but as the grin faded and Paco's expression turned serious, Charlotte's concern turned to fear.

"What was the bitcoin for?" he asked her. "The bitcoin from Perez, I mean."

"Alberto never gave me any bitcoin."

"He tried to," said Paco.

"I had no idea what was on that flash drive."

Paco smiled again, his gaze drifting toward his friends in the kitchen. Then his glare returned to Charlotte. "Were you blackmailing him?"

"Blackmailing him? For what?"

"Oh, I dunno," he said, glancing at Amanda, then back. "Maybe you and the flower lady here had some weird gay sex thing going on with Perez and his boyfriend."

"Shut the hell up," said Amanda.

Paco grabbed her by the jaw and slammed her head back against the wall. "Was I talking to you?"

Charlotte could almost feel her pain; Paco seemed to enjoy it.

"Cuz I don't think I was talking to you, bitch. So sit there and be quiet," he said, as he swung his pistol around, shoving the barrel against Amanda's lips. "Or you can eat this. Understand me?"

Amanda nodded, but only as much as the human vise grip on her jaw would allow. Paco lowered his pistol and released his grasp. Amanda took a breath, and then Paco looked Charlotte in the eye.

"I'm trying to work with you here. I don't know jack-shit about how you elect your president in this country. But I know two things. One, you're important to my boss. Two, you're not too important to be replaced."

He stared a moment longer, as if to see who would blink first.

"I wasn't blackmailing anyone," Charlotte said in a voice as firm as she could muster.

"That's good," he said. "I'll let the boss man know."

He rose, tucked his pistol back into his belt, and walked to the kitchen counter, leaving the two women alone but within his sight.

"Did you see his tattoo?" Amanda asked, keeping her voice low.

"Which one?"

"The skeleton with the scythe."

"Yeah. The grim reaper. I'm sure his mother is proud."

"It's Santa Muerte, not the grim reaper." Amanda

explained the occult roots of the holy lady of death, adding, "I dated a DEA agent for a while. She used to find Santa Muerte statues all the time in drug raids."

"I can't believe Alberto is tied up with drugs," said Charlotte.

"You always had a higher opinion of him than I did."

"I suppose. But why would narcos care who I vote for, anyway?"

"I'm more interested in figuring out how we get out of here alive."

The drunken laughter in the kitchen was getting louder, which only fueled Charlotte's fears. "I'm sorry you're in this mess, Amanda. You shouldn't be."

Amanda gave her a little smile. "Hey, a promise is a promise."

The remark drew mixed emotions from Charlotte. "Why didn't you just call me?"

"Why did you chase after me with a baseball bat?"

"Because I thought I was being stalked."

"By me?"

"No. The way you were dressed, I thought it was a man. The last time I saw you, your hair was longer than mine. You never got close enough for me to tell it was you."

"Any closer, I would have been in violation of the order."

"What order?"

Amanda raised an eyebrow, as if Charlotte were playing games. "Hello? The restraining order you got against me? I never went to court to oppose it, but I should have. It was permanent, which means it never went away."

Charlotte could hardly believe what she was hearing. "What are you talking about, Amanda? I never got a restraining order against you."

Their eyes locked, and the same realization came to them.

"Did that order protect just me," asked Charlotte, "or me and my sister?"

"Actually, you and your entire family. Part of me always wondered if it was your sister or your mother who put you up to it."

"They didn't put me up to it," said Charlotte. "They went around me and hired a lawyer who told the judge you were threatening the entire family."

"Well, I actually did threaten Megan. After she slapped you for having a girlfriend, I told her I'd kick her ass if she ever did it again."

"Oh, my God. The restraining order has Megan written all over it. She's such a coward. She was too afraid to stand up to you, so she made it look like it was me. She got an order to keep you away from the entire family, me included, and she never told me."

Charlotte hoped Amanda believed her.

"I'm sure Megan had no trouble getting Mom to go along with it," said Charlotte. "Mom would rather have had me end up with an abusive man than a woman who loved me."

Those last three words—"who loved me"—seemed to bring Amanda around. "No wonder the court record was sealed. It kept you from finding out about it. My first thought was that you were sweeping 'us' under the rug."

"Amanda, I—"

"Quiet."

"I just want you to know—"

"Quiet," she said in an urgent whisper. "Paco is on the phone."

Charlotte glanced toward the kitchen. Paco was pacing, his cell pressed to his ear. Charlotte could hear him, but he was speaking in Spanish. Amanda was fluent, and from her expression, she appeared to be translating Paco's end of the conversation in her head.

"Alberto is dead," Amanda whispered, her expression turning even more serious. "I think we're next."

Chapter 59

Theo told Jack he needed to check on the inmates at the asylum. Jack dropped him off at Cy's Place and drove home to Key Biscayne. Theo walked straight through the club and out the back door. His car was parked in the alley. In twenty minutes he arrived back at the Tomlins' high-rise on Miami Beach. He was happy to see the same security guard on duty in the lobby.

"Hey, wassup, homeboy?" the guard asked.

"Need a favor," said Theo.

Maybe it was their connection from Theo's days with the Grove Lords, or maybe it was the fact that Tomlin was the biggest asshole in the building. Whatever the reason, the guard was game. "Whatever you need," he told Theo.

The guard dialed the penthouse from the front desk, and Theo listened as he delivered the ruse. "Sorry to disturb you, Mr. Tomlin. But I just finished my walk through the parking garage, and I noticed that someone clipped the fender of your Bentley."

The guard held the phone away from his ear, as he and Theo quietly laughed at the stuffed prick who took pleasure in blaming the messenger. The diatribe ended with Tomlin's pronouncement that the guard was not only incompetent but "grossly overpaid, even at minimum wage." The guard who probably worked two jobs just to feed his family took the abuse without exception, which the penthouse owner seemed to think was part of his job description. Then he hung up.

"Mr. Tomlin says I should meet him by his car in five minutes."

"What's his parking space number?" asked Theo.

"Twenty-two. Level Two."

"Thanks, bro. I got it from here."

If there had been any doubt in Theo's mind that the accountant deserved what he was about to get, the exchange on the telephone erased it.

"Oh, and one last favor?" asked Theo.

"Name it."

"Turn off the security cameras on Level Two for a few minutes."

"Done."

Theo exited the lobby through the door marked PARKING and climbed the stairs to the second level. It was a typical garage, like a vault of unfinished concrete, the walls, floor, and ceiling unremarkable, save for the ribbon of purple paint across the pillars to demark "Level 2." The security lighting was minimal, barely bright enough for Theo to see beyond the long row of Teslas, Range Rovers, Mercedes-Benzes, and the like to the bank of elevators at the other end of the garage. He waited behind a concrete pillar a few spaces away from the silver Bentley Flying Spur, hidden from anyone who might approach from the residential tower elevator.

The elevator chimed at the other end of the row. Theo heard the doors slide open, followed by the echo of approaching footfalls that led to the Bentley. Theo assumed it was Tomlin, and the accountant's muttering aloud to no one—"Where the hell's that lazy-ass security guard?"—confirmed it.

"He's on his way," said Theo, stepping out from behind the concrete pillar.

"What are you doing here? Are you the one who hit my car?"

"Your car's fine, dude."

"Don't tell me it's fine. I don't know what piece of

shit you drive, but this machine goes for two hundred grand, pal, and that's before the built-in champagne cooler and perfumed interior. Somebody hit it. I just spoke to the guard, and he told me so."

Theo took a couple of steps forward and stopped. "You don't even know his name, do you?"

"No, but I intend to find out. Whoever hit this car is going to pay for it."

Theo took a few more steps forward, stopping about a car's width away from the accountant, making their thirteen-inch difference in height even more apparent. "I was talking about the guard," he said, mocking the reference. "You see him every day. And you don't even know his name."

"All I need to know is the name of the guy who hit my car."

Theo stepped even closer, and his voice dropped even lower. "Nobody hit your car."

Tomlin glanced at his vehicle, then back at Theo. "Wha—what are you saying?"

"You lied to us," said Theo, gazing downward at a man who seemed to be shrinking right before his eyes. "I don't like to be lied to."

"I, uh, don't know what you're talking about."

"There you go again," said Theo, adding a mirthless chuckle. "Another lie."

Tomlin licked his lips, his throat going dry.

"Tell me what you and your buddy Dr. Perez have been up to," said Theo.

Tomlin opened his mouth but hesitated, as if afraid to tell another lie. "I honestly don't know what you mean."

Theo crouched low enough to look Tomlin straight in the eye, their noses just inches apart. "If you don't stop lying, I'm gonna snap your little arms right off your body. You won't have to worry about your precious Bentley gettin' hit no more, cuz a man can't drive if he's got the arms of Venus-No-Elbows. That's what I mean."

The accountant swallowed hard. "I told you," he said in a voice that cracked. "I haven't seen Dr. Perez in—"

Theo grabbed him by the wrists, took him down hard to the concrete, and then dragged him to the opening between the Bentley and the Aston Martin in the next parking space. Before Tomlin could even react, he was facedown on the line striping. Theo burrowed his knee into the base of the accountant's spine, immobilizing him. Then he jerked both of Tomlin's arms up and backward like human levers, elevating his hands to a height that sent the proper message: Theo was serious about snapping off his arms.

"Stop!"

Theo elevated Tomlin's wrists a few more inches. It

was as easy as a beer tap in reverse, except that at this fine establishment, nothing flowed but tears.

"Please, stop!"

"Tell me what's going on with Dr. Perez," said Theo.

"I can't!"

Theo raised the human lever another notch, which was more than Tomlin could endure.

"Okay, okay!"

Theo kept the pressure on. "Okay *what*?"

"Just," he said, gasping through the pain. "Follow the—"

"Follow the what?"

"Follow the . . ."

It was beginning to sound like the familiar refrain in politics—one that Theo had heard before. "Money? Are you telling me to follow the money?"

"No. Nanny."

"Huh?"

"The nanny!" said Tomlin. "Follow the nanny!"

"Don't mess with me!" said Theo, and he jerked the accountant's arms a little higher.

"Ow, ow, ow! I swear, I'm not messing with you!"

Theo eased off, but only a little. "What's that s'posed to mean? 'Follow the nanny'?"

"The nanny from Colombia. The one that's gone missing. They got her through Dr. Perez."

504 • JAMES GRIPPANDO

"Who got her through Dr. Perez?"

"Senator and Mrs. Stahl! They got their nanny through Dr. Perez."

Theo wasn't exactly sure what that meant, but he suspected that Jack would. He dropped the "lever," Tomlin's arms fell to the concrete, and the accountant breathed out, relieved. Theo dragged him to his feet, took the car keys from Tomlin's pocket, opened the trunk, and shoved him inside.

"His name is Leonard," said Theo, meaning the security guard. "I'll tell him to come find you."

He slammed the lid shut and left the keys on the bumper, dialing Jack on his cell as he headed for the stairwell.

Chapter 60

The night was young. The *tortillera* jokes were getting old, and the men weren't talking literally about two women who make tortillas. For the first time in her life, Charlotte was somewhat glad she didn't understand Spanish, at least not well enough to pick up slang. She was certain that Amanda was giving her the sanitized translation of whatever Paco and his drunk friends thought was so funny.

"This is going to get bad," said Amanda. They were still seated on the floor, against the wall.

"How bad?"

Amanda looked away. "They're debating which one of us is in most serious need of a dick."

"Oh," said Charlotte, and she realized it was decision

time. She didn't think they could win a gunfight, which was why she'd kept the secret to herself. But it was time to make Amanda aware of their ticket to self-defense.

"How far away would you say that closet door is?"

Amanda seemed puzzled by the question, but she answered. "Twelve feet."

"Take a very close look at the bottom panel."

Amanda's gaze drifted across the room and landed on the three-panel door. She seemed to take Charlotte's meaning, but just in case, Charlotte left no ambiguity as to what was hidden behind the bottom panel.

"Twelve rounds. Nine millimeter."

Amanda nodded, and they sat in silence, thinking. Crossing the room without getting shot by Paco or one of his men wasn't even half the problem. Job one was untying their hands from behind their backs.

"Hey, *tortilleras*," said Paco, staggering his way toward them from the kitchen counter. "Which one of you thinks she's a man?"

Amanda's prediction as to the way things were headed seemed spot-on: this could only turn bad.

"Stand up, *chica*," he said to Charlotte.

It wasn't easy to do with her hands tied behind her

back, but Charlotte used the wall to slide her way up to a standing position.

Paco said something in Spanish to his men, which made them laugh so hard they nearly fell off their barstools. Then he spoke to Charlotte in English. "What you got in your pants, *chica*?"

"More than you got in yours," said Amanda, answering for her.

Paco's eyes filled with rage, and he kicked Amanda so hard in her ribs that she fell onto her side, groaning.

"I'm talking to the pretty one," he said bitterly. Then his attention returned to Charlotte, and he tugged at the waistband of her pants. "Now, let's see what you got in there."

Charlotte had to think fast, and a mad dash to the closet door with her hands bound behind her back was not a plan, unless the plan was suicide.

"Hey, Paco," she said in a bedroom voice. "You ever watch two women make it?"

He smiled, clearly liking the idea. In Spanish, he called across the room to his friends, and they howled with approval. Charlotte stayed with the plan and lowered herself to her knees. Amanda was still on her side, recovering from the boot to her ribs. With a quick glance at the closet door, Charlotte signaled what she was up to.

"Face me," said Charlotte.

Amanda went along with it, rising to her knees and facing Charlotte.

The drunks in the kitchen clapped their hands and whistled.

"Closer," said Charlotte.

Amanda slid her right knee forward, then her left. Their bodies nearly touched. Amanda was the taller, and if they'd kept their eyes forward, Amanda could have kissed Charlotte on the bridge of the nose. But each kept her head turned sideways, Amanda looking up at the ceiling and Charlotte gazing down toward the floor. It was anything but a romantic moment, but it nonetheless reminded Charlotte that on their first kiss—their first real kiss, not the stupid one on a dare—Charlotte had risen up on her toes. Slowly, Amanda turned her head, and Charlotte felt Amanda's breath on the side of her face. Charlotte did the same, lifting her gaze to meet Amanda's, wondering if somewhere behind those beautiful brown Latina eyes, the same fond memory had been triggered by this bizarre and cruel situation.

Charlotte looked away, toward Paco.

"This is going nowhere with our hands tied," said Charlotte.

The drunks at the island were slapping the granite

countertop in a rhythmic chant, as if at a soccer match. Paco blinked twice, apparently taking the problem under consideration.

"You have to untie at least one of us," said Charlotte.

The chant from the kitchen grew even louder. Audience expectations were high.

"We won't disappoint you," said Charlotte.

Paco's men were not to be denied, their chant almost a frenzy, their anticipation rising to the level of Captain Bligh's drunken crew about to witness the Polynesian orgy.

"Her," said Paco. He pulled a knife from his pocket and stepped behind Amanda. With the other hand he drew his pistol from his belt and shoved the barrel past Amanda's ear. As the muzzle settled squarely on Charlotte's forehead, he whispered a warning to Amanda, his gaze locked on Charlotte's eyes.

"You try anything funny, I shoot your girlfriend in the face. How do you like that, flower lady?"

Paco cut the rope, freeing Amanda's hands. Then he withdrew the pistol, holding his aim straight at Charlotte's head, as he stepped back to watch. "Let the games begin," he said, and then he repeated it in Spanish, which prompted another round of shots and more hoots and hollers from the men in the kitchen.

"Save yourself," Charlotte whispered. "Just go for his gun."

"I'm not going to let him shoot you."

"He might miss."

"Yeah, and hit me."

Had the situation not been so dire, it could have made Charlotte laugh. Amanda was good at that.

The men in the kitchen were growing impatient. The boo-birds emerged.

"Just go for it," Charlotte whispered.

Amanda's lips touched Charlotte's, which turned the booing to cheers. It lasted only an instant.

With the voyeurs' rise of excitement, Amanda seized the moment. She shoved Charlotte to the ground, using Charlotte's body like a fulcrum to propel her own body into a roundhouse kick that stretched all the way to Paco, taking his legs out from under him. Charlotte heard a "pop," the sound of Paco's ACL tearing away from the bone, as she instinctively tucked and went into a roll toward the closet. Paco's gun clattered on the floor, followed by his cries of pain and the thud of his body landing like a sack of cement. Amanda was on him, and Charlotte was still rolling, as the crack of a single gunshot sent a spray of red spatter in Charlotte's direction.

"Amanda!" she shouted, fearing the worst, but at floor level she caught a glimpse of the exit wound in Paco's head, the source of the forward spatter—good news, but there was no time to process it. The two men in the kitchen started shooting from a position of cover behind the granite-topped island. Amanda fired back several shots, and one of the men groaned—a hit, for sure. But bullets continued to fly, splintering the frame around the paneled door into pieces that rained down on Charlotte. She rolled right past the paneled door and took cover behind the couch. Two more shots rang out, and Amanda rolled alongside her, having come from the other side.

The gunfire stopped.

"Are you okay?" Amanda whispered, as she quickly untied the rope that bound Charlotte's wrists. It seemed to take all her strength.

"Yes, I'm—"

Charlotte started to say she was okay, then noticed the burst of crimson soaking through Amanda's shirt. Her shallow breathing, her whitening pallor, and the pain in her expression told Charlotte that the blood was not Paco's.

"You need a doctor."

"There's one of them left," she said, meaning Paco's

men. She handed Paco's gun to Charlotte. "Take him out."

Amanda seemed to be moving beyond the pain, but Charlotte didn't like the expression on her face.

"Hold on, Amanda."

Amanda took a breath.

"Don't die," said Charlotte. "I dare you."

It wasn't much, but Amanda managed a little smile. It broke Charlotte's heart to watch it drain away.

"Amanda!" she whispered with urgency. She checked for a pulse. There was none.

The crack of a gunshot stole her goodbye, a terrifying reminder of Amanda's warning that "one of them" was left.

Silence followed.

Charlotte checked the magazine of Paco's pistol. Seven rounds remaining, plus one in the chamber. Paco's custom handgrip—a gold-plated image of the Santa Muerte with pearl-green resin inlay and set in silver—required some getting used to, but Charlotte could handle it.

"*Tortillera!*" the man shouted from somewhere in the kitchen. More words followed, but all Spanish. Charlotte had no idea what the man was saying, but it sounded like he was negotiating.

She was in no mood to compromise.

There were friends back home, even members of her own family, who would have thought Charlotte had no business asking God for any favors. Charlotte said a quick prayer anyway. Then she sprang into action, rolling to her right, squeezing off four quick shots—*pop, pop, pop, pop*—as she crossed the floor from behind the couch to the closet door. In a blur of continuous motion, she yanked open the bottom panel, grabbed the hidden pistol, and continued firing into the island in the kitchen. The gap in time between the last shot fired from Paco's pistol and the first shot from hers was virtually nonexistent, and she didn't stop squeezing the trigger until she was almost out of ammunition.

She listened.

She heard a noise from the kitchen—a swiping sound, like someone sliding against the wall. A man—the one who was left—staggered from behind the island. One step, followed by a failed attempt at a second. And then he dropped to the floor.

His body didn't move.

Neither could Charlotte. She lay there, and the gun simply slipped away from her hand. All the way across the room, in the entranceway from the foyer, lay a flower on the floor, one of the roses Amanda had brought her. Charlotte couldn't look away from it, but suddenly she didn't even have enough strength to hold her head up. She let the side of her face rest on the floor, her line of sight fixed on the flower. And the tears came.

Chapter 61

J ack took Theo's call in the kitchen. Andie was in bed, Jack wanted to be, and he saw no reason not to wait till morning to "follow the nanny." The call from Charlotte changed everything. The police and a team of crime-scene investigators were at her house.

"I'll be on the first flight tomorrow morning," Jack said, and he advised her not to talk to the police until he got there. But Charlotte was tired of that game.

"I've got nothing to hide. Not anymore."

Jack knew what she meant, but any client with three dead narcos in her kitchen had at least that many reasons not to talk to the police—especially a client who was already charged in another shooting. "Charlotte, you are physically, mentally, and emotionally drained. There's no clearer case for self-defense than a home invasion until you say something to the police that could be taken the wrong way, or unless the police write down something you didn't say at all. Tell them that you and your lawyer will sit down with them in the morning."

She acquiesced, and they said good night. Then Jack called Senator Stahl.

The "Florida Electoral College Shootout" was already breaking news on television and the Internet. The senator was more than eager to speak to Jack and get the real story. Jack didn't mention that his visit wasn't about Charlotte Holmes. He definitely didn't mention that Theo was coming with him.

"You want to tell me how you finally got that accountant to talk?" asked Jack.

Theo was driving, and Jack was in the passenger seat. "Nope."

"You didn't bribe him, did you?"

"I did not bribe him."

Jack was almost afraid to ask. "Did you threaten him?"

"I did not bribe him," said Theo.

It was clear that when it came time to talk to the police, there would be no naming of the accountant as Theo's source. But that didn't change the strategy for purposes of the meeting with Senator Stahl.

Gwen Stahl greeted them at the door. Her husband

was on the phone, and she promised that he would join them as soon as the call ended. They gathered in the TV room, which overlooked the swimming pool. Jack and Theo took the matching club chairs, and Gwen was on the couch. Cable news coverage played on the flat-screen. The reporter claimed to be reporting "live" from the street outside Charlotte's house. It was too dark for Jack to tell exactly where the media vans had gathered, but the yellow tape and swirling police beacons in the background confirmed that the house was a crime scene. The medical examiner's van in the driveway, behind the reporter, suggested that it was the worst kind of crime scene.

The senator entered the room, greeted Jack and Theo, then took a seat beside his wife.

"I feel so terrible for Charlotte Holmes," he said.

"I'll let her know," said Jack.

Gwen hit the mute button on the remote so they didn't have to talk over the breaking news from Tallahassee. "Is your client still in any kind of legal trouble?"

It was not the kind of question Jack would normally address with any specificity, but it did provide the opening he wanted. "It all comes down to Dr. Perez," said Jack.

"Whether he was trying to buy her vote for my husband?" asked Gwen.

"I don't think there's any question about the doctor's intent," said Jack.

"Which I had nothing to do with," said the senator.

"Nor did my client," said Jack. "Charlotte never asked for money, and she never agreed to do anything for money. The question is whether Dr. Perez will say something different. Assuming he ever comes back to Florida."

"Has anybody figured out where he is?" asked Stahl.

"Not exactly," said Jack.

"Unless you have," said Gwen. It was directed toward her husband, and not without frost in her tone.

"That's enough, sweetheart," said Stahl.

She accepted his rebuke and dropped the matter, but Jack chose not to let it go. "Is the suggestion really that out of line?"

The senator chuckled. "How would I know where Dr. Perez has gone to?"

"Maybe your nanny told you," said Theo.

Jack didn't need the help, but he let the remark stand.

"We don't have a nanny," said Stahl.

"Theo meant your former nanny," said Jack. But he didn't play his hand yet on her connection to Dr. Perez.

"Unfortunately, that's a sad story," said Stahl.

"Yolanda was like family to us. She went back to Colombia and now, thanks to President MacLeod and his immigration policies, she can't come back. It broke our daughter's heart."

"Why did she leave?" asked Jack.

"Why does it matter?" asked Stahl.

Jack didn't have anywhere near the information needed for cross-examination of a witness, but this was no courtroom, so he played it as best he could: he bluffed. "It's all about the dots."

"The dots?"

"Yeah. I've been very busy in the last twenty hours—connecting them."

"I'm not amused by people who think they're clever," said Stahl.

"It seems nobody wants you to win this Electoral College vote more than Dr. Perez. So I asked myself: Why? At first, I thought it had to do with medical marijuana. But trying to buy Charlotte Holmes's vote is very high risk, and it seems out of line with any potential reward to Dr. Perez."

"People take stupid risks."

"I agree. But what happened tonight at Charlotte's house changed my thinking. Forget marijuana grown strictly for medical use by Florida residents. Swap it for marijuana grown in Florida and sold for recreational use all over the country. Now you're talking tens of billions of dollars. Trying to buy Charlotte's vote might not seem so stupid. Not if Dr. Perez had narcos breathing down his neck. Not if his life depended on a Stahl victory."

"You make it sound like the drug dealers have me in their hip pocket."

"No. I think it's someone else."

"Who?"

"Follow the nanny," said Theo, sounding a bit like a shadowy figure in a dark parking garage.

Jack let the suggestion hang in the air for a moment, gauging the senator's reaction. Then his gaze drifted to the senator's wife. It was time to use the ammunition that Theo had pried from the accountant, albeit without attribution. "Gwen, it's my understanding that your nanny was referred to you by Dr. Perez. Is that true?"

She glanced at her husband, then back at Jack. "Yes. The Perezes' nanny is Yolanda's cousin."

"So, here's what I think," said Jack. "Senator, you don't work for the drug dealers. Dr. Perez does. You work for Dr. Perez and your nanny. Because Yolanda found out your secret. And she told Dr. Perez."

The senator chuckled, but nervously. "Secret? What kind of secret would—"

"Oh, my God, Evan!" said Gwen, rising from the

couch. She took a step back and glared at him, seemingly unable to sit beside him any longer. "Did Yolanda find you in our house—with a man?"

"Gwen, you know that didn't happen!"

"That's exactly what Jack is saying. She caught you, and you were blackmailed by Dr. Perez and his narco business partners!"

The senator jumped to his feet. Husband and wife locked eyes, as if finally ready to have it out, speaking to one another as if no one else were in the room.

"You'll stop right there, Gwen, if you know what's good for you," he said.

"You were blackmailed because you cheated on your wife with a man!"

"Stop the show, Gwen. The audience isn't buying it."

Jack wondered what that meant, but sometimes the best thing a lawyer could do for a client was to stand back and watch the real criminals slice each other to ribbons. Jack let the "show" go on.

"I'm tired of living this lie," Gwen said. "You should know the truth, Jack."

"You're being a fool," said Stahl, but it didn't stop her.

"When I met with you and Charlotte, I told you our nanny had to go back to Colombia—because that's what Evan told me. Yolanda was gone so suddenly, she never even said goodbye to me or Rachel."

"Gwen, that is bullshit!"

"The truth is, when Rachel and I came back from Singapore, she found an ammunition casing in the planter in the hallway. Right outside her room."

"Your ammunition casing!" said the senator, his voice booming.

"You liar!"

"You work for the FDLE, Gwen. You're the only one in this house who owns a gun and knows how to use one."

"I'm sorry, Evan, I'm done protecting you," she said. "Jack, you were exactly right: Yolanda found out Evan had a lover who is not his wife and not a woman. She's dead. Evan shot her with my gun."

"I did not!" the senator shrieked.

"My husband took a play straight out of MacLeod's playbook—the big lie. Everybody was talking about 'Is he gay?' What they should have been asking is, 'Where's the nanny?'"

"Jack, don't be fooled. Yes, we baited MacLeod with 'Is the senator gay?' And like the complete idiot he is, he ran with it. But this wasn't to protect me."

"Don't deny that Yolanda's dead!"

"I don't deny it. That's the reason we sent you halfway around the world."

"See, Jack? He admits it!"

"Yolanda is dead because you shot her!"

"Because you were fucking her in your own daughter's bedroom!"

Dead silence. Nobody moved. Nobody said another word.

Jack watched as husband and wife stood glaring at each other, Gwen breathing a little harder than the senator. The television was muted, and the breaking news was still the shoot-out in Tallahassee. The red-and-white banner headline on the screen read, ELECTORAL COLLEGE CRISIS LOOMS.

"But—but," said Gwen, stammering. "Damn it, Evan! Now you've got me all upset and confused. My mind is all . . . mixed up. Jack, you have to believe me. If I shot Yolanda, if I knew she was dead, why would I have even mentioned our nanny when I met with you and Charlotte?"

It struck Jack as a valid question, but only on the surface. "That's the problem with the big lie, Gwen. Sometimes the liar finds herself believing it."

The senator's gaze drifted toward Jack. "I don't suppose you could see your way fit to consider this conversation protected by the attorney-client privilege. Could you?"

"I'm not your lawyer. I never was your lawyer. I wouldn't want to be your lawyer."

Jack dug his cell from his pocket.

"Not to throw a fly in the ointment," said Theo, "but you do realize that making that phone call means four more years of MacLeod."

Jack knew he wasn't serious, and perhaps someday, looking back, he'd find a way to laugh at the gallows humor that came so naturally to his friend. But not now.

Jack dialed the Miami-Dade Police Department on his cell.

Epilogue: December

Jack's stepmother was laid to rest on a Saturday. It was Jack's second funeral in a week. And what a week it had been.

Gwen Stahl was charged with second-degree murder. It was "a crime of passion," and it had happened on a night when her daughter was on a sleepover at a friend's house. Gwen had taken her FDLE-issued pistol from the wall safe in the master bedroom and walked down the hallway to check on a strange noise coming from Rachel's room. There, she'd caught her husband and the nanny in the act. Senator Stahl was charged as an accessory after the fact for dumping Yolanda's body in the Florida Everglades and creating the phony paperwork that "documented" her return to Colombia. His name was removed from the Electoral

College ballot. The choice was between Malcolm MacLeod and Governor Greer of Wisconsin, the vice-presidential candidate on the Democrat ticket.

There was little doubt that MacLeod would be re-elected. Some Democrats were already calling for the appointment of a special counsel to undo the election. Harry Swyteck's "party that never missed an opportunity to miss an opportunity" would, it seemed, miss another opportunity.

Jack and his father were the last to leave Agnes's grave. They walked in the patchy shade of towering royal palm trees that lined a meandering footpath. The 10:00 a.m. graveside service had been short, and the Electoral College was scheduled to convene at noon in Tallahassee.

"Who is Charlotte going to vote for?" asked Harry.

"You, I hope," said Jack.

Harry smiled a little. "Seriously."

"She's not saying. Charlotte learned her lesson about announcing her vote in advance."

"Amen to that," said Harry.

They continued to walk, passing a row of little American flags that marked the graves of veterans.

"Did you know Amanda Lopez was a veteran?" asked Jack.

"Yeah, I read that."

"Charlotte asked me to file a motion with the court in Pensacola."

"What for?"

"Charlotte's sister got a permanent restraining order against Amanda on false pretenses. The court entered it by default because Amanda never filed an appearance to oppose it. We're going to ask the court to vacate it, posthumously."

"That's a nice gesture. Is Charlotte moving back to Pensacola?"

"I doubt it."

"Will she stay in Tallahassee?"

"Don't know. The good news is she won't be moving to Lowell."

Jack meant Lowell correctional facility, home to over three thousand female inmates. The Leon County state attorney dismissed the murder charge against Charlotte based on stand your ground—a decision hastened by an "anonymous" tip to check the storm drain outside Clyde's for Logan Meyer's missing handgun. The tip had come in the day before Amanda died.

The footpath came to an end, and they reached the parking lot. Andie was with Righley, waiting by the car. Harry opened his arms, and his granddaughter ran straight to him. He picked her up and held her tight.

"Grandpa?"

"What, precious?"

"Did you know that the crosswalk machine by our house can talk?"

"You don't say."

"It's true. Daddy showed me. And when you ask, it will tell you a word that rhymes with 'gate.'"

"Is that so?"

"Uh-huh. And it can also tell you what Max loses when he goes on a diet."

"Really?" he said with exaggerated interest. "Oh, that Maxie McFatty could lose some weight, couldn't he?"

"Do you want me to show you? The machine is right by my house."

"I would love for you to show me, Righley."

"Well, then you have to come visit us."

Jack stepped closer and held Righley's hand. "Sweetheart, that's an excellent idea," he said, and with a quick glance in Andie's direction, he knew the idea was hers. He loved her more for it.

"What do you say, Grandpa?" asked Andie.

Harry glanced back sadly at the footpath they'd followed, then gave his granddaughter a kiss. "I think that's the best idea I've heard in a very long time."

Acknowledgments

Anyone who's read a Jack Swyteck novel in the past twenty-five years knows that this is where I usually take the opportunity to thank my longtime editor, Carolyn Marino. It was at Carolyn's suggestion that the Jack Swyteck series was born, when we decided to bring him back in *Beyond Suspicion*, eight years after his debut in *The Pardon*. Carolyn shepherded Jack through more than a dozen adventures before passing the baton to my new editor, Sarah Stein. I'm so grateful to Sarah for stepping up and leaving her own mark on Jack in *The Big Lie*.

There are still a few "usual suspects" to thank, including Richard Pine, my literary agent, and Janis Koch, my grammarian-at-large who educates me, humbles me, and makes me laugh with her spot-on and often witty copyedits.

Finally, my biggest thank-you is for Tiffany. We celebrated our twenty-fifth wedding anniversary while I was writing *The Big Lie*. I love you. That's the big truth.

About the Author

JAMES GRIPPANDO is a *New York Times* bestselling author of suspense and the winner of the Harper Lee Prize for legal fiction. *The Big Lie* is his twenty-eighth novel. His books are enjoyed worldwide in twenty-eight languages, and his signature character, Jack Swyteck, is one of the most enduring protagonists in the legal-thriller genre. James teaches the Law and Lawyers in Modern Literature at the University of Miami School of Law. He lives in South Florida.